A KNIGHT'S VOW

BOOK YOUR PLACE ON OUR WEBSITE AND MAKE THE READING CONNECTION!

We've created a customized website just for our very special readers, where you can get the inside scoop on everything that's going on with Zebra, Pinnacle and Kensington books.

When you come online, you'll have the exciting opportunity to:

- View covers of upcoming books
- Read sample chapters
- Learn about our future publishing schedule (listed by publication month *and author*)
- Find out when your favorite authors will be visiting a city near you
- Search for and order backlist books from our online catalog
- Check out author bios and background information
- Send e-mail to your favorite authors
- Meet the Kensington staff online
- Join us in weekly chats with authors, readers and other guests
- Get writing guidelines
- AND MUCH MORE!

**Visit our website at
http://www.kensingtonbooks.com**

A KNIGHT'S VOW

LINDSAY TOWNSEND

ZEBRA BOOKS
Kensington Publishing Corp.
www.kensingtonbooks.com

ZEBRA BOOKS are published by

Kensington Publishing Corp.
850 Third Avenue
New York, NY 10022

All Kensington titles, imprints, and distributed lines are available at special quantity discounts for bulk purchases for sales promotion, premiums, fund-raising, educational, or institutional use.

Special book excerpts or customized printings can also be created to fit specific needs. For details, write or phone the office of the Kensington Special Sales Manager: Attn. Special Sales Department. Kensington Publishing Corp., 850 Third Avenue, New York, NY 10022. Phone: 1-800-221-2647.

Zebra and the Z logo Reg. U.S. Pat. & TM Off.

ISBN-13: 978-1-4201-0361-8
ISBN-10: 1-4201-0361-X

First Printing: March 2008
10 9 8 7 6 5 4 3 2 1

Printed in the United States of America

To my family and all my friends,
with love and affection.

Chapter 1

England, Summer 1138

"Sir Guillelm has returned! The son of Lord Robert has come back to us!"

"Thanks be to God, we are saved! The young master has returned!"

Alyson heard the shouts from the surviving men-at-arms and jerked her head up, all thought of prayer forgotten. "My lord dragon," she whispered.

Struggling to rise to her feet from the hard, cold floor of the small, narrow chapel, she repinned her simple veil and pinched color into her gaunt cheeks, feeling her heart begin to race. "Can it really be true?" She had waited for him for so long, she could scarcely believe it. Guillelm, here, in his family's castle of Hardspen. For a moment she felt stunned with happiness.

"My lady!" The reedy voice of her seneschal, Sericus, floated above the hubbub in the great hall of the castle, calling ahead as he tottered on gangly legs to find her, to bring her this miraculous news.

"I am here!" Alyson called, darting from the chapel. Sericus was lame, and to save his withered limbs she picked up the hem of her plain brown gown and hurried down the spiral staircase of the keep. She was a small, slender girl with a mass of long black hair, large, very dark blue eyes and delicate features whose naturally bright, high-colored complexion had been dulled by weariness and grief. Longing to see Guillelm, she was reckless in her haste on the torch-lit stair, where only her natural fleetness of foot prevented a fall.

Would he remember her? She had been fourteen years old when he had answered the call of his kinsman, Raymond of Poitiers, and gone with him to the Holy Land. He had been in the exotic, dusty lands of Outremer for seven long years and she had despaired of ever seeing him again. For the past three years, with no news of him, there had even been the terrible rumor that he was dead. But he was alive!

Was he greatly changed? Would she be the one who would have to tell him that the enemy forces ranged outside the main gate were poised to attack? That his father, the noble and intimidatingly austere Lord Robert, had been dead for ten days? That for the past month she had been living in Hardspen as Lord Robert's intended betrothed?

Chilled and appalled by these thoughts, Alyson halted in the shadows on the final step, raising a finger to her lips as Sericus came out of the hall in search of her. Sericus, understanding her wish without the need for speech, passed by her and limped out of sight of the travel-stained men standing by the log-strewn fireplace in the great hall beyond them.

"Lady, where are your serving women?" he asked in an urgent whisper.

"Gytha and Osmoda remain in my chamber; they are still sick, as are many within this castle." Alyson had left them sleeping, no longer feverish but weak.

"Let me summon attendants to go in with you, a maid at the very least."

"You will be with me, Master Sericus, and that is enough,"

Alyson replied with a smile of gratitude. "You have seen to our guests' comfort?" She blushed at calling the new lord of Hardspen her guest, but Sericus merely nodded his head.

"Yes, my lady. They have ale and bread. Not fresh or fine bread, I fear. The baker's boy has been busy with the repairs and the baker has been sick."

"Then pray allow me an instant to compose myself. And sit a moment, I beg you." Sericus had been without sleep for the past three nights, as she had, helping her with the sick and with the ordering of Hardspen's human and physical defenses—the remortaring of sections of walls, the gathering of stores, the checking of weapons—as their enemy outside the gate waited in arrogant strength.

"My lady, you are ever gracious." Lowering himself onto the stone treads, the wiry, gray-bearded, gray-haired man sat with a tiny grimace of relief.

Standing in the gloomy stairwell, Alyson took in the scene in the great hall, the large, high-ceilinged chamber that was the heart of the keep, where in happier times Lord Robert had dined with his men on the tables and stools that now were ranged to one side. Today, long after sunset, those warriors and men still loyal to Hardspen bedded down there in their clothes on the rush-covered floor to snatch a few hours' sleep. She recognized their plain, honest faces and saw that they remained exhausted, as she was herself, but that new hope gleamed in their eyes—because of the arrival of one man.

Sir Guillelm de La Rochelle. She picked him out easily from the small group of soldiers who drank and warmed themselves—for although it was summer the nights were cold—by the crackling flames of the sweet-smelling apple wood. Tall as a spear, he towered over everyone there, long-backed and long-legged, with broad shoulders and lean hips. He was speaking quietly to one of his men, his back to her and with the dark hood of his cloak still pulled over his head as his powerful body steamed and dripped water from the relentless summer rain outside.

"My lord dragon," Alyson breathed a second time, using the nickname she had given him and which he had made his own. She missed the sight of that mane of bright golden hair and even more his grimly handsome face, but it was enough to know he was alive and safe. Giddy with relief, she now heard him speak for the first time in seven years as a castle defender asked how he and his few retainers had passed through the enemy lines.

"It is my guess that there is sickness and fever in that camp, as there has been here," Guillelm replied in the deep, warm voice that had so often gently teased her in the past. "Your enemy has but few watchmen to stand lookout. On a gray, wet night such as this, those few can see no farther than the rain-water streaming from their caps. We slipped past them simply enough. After that it was an easy matter to bring my commanders safely inside Hardspen; my grandfather devised secret ways into the castle bailey and keep, paths which my father showed to me while I was yet a boy."

"Your commanders, Lord?" asked his interrogator hopefully, picking up on the thread that Alyson had noticed, although she was distracted by Guillelm himself. He had turned to face his questioner and she could look upon the face that had haunted her dreams for so many years.

Eagerly she stared at him, feeling like a thirsty traveler coming to a well of pure, life-giving water. His was a lean, clean-shaven face, tanned by the blazing sun of Outremer, with a faintly aquiline nose that as a girl she had always longed to trace playfully with a finger. If he had changed, it was only to grow yet more handsome, with lines of character and decision etched into every uncompromising feature. She now caught herself wondering what it would be like to kiss that firm, full mouth.

"Some of my commanders, I should say." Guillelm sounded

faintly amused, yet his next words plainly were intended to give heart to the men of Hardspen. "The others are camped with the bulk of my forces in the woods close to the eastern bailey wall. Their presence will give your would-be besiegers something of a surprise, come tomorrow's dawn."

There was laughter, no doubt as Guillelm had intended. Taking advantage of the lighter mood, he called for more ale. There was a scramble amongst the oak tables set against the longest wall to retrieve the pitchers of ale that Sericus had brought up from the winter stores.

Watching how readily the men obeyed him and recalling her girlish hero-worship of the youthful Guillelm, Alyson sternly reminded herself of her duty. She must keep these unseemly feelings of longing within bounds. She was to have been Lord Robert's betrothed, affianced in a ceremony as sacred as marriage, and now almost a widow. How then dare she entertain such unruly desires for Lord Robert's son, a wish that she might kiss him and be kissed in return, enfolded in those strong bronzed arms?

"Let us drink to the vanquishing of all our foes!" Guillelm said, raising his goblet. "Let us drink to a new beginning!"

Listening closely, keen to hear him, Alyson sensed a sadness beneath the stirring words, a sense confirmed when he lifted his cup a second time and said in solemn, tightly controlled tones, "Let us drink to the most valiant of lords. To my eternal grief and shame I did not reach here in time to see and embrace him, as a son should a father, before he was taken by this foul pestilence."

He paused, a tremor of deeply felt emotion passing across his face. Swiftly he mastered it and continued in as strong a voice as before, "To my father, Lord Robert—may his soul already abide in heaven!"

"Lord Robert," came the somber response from the men.

"Robert," Alyson whispered, tears standing in her eyes as

she remembered him and even more painfully, the death of her own father three months before at Easter. For Guillelm's sake, she prayed that whoever had told him of his father's passing had done so with kindness. Dashing her tears away with a trembling hand, she raised her head and smiled at him, hoping that, although he would not see her, he might sense her sympathy.

Incredibly, as she smiled, he looked down the length of the great hall, straight at her. His eyes, deeper-hued and richer than the rarest of velvets, widened as he saw her, capturing Alyson in his dark, compelling gaze.

I could lose my heart to Guillelm and consider the danger of his breaking it well worth the risk, she thought, while an inner voice said, *You already have.*

For an instant both were still, wrapped in each other's glances, but then an indignant shout from Sericus behind her and the raking of greedy, clasping fingers against her shoulder warned Alyson of another, very different kind of danger. Breaking free of the pawing hand, ignoring her foul-breathed assailant's grumbled, "Give me more ale and a kiss, girl!" she whirled away from him and sped into the great hall, furious at the laughter of the other men-at-arms, those who had arrived that night with Guillelm.

Guillelm, she saw, however, was not laughing. She watched his face darken as the stocky, unshaven man from the stairway still pursued her, bellowing in nasal Norman French, "What is an English wretch like you good for, if not for serving your betters?"

"Thierry!" Guillelm shouted, his voice full of warning, and then Alyson heard him curse violently in an unknown tongue, possibly one of the languages of Outremer. She saw him thrust his half-drunk goblet at his nearest companion and stride toward her and her unwelcome follower, reaching them in fewer than ten paces.

"Let the little maid be, Thierry," he growled in French, seizing the other fellow's ever-reaching arm and bending it back sharply. "She does not care for your rough wooing, nor do I. Go back to the garderobe and throw yourself down into the latrine if you can find no better manners!"

He thrust the man aside so violently that Thierry careered into one of the oak tables, where he crouched, rubbing his arm and clearly glad to be out of range of his lord's displeasure.

Guillelm had no time for him. He lowered his head to Alyson, the hood of his cloak slipping down and revealing that glorious mane of blazing golden hair, bright as a dragon's flame.

"He has done you no harm?" he asked softly in English, his deep-set eyes narrowing in concern.

"No." Alyson stared up at her rescuer, more than ever conscious of her rekindled admiration for him while at the same time guiltily aware that her habitually plain clothing had in part caused this confusion. Had not her old nurse Gytha complained that she dressed more like a serving maid than a lady? "No, my lord," she said, knowing she should make some effort to give an account of herself.

She sensed from the abrupt silence in the great hall that Guillelm's men had now been told, in hasty whispers from the others, who she was. She could feel Sericus hovering close by, awaiting his instructions, poised for the slightest signal from her to make a formal introduction to Sir Guillelm de La Rochelle on her behalf. *But what was the use?* she thought bleakly.

He does not remember me!

She felt her eyes fill and averted her face. She had been barely on the verge of womanhood when he had left for Outremer, and they had been only friends: a chaste four-month companionship of an older youth and a young girl. Guillelm had been indulgent with her and she had foolishly taken his kindly dealings as a sign of hope for the future. A false future, as it turned out, for Guillelm did not remember her.

Not even after their trial together in the woods, when they had saved each other . . .

But she would not remind him. Pride would be her savior now.

She felt his fingers under her chin, their gentle touch almost undoing her. She lifted her head, bracing herself to explain who she was and how it was that Hardspen was so lately run down and under threat of imminent siege.

She found herself staring at a brutally handsome, smiling face, dominated by a pair of brilliant dark brown eyes.

"You gave me a rare look of welcome from the stairs just then, almost as if you knew me," Guillelm said, his smile deepening as Alyson felt herself blushing. "If I might presume on your charity, I would beg two favors."

"Yes, my lord?" Alyson prompted as he fell silent. Was he aware of every man in the room avidly watching their exchange? Already ill at ease, she wanted to run from the great hall and keep on running, far into the rain-swept night.

As if he guessed her thoughts, Guillelm gave her another swift smile. "They are nothing terrible, I vow: merely a wish for your company as I reacquaint myself with this keep"—his dark eyes gleamed in the torchlight as he added—"and your kiss of greeting."

The instant he spoke, Guillelm thought, *What am I doing?* Only a few hours earlier he had been standing before his father's tomb in the tiny local church of Olverton where Lord Robert had been buried, his head full of memories and grief. Only yesterday, when he disembarked from his ship at Bristol, had he learned that his father was dead. With that dreadful news and Hardspen castle under threat he had no time for idle, pleasant gallantries, even with a serving maid as pretty as this one.

And yet this dainty, dark-haired serving maid had given

him such a smile of welcome, and of sympathy, that he had been comforted. She had not mocked him or flinched, she had given him instead a look of recognition, as if she knew him. She was familiar to him, he felt; as familiar in some ways as the breath in his body, but his mind was moving slowly tonight, trying to take in the loss of his father and his own sudden coming into his inheritance. He had responsibilities to face; the fate of many lives had been placed by God into his hands, and he must be equal to it, not distracted by this girl who reminded him—of what? Something he had put aside long ago, with pain and regret, as being out of his reach.

But what was the use of these thoughts? he reflected, trying to fight off a well-worn, familiar despair. Women feared him—his elder sister Juliana had been proved right about that. What had Heloise of Jerusalem said to him when she had dismissed his suit? "You are too big and brutal, my lord Guillelm," she had drawled, her hazel eyes widening as she reveled in his frozen expression of shame and distaste. "They call you dragon on the field of battle—you would burn a woman to ashes in your marriage bed." He had stumbled out of Heloise's hot, airless chamber, the sight of her opulent, silk-draped body, artfully arranged blond curls and beautiful, mocking face burning like a brand into his memory, her scornful voice singeing his ears.

"My lord! Only kiss the creature and let us all return to our ale!"

Thierry again—damn the man to hellfire! Guillelm thought, scowling at the interruption and his men's laughter, swiftly stifled as they registered his anger.

"My lord!" The small, skinny seneschal was starting to say something but he was cut off by the maid herself, who observed in a low, swift voice, "Do not be concerned. All is well, Sericus."

To Guillelm there seemed to be a challenge in her words. He took a step closer, amused when she stood her ground. Again, a strange sense of recognition shot through him, an instinct that he knew her very well.

Or was it merely that he found her pleasing? the cynic in Guillelm asked him. Even when she had been standing in the shadowy stairwell, sequestered like a nun by that drab gown and veil, her beauty had shone through, brighter than any torch. She was more than a head shorter than him, small and fine-boned, so that he felt clumsy beside her, and yet she moved and carried herself as boldly as a warrior, as though she had no fear of him.

As she stood before him now, he could smell the perfume of her hair, the scent of rosemary filling his nostrils as he quelled a sudden, powerful desire to tug off her veil. From the few stray tendrils escaping the edges of that plain cloth to frame her flawless, heart-shaped face, Guillelm knew that her hair was black: very black and fine and straight. He guessed it would be long, reaching as far as her slender waist—fine shimmering tresses that a man could lay his head on for comfort, love.

"My lord?" she inquired softly as he took her hand in his. It was a work-roughened hand, resting in his as lightly as thistledown. This close, he could see the dark shadows under her eyes, the taut, bleached look of her cheeks, and was pierced by pity for her weariness. This little maid had clearly done much in this castle but where was her mistress, the new lady of Hardspen? he thought, caught in that instant between anger at the unseen chatelaine and protectiveness for her maid. He had heard rumors tonight that had set his teeth on edge: that his father had married again, that there was a widow in this keep, but he had seen no sign of such a woman.

"Mother of God, why are you alone with this?" he murmured, running a thumb gently down the side of her cheek. He felt her palm, still trapped in his right hand, tremble against his. The heat of her fingers and the warm silk of her skin stirred him afresh, making him forget all else.

Telling himself he was doing this only because his men

would otherwise consider him soft, he lowered his head and
kissed her full on the lips.

Only a few moments had passed since Guillelm had saved
her from the odious Thierry and claimed his reward of a kiss.
In the final instant, Alyson feared to allow him anything more
than the most chaste of embraces, afraid of revealing too
much of her own feelings, but now his mouth came down on
hers and she was lost. As his lips brushed hers, she felt a
shock of feeling tingle down her body in an astonishing wave
of heat. She felt his arms clamp around her slender middle,
gathering her closer, lifting her to him.

The great hall and the men gathered in it fell away to her,
there was only Guillelm and the strong yet tender embrace of
his mouth. She knew that she would probably regret it, but it
was a wish come true. Sighing, Alyson swayed against him,
closing her eyes as the voluptuousness of his kiss overcame
all thought of her duty.

Guillelm, no more aware of the raucous catcalls of his men
than Alyson was, made himself break from their embrace.
After Heloise he had a horror of forcing himself on any girl—
he had not had a woman for some time—but now this slender
black-haired maid was storming his defenses. Her lips were
so generous and sweet, and the way her hands brushed shyly
against his chest and shoulder as if she were learning him was
so fearless that he did not want to let her go. He caught her
back and swung her into his arms, conscious of a terrifying
instinct to bear this woman away somewhere private and
alone and have his way with her. He reached the staircase
without knowing it, the questions and comments from the
men and soldiers in the hall bouncing off him like rainwater.

She laid her head in the crook of his arm, her eyes still

closed, as if this was a dream for her. "Dragon," she whispered. "My golden dragon."

And then he knew her. By her nickname for him and her total fearlessness and, when she opened her eyes, almost as if she had sensed his recognition, by her solemn dark blue eyes. Eyes he had seen fixed on a patch of herbs in her father's kitchen garden, or on the stained glass windows in church, or on his own hands and arms as she soothed his various cuts and bruises from the practice field with her potions. He remembered her as a studious child, quiet and serious, passionate about healing and wishing to tend all living things, yet with a smile brighter than gold. He remembered a day in the forest, when she had saved his life.

She was here with him again, in Hardspen, and in that moment of realization, Guillelm forgot all other grief and concern in a burst of possessive pride and joy.

He kissed her again—he could not help himself. She was the best part of his past and to see her now, safe and adult and even more lovely, made him want to laugh out loud in mingled astonishment and delight.

"Alyson," he said, remembering as he named her how he had loved to make her laugh. "How excellent is this! Alyson!"

She had been so still when concentrating on her herbs and healing and yet so quick and nimble when they had run off together, racing each other to the meadows and woods. As a tall, gangly lad of nineteen he had hoped to make his fortune, earn renown throughout Christendom and then return to her father's manor at Olverton Minor to marry her. But in the end that had been a hopeless quest. Alyson's father, Sir Henry, had seen to that.

The memory of his meeting with Sir Henry blazed through Guillelm. Even after seven and a half years it was a bitter thing that left him sickened inside. All his years in the Holy Land he had fought to put the memory behind him. He had thought he had succeeded, until tonight.

"I will never give my daughter to you, Guillelm de La Rochelle," Sir Henry had told him. "She is a thoughtful, clever girl who, before she knew you, spoke of a sincere desire to enter the church as a nun. Until she knew you, Guillelm, Alyson's steadfast goal was to be a second Hildegard of Bermersheim: a scholar and sacred mystic, a healer. You have almost driven that noble aim from her head, with your endless talk of quests and chivalry. My reeve tells me that you are much in her company, and often without the presence of her nurse. Alyson is on the brink of womanhood. These outings between you must stop—yes, I know they have been so far innocent but I have my child's reputation to consider, and my own.

"Not only that, but I have seen you on the practice field— you are entirely too rash and wild. You will leave my sweet Alyson a widow within six months and your reckless head rotting on a pike. You cannot have her, and must never ask again."

Soon after that painful and disastrous encounter, Guillelm had announced his intention to go with Raymond of Poitiers to Outremer.

"Alyson of Olverton." Guillelm now gave the grown-up Alyson her title, at once entranced and saddened that she should be here. She was glad to see him—but how long would that last? How long would her innocent fearlessness of him last? He could not bear to think of her turning from him with fear in those dark blue eyes, the same blank-eyed fear he had seen in women's faces while on campaign in Outremer.

Slowly, with regret and no lessening of his own desire for her, he left the small landing and, crouching slightly to avoid the low roof-space, he carried her up the narrow spiral staircase to the chapel, where a small candle was burning. He set her down carefully on the stone floor and, so that his fingers would not linger too long on her, or give in to the violent temptation to touch her again, he put his hands behind his back.

"Alyson." He swallowed the urgent questions that he wanted to ask—was she well, had she ever thought of him while he had been away in Outremer, was she still unmarried?—and asked just two things, both equally pressing.

"Alyson, how is it that you are here? And why is there an army pitched outside this castle?"

Chapter 2

Alyson saw the delight in Guillelm's eyes fade and almost cried aloud at its passing. When he had recognized her on the stairs, he gave her then such a look—of glory, she thought, recalling how his whole face, rather grave in repose, had lightened and how his smile had driven all signs of grief from him. She had been carried off by him, amazed by his easy strength, pressed tight against his chest and torso, so close that she could feel his tough leather tunic under his woolen cloak. He smelled of rain, damp wool and his own sharp scent, and she had been torn between a desire to touch him and a wish to rest her aching head on him and sleep within the broad circle of his arms.

But that was not to be. Guillelm, grim-faced again and looming above her with his fists thrust behind his back, had asked questions that needed prompt and ready answers, no matter how painful it would be for her to explain, especially about her near-betrothal to Lord Robert. Putting that hard and tangled matter aside for the moment, she spoke first of the hostile forces ranged against Hardspen.

"The soldiers and mercenaries camped outside the gate appeared seven days ago, as soon as it became known that your father had died," she said, staring down at the chapel floor so that she did not have to watch the growing disappointment and likely horror in Guillelm's face when she told him what she had done to delay an attack from these troops. "They are the liege men of Sir Walter of Enford and the Flemish mercenary Étienne the Bold, who has joined Sir Walter on this . . . enterprise," she finished bitterly.

"I see little evidence of boldness in preparing to lay siege to the holding of a lord who has just died," Guillelm remarked in clear distaste, adding, "I could not see their standards in the rain and darkness tonight, although I think I know something of this Walter of Enford. A local man, is he not? I recall a fat and swarthy round-faced creature who could not manage his sword or his horses."

"Yes, that is Walter. He is a neighbor to your estate," Alyson confirmed, with a small smile at Guillelm's accurate description, "and lately grown very ambitious. He is still not warlike, but the man he has hired, Étienne—" A gust of wind blowing through the keep made the chapel candles flicker and Alyson shivered. "He has raided farms and manor houses hereabouts. There are many homeless peasants sheltering in the castle bailey because of the burning and pillaging of the Fleming and his troops."

"Then he must be stopped," Guillelm said at once. "And I will stop him." Clearly marking her distress, he took her hand in his again, looking startled at his own action but saying smoothly enough, "But this is not a fit subject for a house of God. Shall we move on?"

"Where do you wish to go?" Alyson asked, blushing as she wondered if she should have called Guillelm "lord," even though he now knew she was no serving maid.

If Guillelm noticed any lack of courtesy he said nothing of it. "I have already spoken to the watchmen and the men manning the battlements tonight. I have other duties to fulfill, other people I must see before this night has ended—" His voice tightened and he broke off. "Where are the womenfolk of this castle? Aside from yourself, of course. Are they all in the kitchen?"

Alyson looked up at him and smiled. "At this hour I should think they and the children will all be asleep in the store room downstairs—it is warm and dry there, and is one of the safest places in this keep. As you know," she added hastily.

He gave her fingers a gentle, reassuring squeeze. "Then lead me on very quietly past the store room. I have no wish to alarm them or disturb their rest. I am still hungry, so a visit to the kitchen will do very well."

He always had been famished, Alyson thought fondly, before her wits caught up with the rest of what he was saying. "There has been no real cooking for the last few days," she said hastily. "All food has been moved within the keep—there will be nothing for you to eat."

"But we can talk freely there and I know I will find something in the cooks' house." Guillelm grinned, driving two attractive and unlikely dimples into his tanned, lean face. "I always did in the past."

Apprehensive about their talking freely, Alyson went ahead of him down the stairs, across the back of the great hall to the huge oak door that led out of the keep into the bailey.

Before she could draw the bolt, Guillelm did it. "I can manage for myself." Pulling his cloak from his shoulders, he swept it around her and said gruffly, "It is still raining."

"Thank you." Ridiculously pleased at wearing something of his, even though it trailed past her feet, Alyson hurried down the outer staircase.

As they passed the rough tents huddling close to the keep and sheltering bailey walls, their feet slopping in the mud and puddles, she heard Guillelm mutter another string of oaths in the language of Outremer.

"I am sorry for this," she began in a low, shamed voice that was almost lost in the sweeping, chilly drizzle.

"You have nothing to be sorry for," Guillelm answered, stepping over a soggy, broken sack of beans spilled across their path. "Though in truth," he added, looking round the dark, empty and eerily quiet bailey, where there were no fires, nor indeed any signs of life within the tents, "I thought that I had left such sights as these behind me in the Holy Land. Is this the silence of hunger?"

"Of sickness and weariness. Some brought the sickness with them or, I am sorry to say, caught it here," Alyson answered, relieved that he understood. Peering into the rain, she pointed past a cart, left stranded in the bailey with a shattered axle. "The kitchen is over there, the low timber building."

"That is new since I was here last," Guillelm remarked, offering his hand to Alyson to steady her as she deftly skirted a wide puddle of water. "How long have these poor folk been here?" he asked, as Alyson tried to ignore the disturbing prickle of delight the touch of his fingers gave her, like a spark to kindling.

"A few for over a month." Her people mostly, who had come with her when Lord Robert had bluntly told Alyson that she was no longer safe in her father's manor at Olverton Minor and that her stubborn refusal to leave and join him at Hardspen was putting others at risk. "Most arrived in the last ten days."

"After my father died, the Fleming increased his raiding on those who were left with no protection," Guillelm said grimly.

"Yes." She heard the sudden squeal of a rat and gathered the folds of Guillelm's cloak closer to herself, touching the eating knife tucked through her belt. In the past few days the rats had grown more daring but so far, through shouts and stamping, and even in one case, in the stables, brandishing her knife, she had kept them at bay.

Guillelm reached the kitchen several paces ahead of her

and he shouldered open the door, which had swollen with the water. There was no one inside—the young kitchen lads and scullions who usually curled up snug in the ashes were in the store room by Alyson's express order. If an assault came on the castle, the kitchen would be particularly vulnerable to fire and any left inside easily trapped and burned alive.

While she busied herself finding a horn lantern and lighting it she was conscious of Guillelm close behind her, prowling around the tables, shelves, cooking pots, spits and cauldrons. Dreading but expecting more questions, she still was unprepared for what he did say.

"Sir Henry has gone, too, has he not? That is why you are here. My father would not have left you out in an undefended manor, no more than I would have done. What happened?" His voice was very gentle. "When did he die?"

"Just after Easter." It was easier to admit this without looking at Guillelm. "Not from this sickness and fever that came at the beginning of summer. He was felled from his horse in a hunting accident and never woke from it."

Abruptly she was back with her father in his small bed-chamber behind the comfortable great hall of their manor house, mopping his clammy face, washing his torn hands, speaking soothingly to him while her heart pounded in terror and hopelessness. Memories of that brought more memories—the last few hours of her intended betrothed, Lord Robert, who in his fever had talked to her as if she was his first wife, Guillelm's mother. Guillelm must never know, she thought, while she knew that this strange, precious time together, in quiet before the dawning of a new day and a likely attack from Étienne the Bold, would soon be at an end. *You must tell him you were about to be betrothed to his father,* her conscience goaded, while her heart clamored, *Not yet.*

"I am truly sorry for your loss."

Alyson whirled about, the horn lantern clutched protectively in front of her. "You startled me!" He had come up very close behind her, his feet silent on the stone flags. "I am sorry for your loss, also," she said quickly, meaning the words no less because she gabbled them.

"I know. I could see that from the moment I saw you again, on the stairs." His face, as beautiful to Alyson in the beams of the lantern as the carving of the stone angels in their local church, was earnest. "You always did feel for others."

For an instant he seemed on the verge of saying more, then he gave a bark of laughter. "Steady!" He caught the lamp as it dipped in her hands, the glowing light bouncing over the sooty beams and rafters. "Mother of God, you are not safe with that. You wield it like a weapon." He lifted the lantern from her trembling fingers and placed it on the nearest table.

"Are you all right?" he asked, watching her closely under thick blond eyebrows. His deep brown eyes seemed to darken even more. "Is it perhaps the sickness that has laid the rest of this place low?"

Before Alyson could move or speak, he tucked his cloak closer about her. "Do you wish me to—?"

"No!" Alyson burst out, afraid that he might offer to carry her again. She did not deserve his concern, and she was so tired it would be so very easy to fall asleep in his arms. Their every touch and embrace made it that much harder for her to tell him what she must, for it suggested a growing closeness that would be destroyed soon enough. *Let me keep my pride and not embarrass Guillelm with my unwanted feelings for him,* she thought.

"No one in this castle has been taken ill with the sweating fever for the past three days; the worst of that is over," she said, trying to sound lively and confident. Her face, tense with grief and weariness and now trying to mask her response to the tall, handsome man standing less than a hand-stretch away from her, ached as she forced a brittle smile. "With the help of the blessed Virgin we have come through," she said.

The worst of the sickness might be past, thought Guillelm, but Alyson looked close to the breaking point. He wanted to lift all care from her but knew her stubborn pride of old. He was also profoundly aware of how greatly they had both changed. When he had left for the Holy Land he was a boy and she no more than a girl. Now he was a man and she was very much a woman. Their relationship had changed forever. A few moments earlier he had been about to mention their day in the forest, where she had first teasingly called him "dragon," a title he had since taken as a battle name for himself and a rallying cry for his men. He longed to thank her again for saving his life, but he had decided against it in case such old history embarrassed her.

Yet he liked the grown-up Alyson very much. Perhaps at last the time had come when he could woo her properly—when he had dealt with the Fleming and his over-ambitious neighbor, and when Alyson's grief at her father's untimely death had faded a little. Perhaps with Alyson and her fearlessness he would prove the terrible predictions by Heloise and his elder sister wrong.

For now, to spare her more pain, he asked nothing else about the death of his father. Privately he was relieved that Lord Robert had granted Alyson and her people sanctuary: He knew from bitter personal experience that his father was not usually so charitable. There had normally been a price to be paid for help from the master of Hardspen.

Sending up a sad, regretful prayer for his father, with whom he had never been truly close, Guillelm considered more basic matters. Battles and men-at-arms were things he understood and he turned to them almost with relish as problems he could overcome. Were it not for the danger to others he could almost look forward to the morning.

"My father held this castle and lands as a vassal of King Henry. When the old king died, did he swear fealty to Henry's daughter, the Empress Maud?"

"He did—as did many others who are now foresworn, forsaking the empress for *King* Stephen, simply because Maud is a woman."

Hearing her indignant speech, Guillelm applauded her loyalty but not her sense. "England is a hard realm to rule. It needs a man," he said.

Really, he was her father all over again, thought Alyson, exasperated for the first time with the adult Guillelm. She had expected him to have shown more vision. "So Stephen demonstrates his *kingship* by stirring up civil war throughout the country?" she demanded scornfully. "Setting neighbor against neighbor, friend against friend—those for Stephen against those for Maud? Do you know *King* Stephen is even now besieging Castle Carey, less than thirty leagues from here?"

The sight of her roused struck Guillelm with a low bolt of pleasure deep in the pit of his stomach. Her eyes glittered as she spoke and her natural high color was back, stung into her cheeks and lips by indignation. Her earlier weariness flung off, she paced the length of the kitchen floor, his cloak snapping at her heels. She was so pretty that for an instant he was tempted to make her angrier than ever, but answered mildly, "And do Étienne the Bold and Walter of Enford now claim they are "acquiring" Hardspen as loyal followers of Stephen? That they will wrest it from Maud's men and hold it for the king?"

"Something very like," muttered Alyson, her light footfalls making an interesting counter-rhythm with the falling rain outside. She stopped abruptly and turned to him, lifting her head. The determined, lost look on her face reminded Guillelm of men he had seen in battle, casting themselves into the thick of the fray when all hope of victory was lost. It chilled him.

"What is it?" he asked softly.

"The day Walter and his troops appeared, I put him and the Fleming off by begging their leave for us to bury and mourn your father with all due honors," she said, twisting the edge of his cloak between her fingers until she clearly realized what she was doing and tucked her hands out of sight. "They left us in peace for three days after that."

"Ingenious and not so far from the truth," Guillelm remarked, wondering at her terms—*I put him and the Fleming off*—why her? Why not one of the men or, God forbid, the as yet unseen widow of Hardspen castle? Guillelm shrugged off the last thought. Although the widow, if real, was one of those he must see tonight, he was beginning to seriously doubt the existence of such a female. "And then?" he prompted.

Alyson closed her eyes a moment, then opened them. "I had the men daub a mixture of mud and pig's blood on their faces and hands and let it dry so that it scaled. I myself appeared on the battlements with my face veiled. I told the herald that the fever, which still raged within the castle, had left us this way. Walter of Enford is very particular in regard to his person," she added apologetically. "I hoped our play of blistered faces might dissuade him from too hasty an attack. We had sent messages to the empress by then. With every hour that passed, we hoped for a relieving force to come to our aid."

"I see." The Walter of Enford he remembered had been as vain and strutting as an Eastern peacock, Guillelm thought, his lips itching to laugh aloud at Alyson's clever deception. "And how long did your device win you?"

"Another day." She sighed and resumed her pacing. "In truth, there was real sickness still within the bailey and we were sorely pressed."

"Of that I have no doubt," remarked Guillelm, quiet and serious again. "Did my father's steward die during that time?"

"He did—as did many of his people, which is why my poor Sericus, who is less than nimble, is now seneschal. There was no other left but Sericus with the necessary experience and who could also be spared from possible fighting duty." She was still and staring at the floor again, her earlier brightness dimmed. "All my tending and potions—I could not save them."

It pained Guillelm that she seemed ashamed. "You did all that man or woman could. Do not reproach yourself."

Still she would not look at him. *The men follow her orders,* he thought. *Why? Because she has wit and beauty?* Those alone, although excellent, surely would not be sufficient inducements for grizzled veterans to obey her, even with the castle reeling with sickness. A dark suspicion bloomed in his mind, one he swiftly ignored.

"So the herald of Walter and Étienne returned the following day," he went on, "and presumably he was no longer prepared to wait on any more delays. What reply did you give when Walter and the Fleming demanded that Hardspen should now be held as a castle of King Stephen's? Did you agree and hold them off with your answer?"

"No!" Her eyes flashed pride. "What do you take me for? Lord Robert held Hardspen for the empress. Should I then deny his loyalty and cynically change sides?"

"Men have done such things before."

"Then men are wrong! Oh, I know you think me a child," she went on, jerking her head up to face Guillelm, "but I am one and twenty, two years older than you were when you traveled to Outremer. I have seen the world."

Guillelm whistled one soft low note to himself, a habit when greatly touched and determined not to show it. With her avowal, Alyson reminded him of himself as a youth, idealistic and ardent, but matters did not ring true here.

"Events did not fall out that way?" he asked in seeming innocence.

"No! No." She swallowed and even in the dim light of the horn lantern he could see the beginnings of a blush.

"There were two heralds," she admitted guardedly. "One from each commander, coming at different times. I—I put them both off by saying I needed proper due time to consider their offers, but they have grown impatient."

"They are not alone in that," said Guillelm warningly. She was still not telling all she knew, and time was passing.

"I am supposed to give my answers tomorrow," Alyson said despairingly. "Today," she added, glancing at the closed kitchen shutters, through which the gray wet night was beginning to lighten.

Again she lapsed into silence. Listening to her quickened breathing and the unearthly call of a nightjar in the pounding rain, Guillelm was struck again by the quiet of the castle: a quiet filled with tension and dread. Striving for the ordinary, he placed the scrap of cheese he had found in one of the earthen crocks onto the table and, in an act of deliberate trust, offered Alyson the eating knife from his belt.

"Let us eat. You cut and I will choose my portion." They had done this many times in the past.

"You remembered," she said softly, taking the knife from him and halving the cheese with a swift deftness he also remembered. A smile tugged briefly at her lips. "And you also found food."

"As I always do." Guillelm took the smaller half of cheese, biting into its dry saltiness. It seemed all rind, but Alyson, he noticed, ate her portion with care, as if telling herself to be slow. She was too thin, he thought with pity.

As she returned him his knife, hilt first, he asked lightly, "Those two commanders outside the gates asked for your hand in marriage, did they not? That was their final offer: a wedding or a siege. And who will you choose? Walter or Étienne?"

"Neither, for neither pleases me, nor the rest of the people in Hardspen, which is why we have been preparing for a siege after I tell them both no, and the worst—" She broke off.

"You tricked me into answering! Because I let my guard down when we shared food!"

"I am an experienced campaigner with quite as many ruses as you seem to have," Guillelm replied, amused afresh by her ready indignation and pleased and relieved by her refusal of both men. He pulled an empty barrel out of the shadows and sat down on it amongst the spits of the cold and dusty fireplace. Now, with his face level with hers and looking closely into her eyes, he said, "Sir Walter and the Flemish mercenary each offered you marriage. I tell you frankly, Alyson, that I am wondering why they should do this—unless as a means to secure the castle and its lands."

Under straight and level black brows she met his look boldly. "I have my own lands."

"Yes, and I remember Sir Henry's manor as a well-maintained place with good farmland. But you are at Hardspen and the men here appear to be following your orders. Why is that? Tell me, please. Tell me the truth."

Faced with his direct appeal, Alyson knew she must speak. Hoping he would understand her near-betrothal as, marvelously, he had understood and sympathized with the rest of what she had done, she caught up her courage. "Your father, Lord Robert, graciously—"

"Are the rumors true?" he interrupted suddenly. "That somewhere in this keep there is a new mistress? No doubt she is very comfortable and idle in her solar out of the rain and weather as she counts the gold of her widow's dues. I will need to pay my respects soon to the grieving chatelaine."

His cynicism shook her and she blurted out, "But I am Lord Robert's intended! Your father asked me to marry him and I accepted! We were to be betrothed. Does that make me mercenary?"

Guillelm folded his arms across his broad chest. "My condolences on your recent loss, my lady," he said, without looking quite at her, his voice as flat as the water on a millpond. "Had you told me this earlier, I would have shown you the honor that you deserve."

"I was going to tell you, as soon as I could—"

Guillelm rose to his feet and stepped back. "You seemed in little haste to do so. Were you hoping to gull me, too, my lady?"

His formality hurt Alyson but she was determined to defend herself. "I have told you now," she said, shrugging off his cloak—if he thought her foul, then she should not wear or touch anything of his. "My father made the match with yours."

"And you agreed."

"Yes." After much anxious pleading and more from her father. In the worsening turmoil of the growing civil war Sir Henry had wanted a strong ally and so had offered Alyson's hand to Lord Robert. Failing to bend her to his wishes by the threat of violence or semistarvation, Sir Henry had painted a terrible picture of what would happen to the people if marauders were allowed to roam unchecked over their land, and in the end, Alyson could not bear the thought of their suffering. "I agreed, but asked that our betrothal might be held off, at least until my older sister was safely settled," she whispered, ashamed afresh that she had ever given way.

It was bad enough to hear this, Guillelm thought, but to have Alyson calmly confess that she had consented to a union with his *father* was another blow. Upon leaving for Outremer he had never spoken of his boyish hopes of marriage to Alyson, never entreated her in any way to wait for him, but now in a fit of possessive temper he found himself asking, "How long were you betrothed to my father?"

"We were never formally plighted . . . it was an understanding, for the last five months. There had been no news of you from Outremer for three years." She had mourned him as dead, had finally given way to her father's bullying and wishes because she thought Guillelm was dead, but now Alyson would not admit that and expose herself to more of his cold mockery.

"And before that you had been plighted to no others?"

Did he really think her so easy in her affections? Turning from him toward the kitchen door, Alyson replied coolly, "Until my father proposed the match, I had given serious thought to joining the church. Indeed, my older sister, Matilda, had a true vocation and she has joined the sisters at the small convent of Saint Foy."

Alyson sighed, thinking of Tilda, whom she had not seen for five months. Tilda had been desperate to join the nuns but Alyson knew that without the generous dowry their father had given to the convent, her shy and withdrawn elder sister would have fared far less well—the money, grants of land and jewels had given Tilda a high status at Saint Foy's, and much-needed protection. Here had been another pressing reason for Alyson herself to accept Lord Robert's suit, since her own father could not afford two such dowries and Guillelm's father had waved the whole matter aside. "Alyson will give me more sons," Lord Robert had said.

Hearing her sigh, Guillelm dismissed his earlier ideas of wooing Alyson to be his wife. It was hopeless—she wanted to enter the church, as Sir Henry had warned him all those years ago. *But she agreed to be my father's bride, even if she was not actually betrothed to him,* he thought, and a fresh blaze of anger and jealousy ran through him.

"So you have the choice of two proposals," he remarked through clenched teeth. "I offer you a third, my lady. Hardspen is mine and all who dwell within its bounds. I can and will defend it against all comers and yet it is clear to me that you have ingratiated yourself with the people here."

"Ingra— How dare you? I have done no such thing!"

He held up a hand and overrode her exclamation of protest. "It will be easier for me if you remain as chatelaine, not as Lord Robert's intended betrothed or widow but as my wife. You say you were never formally plighted, so there will be no consanguinity, or spiritual affinity. The priest will marry us." He spoke as if uttering a threat.

"Forgive me if I do not fall to my knees as I offer you my hand in marriage," he went on, as Alyson stood with her back to the kitchen door, scarcely believing what she was hearing, "but the morning is almost on us and I must return to my men outside the castle. Before I go, I would have your answer. Will you be my wife? What do you say?"

Chapter 3

"I must be mad," Alyson said to herself, stalking to and fro on the battlements at noon the following day. "Why did I agree to anything last night? Why did I allow him to take over?"

In truth she had been given no choice. Leading the way from the kitchen and returning to the keep with her hurrying to keep pace with his long-legged stride, Guillelm instantly began to give orders. When Sericus and a few others looked to her, Guillelm said bluntly, "This lady is soon to be my betrothed and she agrees with me."

Before she could draw breath even to suggest alternatives, let alone to argue with him, he turned to her, lowered his head and said in a steely voice, over the ragged applause of the startled but obviously pleased defenders, "I tell you this now, my lady— in private I may give way to you but you will never contradict me in public before my followers. That would make me look a fool and you a scold; it would bring neither of us credit."

"I understand, *my lord.*" Alyson was almost too angry to speak, and Guillelm increased her fury by saying in a carrying voice, "But you are weary with toil, my lady. I pray you, return to your solar and take your rest while you may."

"Try my name, why don't you?" Alyson had hit back. "You

will find it quicker than saying 'my lady' at the beginning or end of your every command."

"As you wish—Alyson." Guillelm's eyes glinted with scarcely concealed mirth as he added, "Soon you and your maids will be busy with preparations for our forthcoming marriage, and I would not have you wear yourself out before our wedding night."

So she had been forced to withdraw, amidst many whispered and no doubt suggestive comments. Storming into her chamber, she was unable even to give vent to her feelings by the childish slamming of the door—not when she spotted the pale sleeping faces of Gytha and Osmoda in her bed.

Joining them on top of the covers, hardly expecting to close her eyes, much less to sleep, Alyson was amazed when she stirred only several hours later, finding herself still on top of the bed but with her maids gone from the chamber and with Guillelm's cloak spread over her. When she later found Gytha and asked her how she had come by the cloak, her round-faced former nurse, as small and plump as a robin and as scarlet-breasted in her russet gown, gave her a shrewd look and a large smile.

"I neither saw nor heard a thing, little mistress, but they do say love is winged, do they not?"

Caught between exasperation and a chill despair, Alyson hid her true feelings and shook her head. "I think they are wrong, Gytha."

"Time will tell," came the comfortable answer as Gytha, moving slowly while she recovered her strength after her fever, carefully shook out their bedding over the battlements. By then the enemy forces had already begun to melt away and the people within Hardspen felt free to go where they wished.

Now, from her high vantage point, Alyson could watch the departing forces of Walter of Enford and Étienne the Bold trundle slowly away over the downs, their battle standards hanging limp in the damp, still air. It was no longer raining, but their passing horses, carts and men had churned up great seams of thick brown mud, and the pale patches of dying grass where they had pitched their tents were clearly visible. Watching them leave gave her a strange sense of anticlimax and unreality, as if these fighting men with their drooping shoulders and bedraggled arms were no more than wool merchants and pots and pans traders, leaving after a fair. Straggling groups of children from the castle and local farms, released from the gloomy safety of the keep's store room, were already outside the castle walls, picking over the shattered pots and broken arrow shafts of the routed enemy.

"What did he say to them, that they should leave so readily?" she muttered, looking over the deserted enemy camp in vain for Guillelm's bright head. When she had last seen him over an hour ago as she and the other castle women swept out the ale- and food-spattered rushes from the great hall—a task impossible in the frantic preparations for a siege—Guillelm had been shouting orders in the bailey. He was without his helmet then, so that all should see and recognize the new lord of Hardspen.

Leaning against the battlements, the stones warmed by a pale primrose sun, Alyson turned toward the woodland growing close to the eastern side of the bailey walls. From there she could see a steady stream of men and horses emerging from the trees and entering the bailey in a shining, well-disciplined array. Battle-seasoned troops, she recognized, noting their tanned faces, gleaming horses and sharp, bright weapons— Guillelm's own men, whose sudden appearance must have given Walter and his ally a considerable shock.

They were wise to give way without a fight, Alyson thought, but she still wondered what Guillelm had said to them. She doubted that she would ever learn what had happened, while she was asleep and Guillelm met the heralds of Walter and Étienne. Had he said, "So be it," when they reached agreement, as he had to her the previous night when she said yes to his unexpected, shocking proposal?

"Why did he ask me to marry him? He does not love me." The spoken words brought her no comfort or understanding. Searching for Guillelm amidst the large and increasingly noisy throng in the bailey, she recalled with a shiver how he'd looked at her when she whispered 'Yes.' His handsome, chiseled face was impossibly suave and unreadable. By no stiffening or even the slightest movement of his large, muscular body or lightening of his watchful dark eyes had he shown any emotion, not even satisfaction.

Alyson stared at the broom in her hand, wondering why she had wasted time climbing to the battlements for a glimpse of a man who did not want her when there was so much to be done.

"You have been a fool," she told herself harshly as she sped back to the staircase leading down to the bailey. But she knew that given the choice afresh, she would do the same. She had loved Guillelm the youth, and surely the man could not be so very changed? He had been far from indifferent when he kissed her. She could not forget the devastating tenderness of his embrace.

He has seen seven years of war, the sensible part of her mind warned her. *He will have known horrors that you can only imagine.*

Yet he has brought no bride with him and he has asked you to marry him, Alyson answered herself with the stubborn, unquenchable optimism of one-and-twenty. "I feel—I know—that I can love this man, that he is well worthy of all love," she said aloud, her feet quickening on the treads of the staircase. "So why should I not agree to this marriage? After all, I risk no other but myself."

Hoping that her bold words would not prove false, Alyson sped out of the shadowy staircase into the pallid sunshine, preparing to make her way to the stables, then to the kitchen.

New strewing herbs were needed for the great hall, and she must check that there was sufficient fodder for the horses and look over the sheep pens and see how Edwin the shepherd was faring. He had been sick with the fever, but not so badly as some of the others.

Approaching the heaving sheep pens, Alyson heard Edwin's panicky, "No!" and she saw a small black lamb leap from the tall shepherd's flailing arms and go jinking wildly across the bailey. With Edwin's shouts and the mother ewe's deep bleating in her ears, Alyson dropped her broom and cut through the milling groups in the yard toward the incoming ranks of soldiers, her outstretched arms reaching for the lost lamb.

The black lamb skidded away from another woman who tried to seize it and bounded closer still to the men in armor and their huge, glossy mounts. Alyson put on a spurt of speed to intercept the tiny, mewing creature before it was trampled underfoot.

"Caught you!" she cried, her spirits lifting for an instant as she snatched the small squirming body out of the way of the hulking warriors, with their spears, scabbards, and iron-shod warhorses.

"You, girl! Get back!"

Too late, Alyson realized just how close she had come to the incoming troops. A warrior in full harness, his face hidden by his iron helm, was bearing down on her, atop a massive bay charger. As the man made no effort to turn or slow the high-stepping horse, she flung herself out of its path, where it passed by her so close that she could smell its shining coat and feel the slap of the embroidered saddle cloth against her cheek. She gasped angrily, a protest echoed more vocally by several in the bailey, especially Sericus, who had just appeared on the outer stairway of the keep.

"Hey! Watch where you are going!" her loyal seneschal bawled, his usually sallow face turning red with indignation. "You almost crushed your own—"

"Stop your blathering, old man," came the cold response from the warrior on horseback, an insolent reply that had Alyson's quick temper boiling.

"How dare you speak to Sericus in that way!" she shouted up at the tall, disdainful figure, quickly handing Edwin his black lamb as the shepherd pushed through the now encircling men and horses to join her. From the corner of her eye she saw Sericus limping quickly down the steps to do the same and called out, "Stay back! I will deal with this.

"Now, sir," she continued, fixing her eyes on the man who had almost ridden her down, "would you care to explain yourself?"

Tossing the reins of his charger to another mounted knight, the warrior on horseback dismounted in a clatter of armor and spurs. "Who are you to demand anything of me, girl?" he asked in the same dry, cold voice as before, glaring down at her in clear disdain. "It was your own folly that caused this."

"And what if the lamb had been a child?" Alyson blazed out in return. "What of my shepherd's livelihood, which is, I deem, as worthy as yours! More, for it is the arts of peace and tending of new life, without which you soldiers would have nothing. You made no attempt to avoid us!"

"Should I ruin my horse's mouth for your stupidity?" Stepping even closer, the arrogant stranger suddenly grabbed her arm. "Perhaps a beating will teach you better manners before you go about your serving duties."

"Do not!" Alyson ordered, appalled that he should actually lay hands on her. Catching a glimpse through his battle-worn helm of a thin, sneering mouth and glinting blue eyes, cold as the sky above them, the thought came to her, *this man is my enemy,* and for an instant she knew real fear. "No!" she cried, struggling furiously in his grip. "Stop!"

"I think not," said the stranger, ignoring cries of outrage and warning from others in the bailey as he drew back his arm to strike her.

"Enough! Release her!" Mowing a path through the soldiers and horses, Guillelm's face was dark with anger, a smoldering rage rising off his powerful frame as a palpable force. Against that, even the fully armored stranger visibly paled, letting go of Alyson as if she burned.

"You are unharmed?" Guillelm asked as he reached her, his large hand brushing her arm where the stranger had manhandled her.

"Yes, but—"

"Then I will deal with this. I bid you go to your room."

He was ordering her away as if she were a child. Alyson's relief and gratitude at his timely intervention turned to indignation. "Did you see what happened?" she demanded in a low, taut voice. "This man has insulted members of my household—"

Guillelm's face stiffened. "This man, as you call him, is my own seneschal."

"That excuses his conduct?" Alyson asked, scarcely believing what she was hearing. "He insulted me!"

If possible, Guillelm's eyes became colder still. "And how would he know what was due to you, my lady? Given the manner of your dress?"

Aware that the stranger was now smirking, Alyson lost her temper completely. "If I dress discreetly that is my choice! As for dues, if I was a serf I would still be owed courtesy and gentleness from this knight. You train your people very ill!"

She turned to leave, but Guillelm overtook her after only two steps. "In here." He half-guided, half-carried her into the stables, not stopping until they had reached an empty stall. "Now, my lady Alyson." He barred the stall entrance with his own body. "You will go to your chamber as I have requested. This is the second time you have been mistaken for a little serving maid by one of my men and it must not happen again. I do not wish to see you in this yard or anywhere in this castle, until you are dressed in a manner more fitting to your station and to me."

That was all he cared about—how she reflected on him, Alyson thought, her mind fizzing with fury at his words, his insulting reference to her as a "little serving maid," and his earlier action, where he had drawn her ahead of him into the stables as if she were no more than a handcart. She was still more concerned with what he had just told her about the knight who had almost beaten her.

"That seneschal of yours—is such a person to replace Sericus, who is worth twice of him?" she demanded.

"Be at peace, my lady. They will work together, or I will know the reasons why not," rumbled Guillelm, his face in shadow.

"I hope you are right, my lord," she answered, angry and alarmed for Sericus and still smarting over what had almost happened. "He should have known I was of gentle birth from the manner of my speech!"

Guillelm frowned but somehow looked less forbidding. "Yes, I am surprised myself that he did not recognize your true station from that," he admitted grudgingly. "Unlike Thierry from last night, Fulk speaks English well and if he had listened properly he should have known at once."

He shook his head, his lips shaping into a rueful smile. "But then, my lady, we both know that I myself mistook you for a maid, and that even after you had spoken to me."

"Then you did not listen properly, either!" Alyson retorted, furious afresh at his admitting this and blushing as she remembered their kiss.

He touched the shoulder of her plain brown gown with a fingertip. "It is the woman we see first—"

"I will dress as I please!"

"And how will it be for our formal betrothal ceremony tomorrow?" he asked with dangerous mildness. "Will you appear in beige, in undyed homespun?"

"No! I—" Alyson had not forgotten the ceremony, but hearing Guillelm speak of it brought their betrothal, and eventual marriage, that much closer. Suddenly, she felt dizzy, light-headed. She pressed a hand to her stomach, glad she had eaten no breakfast. For an instant, she could not say if she was pleased or terrified at the prospect, but then she caught a lost, almost haunted look flicker across Guillelm's face. At once, a great surge of protectiveness rushed through her—she had called him dragon and now if she could she would slay dragons for him.

"I will not shame you," she said tartly, using irritation as a shield to hide these feelings as part of her wished to comfort him as she had as a girl, by flinging herself about his neck and hugging him tightly. "You will have no further cause to re-proach me."

"Mother of God!" Guillelm folded his arms and took sev-eral deep breaths, clearly trying to control his temper. In a gentler, more careful way, he asked, "Why are you in such plain attire, Alyson, as if in training for the convent?"

She had been, many years earlier, and the strictures of the nuns against worldly vanity and needless show were lessons she found hard to shake off, Alyson thought, touched by his use of her name. There was another, closer reason why she had dressed simply, but that was more personal and painful. How could she possibly tell Guillelm, who had just lost his father, that Lord Robert had burnt her better gowns? That he had envied her youth and learning? Guillelm must never know such things, she vowed, determined to preserve his memory of his father.

"You know I have little interest in clothes," she said, which was half a lie and half the truth. Guillelm, however, was not convinced.

"But why so drab?" he continued gently. He studied her a moment, a slight stiffening coming over his long, lean body as a look of wariness replaced his earlier concern. "Was it my father's wish?"

"I—" Remembering Lord Robert's angry and soon-ignited jealousy, Alyson looked down at the hay-strewn stable floor, conscious of the shifting horses and grooms around them. She prayed her face had given nothing away, but Guillelm had always been quick at reading her moods.

"So you dressed to please him," he said, all previous gentleness stripped from his voice. "Then there will indeed be little change for you, my lady. You dressed to please your old lord and now you will dress to please your new lord."

She had to try to make him understand, and without telling him too much that would dishonor his father's memory in his eyes, Alyson thought, as Guillelm unfolded his arms, his face as unyielding as stone. "Please, you must understand—" she began desperately, but he would not listen.

"I must discipline the knight who mistook you," he said harshly, "though I think it hard on him, for he fell victim to a woman's wiles. And I doubt if he will wear your favor too quickly after this, my lady."

With a mocking bow he turned and strode back into the yard, leaving Alyson with the image of his contemptuous smile and, far worse, with the dreadful fear that she had made a terrible mistake in hoping that one day he might ever come to love her as a husband should his wife.

Returning to deal with his own man, Guillelm clamped down hard on the feelings of jealousy that his latest encounter with Alyson had provoked. Bitterly aware of the mutterings and pointings, the scandalized faces of her people in the bailey, he crossed to his knights, warning himself to keep his anger in check.

Only that morning, just after dawn, he had walked into the enemy camp, alone and unheralded, in his long cloak and the jazerant that an Arab armorer had ornamented with his own personal symbol: a dragon rampant, breathing a coil of fire. By the time Étienne the Bold knew that he was there, he was in the mercenary's tent, crouching by the man's rough pallet of straw, his knifepoint at his enemy's throat.

"The Lady of Hardspen is to be my lady and I will suffer no insult, no slight to her," he told Étienne. "You will leave now or fight me, man to man, in single combat."

"But how did you come here?" Étienne stammered, his lean, weather-beaten face breaking into a sweat as he realized that none of his men were about to rescue him.

Guillelm smiled. "Straight through your lines, even as I am. Several of your guards will have thick heads until sunset today; I had to knock them out to prevent them raising a general alarm."

"You are mad!" Étienne the Fleming gasped, his neck reddening where the point of Guillelm's hunting knife rested. "Alone in an enemy camp—"

"I can move silently enough," Guillelm answered, "and when no one conceives of a thing being possible, it is relatively easy to accomplish. Men see what they want to see, and none of your knights wanted to see me."

"It is mad!" Étienne repeated. "Reckless!"

Guillelm grinned at the charge, remembering Sir Henry's bitter words and taking a certain satisfaction in proving Alyson's father wrong. "Reckless perhaps, but my head is still firmly on my shoulders, as you see," he observed. "This way is quicker and quieter, Étienne. Join one of King Stephen's or Empress Maud's war-bands; either will give you welcome and richer booty than you will get hereabouts."

"The pickings have been scanty, certainly," Étienne muttered in French. "Not what I was promised."

Giving the mercenary another moment to reflect on that self-interested thought, Guillelm returned to his main point. "You can give Walter the same message: he leaves or fights. *My* men are fresh and seasoned from the Crusades. I suggest you both leave."

Recalling Étienne's widening eyes as the Fleming imagined the likely outcome of such a contest, his stammered word of honor as a knight that he would stop the siege and leave the district, Guillelm permitted himself a grim smile. He had gauged the courage of the two men correctly. After he had stunned the Fleming with a deft blow and walked slowly through the stirring camp in the same easy way as he had come, he watched Étienne and Walter turn tail and leave without further struggle.

Men he could always deal with, he thought. Perhaps that was how he should treat Alyson, as a kind of youth. He snorted, knowing the idea was impossible; she was too feminine. Yet brave. He had seen the end of her clash with Fulk—she had stood up to an armored knight and flung back just, round answers to Fulk's arrogance and all for the sake of a stray lamb.

In those moments, he had been so proud of her, and so furious at Fulk. If the man had actually hit her, he would be spitting teeth or worse by now, Guillelm thought, his hands tightening into fists. As he had closed with Fulk and Alyson in the yard, he had found his sword hand going straight to his belt, and if he had been armed, things might have gone very badly for Fulk. Yet Fulk was a man whom he trusted with his life, whom he had fought beside in the Holy Land, who had been his own second-in-command for six of his seven years in Outremer. Fulk would be his seneschal here, a reward for true service, and he could not have the man humiliated because of one sorry misunderstanding. That was why he had taken Fulk's part in the bailey and remonstrated Alyson on her dress, an act he now regretted, for Alyson was right: Were she only a cottar's child, Fulk should not have treated her as he did.

He had been wrong himself, Guillelm admitted. She had not started the incident but, after his relief that she was unharmed, he was unfairly angry with Alyson also, and scolded her without cause. "She has bewitched me," he growled under his breath.

Yet he was not wrong to have offered her marriage. Her kiss had stirred him as the embrace of no other woman had ever done, even the voluptuous Heloise. The thought of her even smiling at another man acted like poison in a wound; he had to possess her or he would have no peace. And the people here loved her. He had been unjust when he called the Lady of Hardspen idle—Alyson was none such, and her servants repaid her with loyalty. Everywhere he went in the castle he had heard the same words, "The little mistress helped with that; she is a good, true lady." He had seen her own weariness for himself, when he looked in on her sleeping in her chamber just after her maids had risen. She had not stirred when he placed his cloak over her, except to sigh and curl the fingers of one hand about the collar.

When he thought of those same narrow, work-worn hands touching him, he marveled at the idea. She was still unafraid of him, fighting him even in the stable, where for a dreadful moment she had seemed confounded, genuinely terrified, before she rallied, tossing words at him as if they were spears. He had been torn between amusement, a guilty shame at the justice of her complaints, and irritation at being so wrong-footed by a girl of one-and-twenty. Perhaps with her he would prove Juliana and Heloise wrong; perhaps he might even be able to woo her, as he had thought of doing ever since seeing her again.

But only if you can quench your own envy of your father, Guillelm's conscience warned. "I know that," he said under his breath, anger stirring in him again. Dressing to please his father, that miserly, crabbed old man! "She will do the same for me and more," he vowed darkly, trying to put all thought of Alyson from his mind as he walked up through the lines of his own men to a glowering but distinctly nervous Fulk.

Chapter 4

Stalking into her chamber, Alyson was disconcerted to find her nurse kneeling at one of the store chests, lifting out bolts of cloth, belts, gloves and other clothes. Two cloaks, three veils, a linen apron and a dark woolen gown were heaped across the bed as Gytha plunged a plump arm into the depths of the oak chest, murmuring, "I knew I kept these as more than a keepsake! I think the new lord will be very pleased, especially if Osmoda can find a matching veil for the blue-green gown . . ."

Had Guillelm spoken to her servants already, given them orders? Alyson put down the spark of anger that bloomed within her; if he had there was little she could do about it. But no, it seemed she had done her soon-to-be-betrothed an injustice—Gytha chattered on, oblivious to her mistress's entrance.

"At last I will robe my lady as she deserves! The new lord will surely not be as wretched and miserly as the old—"

Alyson gave a gentle warning cough and Gytha swung round, giving her former charge a gap-toothed smile.

"There you are, my bird! Come, help me; my eyes cannot see so well these days and I do not want this material to tear."

Crouching, Alyson did as she was bid and together she and

Gytha lifted out two gowns, spreading them on top of a second, flat-topped chest.

"You remember them," Gytha remarked quietly, as Alyson trailed a fingertip over the flowing skirts.

Alyson nodded. "Tilda never wore these," she said, and at once her head was full of memories for her troubled elder sister. She missed Tilda—her slow smile, the shy way she ducked her head before answering a question, her kindness. When they were small, she and Tilda had slept together; Alyson still missed her sister's warmth and scent.

"The convent was the best place for her," Gytha said softly, "with her . . . unease around men."

Terror of men was the more accurate, Alyson reflected bleakly, recalling how Tilda had shrunk back even from their father. Given their mother's tragic history, Alyson understood it but it made her acceptance of Tilda's final choice no easier. She had relinquished the world gladly, entering the closed order of nuns seemingly without a thought for those she was leaving behind.

She is safe in a holy place and you should be pleased for her, Alyson told herself sternly, while she shook her head violently at Gytha's suggestion that she try on the two gowns.

"Your sister would be happy if you wore them," her nurse coaxed, "and you surely cannot grace your betrothal ceremony in that ghastly, plain attire," she went on, tugging on Alyson's homespun for emphasis. "Your hair is so pretty and that dull veil does nothing for it, and yet I have seen how the new lord looks at your raven locks."

"Raven!" Alyson scoffed, giving herself away when she asked, "Guillelm has noticed, you say?"

Her red-cheeked nurse gave her a knowing glance. "Your hair will be prettier still when it is washed. I saw that your lord has set some of his men to clearing out and preparing the bathhouse. Do you think you will bathe each other tomorrow?

No?" Gytha chuckled at Alyson's scalding blush. "Perhaps later, when you are truly married."

If only to silence her nurse, Alyson swooped hastily on the nearest gown, of rich blue wool, hemmed with vermilion. Fumbling with the ties of her rough gown, she muttered, "I will wear this today and the other tomorrow." The green-blue of that gown would look well against Guillelm's bright golden coloring.

"A good choice, my lady," her nurse soothed. "It shows off the color of your eyes, and I have found a gold belt that Lord Robert did not know you had, else no doubt he would have taken that from you, as well as your other jewels—"

"Gytha!"

"These things should be admitted, my lady." Her voice faded and she busied herself with helping Alyson unpin her veil.

Alyson said nothing. At tomorrow's ceremony she would have no family due to circumstances but no female friends either, because of Lord Robert. His grasping jealousy had made it impossible for her to keep any friends.

Almost as an echo to her thought, Gytha said, "There will be few folk to attend your betrothal, not with your lord so lately returned from Outremer and knowing so few nobles hereabouts. I cannot remember if he has a large family, but even if he has, they will not be able to come at such short notice."

"No," Alyson said faintly, blushing afresh as she now considered the haste of their match. "Guillelm has few close kindred; no brothers or cousins. His only sister is married and settled far off, somewhere in the north."

"No need to catch your breath, my bird; I've done the lacing up as tight as it will go." Gytha stood with her head on one side and then clapped her hands. "We need a fresh veil."

"The old will have to do for today," Alyson said hastily, recollecting the many tasks she had yet to do and oversee. "Quickly, Gytha! Help me reorder my hair a little."

"All done," said her nurse a few moments later, catching

Alyson's arm before she sped from the chamber. "Look at yourself! You have not taken one peep at your reflection." She pointed to the deep basin standing on a low table close to the bed—washing water left from the morning, Alyson recollected guiltily. With most of the maidservants in the castle still recovering from the sweating sickness it had become her habit to empty the basin herself. Now, however, at Gytha's insistent prodding she leaned over the bowl, seeing a murky, blue-gowned stranger.

"My thanks," she said, and hurried off.

Her mind once more on strewing herbs for the great hall, Alyson found herself drawn to the bailey. "I have to find my broom," she murmured, although that was only part of the truth. If she was honest, she was also hoping to see Guillelm—and that he would see her.

With his height and breadth and dazzling hair she spotted him at once, the sight quickening her breathing and already hurrying steps. Working in the increasing warmth of the sun, he had stripped his brown wool mantle down to his waist, revealing a linen undershirt so fine as to be almost transparent. She could see the hard, sinewy contours of his back, the mat of chest hair that she suddenly longed to touch, teasingly running her fingers through those fine gold strands while tracing the pattern of his muscles . . .

Blushing, Alyson shook herself and tried to concentrate on what Guillelm was doing. He was dismantling the stranded cart with the shattered axle, while at the same time shouting orders to his men who were distributing bread and ale to the tented poor who had crowded for shelter within the bailey. As he roared out an incomprehensible mixture of French, Arabic and English to his seasoned followers, he was hammering at the cart—even as Alyson watched, he dropped the hammer and lifted the entire planked floor of the cart free of the broken axle, hefting it into the waiting, eager arms of two men whom she recognized as farriers from one of Hardspen's nearby hamlets.

"That should serve as a new door for your mother's house," Guillelm called, while the farriers braced themselves to receive their gift. They were panting with effort, but Guillelm was scarcely out of breath. Straightening, he surveyed the milling crowds within the bailey, picking Alyson out at once. His dark eyes gleamed and he beckoned.

"Still no attendants with you, I see," he remarked, as she approached.

"The sickness, my lord," she began, aggrieved that he should fault her for something she could not help.

He grinned, as if sensing her irritation. "Peace, bright-eyes," he said, giving Alyson the nickname he had coined for her years earlier, when he had been a gangling, big-jointed youth. "Have you seen a saw anywhere close?"

Silently, Alyson deftly scooped up a saw from beneath the cart's wheels and held it out.

"My thanks." Taking the tool, his fingers brushed against hers, their brief touch deepening the luster in his eyes, as he added, in a voice only she could hear, "The gown is fine."

Was that a stain of color in his tanned face? Alyson scarcely dared hope that it was; if he was shy of her that was worth more than polished compliments, although for him to say so little—

"You approve, my lord?" Heartened by the fact he was no longer angry with her, she twirled on the spot for him.

"Greatly." His lips quivered. "If the Empress Maud could see you now, doubtless she would be envious. I have sent word to her this morning of our betrothal."

As a fact, Alyson noted, and not in any way to ask Maud's permission. She nodded and recollected her manners. "Thank you for sharing your men's rations with my people."

Guillelm inclined his head. "My people, also," he observed,

regarding the ordered handing out of foodstuffs for a moment before saying, "Food is as good a way as any to ensure loyalty."

"Is that your only reason?" Alyson burst out, realizing by Guillelm's expression that he was teasing. "You tricked me!"

"Only to check if you still wrinkled your nose when you do not approve—which you do."

"And your eyebrows still meet when you frown," Alyson replied, deliberately baiting. "You are doing it now!"

"Enough of your pretty insolence, my girl. I have work to do."

"Yes, and I have a great many fresh strewing herbs to collect and a great hall to make ready and one of the cooks to find, but you only say that because you have lost the argument," Alyson rejoined, stepping back swiftly in a swirl of skirts.

She had been taunting a little but did not expect the speed or power of his reactions: Guillelm dropped the saw and snatched her into his arms, jerking her right off her feet. "Was that a challenge, my lady?"

"Do you see my gauge on the ground?" Alyson's heart was thundering in her chest but not from fear. It was so tempting to rest her head in the crook of his arm, or perhaps tease even more and sting him into kissing her. She could feel his heat and strength, and the touch of his body against hers made her tingle all over. Truly, for all the covering his thin linen shirt gave, he could be naked, she thought, scandalized and delighted at the thought. But people were watching; it was time to remember who she was, the lady of Hardspen. "If you release me, you will be able to search for it."

"Not so fast." Guillelm lowered his head to hers. "Maybe you have hidden it somewhere about your person. Under that nunlike veil, perchance."

Did he think her still a child, that she could allow such horseplay? "I must make haste to see Sericus," she said quickly, clamping a hand on top of her veiled head.

"You cannot do that," he said seriously. "Your seneschal is engaged in a task for me."

"You ordered my Sericus?"

"Mine, too, now. As are you."

Idly, he swung her back and forth, but Alyson refused to be pacified like a babe in arms. For an instant she could not speak, she was gagged by her own rush of temper. "You had no right!"

"Indeed?" Abruptly, he tickled her under the arm and she automatically squirmed, withdrawing her hand, then gasping as his fingers tugged at the pins securing her headrail.

"No!" she cried, genuinely disturbed.

"I know it is an insult to remove a married woman's veil, but not, I think, that of my wife-to-be," Guillelm replied, setting her back down lightly onto her feet. "I would see your hair."

"But—" The gentle touch of his fingers against her forehead distracted Alyson, making her forget the rest of her protest. *I am drowning in sweetness in his arms,* she thought despairingly, dimly aware of the farriers staring, of a conspiracy of children pausing in their game of throwing sticks to giggle and point. "Would you make a show of me, dragon?" she whispered.

Instantly his hand was still. "Not for all the jewels of Outremer, if it truly troubles you." He cupped her face. "But then, you were merely to be plighted to my father, were you not? You told me you had not been formally betrothed." *Why not?* Guillelm wondered. In his father's place he would have been very keen to make all fast between Alyson and himself, but then that was not the important matter here. "You can wear your hair loose, like a true maiden." As swiftly as it had come, the shine of tenderness vanished from his dark eyes and a hard, quizzical look settled over his stark features. "Or did you and my good lord Robert anticipate your wedding?"

Never! Alyson wanted to shout, appalled at the very question. The mere thought made her shudder inside. "What do you think?" she hit back, adding, "If my father were alive, you would not say such things to me."

Guillelm became dangerously still. "You think I would not dare?"

Deciding that actions spoke more than words, Alyson reached up and unpinned her veil, holding it out. "I am as I was born," she said quietly.

A brief look of shame flickered in Guillelm's eyes as he took the cloth from her, screwing it into a tight ball. "That is better," he growled. "And you must admit I have a right to ask."

"As I now have the right to ask for an apology," Alyson replied steadily. She tried not to stare at the faint line of blond body curls that was revealed as Guillelm thrust her veil into his shirt. It ran right down to his navel . . . She closed her eyes briefly, then opened them as she heard him say, "I am sorry. I was wrong."

Forgiving him at once, she raised her head to say as much and so caught the far softer, "Your hair . . . it is amazing."

She was pretty enough and provoking enough to be kissed, thought Guillelm, eager to do just that, and more. Only the fact that he was already aroused and had blundered badly with his wretched jealousy—how could he even have asked such an insulting question?—made him pause. But she was so pretty. Her new gown, the color of a summer twilight, mirrored the rich depths of her eyes and flattered the flawless rose-and-cream of her skin but did not quite do justice to her lissome figure; it could be tighter here and here, he decided, longing to run his hands over those very points. Hastily lowering his gaze, he caught a flash of red, like a teasing tongue, on the hem of her gown as she moved slightly back from him and instantly marveled at her slender feet, so tiny. "You are a wonder," he longed

to say to her, but seasoned warriors did not talk that way—
if his men heard him they would think him mad.

"Guillelm—" The new music that she made of his name
made him almost miss what she was saying, but it was, as ever
with Alyson, direct and pertinent. "I am sorry, too, for being an-
gered when you mentioned Sericus." She smiled. "My sister
Tilda always said I was too hot-tempered; she taught me a convent prayer to recite when I was angry, but often in the heat of
the moment I forget it. Of course you are lord here, and Sericus
is your servant as well as mine, only"—she spread her work-
worn fingers in a further, silent plea—"grant me, I beg you, a
little time to become accustomed to this new order."

He grunted an acknowledgment, ashamed afresh at his
apology, clumsy compared with hers. "How is your sister?"
he asked, avoiding the thorny issue of what Sericus was actually doing for the moment.

"Happy, I think. The spiritual and contemplative life suits
her." Alyson looked pensive. "I must admit—"

Please do not say you envy her, thought Guillelm, relieved
when she merely went on, "I would dearly like to see her again."

"That is easily arranged," Guillelm said quickly, feeling his
heart steadying in his chest. This was folly; he had to keep a
tight rein on his emotions or this beguiling ragtag of a wench
would wind him like a ribbon round her fingers. "But come,"
he heard himself saying, in direct contradiction to his previous thought, "is there anything I can grant you now—in
thanks for shedding that old-fashioned head rail?"

"Old-fashioned?" Alyson tried to look affronted and then
laughed. "I suppose to a lord lately returned from exotic lands
it will be. Doubtless you will have seen many ladies in fine
silks. What is silk like?"

He lifted her hand to his lips and kissed her fingers. "Wait
until tomorrow, then you will know," he promised, thinking
that no silk was as glorious as her hair. Even as it was now,

plaited into a single simple braid thicker than his wrist, it was such a mass of long, fine stuff. "Your favor, my little sweet?" he prompted, delighted when she teased back, "A present for me, my lord? Or should that be a forfeit, for stealing my veil?"

"Your choice," he said, aware of his men and the farriers and not caring a jot for any of them. Then Alyson herself brought them out of this strange, dazzling inner world by saying carefully, "Could you then introduce me to your seneschal?" She gnawed at her lower lip. "I would heal the bad blood between Fulk and myself."

She was ever a healer, Guillelm recalled, but her request revealed a new difficulty. "It may be better to wait until sunset," he replied, hoping she would let the matter go, but such was not Alyson's way any more than it was his.

"Why?" she asked reasonably, then she caught her breath as she clearly remembered. "The discipline."

"For the grave discourtesy Fulk did to you, yes." Guillelm felt his jaw clench and told himself again that the task he had lain on his follower would be punishment enough. "Sericus is overseeing it for me."

Alyson's eyes widened. "What is it?" she whispered.

"No more than he deserves." Guillelm pointed to the outer wall of the bailey. "We can go watch, if you wish."

She wrinkled her nose at him. "What have you had him do?"

"It is a common punishment for a knight; I have endured it myself. Listen! Can you hear galloping?"

They were both silent, Alyson cupping a hand to her left ear to block out the closer sounds of chattering voices, hammering and, overhead, a thread of birdsong. She frowned. "I think I can."

"Outside Hardspen's walls, Fulk is practicing in full armor on his warhorse for the rest of the day. I have told him to keep at a gallop; if he stops for any reason I will hear of it, and he will regret it."

Alyson gasped. "You have made Sericus your spy?" she demanded.

Her tone irritated Guillelm. "Not so—he is my guarantor and a witness. It will do Fulk good to be humbled a little in front of your game old man. I know Fulk; he will see the justice of it."

"But . . . full armor, all day. That is barbaric!"

"It is sweaty and hot and cramping, and he will ache abominably for days, but it is still better than the public flogging Fulk would have given you. It casts no slur on his status and it exercises his horse."

"Even so, it seems harsh," Alyson demurred. She bent her head a moment, then raised her face to his. "Please! Will your knight not have ridden enough by now?"

It was hard to resist her pleading and Guillelm did not try. "Very well. We shall go together." He held out his arm. "Do you remember how we used to walk in your father's fields?"

Blushing slightly, she nodded and unerringly placed her hand in his, proving that she did remember. Side by side, Guillelm careful to keep pace with her and not drag her along in the wake of his natural long strides, they strolled through the bailey, very companionable.

It was going to be all right, Alyson told herself. She had not made a mistake in agreeing to marry Guillelm. With the optimism of one-and-twenty, she felt proud and happy walking beside him, hand in hand. It was as if the years they had spent apart had never been. Her people smiled at her; his men nodded to her, a wary respect showing in their weathered faces. It was going to be all right.

Her joyous mood lasted until she and Guillelm had passed through the bailey gate and they were out on the rolling grasslands with a few bleating sheep and a swineherd driving a herd of pigs into the nearby woodland. As she crested a steep rise, slightly out of breath with the warmth of the climb and simply because she was so pleased to be with Guillelm, she felt the ground shift beneath her, felt the heavy, relentless drumming of hooves. A divot of loose earth and grass reared up at her as a dark-helmed rider on a big bay stallion thundered by, racing over the cropped turf as if charging for the gates of Jerusalem itself.

"Hey, Fulk!" bawled Guillelm, and the rider turned and galloped back, even as her own man Sericus seemed to grow out of a patch of oxeye daisies and long grass, where he clearly had been taking his ease.

"My lord—lady—" the withered old man stammered, furiously rubbing his rheumy eyes. "I did not hope to see you here."

"Peace, Master Sericus," Guillelm answered, above the plunging hooves. "I believe you were going to have an answer for me about furniture?" And leaving Alyson to puzzle over that cryptic remark he drew the aged seneschal to one side, both of them walking over the downs—more slowly than she and Guillelm had done because of Sericus's lame leg—and talking softly with their heads close together.

Which meant it was she who had to greet the hapless Fulk when the man finally reined in, stopping less than an arm-length away from her.

"You ride well, sir," she remarked, as he slowly lowered himself from his charger, clearly wincing through his helm as his feet touched the ground.

"My thanks, Lady." With the same careful movements, as if his every joint pained him, he began to rub down the massive sweating warhorse with the saddle cloth. "My lord Guillelm also rides and fights well, as you would know if we were still in Outremer."

If Fulk wished to begin afresh or make peace with her he was going about it in a strange way, Alyson thought, glancing to ensure that Guillelm was out of hearing. Fulk had not removed his helm, nor made her any kind of courtesy. Since he had mentioned war, she decided on shock tactics.

"Do you resent me, Fulk?"

Her use of his name and the direct question made him swing round, but to Alyson's surprise he was laughing. "Hardly, my lady." Now he did take off his helmet, revealing the same cold blue eyes and narrow mouth she had encountered earlier, a shock of gray hair and a narrow, thin face that might have been pleasing were it not for its sneering expression or the band of small red pustules running across his nose and cheeks.

Seeing the skin disease, Alyson instantly ran through potions in her mind that might help, but Fulk was not interested in anything of hers, as his next words made insultingly obvious.

"Why should I resent you, a mere distraction and the leavings of another man? My lord has taken such fancies before, but they never last. Once he thinks he has won you from his father's memory, it will be over."

"Guillelm has asked me to marry him," Alyson said, determined that Fulk would not make her angry a second time.

The man shrugged, scowling as his chain mail rasped and shifted on his body. "My lord belongs in the Holy Land," he said, turning away from her again and resuming the care of his horse. "That is his true work, as a warrior for Christ."

"You wish, then, that you had stayed in Outremer?" Alyson demanded.

"I do. Every moment away from that sacred place is a triumph of evil and the infidel." Fulk paused in his rubbing down to cross himself piously.

"Then why did you not remain there yourself? I am sure Guillelm would have released you from his service."

"You are sure—" Fulk's words were a cruel mockery. "No doubt you are, *my lady,* but I have made my own promises before God. Within one year, I will return to Outremer with Lord Guillelm de La Rochelle, where we shall resume our noble struggle against the enemies of Christ."

And you shall not stop me, Alyson finished for Fulk in her own head. Clearly in this man's mind she counted as one of the enemies of Christ—a disconcerting thought, seeing that she had once yearned to be a nun.

"Then we understand each other," she responded crisply, stepping away from Fulk and his stamping, bad-tempered horse and scanning the downs to find Guillelm. She would say nothing of this to her husband-to-be, but she made her own vow then and there.

Fulk would not win. She would.

She did not find Guillelm but met Sericus coming back to the rough stretch of grass designated by the new lord of Hardspen as the tilting ground. He hailed her, offering his arm.

"My lady, my lord wishes me to escort you to the water meadows, where he hopes to join you presently."

"Thank you!" Alyson said, the shadow of Fulk's dark words fading a little as she realized that Guillelm had remembered her need for strewing herbs and was even coming to help. Raised up by this tiny act of kindness, she wandered toward the river with her head full of happy plans. She would take this time to replenish her healing herbs, too, now sadly depleted after the sickness. Also, there might be a chance to find treats for Guillelm—did he still like wild strawberries? She would try to gather him some. Did he still like the smell of meadowsweet? Did he still enjoy being read to?

That memory, although precious, brought a less welcome recollection of Guillelm's father, confiscating her book. Smarting at the thought, Alyson muttered an anxious prayer that her precious herbal was somewhere safe in the castle and turned her attention to Sericus, who was full of his own plans for Hardspen.

The sun was beginning to set when Guillelm finally joined Alyson in the lush water meadows. He had been delayed by Fulk and others and was out of temper.

"You will spoil your gown," he observed, watching her cutting through a swathe of meadowsweet, but she only smiled.

"I think not," she said. "I never have before."

"That's true enough," Guillelm admitted. Even as a child, Alyson seemed to have the gift of deftly threading her way through mud and muck that would leave him mired almost to his eyebrows and herself untouched. Now, as he sent Sericus off with a brisk, silent gesture and a bulging cloakful of herbs, he saw her step away from the riverbank with another armful and knew that once she had dusted herself off for pollen she would be as pristine as a jewel. "You have the devil's luck," he remarked.

She blushed, fumbling slightly with her knife. "I have some strawberries for you," she said softly. "If—If you still like them, that is."

Her diffidence made him ashamed. "I do not know," he said brusquely. "It is years since I considered such trifles."

Her color deepened but she gave him a piercing look. "Why so sour?"

He shook his head. Fulk had said much to him—too similar to his own fears for comfort. He stared at her bare head, trying not to imagine Alyson with his father, while the gouge of jealousy jabbed somewhere deep within his chest.

"Fulk doubts that all will be ready for the betrothal ceremony tomorrow," he said.

He expected her to flare up, but Alyson finished trimming the meadowsweet and said calmly, "We can only do our best.

What else did he say?" Her tone sharpened. "That perhaps I should be veiled tomorrow?"

She was too quick and saw too much. Cursing under his breath, Guillelm grumbled, "Not even he would dare say that."

"He implied my purity was not beyond reproach?"

"Mother of God, no!" But Fulk had, not in so many words, but in sly references to Lord Robert's "vigor." Now, meeting her hot, indignant gaze, Guillelm utterly rejected his seneschal's foul insinuations. More than that, he realized it didn't matter. He wanted Alyson, however she was. "Shall I carry those flowers for you?"

"No, thank you."

Silence stretched between them, heavy as thunder before a storm, and Guillelm found himself keen to break it. "He saved my life once."

"As doubtless you did his," Alyson answered. "And many times."

It was true, but Guillelm felt his jaw tighten. He was angry at Fulk and yet knew he was obligated to him, by ties of custom, habit and fealty. And Fulk had saved him on the field of battle, had been a brave and competent second-in-command.

Fulk has stood by me for years, in ways my father never wanted to or did, he thought. *I trust him with my life. I hoped he would approve of Alyson, and she of him, that they could be friends.* It seemed that was a forlorn hope, and he had no tactics to bring them to any kind of reconciliation.

With a sigh, Alyson placed the cut herbs on the lush grass of the water meadow and stepped toward him. The westering sun flared on the red hem of her gown. "I am sorry, my lord, that you are caught between the enmity between Fulk and myself. It cannot be a pleasant place to stand." She raised her hand, her fingers cupped in a small gesture that was almost a silent plea. "I will try to be his ally and I will give him all due respect. Your seneschal is unused to women, I think."

"Fulk wishes to join the Knights Templar, a recent holy order of fighting monks, pledged to protect pilgrims to the Holy Land."

Surprised as he was to find himself admitting this, Guillelm was further disconcerted when Alyson remarked, "He also wishes you to join, does he not?"

"He has spoken of it." Guillelm frowned. "But it is not—" He broke off, ashamed of the rest of the thought.

"He is a powerful advocate for the Christian cause," Alyson said, lowering her eyes so he could not see their expression. "Are all men like him in Outremer? So vehement?"

"Some are," Guillelm admitted, ashamed now that he was not the same. Within the Holy Land he had made friends with Jews and even with Arabs. "We all use Arab physicians."

"Indeed! I would know more of them." Clearly at ease now that their talk had strayed into her own area of expertise, Alyson settled on the ground by his feet and hugged at her knees, another youthful trick of hers that he remembered and that still delighted him. "What do they use to cure fever? Toothache? Sprains?"

"Steady!" Touched by her eagerness, Guillelm was tempted to sit with her but knew they could not linger; his men and the folk of the castle would be waiting for them. "We must leave that for another day."

He held out his hand to help her up.

Chapter 5

Alyson stared at her gold betrothal ring. It was plain and heavy, without any gemstones, but utterly precious to her. Under cover of the trestle table she touched it to convince herself it was real.

All day she had felt to be in a dream. Even this evening, at her betrothal feast in Hardspen's great hall, surrounded by people—mainly Guillelm's men—listening to their jests and good wishes, she felt apart, somewhere beyond joy or calm.

Another dish was set before her to try. Where had the food come from? She had asked Guillelm, who had lightly tugged at her hair and said that years of foraging in Outremer had taught him everything he needed to know about finding victuals, then grinned at her expression of shock and reassured her that no one went hungry at their expense. "Your cook was not so anxious," he had chuckled. "But he saw the provision carts arrive while you were in the bathhouse."

Since then the cook had been busy, Alyson reflected. She picked up her spoon. Alert to the slight movement, Guillelm turned to her.

"May I try some, too?" he asked softly. "It looks intriguing."

He spoke with such tender pride that she felt tears stand

in her eyes. Hastily—for it would not do to be seen weeping at her plight-troth feast—Alyson nodded and, ignoring a vulgar catcall from Thierry, she swiftly broke the crust of the sweet curd flan and offered Guillelm a spoonful.

He leaned forward and ate, his dark eyes never leaving her face as he swallowed. "Delicious," he murmured.

When she smiled, his mouth crinkled in return and a glaze of indulgent happiness transformed him from the seasoned warrior to the youth she had known.

"We will be well together, Alyson," he said, voicing her own hope. "My betrothed."

"May I try some of that?" She pointed to the wooden plate of date slices positioned beside the richly decorated covered salt cellar immediately in front of Guillelm, and he cut her a portion, holding it out to her in his fingers and teasingly withdrawing his hand as she came close.

"Unfair!" she protested, laughing as he waved the sweet under her nose. "You should pay a forfeit for that."

"I have another gift for you, when we have a moment alone." His free hand hovered toward her hair. "You are so—"

A crash on the staircase outside the great hall had Alyson and Guillelm breaking apart and starting to their feet, Alyson instinctively shielding him with her raised arms.

"No, little one, it should be the other way round." Gently but firmly, Guillelm drew her behind him, tensing as a cowering figure stumbled into the hall.

Alyson gasped and darted forward, too quick even for Guillelm's rapid reactions. Evading his snatching hand and the startled servers, she flew from the dais to her former nurse, gathering Gytha into her arms. "There, you are safe," she crooned, rocking the trembling woman as consternation broke out in the rest of the hall, men flinging back the benches and jumping up, looking round wildly for weapons in case of some attack.

"What is going on?" Guillelm demanded, hands on hips as he strode to meet the shadow emerging from the top of the stairs.

It was Fulk. He was carrying a silver cup that clearly was empty—the bulk of the former liquid stained the red-cheeked nurse's bodice and had splashed onto her shoes.

"A collision on the staircase, my lord," Alyson said, relieved it was no worse, but even as she spoke Fulk overrode her, his voice strident.

"This creature is a poisoner! I saw her with my own eyes, tipping some foul powder into your cup, my lord! With my own eyes!" White spittle collected in his mouth corners as he pointed at the now-sobbing Gytha. "A witch!"

"Not so!" Alyson's clear denial rang out above the hasty prayers of the younger squires and knights. The older men and women, she noted, were silent and still, watching carefully. Guillelm was also watching, his face an unreadable mask.

Shocked at Fulk's sheer malice, Alyson bit hard on her lip. The pain reminded her to keep her temper; she needed her wits about her, when part of her longed to knock Fulk back onto the rushes.

She held out her hand. "Give me the cup."

"My lady, I swear to you . . . you know I would never . . . never . . ." Gytha broke down again.

Furious at Fulk for abusing a helpless old woman, Alyson snapped her fingers. "The cup, sir!"

"There is no liquid left. She spilled it deliberately," Fulk replied smoothly, holding the silver goblet so all could see inside.

"Even so, my lady will know from the dregs," Guillelm observed in a deadly calm, speaking for the first time since his seneschal had made his outrageous accusations.

Paling slightly under his mottled, pockmarked skin, Fulk

almost tossed the goblet to Alyson, who righted it before any more of the sticky lees could be lost.

She held it under her nose. "Spices, my lord, and a good wine." She licked a finger and dipped it into the cup, showing the trace of white powder to the assembled company and then tasting it. "The powder is from the dried flower heads of yarrow." She drained off part of the lees, licking her lips. "It is harmless."

"Yarrow is much used by witches," Fulk countered.

"And in loving cups," Alyson replied.

"'Tis true, Lord," Gytha gabbled, fixing tear-streaked eyes on Guillelm. "I used the yarrow for your marriage. Seven years of happiness, my potion will bring. I meant no harm, before God—"

"Peace!" rumbled Guillelm, as if wearying of the whole affair, and he lifted the goblet from Alyson's clasp and drank down the lees. "Though in faith I need no potions, old dame. Did you think perhaps that I was lacking?"

The hall erupted into laughter, releasing the tensions of the past few moments, and Alyson drew in a long, calming breath.

"I will take Gytha to my chamber," she murmured to Guillelm, and he nodded. Both of them knew they could not talk until they were private.

Alyson did not return to the great hall. She comforted Gytha as best she could and made up a sleeping draught for her nurse. Afterward, listening to Gytha snoring gently, she wondered at Fulk's spite. Had Guillelm not intervened as he did, would Fulk have been able to turn the castle against Gytha—and by association, herself?

Peering through the wooden casement, Alyson watched the moon rise and set while she listened to the increasingly rowdy drinking games of the men. Was Guillelm often in his cups?

The idea made her shiver, especially when she remembered how his father, Lord Robert, had been whenever he had too much malmsey . . .

Before dawn, she laced her gown again and rebraided her hair. Taking her favorite mortar and pestle from the smallest oak chest, she slipped out of her chamber and down the stairs, determined to do something useful, if only as a distraction from her thoughts.

Lord Robert had not allowed her a still room in which to make her potions, but Alyson had found a small place for herself in a small lean-to off the stable block. In this she had a chopping table, and earthenware crocks, and even some glass bottles, more precious than gold to her. In the lean-to she had bundles of drying herbs hung from the slanting roof and fresh herbs laid on shelves, a small brazier for stewing herbs and bowls for steeping them. It was a cramped space, even for her, but with its comforting smells of lavender, rosemary and thyme it always felt like home to Alyson, reminding her vividly of the still room at her father's house. Now, when she crossed the threshold and pushed open the door to the lean-to to its fullest, she opened a sack of rose petals and ran her fingers through them, simply for the pleasure their silky texture and delicate scent gave her.

"So this is your secret place." With that disconcertingly silent tread of his, Guillelm had approached without her realizing. He was dressed in a plain mantle and leggings, very different from the dark red robe with golden thread round the neck and sleeves that he had worn at the feast last night. The change made him look younger, easier to talk to.

"Careful!" she warned, automatically stepping sideways to protect her glassware.

"You did that last night, using yourself as a shield."

"Yes." Suddenly they were straying into more difficult territory; she did not know quite how to go on, or what to say about Fulk.

"My seneschal was wrong. He understands his error. He will not do anything like that again."

Seeing him stare down at his bunched fists, Alyson could not suppress a shiver.

"How is Gytha?" Guillelm asked gently.

"I left her sleeping. Osmoda will be with her today."

"Excellent." Guillelm grinned, crouching so that he did not loom in the doorway. "Never fear, Alyson. This is your domain," he reassured her, meaning more in his answer than the simple lean-to. "How many mixtures do you have here?" he went on, inhaling deeply. "I can smell spices."

"That will be my cinnamon, no doubt, and pepper." Alyson tried to count on her fingers the number of tisanes and potions she had made, but gave up, shrugging. "I do not know. Not as many as I had in my father's house at Olverton." Her mouth dipped as she remembered her loss afresh.

Guillelm nodded. "Sir Henry was a good man."

"I miss him."

"As is right, and natural."

They were silent, joined together in mutual grief for their dead fathers, although from Guillelm's frown it seemed his recollections were more troubling than sorrowful. After a moment, he raised his left hand, pointing to where a patch of early morning sun flared against the thatch. "I think it will be another hot day and I wondered—"

He stopped as a scullion boy, in a ragged loincloth and with a sooty face split by a huge yawn, tottered past the lean-to, his bare feet stirring up seams of mud and dust and hoards of small, buzzing flies. When the child was out of earshot, Guillelm resumed, a little faster than before.

"I thought perhaps we could leave the setting right of Hardspen for a day or so—or at least leave it to Sericus—and go out? You will not have left the castle grounds for weeks, and you mentioned your sister Matilda. I am sure her convent would welcome us as guests, at least for a brief space, and especially if we go bearing offerings."

He sprang to his feet. "I thought we might set off presently; our attendants can catch us up. The way to St. Foy's is safe, well out of the reach of any forces claiming allegiance to King Stephen or Empress Maud, and we do not have to hurry. What say you?"

She and Guillelm would be alone. Alyson hugged the idea to herself and nodded, afraid her voice would be too breathy to answer.

"Excellent!" he said again—it seemed a favorite saying—and he turned to the stables, adding, "I will saddle some horses." A quizzical, teasing light stole into his eyes. "You can still ride, I take it?"

"Of course!"

Guillelm was laughing as he stalked lightly away, supple as a tawny cat, the rising sun gilding his hair to an even brighter gold.

He had found her a tall black palfrey to ride, handing Alyson the reins and cupping his hands to invite her to mount.

Alyson stayed a moment, a smile lurking about her mouth. "This is not one of Fulk's?" she asked, taking in the height of the glossy, wide-eyed beast with its silver and gold horse trappings.

"Jezebel is mine and now yours." Clearly impatient to be off, Guillelm plucked her from the ground and set her on the saddle, giving Alyson no time to recover from the heady rush of being in his arms, however briefly, before he demanded, "Do you question everything?"

"Always. Have you forgotten?" she teased back. "I hope Jezebel does not refer to the temper of my horse," she went on, guiding the palfrey gently with her knees to see how responsive she was.

"Only when she is in season—which she is not."

"What is your horse called?" Alyson asked as Guillelm took Jezebel's bridle and the reins of his own big white-and-gray piebald to walk them to the main gate.

"Caliph." Guillelm rubbed a finger at the side of his long nose—a sign Alyson had come to recognize as a form of embarrassment. "He is from part Arab stock, and I named him before I understood what the title meant. 'Caliph' is a form of great respect to the Muslims."

"And you do not wish to slight a worthy enemy?"

He laughed. "How well you know me, wench!"

Alyson felt a glow of satisfaction as they passed the guards on the gate, glancing again at her betrothal ring and daring to hope that all would be more than well between them.

She had filled out a little more in the past few days, lost that grayness under her eyes and in her face. In her new blue gown and with her hair streaming out behind her as they cantered over the downs, Alyson was more vivid than the fresh summer green of the trees, so bright to his eye after the muted, dusty colors of Outremer. She was more delicate than the scattered cowslips, speedwell and orchids that bordered the chalk track they were racing along, giving the horses their heads. She rode superbly—but then, what did Alyson not do superbly?

And she is mine. Guillelm wanted to utter a war cry from sheer bravado, utter pride and joy. At the castle gate, one of his guards had asked if he was hunting today and he was, though not with hawk or dogs. His present quarry needed more subtlety and patience. Patience above all, Guillelm reminded himself, thinking once more of Heloise of Outremer and her dreadful warning.

Desperate to avoid that fate with Alyson, he had planned this day as he might a military campaign and only prayed that his preparations would be to her liking. He knew the arts of war but less those of peace. How did an English lord entertain his lady?

He had taken food from the kitchen for them but now, as he spied a stand of oak trees where they might shelter from the midday heat and relax, he was unsure. As a girl, Alyson had enjoyed romping and eating out of doors but as a woman perhaps she would consider those things too unmannerly, even coarse.

"I thought we might stop here, allow the horses to graze." *Fool! It must be obvious that is only an excuse,* he thought, scanning the sparse grass under the trees. "If that is acceptable?" he went on, compounding his error by actually asking permission.

Alyson nodded and reined in. Swiftly dismounting, perhaps so that she did not have to endure his touch, she knelt by one of the oaks. As he wondered what she was doing, Guillelm watched her take a worn knife from her belt and begin sawing at the bracket fungus growing at the base of the trunk.

"This may be useful for my healing," she explained, lifting the fungus onto a clean scrap of cloth she had produced from somewhere about her person.

"Healing is surely in God's hands," Guillelm began, recalling old childhood tales of poisoned toadstools, but Alyson wrinkled her nose.

"It may be, but Christ gave us wit and nimble fingers to aid ourselves," she said.

He knelt beside her and took her knife, plunging it into the grass.

"That is a very round reply, mistress." Would she be teased by him, Guillelm wondered. Dare he tease?

The matter was resolved when Alyson thrust her tongue out at him.

* * *

What was she doing? Guillelm was no longer nineteen. Because they had stopped beneath the dappled shade of an oak tree, had knelt close to a small, gurgling stream that she could hear but not see, it did not mean that he remembered what she had never forgotten. She had allowed the memory of that afternoon, by another oak wood, on another sultry summer's day, near to another clear, swift-flowing brook, to govern her actions.

Appalled at her folly, Alyson tried to rise to her feet but was snared in a pair of arms that pinioned her own hands helplessly by her sides.

"The last time we were this way together, you saved my life."

"No, no," Alyson demurred, pleased and at the same time alarmed that he did remember. She tried to squirm free of her captor.

"None of that." Still clasping her—so strongly that she felt bound by fetters of iron—Guillelm lowered his head. "I mind it well, bright-eyes."

"Dragon—"

"You called me dragon then, too, when I was ready to confront the royal foresters, and you dragged me under cover. Into brambles, I do believe." He was smiling, but then he added seriously, "Had those woodsmen caught us, straying into part of the king's forest, there would have been no mercy for me."

Alyson nodded, thinking how Guillelm had found a dead deer and had dressed it for meat, recalling how stubborn he had been to keep the deer, although by law all such game was reserved for the king. He was even ready to fight the foresters, whom with her quick hearing she heard riding across the stream before she and Guillelm were seen.

"You flung yourself on me and brought me to my knees. I remember your words: "You cannot fight five armed with bows and swords and you with only a hunting knife, even if you are as brave as a dragon." Your good sense saved me. And at the time I was astonished that such a slip of a girl could take me down so easily." Guillelm brushed her cheek with his, whispering, "Your quick wits made me think, reminded me of what really mattered. Your own safety."

Alyson blushed, aware, as she had not been at fourteen, of the truth of Guillelm's statement. Then, her only thought had been to save him from the harsh laws of the forest and the king's justice; she had not considered her own position, or vulnerability, a girl at the dubious mercy of six men, all strangers to her and she to them. "I was naive," she said.

"We both were."

"You really saved me," Alyson went on, but Guillelm shook his head.

"We saved each other," he said. "Did I ever thank you?"

"Of course."

"Did I kiss you?"

Alyson's heart felt to leap almost out of her ribs. Breathless, all eyes, she waited as his mouth touched hers. She sighed, leaning into the kiss and he gave a mighty groan, gathering her closer, his hands releasing hers to cup her face.

Dazed with the sweet pulse of pleasure coursing through her as their kiss intensified, Alyson did what she had dreamed of doing for years and playfully traced a finger down the length of Guillelm's nose. Then, as he started slightly with surprise and drew back a little, she teased her thumb over his upper lip.

"Little witch." In his mouth, the words were an endearment. He nibbled her finger and softly drew her hand away, claiming her lips a second time with his own.

Tingling with sensation, Alyson wondered if she was experiencing anything akin to what the great mystic Hildegarde of Bermersheim had once described as being like 'a feather on the breath of God." There was something almost unearthly to their embrace; the very air about her and Guillelm seem to crackle. When they broke apart to look at each other, the sun seemed brighter, the scent of the bruised grass beneath their knees fresher, the luster in Guillelm's eyes deeper. His whole face glowed, the fine bristles trembling on his upper lip.

"You are . . ." He swept a hand along her arm, raised her hand and kissed the knuckle above her betrothal ring. "I wanted to do this seven years ago."

"And for so long I feared you dead." In a chilling flurry of remembered horror, Alyson pressed herself against Guillelm, hearing his heart but wanting still more, to be closer, flesh against flesh. "Dead!"

She shuddered and he rocked her, crooning a snatch of song. "Remember this little tune?" he asked.

"'My Lady's White Rose.' It was on everyone's lips that summer." At fourteen Alyson had not known the name of the song. "You would whistle it sometimes, to tease me."

"Do you still snap your fingers when you are angry?"

"You will have to wait to find out," Alyson replied.

"If you do, then as your betrothed I may devise some suitable punishment for you."

"You can try," Alyson answered lightly, hoping her face gave no hint of her darker thoughts and Lord Robert's 'punishments.'

Guillelm glanced at her keenly and she shifted slightly, disturbed by memories and by more direct physical discomfort as the dull ache in her knees finally registered.

"Ach! My legs have gone to sleep!" Guillelm scowled, then laughed as Alyson said quickly, "Stamp your feet and rub your calves. That will bring them back to life."

"What else do you suggest, physic?" Rising, he lifted her with him, dangling her from his arms.

"Food," Alyson answered determinedly. "For you will have brought some victuals for our journey, I think. Now, are you going to set me down?"

Guillelm grinned and did so.

* * *

Out of his pannier came a meal that threatened to rival their betrothal feast. As the cold meats and bread, flagons of wine and nuts, cheeses and rare raisins were spread by Guillelm before Alyson—using his cloak as a table between the spreading roots of *their* oak tree (it was theirs now because they had kissed beneath it)—she found herself snapping her fingers in sheer delight and wonder.

"Amazing!" she cried. "So much! You are a worker of wonders."

"Every dragon is," Guillelm replied, a little smug but glad his plans had met with her approval. He thought of the final gift he had for her, tucked into his shirt, but then decided it would be better after they had eaten. He drummed his fingers on the earth. "The banquet is ready. Come."

They sat with their backs resting against the oak tree, close enough so that Guillelm could feel Alyson's long sleeve brush against his arm whenever she stirred: a delicate, tormenting pleasure. She sampled everything, praising especially the wine and the freshness of the soft cheese, and seemingly happy to have nuts cracked for her and to be fed raisins by him. She offered him a slice of pork off her knife, giggling as he pretended to gobble it, and was altogether easy with him.

Of course she is, nagged the devil of conscience and dread that whispered in his mind in a strange mingling of Heloise and Fulk. *Alyson treats you as an older brother.*

Brother and sister do not kiss as we have done, Guillelm told himself, but some of the sparkle of the day diminished for him and, turning their talk away from the spice markets of Outremer, he began to speak of a more practical concern, the digging of a new well at Hardspen.

"That would be a good thing." Alyson went along with his abrupt change of subject without any pause. "Last summer, my father gave the villagers of Olverton Minor a new well."

"Oh, yes, a village." Preoccupied with this new goal, Guillelm spoke dismissively. "The castle well would need to supply hundreds, not merely a few cottars and passing tinkers."

"What do you mean?" Alyson asked, sitting up straighter and hugging her knees.

"The needs of Hardspen are not like those of your father's holdings," Guillelm began reasonably, "a single unfortified manor and some modest lands—"

He was astonished when Alyson bridled.

"Are you saying that my family are little more than serfs? We may not be rich or powerful but we are loyal and we look after our own!"

"That is your family motto, is it not? To look after our own?" Guillelm said quickly, but Alyson would not be placated.

"Answer me." She whirled to her feet, casting a half-finished daisy chain to one side. "What am I to you?"

Everything, Guillelm thought, but now behind them came the pounding of hooves and creak of carts and Fulk, bawling in a voice designed to carry even over the field of battle, "Well met, my lord! We have finally caught up with you!"

Chapter 6

St. Foy's was a closed order, but the prioress allowed Matilda and Alyson to meet in the small infirmary garden. Guillelm and the other men were kept out of the convent and were kicking their heels somewhere beyond the high walls, but Guillelm had told Alyson not to hurry her visit.

"Stay until after sunset and compline if you wish," he told her. "I have our sleeping arrangements already in hand." Ignoring her blush, he went on, "A friend of mine has a manor no more than a mile from here. Your sister is welcome, too, if the prioress allows it."

"Who is your friend?" Alyson had asked, wondering if he had been at her betrothal feast, and if so, why he had not traveled back with her and Guillelm.

"Thomas of Beresford. He fought with me in the Holy Land, losing a hand and a foot, and is much scarred besides. He does not like to travel, or to subject himself to the pity of strangers, but former comrades from Outremer are always welcome in his house." Guillelm must have guessed something of her disquiet, for he had grinned and added, "Steady, there, bright-eyes. Tom knows we are coming."

"The prioress will not allow me to undertake such a secular outing, especially in the company of men-at-arms," Matilda said.

"But they are former crusaders," she protested.

Matilda smoothed away an imagined crease on her dark sleeve. "You must be content with what we have here," she said. "It is the will of God."

"Tilda—" Alyson tried the childhood nickname, but her sister said quickly, "I am Sister Ursula. That is my true title and you must call me by no other. Nor should we indulge in any worldly gossip. Indeed, after today, it is my wish that we should not meet again, unless there is urgent need."

The reminder of her religious name and purpose, the sober habit, which accentuated Matilda-Ursula's natural pallor, throwing her handsome, somewhat sharp-featured face into even more desolate relief, and most of all that final, cruel instruction brought home to Alyson how distant her birth-sister had become after only a few months' separation. Her kindness and slow smile were gone—or did she share these only with her sisters in Christ? Whatever the truth, this sudden blow was like a second bereavement: First she had lost her father and now this.

"Are you happy here?" she stammered, at a loss for conversation.

Sister Ursula inclined her head. "It is what I always wanted." She walked through a wattle arched gate into another part of the garden, calling over her shoulder, "Come, look at our vine walk. It provides us with welcome shade on warm days such as these."

Alyson had little choice but to follow, passing the elderly convent infirmarer who was weeding the beds of leeks, celery and parsley. The scent of coriander was heavy in the still air and she was acutely conscious of her own footfalls on the beaten earth paths.

"You could have been a part of this," her sister remarked as she drew near. "You once wanted to be a great healer, a scholar—as I am." Sister Ursula held out her right hand, showing her thumb and forefinger, stained with the inks of the scriptorium. "Why did you break your vow?"

"What vow?" Alyson did not understand the question.

"You swore to join the nuns. Why did you break that promise?"

"I never—" Aware from the infirmarer's puzzled glance that she had raised her voice, Alyson forced herself to speak more quietly. "As a girl, yes, I wished to be part of convent life, but I made no formal vow."

"You were seduced by secular pleasures." Sister Ursula gave her gown a look of undisguised scorn. "Pretty clothes!"

Just in time, Alyson stopped herself from saying that the gown was once Tilda's; that would be a most unwelcome reminder. Instead she tried reason. "It pleased our father for me to take another path in life."

"I agree our father was morally weak, as are all men, but do not blame him for your own forswearing."

"I do not," sighed Alyson, staring at the patch of poppies in the physic garden and trying to remain as calm as if she had swallowed a draught of poppy juice. By her own choice she had made it possible for Sir Henry to allow Matilda to enter the convent in some style, but she did not say that. She knew there were other, darker and more urgent reasons why her elder sister had been so desperate to remain unmarried.

"Our mother died in childbirth. Have you forgotten?"

Tears stood in Alyson's eyes at the unjust accusation. She shook her head, but her sister was deep in the past, reliving those terrible three days.

"She screamed so loud and she was pleading with God and all the saints for the pain to stop. Our father was out hunting, taking his ease as do all men, and mother was shrieking in their chamber, with no one to help her but a few twittering old women."

"Please, Tilda," Alyson begged, the memory that forever haunted the dark spaces of her mind rising up and striking her afresh.

She had been just four years old. To know those pitiful cries had been made by her mother, to see the pallid, sweating faces of the helpless nurses and midwives, to be shut out of her mother's chamber had been truly terrifying. It must have been worse for Matilda, the older by five years and so more aware of what was happening. They had clung to each other, hiding out of sight under a trestle in a corner in the great hall while in the small, narrow room off from the hall their mother labored and suffered. Alyson remembered Matilda weeping; she was weeping now, tears coursing down her thin, sallow cheeks.

"It is a judgment of God upon women. The only way to escape it is to avoid the contaminating sin of marriage and to take the veil, as I have. As you should have done!"

"Sister—" Alyson tried to enfold the slim, sobbing figure in her arms, but although they were a height and similar in build, if not in looks, her sister tore herself away with the strength of desperation.

"Do not touch me! You did not see our mother when she was dead! I did and she was white with loss of blood! Her bed and chamber reeked of it! Even now, I can smell it." Distracted, Sister Ursula thrust past Alyson and fled back to the main church of the convent, ignoring Alyson's calls for her to return.

Some time later, after she was forced to admit that her sister would not emerge to bid her farewell, Alyson took her leave of the prioress of St. Foy's. Feeling battered and rather degraded by Tilda-Ursula's accusations, she responded as briefly as possible to Guillelm's greeting, aware of Fulk's avid interest.

Guillelm took in her sunless demeanor in a single piercing glance and lifted her onto her horse without comment. He asked no questions on the journey to the manor of his friend, but spurred on his piebald so that his men had to gallop to keep with him. Alyson was grateful for his tact and glad of the hard ride; concentrating on that blotted out some of her grief.

Soon enough—too soon for Alyson—the party had reached the home of Thomas of Beresford. The former crusader was as Guillelm had described, with many ragged scars blazoned upon his forehead, the tip of his nose missing and a deep groove hacked from his jawbone, where the rest of his curly black beard would not grow. He stumbled down the manor steps to clap Guillelm on the shoulder and roar out a "Well-met!" wielding a stump of a right arm and a peg leg for his right foot, but Alyson sensed a warm and genuine welcome beneath the fierce, battle-hewn countenance. She liked him at once, even before Guillelm drew the man across to her horse, so that she would have the advantage of looking down on them, two hulking, seasoned warriors with skins the color and texture of polished beechwood.

"My betrothed, the lady Alyson of Olverton," Guillelm said formally, smiling at her while Alyson prayed that her face was not filthy with the dusty ride. She put out her hand to her lord's stocky, barrel-chested companion.

"Thank you for allowing us to stay at your house, Sir Thomas," she said.

Guillelm laughed at the look of mingled awe and shyness on his friend's rough-hewn face. "Mother of God, Tom, make some answer or my excellent wife-to-be will think you dumb as well as ugly!"

"No more brute than you, my lord," Alyson flashed at him, an answer that had several of the nearby men-at-arms who were still riding round the manor yard, cooling their foam-speckled horses, glance at her with some astonishment. Fulk even scowled but not Thomas.

"Excellent indeed!" He clasped her hand in his left and stamped his peg leg in sheer good humor. "She is a match for you, Guido, and more! Welcome to my home, my lady!"

"Thank you, sir," Alyson responded, wondering afresh if Guillelm really did consider her his equal, given the difference of their lands and titles. But she had no time to consider the question before she was swept off her mount by Guillelm and set down beside Thomas with the growled warning from her lord dragon, "There shall be a reckoning later for that pert answer, mistress. Now go in with Tom and try to be good, eh?" He sent her on her way with a teasing pat and turned to bellow instructions to his men.

Staying at the manor of Thomas of Beresford was a bittersweet occasion for Alyson. Still grieving after the painful encounter with her sister, she found the manor contained many echoes of her old home at Olverton. It was the same kind of house, with a great hall and solar, a small pantry and buttery, a staircase to a series of small upper rooms and the kitchens and bakehouse across the yard. The furnishings were those that reminded her of her childhood: sturdy oak tables and trestles, earthenware crocks, a few faded wall hangings. She missed the flowers that she had spread about Olverton hall, and the scents of her old still room, but otherwise she could have wandered through this place blindfolded and known where she was.

In one way, however, it was strange—very strange. There were no womenfolk, no maids, no lady of the manor, no laundresses or spinsters.

Her host remarked on it as he showed her to the narrow chamber that would be hers for the night. "I had my steward put you in here, my lady, you being a lone lass among men. It was my mother's sewing room."

"Thank you, sir." Alyson glanced about, taking in the fresh thatch over the window shutters, the recently redaubed wall by the bed, the stout bar to place across the door. There was even a candle for her and a small brazier, in case the summer night turned cold. "You have made me most welcome."

"No, 'tis nothing for the woman who can look at me without flinching. That is a rare skill, and one none of the village maids have mastered." He scratched uneasily at his patchy beard, ducking his head under the low roof beams. "I would have women here, but they do not stay. The last washerwoman to work here told me straight out before she left that I had the evil eye and would sour milk."

"How cruel!" Indignant on his behalf, Alyson crossed the floor in two steps to lay a hand on his arm. "That is folly, utter superstition. You must never think it true."

"I am used to it. Do not let it trouble you." Thomas grinned, the scars on his forehead seeming to crack open afresh once more. "But you are as fiery as the dragon himself! Tell me, are you the wee maid who gave him that title?"

Startled, Alyson dropped her cloak on the bed. "I did not realize he had mentioned it."

"Once only, my lady, in Outremer, when he was a lad of twenty and we were making camp before our first siege. The talk round the fire fell to those remaining at home. The other men spoke half in jest as they bragged of women bedded and left, but not Guillelm. 'If I could have the girl of my liking, she would be a small, dark elf, a clever girl, with eyes the color of a rising storm. She knew and recognized me before any other,' he told us then, and he tapped the dragon on his shield." Thomas of Beresford regarded her closely, his battered head on one side. "I thought then Guillelm spoke of his ideal, but here you are, in the flesh."

"Please, sir—" Alyson knew she was blushing and fumbled with her riding gloves. She was stopped by her companion.

"I am glad you are real, my lady."

"Please, call me Alyson."

"Then you must call me Tom, as Guillelm does."

"Sir—Tom," Alyson faltered.

"Sir Tom will do very well." He peered at her in the dim light of the chamber and nodded. "The good thing is that you are so different from the other one."

Alyson felt the scrape of a sudden chill across the back of her neck. "What other?" she whispered.

"Never mind, it is years past and best forgotten." Sir Tom squeezed her arm, his eyes very kind behind their mesh of angry scars. "Now we should return to the hall, or Guillelm or his miserable shadow Fulk will have something to say."

They walked downstairs, Alyson beset with a new fear. Who was the other one? What woman had Guillelm known in Outremer that she should cast so long a shadow? "Who was she?" she demanded.

"Her name was Heloise."

"What was she like?"

"Proud and blond—but I will say no more, so do not ask."

"Then I will ask Guillelm."

"No!" Sir Tom stopped her on the stairs. "Swear to me now you will say nothing to him! He was so mauled by her, it would do him no good even to remember!" His earnestness was painful. "Promise me, Alyson. This is no idle thing I ask. I beg you to believe me when I say it would do great harm."

"But surely for him to speak would bring relief?"

"So women ever think. It is not the same for men. Guillelm needs to forget. Promise me, please." A bead of sweat trickled down his forehead, running past his ruined nose.

In the teeth of his distress Alyson felt the worst kind of gossip. "I promise," she answered swiftly. "I will not ask him direct. If he wishes to tell me . . ." She spread her hands.

"He will not!" Sir Tom spoke in heartfelt accents that pained and alarmed her.

I must know more, she thought. *Somehow I must find out. Or I will have no peace.*

Although it would be painful, she knew whom she could ask and get some answers—perhaps not all true, but certainly full. Guillelm's miserable shadow and her own nemesis, Fulk.

Guillelm watched Alyson enter the great hall on Tom's arm and cursed again his lack of foresight in providing her with no maids. He should have remembered the masculine nature of his friend's household; as it was, Alyson was the only female present. Even the wolfhounds slinking round the great unlit fireplace were male.

He was jealous, Guillelm realized and was ashamed of the emotion, for Alyson gave him no cause. In this situation, a single woman in a melee of menfolk, Heloise would have reveled in the attention, would have ensured that all eyes were on her. Quiet and grave, concentrating on what was being told her, Alyson strolled about with Tom, utterly unaware of the stir she made.

The stares of his men irked Guillelm. He wanted Alyson all to himself, wanted her alone. He strode across, deliberately heavy-footed so all would know he was coming.

"I will take her now, Tom," he said, closing fast.

"Aye, no doubt you will." The former crusader stepped back without breaking off from feasting a pair of very busy eyes on Alyson. He wore a look on his mangled face that could only be described as foolish. *The man is besotted,* thought Guillelm, jealous afresh.

He turned on his men. "Have you no tasks to be doing?" he barked at the astonished company. "Must I order everything?" He snatched at Alyson's hand, almost dragging her away from Tom. "Come, mistress, I would have a word."

He walked her behind the screens separating the great hall from the pantry and buttery, where a glower at a dice-throwing page had the boy scurrying off. Checking there was no one lingering in the buttery or pantry, he threaded his thumbs into his belt, taking pleasure just in looking at her. He had his second betrothal gift ready; he had wanted to give it to her earlier in the day, when they were alone in the woodland, but Fulk's battle roar had interrupted him. Now he and Alyson had a moment and he intended to make best use of it.

"Yes, my lord?" Alyson asked. "It is ever your custom to call me mistress when I have displeased you, so in what way have I offended now? I would know."

Quite apart from the justness of her mild reproof, the weariness in her voice startled him. Clasping her by the shoulders, he swiveled her toward the greater light streaming into the pantry and saw how bleached-out she was about the eyes. Her face had a suspiciously scrubbed look and her lips were pale.

"Your meeting with your sister?" he prompted, utterly changing what he was about to say. His gift would keep, but Alyson's distress would not. "Was she not pleased to see you?"

It was a shrewd guess. He felt her tremble, saw the sinews in her neck stiffen as she clenched her jaw. "She saw me."

"And?"

"We spoke for a while."

"What about?"

"Family matters. Very little, really."

"You have less in common than you thought?"

Alyson rubbed at her eyes. "Our lives are very different."

She moved to go past him and return to the hall but he stopped her. "Please, tell me what happened. I cannot bear to see you so . . . so beaten down."

She stared at him for so long that Guillelm wondered if he had changed into a hippogriff, or unicorn, or some other strange beast. "Please, sweeting," he said, the endearment feeling as if it had been wrung from him.

Out it came in a low tumble of words: her sister's anger that

Alyson had not also joined the convent, that her sister saw marriage as a sin.

"Why should she think that?" Guillelm knotted his forehead, trying to remember Alyson's sister, Matilda. A fleeing shadow in a dark dress was all that came to him and now he was all attention because Alyson was speaking.

"Our mother died in childbirth."

"Ah." Inwardly, Guillelm cursed his own memory; he should have remembered why Sir Henry had been a widower when he met him. "I am sorry."

"It frightened my sister greatly. She was older; she saw and understood more than I did. I was only four."

Old enough to be petrified, thought Guillelm grimly, sensing her taut as a harp string, while a small selfish part whispered that he was glad to be a man. He cleared his throat, embarrassed and yet wanting to offer some comfort. "In Outremer there are many skilled doctors who understand such things."

Alyson smiled. "We are not in Outremer." With that simple reply she drew away from him, adding, "Do you not think we should rejoin our host? Or he will perhaps consider the excellence of his welcome is lacking."

"You are right." As ever. Taking only a small pleasure from the fact she had used one of his own habitual phrases, Guillelm offered her his arm and they walked out from behind the screens.

Preoccupied, he did not notice Fulk emerge from behind a barrel of wine in the buttery and slip off to the chambers upstairs.

Chapter 7

Alyson pushed open the door to her night's lodgings, relieved that she was upstairs, beyond the tumult of the men. Below her, the noise in the great hall abated slightly as another dish of roast pig was carried in from the kitchen and the drunken diners fell on it with much hacking of knives and belches of satisfaction. Barring her chamber, Alyson unlaced her gown with a sigh, glad she was nimble enough to do this on her own.

No doubt Guillelm would have helped and played the part of lady's maid, if she had asked. Throughout the evening, with its noisy toasts and loud reminiscences of old campaigns, she had sensed his dark eyes ever straying to her. Had he watched the mysterious Heloise in the same way?

At least Fulk had been civil, Alyson reflected, shrugging off her shoes. He had been sitting beside her on the dais at dinner and had passed her several platters. He had even asked if she was warm enough.

Perhaps he is coming to accept me, she thought, glancing round the bare room for a comb or brush. She did not want to waste the candle in closer search, or lose the heat of the chamber by opening the shutters. Besides, the midsummer night was almost light enough to see by.

Finding nothing to do her hair with, she left it in its usual thick plait and sat on the edge of the bed, still considering Fulk. He had been almost suave tonight and certainly less hostile. If she could have devised a way of asking him about Heloise without Guillelm overhearing, she might have done.

She lifted back the woolen blanket—

And was off the bed in an instant, lunging for the shutters. Through her own shocked, harsh breathing she heard the catch give and she pushed, admitting a spill of moonlight into this sudden chamber of horrors.

I could have climbed into bed with that. Her stomach rolled at the thought and she gagged, turning toward the window to gulp down the fresh night air. What was it?

Setting her back to the window, she forced herself to look again. Shudders ran through her and her mind snatched at one piece of comfort: She had not touched the thing.

Below her the rafters shook as Guillelm bested two men at once in a wrestling match. She heard the shouts of congratulations with only a brief fizz of pleasure. She had her own contest here, with an unknown enemy. What had been left for her in the bed?

Alyson crouched and tugged slowly at the nearest blanket. With a queer sucking sound the mound of flesh hidden beneath the coarse wool shifted, as if alive, and then was still.

"Imagine it is the ingredients for a potion," she said aloud, but still she could not take any steps closer. She peered at the ruin of sheets.

It was offal, she decided. Lung, heart, liver. All washed. Filched from the kitchen and brought up here as what? A warning to her? A spiteful joke?

What had Fulk hoped to achieve? Even as Alyson's reason pointed out that she had no proof that it was Guillelm's seneschal who had done this, her instincts all agreed that it would be no other man. But why?

Working swiftly, Alyson bundled up the parcel of lights into a blanket and tossed it out of the open shutters. She would have to explain tomorrow how she had lost a sheet but she would think of something.

Or should she go down now and confront Fulk?

"With what?" Alyson scoffed. "You have just hurled the evidence out of the window!" And to judge from the chanting and foot stamping that was now going on in the hall, the men there were deep in drink. What if they merely laughed at her? What if Guillelm laughed?

He would never do that, she thought, but it would be a bad business, to accuse his most loyal follower of such a low trick. Fulk would deny it and she had no proof. Worse, Fulk could blame others, perhaps even Sir Thomas.

The thought of that kind, good-hearted man realizing that his home and hospitality had been so abused stopped Alyson on her way to the door. She could not do it.

Better perhaps to act as if she had found nothing amiss. That would annoy Fulk. And she could tell Guillelm in the morning.

But she would bed down on the floor tonight.

Although she was spent with the long ride and the emotions of the day Alyson did not expect to sleep. It was with shock that she was awakened early the next morning by a greenfinch fluttering around her room in a panic. The poor bird had flown in through the open shutters and kept beating itself against the roof thatch in its efforts to escape.

Alyson tossed her veil over the finch and gathered it gently, setting it flying free into the dawn. She wished she could rescue herself as easily; her rest had been troubled, plagued with dark dreams of blood and her dead mother.

Had Fulk somehow overheard what she had told Guillelm?

Had he left the offal as some kind of grisly token of childbirth—a future warning to her?

"It may not have been Fulk," Alyson told herself, but she could conceive of no other doing such a thing. Still, it shamed her. Her nightmares shamed her. Telling Guillelm would only spread the pain, she thought. She must deal with this herself, in her own way.

Once she had made that decision she felt a little easier and unbarred her door with more confidence than she might otherwise have had. Which was good—Guillelm was sleeping across her threshold, snoring and twitching like a great golden shaggy guard dog.

He stirred the instant she opened her door, flinging up an arm to prevent any entering her room from the stairs and blinking a baleful eye. "What?"

"You have no need to defend me from me, Guillelm." Somehow calling him "my lord" seemed inappropriate, especially now, with him yawning and rubbing at his bristling jaw.

"Excellent girl—"

"You want something."

"A cup of water or weak ale, if you have it."

"Not here; we must go downstairs." Alyson shook her head, astonished at how indulgent she felt toward this large oaf. It could not have been comfortable for him last night, napping on the stairs, and yet he did so in order that she would be safe. The thought touched her in spite of her disapproval of his carousing. "Did you win all your wrestling last night?" she asked.

He grinned and lifted an arm, showing off several cloak-pins skewered through his sleeve. "All fairly won. The others can show you their bruises." He blinked and knuckled his eyes. "Mother of God, it was quite a night."

"You should have drunk less," Alyson said, nudging him with her foot. "You will feel better outside." She held out a hand.

"You will not pull me up," he protested, using the wall instead as a brace as he swayed to his feet. "No, I am fine. I will be."

"Let us go, then," Alyson challenged. "Your breath is not so sweet this morning."

"Saucy wench!" Guillelm grumbled, but he was moving, picking up his feet lightly enough so as not to disturb the other twitching sleepers sprawled over the trestles in the great hall. Alyson passed by their slumbering forms as she sped from the stairs to the main doorway set in the middle of the hall, opposite the fireplace. There a few ash-covered firedogs, discarded cups and empty earthenware jugs, plus an over-turned small cauldron leaking a spill of stew, showed that it had been a very rowdy evening indeed. She glanced at Guillelm with raised eyebrows and he had the grace to color slightly and hurriedly push open the door for her.

"There were many toasts to our betrothal," he said sheepishly. "I could not deny or gainsay them."

"No?" About to tease more, Alyson noticed Fulk sleeping on the floor close to the stairs. He was sullen and frowning even in sleep and the sight of him, coiled into a tight, unyielding ball, made her shiver. What if he had attempted to do more in her room last night, when the rest of the company were making merry? If Guillelm had not lain by her door, would Fulk have tried to harm her?

I need to find absolute proof that he is my enemy, and quickly, she thought, but for now she was glad to step out of the beer-fumed hall into the early morning sunshine.

To her surprise, she and Guillelm were not alone. Thomas of Beresford was already outside, chopping wood.

"Guido!" Tom buried the axe in the thick trunk of oakwood that he was trimming. "Come work off that hangover by cutting some of this timber into manageable logs and I will fetch us breakfast. You, too, sweet Alyson. I trust you slept well?"

"Very, thank you," Alyson lied, watching the man hurry away to the kitchen block with a jaunty strut to his step.

"I know not how he does it, but Tom is ever good-tempered on a morning." Beside her Guillelm took up the axe and tested the blade with his thumb. "'Sweet Alyson,' eh?"

Without waiting for an answer he peeled down his tunic, stripping to the waist, and resumed the task Tom had started.

Alyson blushed; she could not help it. How often had she wondered in daydreams what Guillelm might look like? Not naked—she had never been so bold as to imagine that—but as he was now?

He had his back to her and she had a good view of him before a shout from the returning Tom made him twist round for an instant. The flesh across his back and shoulder blades shone in the ruddy dawn. He was beautiful as a wolf or wild-cat is beautiful; a marriage of spirit and sinews and animating grace. Light flashed from the metal head of the axe as he swung it back for another blow. The cry of splintered wood sang in her ears and she stumbled forward.

Guillelm spun about, axe automatically raised to attack. Seeing her, remembering she was there, he laughed and returned to his work. The curved bough he was working on groaned and fell clear; he tossed the log casually onto the growing pile and examined the rest of the tree trunk before laying aside his axe.

Alyson went to him, brushing shavings from his downy beard. His eyes were red with sawdust, but he grinned at her.

"The oak is my favorite: handsome in leaf and laden in the fall with sweet, full acorns. It grows strong wood." Guillelm's fingers spread across the tree bark and Alyson grinned at his obvious delight—she was happy again, her doubts dismissed. Arm in arm, they walked back to Tom, Guillelm shaking wood chips from his hair and talking.

"There will be a great tree harvest this season, I think, and

apple wood to burn, bark for your poultices, timber to shape."
He patted Alyson's rump as he had patted the oak trunk.
"Maybe a crib for a young one, and toys. What is it? Your
cheek is as fiery as the barberry. Have I spoken too soon?"

He had stopped walking and transferred the axe to his right
hand to clasp her shoulder. He smelt of sweat and musk, and
a familiar ache stirred in Alyson, but she answered clearly.

"I wish it was that, Guillelm. Your words—I thought then
of my sister."

"Ah. Of course." Guillelm withdrew his hand. "Forgive
me." He smacked his palm onto his forehead. "How could I
forget what you told me only yesterday? I am such a fool!"

"No—" Alyson began, but Tom interrupted, proffering two
cups of ale and saying in an over-hearty voice, "There is
bread and meat ready in the kitchen; we should go there
before the scullions eat it for us."

"My thanks, but I must visit the stable first." Guillelm
downed his ale in a single swallow and strode off, tugging his
shirt and mantle back over his head and leaving Tom and
Alyson to follow.

"I think he means the latrine," Tom remarked, catching
Alyson's disconcerted look. "Guillelm is shy when it comes
to women."

He offered her his arm, adding, "I am glad we have this
moment, Alyson. I have a question for your ears alone. Early
this morning I found two of my hounds eating something
beneath the window of your chamber. Do you know what it
could be?"

Alyson, heart thudding in her chest, looked into Tom's guile-
less, kind eyes. She could not lie, but how could she speak?

"No matter," Tom continued. "The dogs will scavenge anything. But if"—he glanced ahead to ensure that Guillelm was
still out of hearing and dropped his voice—"if ever you require

help, you need only ask. It will be given without question. And now you need say nothing; it is enough that we both know."

Tom moved ahead, pushing open the door to the kitchen and allowing Alyson to enter first.

After breakfast, Guillelm spoke to his friend. "I would take Alyson and be gone from here soon, before the others. Her palfrey needs more rest than my men's horses."

"That would make sense," Tom agreed, while he thought, *You hide your true feelings even from yourself! It is a thousand pities you ever met Heloise.*

"Stay here in the yard a moment first," he said. "There is something I want you to see, you and your lady. Wait—I will bring it to you."

"This is my betrothal gift to you both," Tom said.

Alyson heard Guillelm's whispered, "Mother of God," and understood his amazement. He slowly put out his hand and gently stroked the breast of the creature. "It is so fine," he murmured.

"To replace the hawk you had in the east," Tom said. "At first, I was to give you a pair of hounds, but knowing how hard you took the loss of your last dog on our homeward voyage from Outremer, I thought this better."

Alyson had wondered why he had no dogs with him and now she approved his constancy. "Is it a merlin?" she asked softly, as Guillelm donned a glove and took the hooded bird from Tom's fist.

"A very beautiful one," Guillelm answered, smiling at the little hawk's soft cry. "Her plumage is wonderful, such a rich mosaic of browns and creams!" His widening eyes found

Alyson's and he smiled at her. "If Tom will have her back a moment, you may have my glove—"

"No need." Tom handed Alyson a finely tooled glove.

"Fulk must ride ahead, ensure the hawk house is made ready," Guillelm went on. "Is David of Jeston still at Hardspen?"

"He died of this year's sickness," Alyson said, reluctant to pierce Guillelm's moment of giddy joy but remembering the falconer's fevered end all too well.

"Fulk knows something of the care of hawks," Tom said, covering the awkward moment of silence.

"I know, too," Guillelm remarked. He thrust out his free hand and caught Tom's fingers in an enthusiastic, whitening grip. "My thanks to you, Tom."

"It is a trifle," Tom demurred.

"It is a generous gift, Sir Tom," Alyson said, delaying handling the bird by not pulling on the glove. Her father had spoken of hawks in a tone of longing; peregrines and such were kept by great lords. She had never seen any bird of prey so close before, not even the red kites that scavenged on the midden heaps. For herself, thinking of the talons and that tearing, hooked beak, she was glad the merlin was hooded.

"Perhaps you can carry the perch?" Guillelm had noticed her reluctance; a half-amused, half-indulgent smile played about his lips. Tempted to thrust out her tongue at him again, Alyson said only, "You have not tied your own jesses," and pointed to the loosened throat strings of his shirt.

With a grunt of amusement, Guillelm attended to his clothes.

She and Guillelm set off soon after, Sir Tom supplying them with a generous pannier of provisions and wine, and long, needless instructions for the best route back to Hardspen. When it came to their farewells, Alyson was swirled off her feet into a rough hug, then as swiftly put down.

"More and Guillelm will be challenging me," Sir Tom rumbled against her hair, his scars tickling her ear. "Come see me again soon, do you hear?"

"We will," Alyson promised, springing lightly onto her horse before Guillelm could scold her for tardiness. She did not want either man to see the ready tears that had filled her eyes and even now threatened to spill onto the rough mane of her black palfrey. She would miss Sir Tom, more perhaps than her sister, and that was a bitter lesson to learn. Leaving Guillelm fussing with the merlin, she spurred her horse on, eager to be on her way before she broke down and disgraced herself completely.

Chapter 8

"Her jesses must be tangled in the branches. She cannot break free!"

Shading her eyes, Alyson bit down on the rejoinder that he should not have been flying the merlin while they were traveling and reached across their horses to seize Guillelm's arm.

"You cannot scramble up there," she warned. "That half-rotten tree will not take your weight. I will go. Give me her her hood and some meat to tempt her."

"She needs to be fed, certainly." Dismounting, Guillelm squinted up at the bird, which had stopped baiting and thrashing about the intermingled oak and hawthorn branches and was quietly roosting, seemingly oblivious to the alarm calls of the woodland crows and blackbirds. "You will take care?" he added, handing Alyson the soft leather hood without checking how she alighted from her horse and without breaking eye contact with the merlin.

"I climb well."

"I know that! I remember. I mean of her."

"Of course." *Your precious merlin will be quite safe,* Alyson thought.

Guillelm reached her as she was about to duck under the oak tree's low canopy. "Good luck, bright-eyes."

She nodded, mollified by the nickname and the mute appeal in his compelling velvet eyes, and began to climb.

"She is baiting again!" Guillelm shouted from below. "She will pierce herself!"

"No, I see her now and she is not so close to the hawthorn!" Alyson called back, cupping her hands round her mouth so as to cut down the sound the merlin would hear. "She is not hurt."

"And watch yourself!" Guillelm continued, crashing about the base of the oak with the hawthorn sprouting through its mat of branches as he tried and failed to shin up after her. She heard him cursing as he flailed in the undergrowth like some angry wild pig and felt a bubble of amusement soar in her throat.

"What in God's name are you giggling about?"

She playfully stamped her foot, kicking off a strand of lichen that drifted down onto Guillelm's nose. Seeing his indignant upraised face smeared with green, she laughed heartily. "You look like a pagan."

"Well, from down here, mistress, I can see a great deal of you, too." Guillelm was also laughing.

"You exaggerate," she replied, certain of her modesty.

"Alyson—"

"Hush, I am within a fingertip of our hawk." Should she try to tempt the bird with a morsel? Swiftly, at full stretch, she jammed a piece of raw meat into a jutting, sheared-off twig close to the merlin and backed up several paces along the main branch.

The little female hawk fluttered her handsome brown and cream wings and, with a soft jangle of the delicate bells on her jesses, hopped toward the tempting snack.

While she was occupied, tearing at the meat, Alyson was able to free one hanging strip of leather jess that had become snared on a mesh of hawthorn spikes. Having no desire to be torn at herself by that bright yellow beak, she called down to Guillelm.

"She will be able to fly now. Have you something you can use as a lure?"

"No need!" Guillelm answered, for the merlin suddenly swallowed a huge gobbet of meat and launched herself in a stoop, falling like a fiery arrow through the tree branches, straight back onto the bow perch she had been fastened to all morning: a familiar, safe haven. When Alyson tossed down the hood, Guillelm had already secured the bird and the adventure was over.

Not quite over, for when Guillelm raised his golden head to look at Alyson again, an "Excellent," forming on his lips, he stiffened, then began wildly pointing.

"What?" Alyson looked over herself and the branches she was "walking" on and clinging to. Nothing to be alarmed of here; no rotten boughs or wasps' nests. She took another step—plummeting into empty space as the part of her gown that had already snagged on an oak bole remained caught, throwing her off-balance and pitching her off the gently swaying tree. She heard a hoarse yell and then hit a shimmering mass of blues, greens and browns, choking as ice-cold water poured down her throat.

Praise Christ the river was here to break my tumble, was her first thought, followed at once by the realization that she was sinking. She thrashed and pounded but her shock-stiffened limbs would not answer her wishes; she went under again, heavy, calm, unable to breathe.

Another yell, and a pair of strong tanned arms scooped her out of the drowning murk.

"There, you are safe." Guillelm lifted her clear of the water. "I have you, dear one, and all is well."

* * *

He cradled her tightly, hoping she would not feel him shudder. He had seen the thorn branch hooking into her gown too late. Watching her fall, helpless to save her, had been the worst moments of his life. He had forgotten the river flowing beneath the oak—how foolishly preoccupied he had been with the merlin! A bird, when Alyson might have been lost. He had heard her hit the water, then clawing through the undergrowth to the water's edge, he had seen her slide into the stream's deep embrace. His Alyson was ever a fighter but she seemed unable to stop herself being dragged under in a deadly mesh of heavy skirts. Most eeric of all, a long, trailing skein of hair bobbed on the top of the water. Never before had he swum so rapidly, never in such terror.

Her small white hand was still hooked beneath his mantle, clutching his sodden undershirt. Shiver after shiver ran through her, though she did not seem to notice, whispering with her head against the crook of his arm, "You have briared your face."

"You think that matters?" The cuts and weals that stung on his nose and jaw, the result of beating desperately through the web of ferns, alder saplings and God knows what else, were nothing. "I saw you gone!"

"But you saved me." Wonder and gratitude warmed her voice where Guillelm would have had her berate him for putting her life in danger for a bundle of screeching feathers. For an instant his arms clamped tighter still about her small, willowy form as he thought of wringing the merlin's neck, then decided there would be more justice if he could wring his own.

"I was a fool!" he said.

"Then we both were, for I cannot swim."

That stopped him in midrage, as she hoped it would.

"Truly?" He paused in midstream, his feet rocking on the

river pebbles. "For all your clever book learning, there is something I know that you do not?"

"Will you teach me?" The words were out before she could drag them back. *I must be more shaken than I thought,* Alyson reflected, appalled at her own question. Each time she was in Guillelm's arms she forgot herself; it was a dangerous habit.

"We should feed the merlin," she went on, but the hawk, which had been Guillelm's great concern all that morning, no longer was a distraction. He merely grinned at her in that way of his that always made her feel as if her heart was suddenly lifted and jammed into her throat, and he said lightly, "I will tend the spoiled little brute, while you prepare yourself." He raised a thick gold eyebrow. "If you are certain you want me to teach you. My men will tell you I am a lethal taskmaster."

"Hard work never frightens me."

She was no longer shivering but languid in his arms, smiling at him with absolute trust. Guillelm had a sudden, disturbing vision of himself as tutor, pulling a squirming Alyson over his lap while he applied a schoolmasterly discipline to her pert backside. He flushed, ashamed of his thoughts— Heloise was surely right about him—and plucked at the clinging sleeve of her gown.

"You cannot swim in that," he remarked, determinedly averting his eyes from her bodice. The water had sculpted Alyson's clothes to her closer than a second skin, making him even more acutely conscious of his own aroused state. Fervently he wished the river was cold, blanketed with ice.

"What is the salve for earache?" he asked desperately as he attacked the gently shelving slope of the riverbank. Perhaps hearing her voice would bring him to reason, or at least be a comfort. Part of him was still grasping the dreadful marvel of her too-near escape from death.

"I have heard doctors swear by bloodletting and a tincture of mercury, poured into the ear. But for myself, I have found the gently warmed oil of the olive a good remedy."

"And for backache?"

"A hot bath to start." Alyson broke off, frowning at her dripping plait and checking with a swift downward glance that she had not lost her shoes. "Why all these cures? Are you going to shout at me so much or make me swim this river to the sea?"

"Worse." Guillelm deposited her onto the grass. "I am going to make you as hungry as the hawk."

She chuckled, that warm, throaty giggle that made him want to kiss her. "So 'tis well Sir Tom gave us generous provender. Do we eat first or later?"

"Later," said Guillelm.

The day was warm—more than warm, blisteringly hot, with a humidity that put Guillelm in mind of the East. It was airless under the trees by the river, or perhaps that was just him, he thought, as he kept busy, feeding the merlin, checking their horses, while Alyson shrugged off her soaking gown. It was at least a good day for a new swimmer, he told himself, tempted to ask if she needed help while he counted moorhen and coots with their young; bits of dark fluff swimming earnestly along the far riverbank. In these shallows the water would be perfect.

He heard her splash into the river and swallowed, his ears buzzing with heat and barely thwarted desire.

"I am ready." She was sculling the water with her hands. Would she be naked? No, for she was already growing nervous, perhaps even regretting her impulsive suggestion. "Guillelm, do you think this is right? I mean, is it seemly?"

"Why not?" He turned to reassure her and almost laughed:

Alyson had sat down in the shallows and he could see little of her. "We are, after all, betrothed."

"I have spread my gown on the hazel to dry." She pointed and he could see she was still wearing her undershift, a modest choice. "Will you swim as you are?"

"My stuff dries fast." His clothes were little enough of a barrier but they were something, a reminder he needed that Alyson was an innocent. *Or is she?* muttered Fulk in the baser recesses of his mind, a thought he resolutely thrust away. He strode to the river, willing himself to be a perfect gentle knight while he felt anything but chivalrous.

Be a lady, Alyson thought, both relieved and disappointed when Guillelm stalked into the river fully clothed. He was so swift-moving when he needed to be that she forgot his size, but now he was beside her again he towered over her, an eagle to her merlin. And how that gift of Sir Tom's had caused trouble! They were a good half mile or more off the recognized track through these woods and both of them had endured a wetting. *Fulk will wonder what we have been doing,* she thought, but then she forgot him in the face of Guillelm's grim stare. *Perhaps he dislikes this, perhaps I have been too forward.* The fears scurried through her mind like dandelion clocks blowing in the breeze as she tried not to shrink from him.

"Peace, girl." Kneeling in the water beside her, he had spotted her slight movement. Alyson, knowing him sensitive to the point of wariness over her possible dread of him, was tempted to slap the river back into his scowling face, to prove she was in no way scared. Had she been younger she might have done so, but at one and twenty she knew she ought to have more finesse.

"Did you swim the rivers in Outremer?" Not a very original question, but when Guillelm was apt to make her tongue-tied Alyson was proud she had managed so much.

"There are no such streams as these in the East." An evasive answer, made more mysterious by the ready stain of color that bloomed along Guillelm's jaw line and chin. "What is that strange scent? Like a spice or perfume."

He did not think it was anything to do with her, Alyson noted, disappointed, but she breathed in deeply. "It is fennel," she answered, nodding toward the bank where a stand of the tall, yellow flowers swayed among the cobwebbed beauty of the white elder blossom. "I use it in eye baths and for the colic. I dare say you have forgotten it, being so long away."

"And those birds?" he asked, but there was a gleam in his eyes that made Alyson click her tongue.

"Ducks, and you know it, you big oaf."

"Oaf, am I?" He lifted his feet from the river pebbles and stretched, floating full length on his back on the sparkling, tranquil surface. "Can you do this?"

She set to his challenge at once, only to sink as she tried to follow his example, wallowing in an ignominious stream of bubbles onto the sandy base of the stream.

"Steady, little swimmer. Up with you." Two hands buoyed her to the surface, their strong palms supporting her across her shoulder blades and the small of her back. "Relax. Imagine you are a bird and this water is the air beneath your wings. It will carry you easily. See?"

She was floating, the blood-warm water eddying round her limbs. Feeling safe, she closed her eyes, dimly aware that Guillelm had lowered the hand beneath her back.

"There," he said.

"This is marvelous," she said. "It is like reading a new book!"

"Only you would compare such things." His tone was indulgent. "I would have said riding a fresh horse, or petting a new dog."

The hand beneath her shoulder blades swept down the length of her spine and away. Alyson's eyes flew open and, with considerably less grace than her partner in the water, she put her feet down hastily, sighing with relief as her bare toes dug into the sand.

"Over with you." Guillelm gave her no time to protest, catching her round the middle and turning her, resting her stomach on his bent knee and saying, "Put your arms like this—that is good! Now work them so."

He showed her and she copied his movements. They paused a moment while he explained how to kick her legs and then she tried again.

"I am swimming!" she cried, delighted at her progress.

"Something, certainly," Guillelm answered, amused by her jerky dog-paddling and making sure he had her safe at all times. If he released her now, she would drop like a stone and he did not want her to lose confidence.

But she was a distracting thing and she did not even know it. Her linen undershift had turned half-transparent in the water, molding to her limbs in a way an Eastern harem beauty might envy. Attempting a churning, uncoordinated breaststroke on her front displayed her wildly kicking haunches and shapely legs to best advantage, while her breasts, cupped teasingly by the water and shown off by her beguilingly arched neck, were soft mounds he ached to caress. Their nipples were pink, he thought, although he was not entirely sure and did not trust his own countenance or continence to sneak a closer look.

He knelt again on the river bottom, gently withdrawing his hand from her trim stomach. Even through the water and linen, her skin was smooth and flawless as the inside of a freshly split apple and smelled as sweet, as good to taste. It would be so easy, to brush his fingers lower—but that was outside his role as teacher, for now at least. Trust was everything, as Alyson herself proved, swimming three genuine strokes as he came round in front of her, stretching out his arms.

"Hang on," he coaxed. "I will give you a lift."

She caught his hands willingly in hers and he drew her along, swimming on his back and praying there were no overhanging branches for him to blunder into and sink them both. "Do you like it?" he called.

She laughed, showing her white even teeth, giggling more as he accelerated in the water. "It is flying!"

If you think that, wait until we have the nights together, Guillelm thought, but then he struck his head against a boulder and went under, swallowing a good yard of river.

Strong fingers yanked his hair and tugged; he surfaced, coughing, and with part of his skull feeling as if it had undergone an ordeal with a hot iron, but still afloat.

"I have you," Alyson crowed. "I am swimming for us."

"Peace, wench, and get me to the bank," said Guillelm. That was enough of lessons for the day.

Chapter 9

Three weeks later and there had been no time for more swimming, Alyson thought with regret, but with pride, too, for she and Guillelm had not been idle. The new well at Hardspen was being dug, the stores had been checked and added to, everywhere had been cleaned, including the stables, the sheep had been clipped, the hay harvest gathered, the wheat was growing well, firewood and timber laid by and folk were seen in the great hall with their appeals for help and justice.

Though Alyson had no doubt that Fulk disapproved, Guillelm often sought her out to ask about the background to the various complaints from the local people. "You will know who is rumored to steal from the fish ponds and who gives light weight to their measures," he remarked, a comment she hugged to herself. Guillelm's father had never involved her in any way in such disputes.

Her only cloud was her nights, where she had bad dreams. She begged her nurse Gytha to say nothing of her nightmares of blood and screams. They would pass, she thought. They must, or Fulk's malice with that vile parcel he had left in her bed at Sir Tom's would leave too great a shadow.

She was also no closer to learning about Heloise. She had

promised Sir Tom that she would not ask Guillelm directly and she had kept that vow. More oblique questions to him—Had he known many ladies in Outremer? What fashions did the women of the East wear? Were there any female crusaders?—had yielded only one-word answers or, in the last case, a grunt of laughter.

But perhaps she was being foolish. On the evening of the day they had swum in the river, Guillelm had asked her to join him in the chapel at Hardspen.

There, with the last of the evening sunlight casting shadows on his face and hair he had knelt before her on the stone flags so that their eyes were almost level.

"This is for you. I meant to give it you earlier."

He had handed her a scrap of cloth. His eyes gleamed with the same suppressed excitement that she had seen in them when he was a youth, when he was about some quest or mischief, and she heard the tendons of his neck crack as he lowered his head to watch her fingers.

"I hope you like it," he murmured.

Wondering what it could be, she opened the roughly tied parcel. Inside the cloth had been a delicate web of something, thin as the wings of a butterfly. Alyson blew on it, watching the filmy stuff billow.

"Silk?" she asked.

Guillelm nodded. "Bartered from a trader in Jerusalem with a stall close to the spice market."

"It is a gorgeous color. Like a fall sky at twilight." Almost afraid to handle the purple-blue haze, she unwrapped it fully. "It is beautiful. So smooth and light."

"The only thing I thought worthy of covering your hair," Guillelm said quickly. "It is a veil," he added unnecessarily.

"Thank you." She touched his cheek with the silk, feeling the rough grain of his tanned flesh through the rare fabric. "I shall wear it at our wedding," she continued, catching her breath as Guillelm had turned his head and kissed her hand close to the wrist.

Thinking back, Alyson smiled. Whatever memories Guillelm had of Heloise, he had given the silk to her. And proud, blond Heloise was in Outremer; it was she who was marrying the lord of Hardspen.

Tomorrow.

But what if she could not make him happy? What if her sister was right and God was angry with her for not entering convent life? What if she died in childbirth, like her mother? What if at some fatal moment, Guillelm did something that reminded her too closely of his father? What if he saw the scars on her body? What if they repelled him?

The questions had driven her back to the castle chapel. She had been on her knees here since the midday meal, telling Guillelm that she was keeping a vigil.

"That is what a squire does, before he is knighted," Guillelm had said. "He spends the night at prayer and fasting. Do you think our marriage will be such a battlefield?"

His question had seemed innocent enough, a tease, but she had sensed his disquiet and answered seriously, "I will pray for those things a good knight prays for: faithfulness, fellowship, generosity of spirit." Then she had grinned. "A good defense."

"Off with you, horror," Guillelm had said, tugging her plait as she mounted the stairs.

She had been praying before the simple stone altar for several hours. Beyond the chapel door the daytime bustle of the castle had given way to the scurry of the evening meal in the great hall, then quiet. Guillelm was not drinking tonight and neither were his men. Presumably he did not wish to appear at his wedding thickheaded, she thought, but the lack of merrymaking made her wonder if he was having second thoughts. Where was he tonight? With some woman? His final bedding as a free man?

Alyson tried to quell the thought, ashamed of her own jealousy. And in church, too!

There was a knock on the chapel door. Alyson rose, rubbing her numb, cold knees, as Fulk entered.

"I have brought you some mulled wine, my lady."

The wine smelt good and looked harmless. More surprising still was Fulk himself, very fine in a gold and silver mantle, smelling of fresh soap, and smiling.

"Thank you, sir." Alyson could think of no legitimate reason to refuse his apparent kindness and could only delay. "Would you leave the wine outside the chapel for me? To drink here does not seem quite appropriate."

"Yet we will take communion wine in here tomorrow, my lady." He proffered the goblet again. "Please, for the sake of my lord. He would not have you catch your death of cold."

Guillelm had sent the wine? Perhaps he had, but then why had Fulk brought it and not a page or squire? Or even one of the maids—there were plenty about the castle now, for all had thrown off the summer sickness.

"My lord is ever kind," Alyson responded stiffly. "As are you, sir, for carrying it to me yourself." She took the goblet from him, making great play of inhaling the steaming beverage. "I love the smell of warm spices." Which was true, although the reason she sniffed so heartily was to catch any trace of something unwholesome in the mixture. Alyson had not forgotten Fulk's accusation of poison against Gytha.

Nor it seemed had Fulk. He took a step closer to her. "I swear that it is safe."

The very fact he did not add "my lady" convinced Alyson, that and the flush that tided up into his gaunt face, submerging the angry red spots on his sallow cheeks beneath a rush of shame.

"I have wronged you."

His words were almost indistinct, yet his gesture was plain.

Much to Alyson's embarrassment he fell on his knees before her, his hands reaching in supplication for the hem of her gown. "Forgive me. For my pride, my arrogance, my malice. I have sinned against a purely virtuous lady and now I see my error. Forgive!"

He was clutching at her skirts, his hard blue eyes wide in seeming distress. But why the change of heart? Had Guillelm spoken to the man?

Almost as if he had divined her thought, Fulk prattled on. "Please, my lord knows nothing of my trick against you at the house of Thomas of Beresford. I beg you not to speak of it to him."

Sickened by his admission, Alyson yanked her gown from his clasping fingers. "I am no telltale."

"No, you are a mate worthy of my lord. I understand that."

Alyson sniffed the wine again and tasted it. "I think less cinnamon next time." She rippled her fingers at Fulk. "Rise, sir, or you will be the one to catch your death of cold.

"Tell me," she said, when Fulk was on his feet. "How did you arrive at your revised conclusion?"

"You speak like a master of logic, my lady—"

"And you put pig's guts into my bed. Answer the question."

Fulk scowled, clearly put out by her directness. "I was not myself that night," he muttered. "Too much wine."

It was the nearest, Alyson sensed, that he would come to an explanation or apology. "Go on," she said, sipping her wine.

Fulk stared at the altar candles. "Guillelm is happy."

"Your lord's joy is important to you, then? Even if it means a different destiny from the one you wanted for him?" Waiting for Fulk's reply, Alyson found herself looking at the altar, with its bare white cloth and small, roughly carved, garishly painted wooden crucifix. Gytha and Osmoda had promised her many flowers for her wedding day but so far the chapel was as plain as it had ever been.

"Perhaps it is the will of God," Fulk conceded.

"Yet you told me Guillelm's fancies did not last, so why should you think differently of me?"

"He is marrying you. You have no family, no important friends to force your case with him had he chosen to keep you as his leman, instead." Fulk shrugged—it seemed that begging her forgiveness and his earlier groveling had depleted his small store of courtesy as he now added, "It is certainly nothing to do with honoring your own lands or title, neither of which can be described as significant."

"It is well for you, Fulk, that our lord is not here, or you would suffer for that ungentle remark." Alyson's mind turned cold, her body clammy. Guillelm's mistress. She had not considered that possibility, although in truth, considering what had so nearly happened between her and Guillelm's father, Lord Robert, she should have done. For an instant her own vulnerability weighed on her, then she rallied.

"What of your vow to me, to win places for yourself and Guillelm on a further crusade to Outremer? Do you still hold to that promise?"

"It seems I cannot."

"Do you give up that vow?" Alyson persisted. "Do you?"

"It seems I must."

"Not the most extravagant of new promises, Fulk."

"I know I must do better." Fulk clasped his shaggy gray head briefly between his hands and then began to pace about the chapel. "I cannot easily praise women."

"Not even the delicious Heloise of Outremer?"

That stopped him dead, in midstride. "You know of her?"

"Of course." Alyson waited; this was more teasing than the most delicate of potion making. If Fulk guessed how badly she wanted to know more of Heloise he might deny her. "She was blond and beautiful and she injured my lord."

"That is true—I know nothing of what passed between them, but Heloise was the very devil."

"To you we women are all the snares of the devil." Alyson did not smile at Fulk's startled expression; it gave her no pleasure to admit this. She knew that to him there was nothing about her of value. To him, she was simply a dark Heloise. *Heloise, who remained mysterious . . .*

"If you get Guillelm a son it will be enough." His previous fulsome speech had entirely deserted him. "If you have the courage for such work."

So he had overheard her talking to Guillelm and knew the tragic history of her mother! Yet there was no sympathy in his look or words. To Fulk she was a vessel for a man's seed, nothing more. "And my people and I will be safe from you?"

A trace of white spittle appeared at the corner of Fulk's mouth as he whipped round to face her. "What do you think me? You are my lord's!"

"Perhaps worth even as much as his merlin," Alyson agreed.

That wrung a grudging smile from Fulk. "I swear I will make no move against you." He signed the cross in the air.

"Nor against my people?" Alyson demanded, remembering Gytha.

"Nor against your people."

"You will serve me faithfully, as a true knight to her lady?"

He sighed. "Even that."

Should she demand an act of fealty from him? Alyson wondered, but the idea of Fulk kneeling before her a second time, of her hands clasping his while he swore an oath of allegiance, was abhorrent to her. He had sworn and signed the cross; that should be sufficient.

"I would serve you now, my lady," Fulk's attempt at gallantry was back and Alyson chose to take the wish for the deed.

"How so?" she asked, finishing her wine. It had indeed been excellent—she and Fulk might yet muddle along, she thought, praying that she was not being too optimistic in her assessment. Yet she had to try, if only for Guillelm's sake. "What would you do for me?"

Fulk walked away. For an instant, Alyson thought he was leaving and was uncertain if she was relieved or annoyed, but then he crouched in the shadow of one of the chapel's stone pillars, plucking something from the floor. He returned to her, holding it aloft between his hands. "I would tell you of this diadem, which the chatelaines of Hardspen have ever worn on festal days. My lord thought it lost, but I have sought and found it and now I offer it to you."

He held out the diadem. "It was in one of the store rooms, thrust into a sack in a corner. I think the previous steward of the castle must have brought it there for some reason of his own and then died of the fever before telling anyone where he had put it, or why, but no matter; it is recovered."

"A prodigal diadem," Alyson observed, but her small joke, at which Guillelm would have laughed, earned her no smile from Fulk.

"It is an ancient thing, my lady." He spoke as if she had said nothing. "My lord has spoken of it to me, with sorrow at its disappearance. He did not mention it to you," Fulk went on, turning the diadem in his hands, "because he did not wish to cause you distress."

Alyson waited and after a pause, during which the unearthly shriek of a nightjar filtered through the only window in the chapel—a simple three-lancet affair but with rare colored glass—he picked up his tale.

"There is a story attached to this jewel. It is said that if the lady of the castle does not wear it on her wedding day, the marriage will be barren."

"Guillelm told you this?"

"On the first night we returned to Hardspen, my lady." Fulk inclined his gray head, his fierce blue eyes narrowed into slits

as he considered the diadem. "He looked for it himself after
he had made his suit to you, and when he did not find it he
sought to laugh off the story, saying it was naught but superstition. But I could tell he was disquieted." Fulk flung her a
cool, assessing glance. "When Guillelm was in his cups, the
night before we rode to St. Foy's—"

"The evening of our betrothal," Alyson dropped in coolly.

"—he spoke of it a second time. He said it was an evil loss.
I do not think he would have spoken so had he not been made
unguarded with drink, but it is certain that it has preyed upon
his mind, do you not agree?"

"Perhaps. Is there more to the legend?" Alyson thought it
sounded bald and a thread of suspicion wound about her
mind. She was little reassured when Fulk shrugged.

"Something of two crossed lovers—a womanish fancy. I
forget."

Reluctantly, Alyson put her empty goblet on the stone flags
and held out her hands. "May I?"

Fulk gave her the diadem and stood back a pace with legs
apart and arms folded—a curious stance for a pious man in
a holy place. She would certainly not take just Fulk's word on
this. She would ask Gytha to question the old servants of
Hardspen, see if this "legend" was more than a product of
Fulk's devious head. Yet if that were so, for what purpose?

The diadem could not be poisoned; he had handled it too
freely. It was a plain, heavy device in gold, very much like her
betrothal ring. The gold was as yellow as the yolk of an egg.
There were no markings on it yet she guessed that Fulk was
correct. It seemed old, an heirloom.

"Thank you, Fulk," she said.

He bowed, recovered the goblet and took his leave without
asking if she would wear it on the morrow. Alyson waited
until she was certain he was gone on the dim stairway, then
slipped out of the chapel to find Gytha.

* * *

Later that evening, in the modest chamber that after tonight would no longer be hers, her nurse was reassuring. The diadem was indeed a family heirloom, from the maternal line. Guillelm's mother had worn it at her wedding. It was claimed by all the old retainers of the castle that any Hardspen bride who wore it would have a supremely fortunate marriage and bring forth many living sons.

Her lord dragon, with his great size and strength, surely was the equivalent of many sons, Alyson thought, and she smiled. "And the story of the lovers?" she asked.

Gytha patted the bed that she and Alyson were sharing for the last time, encouraging her former charge to snuggle down beneath the sheets to listen.

Somewhere in a story of a young Norman prince and a Saxon lady, who had met on pilgrimage to Rome and then been parted by fate, with the lady kidnapped by a wicked uncle and the prince searching for her, undergoing travails through marshes and being guided to his true love by miraculous speaking birds, Alyson fell asleep. She stirred once, when Gytha reached the climax of her tale, saying that although the lady had been bewitched into the likeness of an old hag by her uncle, the prince recognized her by the golden diadem and kissed her, breaking the spell.

"So they were wed, my bird, and very merry. The lady wore a gown of cloth of gold and a veil of gold and shoes of . . ."

Alyson slept again and heard no more.

Chapter 10

For what felt to be the thousandth time, Guillelm stared at his bride. Where had she found it? He had thought it well hidden, but here she was in her best gown and her silk veil and *that*. Someone must have gone looking for it. Was it in innocence that she wore the diadem, or did she know? Had she heard some whisper? Yet if she had heard and she knew the full history of his mother's jewel, how could she appear before him, wearing it? Sporting it, even? How dare she?

It was always a favorite of his father's, Guillelm remembered. Did she wear it for him, in memory of him? Did she miss Lord Robert? Did she wish she was marrying the father instead of the son?

Round and round, like a child's spinning top, the thoughts tormented Guillelm through his marriage vows. He watched Alyson at their wedding feast, haunted by the fact that she ate little and said less. Nerves or more?

Soon they would be together, once her maids had finished preparing the main bedchamber. Guillelm had never used it, preferring to sleep with his men in the great hall, below the great long sword and round gold-embossed shield of his famous Viking ancestor, Thorkill of Orkney. To him, the main bedchamber still felt like his father's, rather than his.

Tom said something and Guillelm answered, thinking that although his friend had made a special effort to attend their marriage, his own sister had not, sending instead a modest gift of bedding and the excuse, delivered by the shamefaced messenger, that she could not come because of "women's troubles"—whatever those were. None of Juliana's family had attended, either, which saddened but did not surprise Guillelm. He and his elder sibling had never been close.

Down on one of the lower tables, Thierry made a ribald comment and several knights grinned. Thierry and the others would expect to witness the bedding of bride and groom, but Guillelm had already spoken to Tom. He and Alyson would climb the stairs to the bedchamber alone, and Tom would guard their backs. Once, he might have asked Fulk to do the same service, but he knew that Fulk and Alyson were still cool with each other. Again, he was saddened but not surprised.

"That is a battle face for your wedding night! Do you think your bride be so hard to conquer?" Thierry bawled, at which Guillelm clenched his fist so hard that he bent the handle of his eating dagger, brooding on Lord Robert, and Alyson's diadem, and the night to come.

The diadem hurt her head, it was so heavy. How had Guillelm's mother been able to wear it? thought Alyson, wondering if she was somehow lacking. She longed to take it off—that and her shoes, which were new and pinched her toes.

She stretched a smile at Thierry's comment, tired of the expectant faces. It was her wedding day and all she wished to do was find a quiet corner to sleep. The blazing joy she had expected had come earlier, in snatches: when Guillelm said his vows to her; when he placed the wedding band on her finger; when he kissed her, saying softly against her hair, "You are mine now."

You are mine now. Flexing her aching toes inside her shiny new shoes, she glanced at Guillelm beside her, close enough for her to brush his leg under the table, if she was so bold, or to feed him, but so far in other ways! She sensed a gulf between them, widening with each hour and the lengthening shadows of evening. What Thierry called his battle face was also his unreadable face, taut and blank as new parchment. He would not look at her directly, but all through this long feast she had felt his eyes on her. Such scrutiny was scarcely the behavior of a loving groom.

You think too much, Alyson scolded herself, but dread churned in her belly. She snatched at her cup and drank the sweet wine, wondering if she should have more.

Guillelm had noticed. He leaned toward her, coming close but careful that their shoulders did not touch. "I trust you do not drink so readily in order to numb yourself for the rest of tonight."

Shock, hurt and indignation warred in Alyson. She had never expected such a comment from him, would not have thought him capable of such crassness. There was no teasing in his eyes or voice, merely chill accusation. *We are going wrong again,* she thought in despair, while she forced herself to utter a sprightly, "Indeed not!" tapping his foot with hers to make good her words.

He withdrew as if she was a monster, jerking back on his chair and lurching to his feet.

"Dragon—" she whispered, but Guillelm was addressing the company.

"My excellent lady and I will now say goodnight, my friends. Enjoy the rest of the feast! You have earned it."

It was a brief, terse speech, and as if he recognized this, Guillelm began to applaud his own men and the servers.

When they in turn began to clap their hands, he scooped her straight off her chair into his arms and raced for the stairs. There were good-natured shouts, snatching hands, high-pitched laughter from the few women present, as it was realized where he was heading. Breathless from Guillelm's speed and the force of her abduction, Alyson heard a general clatter and scrape of stools as some of the younger men left the tables and tried to follow. She could see little, pressed tight against Guillelm's mantle, but Sir Tom was calling, "Easy there! Let them go!" and she caught a glimpse of Tom's scarred, kind face, creased with concern, as she was carried from the great hall. There were flashes of torchlight and shadow, shouts, ever more distant, a dizzying twist from Guillelm as he turned from one stair onto a second, one she knew led to Lord Robert's former chamber.

Despite her best intentions, her courage began to falter. She had known they would come here, so why was she not more prepared? What had happened here between Guillelm's father and herself—that was the past. It had no place between her and Guillelm.

She was able to suppress a shudder, but her teeth chattered.

"Here we are," Guillelm said unnecessarily, setting his shoulder to the door and pushing.

"Ah!" The exclamation was out before Alyson could stop it.

"You like it?"

"This is wondrous, dragon!"

"Mother of God, you are right. They have done well for me."

"Who?" Alyson recollected and understood. "Sericus and your question about furniture! It was for here."

"Clever creature." He tickled her under the arms before he let her down, play that delighted Alyson. With renewed hope she started round the chamber, touching everything.

* * *

She ran her fingers over the great carved bed, pressed her hands into the soft mattress, peeping at him swiftly through shy, half-lowered eyes. She raised and lowered the lid of a chest, blushing as she saw it contained his clothes. She kicked off her shoes and walked onto the sheepskin rug. "That feels good," she said with a sigh.

He stared at her delicately arched feet because they were pretty and because he did not want to look at the diadem again. Her words—"The flowers are beautiful"—snapped his head up, and for the first time he noticed the great sprays of lavender, hyssop, marigold, poppy and sweet violet wound about the canopy of the bed and draped on the window sill. Their scent perfumed the whole room and that, more than anything, finally put the malign influence of Lord Robert out of his head. The chamber was exorcised; it would never be his father's again.

"I must give the maids some gift on the morrow," he said with a smile.

Alyson nodded. For her the room was superficially changed, the dark aged dresser and sagging bed gone, the flags made warm and human with rugs, but shadows remained. She was glad of the flowers. She was glad, but also wary of Guillelm. Wondering which of them would make the next move, and too shy to approach the great bed, with its crisp linen sheets, she knelt on the sheepskin to spare her aching feet. "Thank you," she said, bowing her head as a sign of respect.

"No!" the cry broke from Guillelm. "You never kneel to me! I am not—"

He broke off, but Alyson knew what he was about to say. *I am not my father.*

"Guillelm, it is all right." She looked up at his tall strong form and heard herself say, "I trust you. How could I not? You saved my life."

"Then why do you wear that?"

Alyson followed his pointing finger and lifted her hand, touching the golden diadem on her head. "What is wrong?" she asked. "I was told this was an heirloom, that you would be pleased if I wore it." Alyson debated and then told the truth. "Fulk gave it to me."

Fulk. His own man had done this. Guillelm could scarcely believe it, but Alyson was still talking, apologizing.

"I am sorry if I have done anything amiss, dragon. Many at Hardspen told my nurse the story of the diadem: how it brings good fortune."

"So people believe, but they do not know the whole."

Guillelm strode to the bed and sat down, sinking into the soft mattress and wishing for an instant that it was quicksand and that he could bury his duplicitous seneschal up to his neck in it. Fulk's cunning appalled him, but Alyson deserved better: better from Fulk and far better from him.

"Come, we are bound in love. Come sit here and I will explain." He patted the bed.

He still looked fierce but no longer with her. Alyson dragged the diadem off her head, ready to throw it into the furthest corner. Why had she even tried to trust Fulk?

Bound in love. Guillelm had used those words. Feeling as if a great light shone within her, Alyson scrambled over to the bed, missing her footing once. It did not matter. Guillelm took her hand and they sat side by side, very companionable.

He put an arm about her shoulder. "Comfortable?" he asked softly.

She nodded, and then, seeing his eyes darken, said quickly, "You do not need to tell me if it gives you pain."

"No, it is best you know."

Guillelm took a deep breath. Years later the memory was raw; he hated to pick at it.

"As I am sure you have been told, the diadem was my mother's. It was part of her dowry and had been in her family for generations."

He smiled. "I remember her wearing it during our Christmas feasts. Her hair was brown, then, not so fine or black as yours, but the gold looked well against it. In her best gown and jewels, my mother was as noble as any queen.

"She died when I was twelve. I was living in the north then, as squire to the husband of my sister, Juliana. I was too late to see her before she died; there were no farewells between us."

Alyson nodded, tears standing in her wide eyes, and Guillelm knew she was thinking of his loss, and of the death of her own mother. He hated to hurt her so, but he knew he had to speak on.

"A month after my mother was buried, my father had me return to Hardspen." He felt his mouth twist downward; even the thought was bitter and in his mouth the words seemed to taste like vinegar. "Lord Robert claimed he could not live without me, that he was lost, missing his wife and his heir. So I was returned for his need, like an extra blanket, only to discover that another lady had taken my mother's place."

He could tell he had shocked Alyson. Her very stillness gave her away.

"You are surprised—so was I! The first evening I served at my father's table, as squire, as I had done at Juliana's, I found myself handing wine to a woman sitting in my mother's place, dressed in my mother's gown and with my mother's diadem upon her blond head.

"She was a merchant's daughter, I discovered. Her name was Margery. She was a plump, cheerful girl, closer to my age than my father's, and trusting as a puppy. Lord Robert doted on her. I did not. I considered her presence, so soon and so openly after my mother's death, an insult to her memory.

"Lord Robert and I quarreled. I kept my temper—which was a hard thing to do!—until I could get him alone and then I laid into him."

It gave Guillelm no pleasure to admit this, nor to recall the sweating fear in his father's face when he had swung him against the staircase wall. Even at twelve he had been a strapping lad and anger had given him more strength. Climbing out of the great hall with his father he had not been able to wait until they reached Lord Robert's chamber before he spoke out. He had pinned Lord Robert on those stairs and raged against him.

"I threatened to throw him off the battlements. Lord Robert pleaded and blustered; much was said between us on both sides that should never be said. I stormed out and rode all night and when I returned Margery was gone. The diadem was gone, too; Lord Robert told me that it had been put away with the rest of my mother's things. Certainly I had no wish to see it. I did not ask what he had done with it. We never spoke of it again."

Guillelm lifted the diadem from Alyson's lap. "None of the servants knew the whole story. I told Fulk many years ago, when I was laid up with fever and talking all kinds of nonsense. He swore then that he would not mention it."

"He did not," Alyson said, "not really."

They sat a moment in quiet, Alyson considering what he had told her. Guillelm's distance from his father, the way he often called him Lord Robert, was now explained. But to lose his mother at twelve! That was terrible, just on the edge of manhood, when youths tended to revere their mothers.

"How did she die?" she asked softly.

"In childbirth. Twins. Two girls. They died the following day." Guillelm turned stricken eyes on her. "I am so sorry, Alyson."

For him to blame himself was almost too much. She was torn between boxing his ears for being so foolish and gathering him to her. She compromised by stretching up and placing a gentle kiss on his forehead.

"It is not your fault," she said.

Yes, thought Guillelm, it was, for being envious of his father and suspicious of Alyson and for trusting the fellowship of old crusaders too much. He had known Fulk disliked Alyson—why had he not seen how deep that dislike ran? Between Fulk's animosity and his own jealousy he had almost spoiled their wedding night.

"I am sorry," he said again, kissing her forehead in return.

"Are we echoes?" she asked, but she was smiling, warm and pliant as he drew her onto his lap.

I care for her so much, he thought. She deserved so much. He longed to protect her, pamper her, make her laugh, share his past, present and future with her. A child with her warm, clever eyes. A daughter with her hair, her wild kindness and courage . . .

"She would be a little heartbreaker," he murmured. He was torn between the desire to kneel at her feet and pour out to Alyson how much he cared for her and an earthier need.

"I am truly sorry about Fulk," he said.

Guillelm looked startled as he spoke, as if he had been about to say something utterly different and was overtaken by surprise at his own words. His face had been so tender before, so ardent, that Alyson had almost framed the answer, "And I love you," but now his statement fell on her like a dash of cold water. She who had only just learned to swim floundered.

"Is there wine?" she asked brightly, wondering if she should climb off his knee and look for some. In some households, she knew that weddings ended in a very public bedding, and much as she was grateful to Guillelm for sparing her that ordeal, she was not quite sure how to behave. She remembered from the few female friends she had—before Lord Robert had forbidden her to meet them—that brides were often put to bed by a gaggle of maids and womenfolk and the grooms brought to them. Guillelm had said no to that, too, overriding Gytha's mild protest that her lady would need her hair loosened and brushed by saying, "I will do it," in a way that brooked no argument. At the time, Alyson had been flattered and excited; now, truly alone with Guillelm for the whole night and for many nights to come, she was almost uneasy.

Heloise. Her blond rival. A devil, according to Fulk. A beauty so lethal that she must not even be spoken of, according to Sir Tom. More and more she regretted her promise to Sir Tom that she would not question Guillelm directly; such matters were better out in the open between them. Instead she had brooded on Heloise until the woman was almost supernatural in her mind—an adversary and a memory she could never defeat.

I am not blond. I am not tall or elegant or beautiful. Was Guillelm comparing me to Heloise? Was he disappointed? Was that why he had not wanted a public bedding?

He has not seen me yet, not really, she thought, and renewed panic stampeded in her mind. Her reason told her that Guillelm cared for her, that he had married her, that he spoke of her with the pride of possession: *You are mine now.* But was it only possession? Perhaps with men it was.

A tiny shake of her hand returned Alyson to herself.

"There is a flagon and cups on top of the flat chest," Guillelm said indulgently, "as I told you several moments ago, before you sank into that serious-looking reverie of yours. What on earth were you thinking? No, wait—" he added, as she tried to push herself off his knees. "With your distracted state, I think I should pour the wine."

With maddening ease and with her still sunk in his lap, he rose from the bed, retrieved the flagon and cups and settled back against the headboard in a single flowing movement.

"Drink," he said, holding a brimming vessel to her lips.

She did so to please him, although malmsey was a wine she disliked. Its cloying sweetness stung in her nose, reminding her too much of her own recent past.

Fearful of looking into Guillelm's eyes lest he see her old fears and believe himself responsible for them, she turned her head, seeking something more to praise.

Then she saw it. The charm meant for her, for her protection, tucked under her pillow. A charm midwives would give women in childbirth, to keep them safe. Gytha must have left it.

She must truly fear I will be like my mother and Guillelm's mother and die in childbirth. Leaning away from Guillelm's sheltering arm, ignoring his, "What?" Alyson drew the charm out of its hiding place.

It was a tiny purse, richly embroidered, containing a small jasper, the stone that gave protection to pregnant women.

"A pretty device," Guillelm remarked, looking over her shoulder.

"Yes," murmured Alyson, glad he understood no more. The charm was kindly given but what was the use? Her own mother had possessed a necklace of jasper and yet she had died.

She shuddered, unable to deny or suppress the memories that now assailed her with their terrible renewing freshness: her mother's terrified screams, her sister's crying. The blood. Tilda had accused her of not knowing about the blood, but she had. She had seen her mother's birthing sheets. She shivered a second time.

Guillelm sensed her withdrawal and a great sorrow welled in him. Even with the wine, even with him trying to be gentle, patient, it was no use. Heloise had been right: He was cursed in his relations with women. Alyson was like all the rest, afraid of him, revolted by his size.

Swiftly, before his baser instincts overwhelmed him and he did something he would regret for the rest of his days, Guillelm gently put his new bride from him, laying her down on the bed.

"I will leave you. Get into bed, Alyson. I will come later."

"When, my lord?"

Her huge eyes tore at him.

"Later!" He stormed from the chamber, and Alyson heard his dreadful vow, wrested from him in darkest despair, when he dreaded even to look at her lest he see the disgust in her face, "We may share the same bed, but we shall never lie together in love, madam, so put all such horror from you now. I will come back later. Later—"

His voice echoed on the stairs and then he was gone.

Guillelm did not return that night. Alyson had no idea where he slept. She did not sleep at all and in the morning when she rose she felt a thousand years old.

Gytha, bustling in with congratulations, took one look at her and shooed the other maids out.

"Not all wedding nights are smooth," she observed when they were alone.

Alyson did not want to admit that hers had been a disaster, although she knew that tongues would be wagging soon enough. Someone no doubt would have heard Guillelm on the stairs and be eager to tell.

Mortified, Alyson wanted to dress in her oldest clothes, spend the day out in the lean-to with her potions, but she knew that was impossible.

"You will win him back, my bird." Gytha smoothed out the already smooth pillows. "There is a wisewoman I know near Olverton Minor, within sight of your father's manor. She lives in the woods there, close to the road between Olverton Minor and Setton Minor, almost a recluse except for her family, but Eva is a very experienced lady in all areas of marriage and menfolk."

Alyson shook her head. "No more charms or potions, Gytha," she said. "It must be love and trust, or nothing."

She flung back the sheets and rose, a new energy and will pounding through her. *I will lie with Guillelm,* she vowed to herself, astonished at her own brazenness, but determined nonetheless, *and on my own terms. Heloise may have made him chary of women and of himself, but with me he will be healed and whole.*

She would save their marriage. She would seduce him back.

Chapter 11

"I heard about your vow."

Guillelm did not pause in his stoking of the bathhouse fire. He had sent the other men and servants out, but Fulk had entered as if he had a perfect right to be there.

"Do you not think it a sign from God?" Fulk continued in that pious, smug way of his. *How had I not noticed this aspect of him before?* Guillelm thought, depressed anew. In everything it seemed he was a poor judge, willfully blind. The only skill he appeared to have was in killing.

"Yes, it is a sign—of my own inadequacy. Boil, damn you," he added under his breath to the already steaming tub of water. He longed to be clean, to feel clean. "I want no one here with me now," he growled. He had not forgotten or forgiven Fulk over the man's mean trick with his wife's diadem.

His wife—what a reckless dream that had been! Heloise was right: No woman wanted him.

"Go!" he snarled, and Fulk paled and went, backing out rapidly and skidding down the bathhouse steps.

Guillelm hurled more logs into the fire. Presently he heard the door creak and bawled, "Out!" without turning round.

"Where shall I put the towels?" asked an achingly familiar voice.

He spun round and there she was, Alyson, his wife. Even as he gawked at her, longing to beg her forgiveness, to snatch her into his arms, to drag her with him into the steaming bath and frolic there until the water turned cold, his tongue felt nailed to the roof of his mouth. What could he say? He had failed her so badly.

She smiled and he was smitten afresh, more stunned than he had been that time in Outremer, when a stone from a sling had struck him on the visor of his helmet and he had almost blacked out. There was no fear of his losing consciousness now, but certainly she mazed his wits.

"I shall put them here, shall I, my lord?"

Nimbly, she arranged her armful of towels by the side of the great tub, scattering something on the lapping water that instantly perfumed the bathhouse.

"An old remedy, lavender," she explained, lifting her skirts to tread lightly over the flags toward him. "I have spearmint, too, for our teeth and breath."

"Our teeth?"

She did not answer, merely passed straight by him, close enough for him to feel the swish of her robe against his legs, and lit two beeswax candles from the torch. She placed these on the stone shelf beside the tub, where most bathers put their trinkets, or goblets of wine.

"I find that bathhouses are always a little gloomy, even in summer," she remarked. "Do you not think the candles add cheer?"

They did, and they put a glow into Alyson's face, warm shadows on the vaulted stone roof of the bathhouse and a flickering play of lights on the water. They added little light, if truth be told, but something else instead, a sense of being in a dream.

Guillelm cleared his throat. "You have done this before?"

She divined his real question at once and answered with the devastating directness of an armored knight on a full-tilt charge. "With your father? No. Indeed no one, unless you count girlish fancies." She looked directly at him, her storm-colored eyes darker than the rarest sapphires. "I have imagined doing this with you, dragon."

He was astonished that she could make him color up, amazed at her words. She seemed shaken herself, for she laughed, adding, "Perhaps my early morning cup of sweet white wine was a mistake, but I needed something."

She lifted her heavy plait of hair away from the back of her neck, draping it over her left shoulder while her fingers picked at the side lacings of her gown.

"Not to approach you, my lord," she went on, tugging off her belt and keys, "I need no wine-inspired courage for that, but in order to free my own tongue—yes." She let the leather belt drop onto the flags and began to slide her arms from her wide sleeves.

In the half-light of the bathhouse he had not noticed the color or style of her dress but now he was all attention. "Alyson, for pity's sake—" he managed to grind out, as she deftly shimmered out of her gown and hung it over one of the lower roof beams.

"A maid could help you bathe, if you prefer, my lord."

There was a slight wobble in her voice that made Guillelm ashamed. She was being braver than he was, risking his rejection and his scorn. *She is leading you on, as Heloise did,* a treacherous whisper mouthed in his head, but he ignored that; the thought was unworthy of her.

"You are all the maids I need," he said. "But are you not afraid of wetting your undershift?"

He winced inside, thinking his attempt at flirting too obvious, but she glanced up from undoing her shoes, grinned and snapped her fingers at him, mock-angry.

"Shame on you, sir! Are you suggesting I am not neat-handed? Or would you do the ungentlemanly thing of dunking me into the water with you?"

She was out of his reach, or he might have done it there and then. "That is a very good idea," he said, striding across the flags, "little scold."

Barefoot and in her shift, Alyson stood her ground as he approached. Closing, Guillelm saw her hands come up, but not, as he half-dreaded, to ward him off. Her fingers fastened lightly on the lacings of his mantle.

"It must take almost a bolt of cloth to clothe you," she murmured, not fearful but admiring. His mantle undone, she now tugged at his sleeve and he followed where she led, not daring to speak in case she changed her mind and whirled out of the bathhouse.

"Am I truly a scold?"

They were beside the tub now and her hands were on him, easing his mantle and undershirt down to his waist. Her silken touch robbed him of answers; he could only shake his head.

"So much," she said softly, tracing the golden threads, running her fingers through the rough mat of fair curls on his broad chest, the branching longer hairs running from his breastbone to his flat, hard stomach, the bits of fluff below his belly button. "You are wonderfully hairy, dragon."

No woman had ever said that to him. No woman had ever touched him as Alyson was doing: gentle yet searching, as if she could not learn enough of him. He felt healed by her hands, saved by her clever, questing fingers, and at the same time helplessly stirred.

He closed his eyes and sank his head against the top of hers, kissing her forehead. Twin needs warred in him: to crush her into his arms and have her here at once, on the flags of the bathhouse, and to stay as he was, rigid in delight, scarcely able to catch his breath. There was the marvelous scent of her: a mingling of rosemary and lavender and a babylike sweetness, Alyson's own ineffable essence. She moved about him like a sultry shadow, weaving her spell with her limbs—not only her hands now, but her legs, too, one winding about his as she balanced against his lean hips. And her mouth!

He gasped as he felt her lips upon his arms, his scarred forearms that for so many years had known only the feel of mail and the shock of sword blows and yet now were tamed and stilled by the butterfly-light kisses of this girl. He trembled like a tree in a gale as her lips moved on, across the great arch of his ribs. Growing bolder, she used her tongue to flick and taste at the hair on his chest.

But not so bold. To Guillelm's disappointment—and relief— she stopped, laying her head against his heart with a sigh. Cautiously, as if she was the wariest of creatures that he had ever hunted, he placed his arms about her, running his thumbs over the delicate bones of her shoulders. He could feel her taut sinews and the stretch of her thigh muscles pressing against his. In her linen undershift he could almost see her body—not quite, for the bathhouse was, in spite of the torch and candles, still a place of shadows as well as light—but he knew her shape now, lithe and wiry, small-breasted and narrow-waisted, with sweetly flaring hips. She was still too thin, he thought, tracing the clear bones of her ribs with a pity and anxiety that almost made him forget his own hard desire, but then her right leg slotted a little tighter against his left and the intimate contact scorched him. He shifted slightly, trying to see her face, and she yelped.

"Mother of God, I have hurt you!" he cried, dropping his hands from her as if she were more delicate than stained glass, but Alyson pressed herself closer, saying urgently, "No, no! 'Tis my own vanity, see?"

She leaned back, and he cursed, seeing where one of her necklaces had dug into her throat. Although dressed in naught but her undershift she seemed to be wearing every jewel she

possessed—three necklaces, a golden belt and two highly
polished copper bracelets. She was also wearing the silken
veil he had given her, secured by a narrow silver coronet.

He kissed the raw place on her neck and she whispered
something.

"Sorry, bright-eyes, would you say that again?"

She blushed and pointed at the tub. "Should you not be in
there, my lord?"

"For sure, my sweet, and you with me."

Before Alyson had the chance to protest, Guillelm had
ripped off his leggings, kicked them and his mantle away and
scrambled into the wooden tub, lifting her with him.

"Now," he said, as she struggled to catch her breath, "do
we chew this spearmint you mentioned?"

"If you wish," she replied, which was in truth no answer at
all, but her courage had failed her. She was in a bath with Guillelm and he was naked. Plans of seduction were replaced by a
paralyzing shyness. She knew she was being foolish—worse,
her seeming reluctance might reinforce whatever cruel tricks
Heloise had played and convince him she did not want him.

"Did you know many women in Outremer?"

The instant the question was out Alyson quailed—what
was she doing? The very last thing she should be asking!

"I am sorry," she stammered, reaching blindly past Guillelm for the comb she had left on the edge of the bathtub.
"That was wrong—"

"You have done nothing. Truly. Why should you not be curious?" In the shifting candlelight, Guillelm's features took on
a wry look she was recognizing as a form of deep embarrassment. "I was the same about Lord Robert, with less cause."

He cupped his hands and lifted them, allowing the water to

trickle through. "The women in Outremer feared crusaders." He answered without looking at her. "Me especially."

And Heloise provided the *coup de grâce,* Alyson guessed. Understanding this, she willed her limbs to move, but her legs would not obey her.

"Come here, little one."

Strong arms wrapped about her, lifting her through the water, and then she was tight against Guillelm, him peeling her damp veil back from her face. "The silk looks well on you, even wet, but I would see all of your blush." He ran his thumb along her black eyebrows and over her cheekbones. "You color up so beautifully."

"As do you," she managed to mumble in return, her eyes drawn to the drops of water beading on that wonderful mat of chest hair. Where was her soap? She had forgotten where she had put it and without that she could think of no other excuse to touch him. *I have less wit than a wren near you.*

"Be glad you have any, for you often make me speechless," Guillelm answered softly, which made her blush harder than ever. She had not realized she had spoken aloud.

"Good!" Alyson could feel his calves against hers. The legs of a runner, she thought, tracing their lean, long muscles with the toes of her left foot. Where was her soap? "I cannot have a man who talks more than I do, or how can you listen to my wishes?"

"Wishes, eh?"

Alyson raised her chin. "Or commands."

He gave a low whistle. "Is that how you think it will be?" He lifted her closer to him so that she lost her footing and floated in the lavender-scented water, him laughing as she tried to kick him. "This is one battle you cannot win."

"Maybe not, but I shall win the war." She stretched up and tried to kiss him on the mouth, missed and bumped noses instead.

"Well, my lady, if those are your tactics—" His lips unerringly found hers and he clamped her along the length of his body, his hands sweeping over her back, her sides, her breasts. She gasped and he kissed her more deeply, flicking his tongue against hers.

"My lord!" A breathless Sericus, bedraggled and clearly distraught, limped into the bathhouse and hastily turned his back on his young mistress.

Alyson tried to break from Guillelm but it was like trying to escape the coils of a dragon: impossible. His body heat was like the blast of a furnace, making her thirsty and dizzy together. *He could take me now with Sericus here and I would not object,* she thought, appalled that she could be so wanton.

"What is it?" Guillelm grunted, sounding no more happy at this interruption than she was herself. "Speak, man!"

"The men were drinking last night," the old seneschal stammered, nervously licking his lips. "Some were drunk this morning and things—"

"Things have become rowdy," Alyson finished for Sericus, sensing he was inhibited by her presence.

Sericus nodded unhappily. "One is on the battlements, with a sword. No one can get near him. He thinks we are the enemy."

Guillelm sighed and lowered Alyson gently to the floor of the bathtub, rubbing his hand across his eyebrows. "That will be Thierry; he drinks and then he fights. Fulk cannot manage him?"

"I do not know," Sericus said loyally. "Sir Tom asked me to come here." He bowed to Alyson. "Forgive me, my lady, I did not realize—"

"No matter, Sericus, you had an urgent summons," Alyson replied, absently crossing her hands across her breasts. She was glad of the high sides of the bathtub.

"Urgent indeed, if Tom told you to fetch me," Guillelm said, boosting himself out of the water. He tied a towel quickly round his middle and offered Alyson a hand, smiling slightly when she shook her head and paid close attention to her fingernails.

"You must bathe without me, sweet," he said softly.

"Of course," she said at once. "Take care."

"I will." Tugging on his mantle and with one shoe still unlaced, Guillelm sprinted for the door, calling over his shoulder, "Guard her, Sericus!"

Alyson waited a moment, hearing his pounding footsteps receding in the direction of the keep, and then she blew out the candles. "Now that my anxious husband has gone on ahead, we shall follow," she told her startled seneschal.

"But, my lady!"

"I have vowed to remain close to Guillelm today, and I shall, whatever happens." As she did when she was preparing a particularly tricky potion, Alyson narrowed her eyes and chewed her lower lip. "It may be that I can help him with Thierry."

"But the man is roaring drunk—"

"Even so. Pass me my gown, Sericus."

Chapter 12

Ignoring Sericus's protests, Alyson dressed swiftly. On the way to the castle, she called to a kitchen maid and asked the girl to send a message to Gytha and Osmoda that a tub of fresh hot water was waiting for them in the bathhouse. Why not? She knew that her old nurse would appreciate the chance to soak her aching joints and Osmoda would welcome the opportunity to bathe. Someone at least would reap the benefits of Guillelm's work and her own.

Meantime there was an armed knight rampaging around Hardspen, convinced that all who approached him were his adversaries. She could hear Thierry as she rushed ahead of limping Sericus and ran up the narrow spiral staircase leading to the battlements.

"Fight, damn you!" Thierry was raging in French. "Come at me, pigs!" He lapsed into Arabic and then into a long, incoherent bellowing, oblivious it seemed to his fellow countrymen yelling at him to stop, to put his sword down, to recognize them as friends.

Guillelm was already on the battlements. His voice was low, steady, comforting.

"You are safe, Thierry. You have fought and won, Thierry. You are ever a brave and noble knight who will do no wrong.

You will know me, Thierry. When I walk across to you, you will know me as you know yourself. And you will be safe. I promise you will be safe."

Alyson paused at the top of the stairs, allowing her eyes to adjust to the bright sunlight after pounding up the shadowy steps and to take in the scene. Her sudden appearance might inflame an already difficult situation and so she would keep out of sight, but she had to be sure Guillelm was safe. And if the chance came where she might help him, she would.

Thierry was on the highest part of the keep, crouching in a corner, below the arrow slits and crenellations and with two outer battlement walls protecting his back. He was a stocky, swarthy man whom Alyson remembered all too well from the time he had tried to kiss her. There were splashes of beer, vomit and wine on his leather jerkin and a huge jagged gash in his leggings. He had black and yellow bruises on his square chin and broad nose and strands of rushes in his greasy dark hair. He was armed with a sword and a dagger, brandishing both in front of him.

On his left a knot of men, including Fulk and Sir Tom, carried no weapons but had their long shields raised against him. Alyson saw Fulk's tense profile and his hard blue eyes blinking over the top of his shield.

"We are your friends, damn you!" he shouted in French, leaping back a step as Thierry swung at him. The point of Thierry's long sword clashed against the rim of Fulk's shield and the two men cursed. The others flinched, including Sir Tom, who glanced across the battlements at Guillelm.

Guillelm was standing alone, to the right of Thierry, the place of danger where a right-handed swordsman most likely would attack. He had no sword or shield to protect him: he was bareheaded and barefooted, his clothes tugged on and still untied, but when he addressed the sweating, dark-browed man he was calm and kind, as if speaking to a child.

"Thierry, you are safe. No one here means you harm. Look

at me, Thierry." He took a step toward the scowling figure, ducking as Thierry struck at him with a wild lunge.

"You know me." Guillelm stopped and whistled a jaunty little tune. "Do you remember that song, Thierry? You sang me all the verses when we were riding to Jerusalem."

He spread his hands and turned full face to the muttering Norman knight, careless, it seemed, of presenting an easy target. "Your younger sister stitched you the embroidered belt you are wearing now," he went on, unmoving as Thierry slashed his dagger so close to him that Alyson had to gnaw on her lower lip to stop herself screaming a warning. *He is crazy,* she thought. Guillelm will get himself killed for the sake of a drunken, lecherous fool. But she had to trust him. Love is trust, and if she intervened now, if she broke the fragile eye contact that had been forged between Guillelm and his man, then anything could happen.

"I have more ale in the great hall, waiting," Guillelm continued. "Drink with me, Thierry."

He took another step closer. Thierry's sword dipped as the man's shoulders sagged and Fulk took the moment to edge forward, but then Thierry jerked out of his crouch and lumbered forward, his sword arm raising again.

"Infidel!" he screamed, but Guillelm merely sidestepped his clumsy charge, caught the man firmly by his left arm as he tottered past and yanked him back, preventing Thierry from taking a lethal plunge off the battlements into the inner courtyard.

"You know me, Thierry. Look at me." Guillelm was scarcely out of breath, although for an instant his man had been within two steps of the edge. Glancing at the anxious upraised faces below them, hearing the stifled gasps, Alyson felt momentarily sick. If Thierry had gone over he surely would have been killed.

"Come drink with me, Thierry. Infidels do not drink. You know it is forbidden to them."

"More fools they are," Thierry slurred, appearing almost cross-eyed for a moment in sheer bewilderment. "I know you."

Guillelm took another step closer, his blond hair glinting in the strong sunlight. "We are crusaders, brothers in arms."

"You owe him your fealty," Fulk dropped in, at which Sir Tom pulled a face behind his shield, for Fulk's alien, nasal voice broke the spell.

"Liar!" Thierry screamed and waded toward Guillelm, stabbing and hacking while Guillelm dived this way and that, weaving around Thierry's frenzied attack and keeping out of range of the deadly, flashing blades. He barged into Thierry, shoulder-first, almost knocking him clean off his feet, but the stocky Norman staggered a few paces back, his sword grating over the stone walkway, and then he regained his balance. He grunted and shook his head, clumsily patting himself over to check he had not been cut.

"I am unharmed, Thierry," Guillelm said steadily. "I am Guillelm de La Rochelle and I swear by the Mother of God that I would never harm you."

"Mother of God?" Thierry's lips moved slowly. "That is a familiar oath. My lord uses it often." He peered at the tall blond warrior standing fearlessly in front of his sword point. "Are you he?"

Guillelm remained stock-still, hands on hips, ignoring Fulk's muttered, "The fellow is worse than blind drunk this time. You are mad to approach him, my lord." Guillelm did not recoil as Thierry swayed toward him, the dagger in Thierry's left hand exactly level with his guts.

"Mother of God, please keep them safe," Alyson prayed urgently, starting as a gnarled hand flopped against her shoulder.

"My lady," Sericus wheezed, "you should not be here. You—" He coughed, his whole body shuddering with the long climb of the stairs.

"I am safe enough." Swiftly, without taking her eyes off Guillelm, Alyson stepped around Sericus, bracing her arm against the spiral staircase so that the poor man should not fall. "Do not be troubled."

"But my lord said—"

Alyson did not listen to the rest. Placing a hand on his shoulder she motioned the seneschal to sit on the stairs with her, her eyes never leaving her husband. If Thierry struck at Guillelm now, would her dragon have time to save himself? They were less than a spear's length apart from each other, Thierry making stabbing movements in the air, shaking his head as Guillelm did not react.

"I am Guillelm, Thierry, and you are always safe with me."

If possible, Thierry looked more bewildered than ever. "But I am in the dungeons of Hasim, where no one escapes."

"Except for you, Thierry."

"No, my lord is storming the castle of the infidel . . . can you hear the crash of the rams and siege engines?"

"That is long ago, Thierry. Listen, now: I can hear birdsong."

Thierry knuckled his eyes with the fist that was clutching his dagger. After a moment, he hissed, "You are right! A sky-lark, very high."

"We are not in Outremer now, Thierry."

"No? But my lord came down into the dungeon of Hasim to lift me out. I had been there for three months and Guillelm broke my fetters and carried me out in his arms like a child, carried me out into the sunlight and the fresh free air."

Alyson gasped, understanding now why the Norman should be so disturbed. Of all punishments that men could inflict on each other, imprisonment in the windowless, airless dungeons of their castles was surely the worst. She had heard of men driven mad in such places; it was no wonder that, deep in his cups, Thierry might remember his long confinement and confuse past and present.

"Come with me now, Thierry," Guillelm said, adding more in a French dialect that Alyson did not understand.

Thierry dropped his dagger. It skidded onto the battlements and bounced on the stones. Fulk made a grab for it, which Thierry interpreted as a fresh threat, regripping his sword and pitching forward at Guillelm, his face twisted into a terrible snarl of fear and anger.

"No!" Sir Tom yelled, as Guillelm twisted swiftly and harmlessly away and Thierry blundered on, ever closer to the four-man-high drop over the battlements into the inner courtyard. As Guillelm spun round, his hands reaching and grabbing, trying for the second time to stop his man falling, Alyson launched herself from the dark stairway and darted at Thierry. She had no plan, simply the wild desire to stop him.

"Thierry!"

At her high, clear voice, Thierry slewed awkwardly, his feet scrabbling on the stones. Finally and with a roar he slipped and sat down heavily. "A girl!" he bawled in French.

The distraction was enough for Guillelm. Seizing the moment that Thierry's attention was on Alyson, he wrested the man's sword out of his hand and pinned him to the battlements. Thierry flailed about for an instant and then lay back, panting and repeating in French, "A girl, a girl."

Guillelm clapped Thierry on the back and pushed him toward the waiting Fulk and Sir Tom. "Sleep it off, man, and think no more of it."

He turned to Alyson as the subdued Thierry and the rest of the men filed silently down the stairs. "Are you all right?" he asked her.

"Perfectly," Alyson lied. Now that her initial jubilation that Guillelm and Thierry were both safe had passed, she felt clammy. "Are you hurt?" She countered question with question.

"Unharmed, save for the fright you gave me when you hurled yourself out of the stairwell!" He chuckled. "That was a brave act, if foolish."

"No more than your own," Alyson began, but reaction caught up with her and she quickly turned her head, clutching her stomach. "I feel sick."

To her mortification she was sick, straight over the battlements. As she spat and shuddered, she felt Guillelm's hands on her shoulders.

"Here, little one." He uncorked a leather flask for her, holding it as she rinsed out her mouth and took a drink of the weak ale. "It can take you like this after a fight, or danger. Coming alive again is a shock." He patted her shoulder.

"Thank you for saving me."

Expecting a scolding, Alyson stammered, "But I did not do so much, dragon, and if you had not been so quick, things may have gone amiss."

"Aye, they may." Guillelm gave her ear a gentle tweak. "You are running up a mighty debt to me: waspish answers, disobedience—"

"Disobedience!"

"—not to mention the bullying of my servants. We agreed that Sericus is my servant, too, did we not? And yet you have that lame old man galloping about the bailey as if he were a warhorse. No, you are greatly in debt." He overrode her protest. "Nothing else will do in repayment except that you bathe me as you promised. Or are you one who reneges on vows?"

"You will have to test me and see," Alyson quipped. She smiled up at her new husband, her sickness replaced by a light-headed joy. Her strategy was working; Guillelm was becoming less wary of her, less guarded in his replies. Surely he must realize how much she loved him, how much she desired him. If he so much as clicked his fingers she would cast herself into his arms right here on the battlements and smother him with kisses; she did not care who might be watching.

The wanton thought made her blush and laugh, which was a pity, for Guillelm had been lowering his head to her and now he stopped.

"I see you are still affected by this morning's misadventure," he said abruptly. He turned on his heel. "Forgive me, I know I must give you time. I will be down in the great hall, whenever you wish to join me. Now I must make certain Thierry is settled."

Listening to his rapidly descending feet Alyson snorted and uttered an unladylike curse under her breath. Things between them had been going so sweetly . . . but it was not all lost. Guillelm had said "whenever you wish to join me." He desired her company and that was an excellent beginning, was it not? She could only hope so!

Patience, Alyson counseled, determinedly telling herself that this way she could slip into her new marital bedchamber, change her gown and restyle her hair before she reencountered Guillelm.

Fulk, who had sent his own page to spy on Alyson, drew the boy off to the stables and listened impassively to the lad's latest report. The lady, cloistered in her chamber with that aged, crabbed nurse of hers. Womanish scents. Whispers and laughter. The lady emerging in a new gown and with ribbons in her hair . . .

Women really were the devil's work, Fulk concluded, sending the page off to watch some more. He had sworn to the lowbred Alyson of Olverton that he would not act against her. Nor would he, but for his lord to break a solemn vow of abstinence after only one day would be unseemly; he would remind Guillelm of that. *And I must also ensure that when he goes to his chamber to rest, he is not disturbed by anyone,* he thought, and smiled.

Chapter 13

The baker of Hardspen was recovered of his fever and hard at work. Guillelm had heard no complaints of him, but now another local baker, accused of selling short-weight loaves, had been brought to the castle from the nearby village of Setton Minor. The four men—and one woman—who had dragged the fellow into Hardspen and pitched him onto the rushes in the great hall had been vocal in demanding justice. Guillelm, fresh from disarming Thierry and wanting to spend more time with the former crusader to make certain all was calm and well with him, was forced to listen to the disgruntled villagers' complaints.

Sitting on the dais, keeping a wary eye on Thierry, who was crouched by the central ash-covered fireplace playing dice with a worried-looking Tom, Guillelm gripped the arms of his carver chair and tried to follow a rambling tale of bad flour, moldy loaves sold as best and bread not fit even to be used as trenchers. The woman, whom Guillelm was surprised did not bake her own bread, was the most vocal of the five, but her quick patter and the baker's rasping answers seemed to make no sense. Some matter of pies and rats and a brown bread that crumbled into . . . was the word dust? Guillelm wondered. It did not help him that their local dialect was so thick as to be almost incomprehensible. After seven years abroad, away from these habits of speech, he had a struggle to understand more than two words in ten.

Listening, Guillelm felt a renewed surge of irritation against Fulk. His seneschal might have dealt with this, had Fulk's command of English been better. But Fulk had retreated to the stables and then to the tilting ground, claiming he could not understand "these mewling peasants," and Sericus was off tending the merlin—a task Guillelm had expected Fulk to undertake whenever he himself could not.

The woman had asked him a question. As Guillelm resigned himself to ask her to repeat it and risk enduring the whole rigmarole again, Gytha and then Alyson walked into the hall.

Habituated by war to watching movement even at the edge of his vision, Guillelm realized that Gytha was offering Thierry a vessel—doubtless one of her mistress's potions. A calming draught, perhaps. It was a good thought, and for the first time in the great hall that day he smiled, allowing himself the pleasure of gazing upon Alyson herself.

He could do so at length, for she had brought four pages with her, each lad carrying cups and jugs of ale. As they proceeded to serve everyone in the hall, including the villagers, Alyson approached the dais, bearing a silver chalice. A maid, scurrying a few steps behind her, clutched a large pottery jug. The maid would not look at him directly and her pinched, pox-scarred face had that blank look of fright that Guillelm was only too familiar with from the women who had crossed his path in Outremer, but Alyson met his eyes.

"I have brought you a tisane, my lord." Her clear, low voice broke into his reverie. "For your refreshment." Beside the dais, she lifted the chalice toward his reaching arms, raising her head and adding swiftly and softly, "I beg mercy for the baker, Stephen Crok. He is losing his wits before his old age and cannot help what he does. The widow Isabella who accuses him most sharply has a younger son who would be a baker."

"Would the widow want her son to be taken on as Crok's apprentice?" Guillelm murmured, masking their conversation by making a play of sampling the tisane. The elderflower cosseted his nose with too cloying a scent, and he prayed that he hid his dislike of the draught. Alyson deserved better.

Shame at his cowardly behavior last night tore into him again, but he forced himself to attend to her rapid, whispered answer.

"Stephen Crok's wife has been bedridden these past two years but she knows how to bake bread. Isabella would be glad for her son to learn from such a teacher, but she cannot pay any 'prentice fees." Alyson bit her lower lip. "I would do so for her, if it please you."

"I will pay," Guillelm said flatly. "But what can I offer to the others?"

"A week of dining in your hall—my lord?"

Guillelm nodded. "So be it. Will you translate for me?" he added, rising to his feet.

"With pleasure!" Her eyes sparkled and her joy pierced him. So simple a mercy to give her so much delight. What had her life been like with his father? Guillelm wondered again.

He was still wondering as he dispensed justice—if Alyson's suggestion could be called such. It seemed so, especially as his new wife smoothly switched to the local dialect and repeated what he said. The manner of the widow Isabella changed in moments from thin-lipped scowls to effusive thanks, the men with her licked their lips and held out their cups to the pages for more ale and the baker tugged on Alyson's gown.

"Can I go home now?" he asked, his slow, heart-wrenchingly simple request comprehensible even to Guillelm, who answered, "You may."

He swallowed the elderflower draught and came down from

the dais as the villagers prepared to leave, sorry for the tisane but glad that Alyson had been with him. She knew many people here and, more important, understood them: their needs and irritations and hurts. Even in this she was a healer.

"My thanks for your potion for Thierry," he said quietly, "and for the rest." His smile deepened; it was so easy to smile at her. "You have the sense of King Solomon. I would not have thought a woman—"

"Capable?" Alyson finished archly. "You do me too much honor."

He had been about to say something quite different, but her mettlesome answer demanded a more physical response. He reached for her but she nimbly stepped back.

"The chalice, my lord?" She pointed past him to the high table. "I would return it to our chamber."

At the word "our," a faint rose stained her cheeks and Guillelm was snarled anew—like a fly caught in fresh resin, he thought, aggrieved. But although he was ever wary of her possible rejection and she in turn clearly careful of him, he was more than glad of her presence.

"A moment, wife." He said that to make Alyson blush more deeply, and to his mischievous delight she did. "I am for the tilting ground soon, and will I have your company?"

Alyson's face was now as scarlet as the embroidered hems on her sleeves, but she answered readily, "If it please you." Her eyes glittered. "Then when you take a tumble, I shall be there to tend your hurts."

"Provoking weasel," he said affectionately, adding as she made to move off, "Is the way you wear your hair the English style? I am out of touch with such fashions."

"Such country fashions?" she suggested, clearly taking his question as a criticism, where none was intended, where he had only wanted to keep her by him. "It is my own style, but no matter. I will change it to suit your wishes. You need only instruct me, though I beg not here, in the hall, with your men hard by."

"Alyson—"

"I know I am only a simple creature to you, my lord, nothing like the grand ladies of the court. I will do as you command."

Exasperated, Guillelm told the truth. "You need change nothing, little idiot! Shall I tell you of these grand ladies? The women of my uncle's court in Poitiers had bad teeth from too many sweets and hair as brittle as straw from spreading their sparse locks in the strongest sunlight to bleach them."

Instantly, he regretted this ungallantly, but it was too late. Alyson closed her sagging mouth with an audible snap. "Women torture themselves to change their locks to gold because men ever prefer them so."

"Not this man," Guillelm said steadily.

She shot him a strange, bright glance but said nothing. Did she know anything of Heloise of Outremer? The notion she did grazed his heart but his feelings did not matter now— Alyson was turning from him, motioning some silent instruction to Gytha and her other maids.

"Alyson?"

She looked at him, her face stricken.

"Mother of God." He could not leave her thus. "I am sorry. I spoke badly. Let me make amends." Desperate for something to bridge the sudden yawning gap between them, he said quickly, "Wear my favor at the tilting ground. Please?"

Solemn as when she had been a child, she nodded and he breathed afresh. "Will you walk with me to the ground?" he asked.

She fell into step with him. Strolling together, down the stone stairways and out past the stables, he studied her again. Alyson was a lesson he never grew tired of, and his. If only he might make her truly his.

Her gown was new to him, he thought, or perhaps he was

seeing it clearly for the first time. It was that green-blue color favored by many ladies and marvelously snug about her bosom, waist and hips. Her long sleeves were trimmed in scarlet and, as she pointed to a dove strutting by the stables, muttering, "The dovecote here needs some repair, my lord," he was distracted from her highly practical observation by a glimpse of her wrist, smooth and burnished and white as a pearl. Quickly, to try to stop the inevitable stirring below his belt, he followed her pointing finger to the dove. Its feathers were as milky as the flesh on her wrist. Did she know how the scarlet embroidering set off her hands? Her gliding, high-arched feet, too, for now he caught a flash of her trim ankles as she lifted the scarlet hem of her gown to negotiate past a pile of trodden sheep dung.

"Do you think, my lord?" she was asking, "that the emperor of Germany is really a woman?" and he said hazily, "Yes," starting as she laughed.

"You have not been paying attention, Guillelm, and now I have proved it!"

"Attention, eh? Then I must give you some." Inspired by her teasing, he went further. Ignoring her choked-off giggles, he flung her over his shoulder and twirled them both about. "Is this enough attention for you?"

"Let me down!" She hammered her palms against his back but he felt the blows as if they were the lightest of embraces, overwhelmed already by the scent of her, the taut, firm bow of her body on his. Her long braids swung against his calves, a piquant series of strikes that made him want her even more.

Enough! Do you want her terrified again? You have seen women raped in Outremer—will you be no better? Are you a Viking who seizes what he pleases? Slowly, reluctantly, he lowered her to the ground.

"More of that and no doubt I should undo some streamer

from your hair and be nagged all the way to the gallops," he said gruffly. "We should get on; 'tis past noon already."

She snapped her fingers at him. "I am no scold, dragon, as well you know, but I will race you—now we are fairly matched since you are clearly exhausted by your lifting."

Giving him no time to answer, she sped ahead, her dark plaits flying out behind her. He let her go, amazed at her fleetness, then started after her, aware he was chasing and happy to chase, for Alyson did not mind if she was caught.

They had a tranquil afternoon at the tilting ground—which was odd, Alyson thought, because Guillelm and the other knights there were in training for war. Content merely to be close to him, she watched him on Caliph, galloping at targets, practicing with spear, sword and shield and working himself, his men and their horses into great steaming sweats.

Halfway through the afternoon, Alyson sent a messenger to the castle to have the bathhouse readied again and instructed pages to bring ale to the men. Ducking under a tourney target, she walked across the churned-up ground, waving to Sir Tom and stroking one of his panting hounds, avoiding Fulk, whose bay stallion had already bitten another horse, to hand Guillelm a drink.

"My thanks, sweet." He took it with a tiny brush of his callused thumb against her palm, a gentle touch that told more of his gratitude than any number of words. He wore one of her hair ribbons pinned to his shoulder, a bright blue favor. She in turn had asked for and been given one of Guillelm's small brooches as a favor. She flicked it with a finger.

"The dragon on this brooch looks to have indigestion," she remarked, which earned her a guffaw from Guillelm. He leaned down from Caliph, hooking his free hand under her belt and lifting her off her feet again—any excuse to carry her was good enough, it seemed, and that was fine to Alyson.

"It is a pretty brooch, all the same," she said, balancing on his stirrup and giving the rather portly gold dragon design a cleaning rub with one of her ribbons.

"How many ribbons are there in your hair?" Guillelm muttered.

Alyson smiled. She had spent more than an hour arranging her coiffure; it was gratifying to behold her husband's faintly stunned look whenever he saw it—that and the many quicksilver glances he sent her. In truth, she had no idea if what she had done was fashionable, but she had tried to tread a narrow path between modesty and instinct.

Although it was a bitter truth that all in Hardspen doubtless knew of the wretched wedding night between Guillelm and herself, she saw no reason to proclaim the tale. Modesty and self-protection—protection for Guillelm, too, against possible sly jibes—had prompted her to place her silk veil on the crown of her head, as befitted a married woman. Instinct, though, had suggested she fold the veil into no more than a small square, held by a narrow copper coronet.

Below this delicate, narrow head rail she had divided her hair into four plaits, each spiraled about with ribbons. Lord Robert, Guillelm's scarce-lamented father and her former "protector," had taken her hair ornaments from her, along with her jewels. She had made more by sacrificing two scarves and cutting them into ribbons.

Quickly, Guillelm brushed his lips against one of her plaits and then, almost as if that contact would be too much for her, swung her gently to the ground. "I must continue," he said. "I would see Thierry soon, make certain he is still sure of where he is, and who he is with."

"I understand completely," Alyson replied, briefly envying Thierry his lord's concern before good sense took hold of her again. There was a difference between being attentive to Guillelm and becoming his very shadow. Besides, if she left for the castle first, he might wonder where she had gone, and surely a little doubt on his part was good?

Quitting the tilting ground, aware of Fulk watching her leave, Alyson could only hope so.

Chapter 14

As Alyson was passing the bathhouse, encouraging a lagging page to keep up, Sericus stopped her.

"My lady." He drew her apart from the pages, his wrinkled, gray-bearded face warped with concern. "Grave news."

Alyson braced herself. Was Tilda safe and well at St. Foy's? Had Thierry gone berserk again? Or did the news concern King Stephen or the Empress Maud? Had the warring forces come closer to Hardspen?

"Yes, Sericus?" she asked, when her gray-headed seneschal did not speak.

"Edwin the shepherd has seen a wolf at the edge of the common land and forest. He is sure," Sericus continued, guessing Alyson's first question. "He knows there have been no wolves in these parts for many years, but he saw a pack when he was a boy. He swears to me there is no mistake." Sericus hopped nervously from one foot to the other, favoring his less withered leg. "Already he is short a dozen lambs."

Alyson sighed. "I am sorry for that." She was, too, and there was no easy answer. Edwin was keen-sighted but had no skill with bow and arrow and less with a sling and slingshot.

"He has no shepherd lad or lass with him to guard his lambs?" she asked.

"I fear not—and now the wolf grows bold, my lady. Only yesterday, Edwin saw it carry off a lamb in bright daylight. Also, he says that a widow from Setton Minor was terrorized the day after the feast—day of Saint Mary Magdalene—by a 'huge black beast, like a dog but with more teeth,' as she took flowers to a wayside shrine of St. Foy."

And was the widow also paying a visit to Eva the wisewoman in the woods there? Alyson thought, but she said nothing.

Sericus crossed himself and continued. "The woman was on the road when the beast came at her; she managed to toss a stone at it and drive it into the thickets, but she was badly shaken."

"So it may be only a matter of days before it attacks someone: a child gathering berries, an old woman seeking firewood." Alyson frowned, imagining the damage a hungry wolf could inflict on such innocents.

"I shall speak to my lord," she told Sericus, with more assurance than she felt. Guillelm was kind and mindful of his people, but whom could he spare to go on a wolf hunt? Perhaps that was how she should ask—present it as a challenge and "good sport" to tempt Guillelm and his men into tracking the beast.

"I will speak to him when I may," she promised, squeezing Sericus's shoulder in brief reassurance as she continued on her way to the castle keep.

For the rest of the afternoon, Alyson was kept busy with questions from her maids concerning the flax and wool spinning and also the anxious head cook, who seemed convinced that with Guillelm and his men having lived in Outremer, they would expect an Eastern feast every day. She spent an hour in the lean-to where she made her potions, checking the drying and steeping herbs, then time in the shade of the bathhouse with the oldest laundress, who had a complaint that "some vile, low knaves" had smeared fire-ash onto the bed linen she was drying on bushes by the river. As a piece of malicious mischief, Alyson thought it grotesque, and she listened most sympathetically to the woman's tirade, promising to speak to her lord about it and offering her the copper bangle from her own wrist in recompense of the laundress's wasted labor. She would have liked to have given the laundress money, but she had no coins. Lord Robert had taken the few silver pennies she owned.

With these matters and other tasks, Alyson realized with a start that it was close to sunset. Expecting to find Guillelm in the stables, tending to Caliph, she was surprised he was not there. Jezebel, her own horse, whickered happily to see her and she could not resist giving the mare some attention, brushing her coat and combing out the tangles in her mane. The stable lad protested when he found her working, but not too much. She was the well-loved lady of Hardspen and, moreover, he knew that she would willingly tend his hurts if a horse kicked or bit him.

Backing away from the stables, Alyson thought too late of her gown. Berating her own folly, she looked herself over, relieved that the dress was still clean and wholesome. Not so her hands—they needed a soak.

Within the keep, she climbed the stairs swiftly straight to her chamber, longing to see Guillelm again as she passed the entrance of the great hall but not sneaking a peep in case she was spotted. True, her dragon had seen her with potion-stained fingers when she was child, but she doubted if the mysterious Heloise had ever appeared to him thus. Perhaps she should add even more ribbons to her hair, or would that merely make her husband laugh?

"I could try it and see," she said aloud, stepping off the stair

onto the narrow stone landing outside the main bedchamber—
hers now, and Guillelm's, if he should ever rest in it again.
Would he do so tonight? Where had he slept on their wedding night? Had he slept?

The panic had been with her all day, the dread unacknowl-
edged but horribly present. She had tried to keep occupied,
but that and all the foolish beauty aids and girlish plans had
been no more than ploys to stop her dwelling on the question,
What would happen between them tonight? *Would he come?*

Her fragile confidence faltered, crashing completely as
she saw the figure standing outside the chamber, "guarding"
the door.

Checking that the door was indeed closed, Fulk stepped
toward her.

"My lord is resting and would not be disturbed," he said.

"But he will come to supper soon," Alyson observed.

"I am to be in his place at the high table this evening, by
his own order. Sericus too," Fulk added negligently.

This was against custom but Alyson did not want to ask for
explanations from Fulk.

"We have fought hard today," he went on.

Alyson saw the sheen of sweat on the man's glib, triumphant
face and answered with unusual spite, "For you it was hard. For
my husband it is no more effort than blowing away the web of
a spider. I have news for Guillelm." She thought of the complaint of the laundress but put that aside to speak of the greater
threat—something that could not wait. "There is a wolf at
large, terrorizing the country close to Hardspen. It needs to be
found and stopped, before a child is killed."

"I will tell him."

"You are not my messenger, and I will enter my own bedchamber."

"No!" Fulk raised his hands, blocking her way. "Do you

not understand your own language?" he demanded. "My lord is exhausted."

"Speak a little louder, Fulk. I do not think Guillelm heard that. If he did, I do not think he would be pleased."

His blue eyes widened, then narrowed, a sign of anger she was coming to recognize only too well. "To fight even in practice is a furious labor, something a female never understands."

Alyson smiled, conscious at this moment only of her dislike for Fulk. He must be an excellent warrior. Nothing else would have compelled Guillelm to favor such a man with any kind of preferment, but she would have him away from the door.

"When you have undergone the trials of childbirth, Sir Fulk, then you may speak of labor to me," she remarked sweetly.

"What would you know of that? The women of your family bleed, not breed, each miscarriage proof of your sins, or drop only daughters. You doubtless will be as useless and barren."

Nasty and clever—his voice was now no more than a whisper.

"You would not say such things to me in the hearing of our lord," Alyson said, struggling to keep the memory of her mother's death at bay, terrified at the thought that perhaps the women of her family were somehow cursed, steeped in sin. "You would not dare."

He snorted. "I would not need to! Guillelm will learn soon enough. That is, if he ever breaks his vow and troubles to bed you."

Such affront was more than Alyson could bear. "You are without honor!" she blazed out, turning so Fulk would not see her cry. She stalked away. Reaching the stairs and out of sight of the landing, she ran.

"Wait!" Guillelm called out urgently, but she was already gone, vanishing into the long evening shadows. He seized

Fulk, slamming the man against the wall. "What are you doing here? Why did you not let her pass?"

"I was about to, my lord! I swear."

Fulk lapsed into French, a bead of sweat trickling down his nose as he made excuses that Guillelm was too angry to hear. Struggling with a locked chest in the chamber that he could find no key to and could not open without force, he had not realized that Alyson was outside until he heard her raised voice.

Abruptly, he released Fulk, thrust him off. "I have no time for you," he said, cutting through the man's declarations that he had caused the lady no offense. "We shall speak later." Guillelm made the promise a warning as he followed his fleeing wife.

Alyson retired to her former room, where her nurse Gytha took one look at her and silently guided the gawking Osmoda and the sharp-eyed maids out of the chamber. Alyson knew she had taken their sleeping place for the night but could hardly feel sorry for them—she was pitying herself. She threw herself onto the nearest bed and wept, pummeling the mattress with her fists, imagining the yielding pallet as Fulk's smirking face. Why should women have always to give way to men? How could she reach Guillelm and tell him of the wolf?

But then, why should she try? "I will catch the wolf myself," she said, and cried again.

Presently, she wiped her face and sought to compose herself. If Guillelm truly was weary, then she should go to supper in the great hall. If the lord of Hardspen could not show himself to his people, then the lady must. Yet it hurt her that Guillelm had not sent her a message to say he would not be dining in the hall, that he should tell Fulk and Sericus ahead of her. Or was he perhaps planning some surprise for her within their chamber? A sweet thought, but was that merely her own desperate hope?

She heard a muffled cough outside and guessed that Gytha

would be hovering by the door. She should at least tell her nurse to find a sleeping place, she thought, ashamed of her own self-seeking concerns as she unthreaded some of the ribbons from her plaits. To appear before Guillelm's men in the great hall with such silly trinkets in her hair seemed foolish.

There was a soft knock on the door. "Come in, Gytha," she called out, but it was Guillelm who entered.

"I did not know you were outside our chamber," he was saying, stopping as he saw what she was doing. He grimaced. "Forgive me, I did not realize you were retiring."

When he started to back away, Alyson understood. He thought she was sleeping here, in her old room, without him!

"No, dragon," she said quickly. "I was about to go to the great hall."

"I looked for you there first. I wish us to dine in private this evening, within our room. I know it is not the custom in England, but for one night, where would be the harm?"

He smiled but seemed ill at ease.

"What was Fulk saying to you just now?"

That I was a barren, useless female on whom you would never get an heir. Alyson bit back the answer, clinging to the marvelous idea that Guillelm wanted them to eat in private. Slowly, she drew out one of her ribbons, hoping Guillelm's fascination with her hair would distract him. "Is Gytha outside?" she asked in turn.

"No. Shall I summon her? Do you wish her to attend you?"

"No!" She had asked because she did not relish the idea of her nurse overhearing anything. "You could attend me—only if you have the time," she added.

Was her question a test, or mockery, as it would have been with Heloise? The last time he had been in a woman's bedchamber it had ended in disaster. Scorning his own cowardice,

Guillelm saw the ribbon in her hand tremble. She was shaking, ever so slightly. Nervous of him, or of her own perceived boldness? Pity warred with desire in him but he was guarded. He wanted neither to force his attentions on her, nor to make a mistake. The thought of last night scalded him with humiliation. He had no desire to repeat that experience.

"Fulk and Sericus are sitting in our places in the hall tonight," he explained.

"Fulk and Sericus?" She gave him a teasing look, her face full of mischief but no fear. "Think that they will be peaceful together? And who will be the lord and who the lady?"

Guillelm laughed, his fancy caught by that droll idea. "They will need to sort that between them, but 'tis only for one night. So there is no need for us to stir from our chamber. Or indeed from here, if you wish." When Alyson did not seem panic-stricken at the prospect, his hopes revived further. "What say you?"

"That pleases me," she said quietly. "I would be pleased to stay here with you, Guillelm."

"Excellent!" He need only put his head out of the door and shout for a page, summon servers, and their supper would be brought to them. It had been his plan: an intimate meal between them, at ease within their own chamber, but now he found his breath stuck in his throat. He did not want to speak to anyone else, or move even a finger-width farther apart from her.

"Mother of God, you are beautiful."

She wound the ribbon around his wrist and, using it, gently pulled him closer. "I have made a vow, too." She blew softly across his bare forearm, warmly stirring each and every hair, the contact-that-was-not-contact making him shudder.

"I have vowed to win you."

She stood on tiptoe and kissed him, her mouth tasting of strawberries.

Desire rammed through him, stronger than a siege engine.

Stronger still was the marvelous delight that Alyson cared—she truly did. He wrapped his arms about her, embracing her, his lips finding the rapid pulse at her throat, the soft crease behind her ears.

There were running feet on the stairs outside. "My lord!" A breathless page was shouting, "My lord Guillelm!"

The lad pounded on past the room, racing in error for the main bedchamber.

"My lady!" A maid hammered on the door. "My lady, you must come!"

As one, Guillelm and Alyson lunged for the door and the maid tumbled in, teary-eyed and shivering.

"What, girl?" Guillelm barked, and now she did burst into tears, sobbing into her hands.

"You must come!" she cried, cringing away from Guillelm's towering figure. "The news! Such terrible news—"

Alyson pushed past Guillelm and took the maid by the shoulders. "Hush, there, Mary. Catch your breath."

"What news?" Guillelm demanded.

The maid gulped and raised her head. "The Fleming has returned, my lord. The convent of St. Foy is under attack."

Chapter 15

Guillelm sprinted from the chamber, shouting for his sword and armor, leaving Alyson with the shivering maid.

"What has happened?" Alyson asked, desperate to know more, but Mary could only cry against her shoulder.

"Terrible thing, my lady. Dreadful!" Mary wailed, leaning so hard against her smaller, slighter mistress that Alyson almost lost her footing. She hooked a stool with her foot and dragged it closer, encouraging Mary to sit, put her head down, take deep breaths.

"Easy, easy," she soothed, ruffling the girl's thin brown curls, trying to calm her while her own imagination was bursting with horrors. Mercenaries attacking a holy place: it was unthinkable, unspeakable. Unbearable, that her own sister should be there. What was England coming to, if a convent could be attacked? Was Tilda alive? Was she safe, undespoiled?

Alyson dropped to her knees, praying, the Latin words freezing on her tongue as the maid moaned and blubbered, her nose running. Rising to her feet again, Alyson tore a wide ribbon from her own hair and pressed it into Mary's cold fingers.

"Here, Mary, blow your nose," she said, gentle as if the

maid were her daughter. "All will be well. Your lord is a great fighter; he will see the convent safe."

She swiftly bound her hair, still with its many ribbons, into a single plait. "Pray, Mary, but be not so afraid. The convent is close; it will be saved." She looked about for her cloak. "Have you people at St. Foy's?" she asked, wondering if that was the reason Mary seemed so undone. She slipped a cloak belonging to Gytha, short on her, its narrow trimming of rabbit fur riddled with moth, over her shoulders and tied the throat strings.

Mary shook her head. She was quieting and less pale, regaining some of her native wit, too, for now she whispered, "I am sorry, mistress. I know your own dearly missed sister is there—would that she were not! But I have seen the handiwork of Flemish troops before."

"We all have these days," replied Alyson bleakly. Forcing some kind of smile to her lips, she said gently, "Stay here tonight, if you wish. I will send Gytha and Osmoda to join you."

"But where are you going, my lady?" Mary asked, holding out the sodden ribbon, which Alyson gently refused.

"To join my husband," she almost said, but stopped herself. "To pray," she answered, which also was true, but was not the whole truth.

Alyson did not look to find Guillelm in the keep. Pulling Gytha's sparse hood over her head, she sped out to the stables. All there was a riot of comings and goings in a flicker of torches: men saddling horses, checking girths and gear, pulling on armguards, squires scampering for armor, helping their knightly masters onto their mounts.

Lingering in the shadows of her lean-to, Alyson noticed the lad she had spoken with earlier that day. Sadly, he also noticed her.

"My lady!" He darted across to her. "You should not be here!"

"I have a token for my lord, for his good fortune," Alyson lied quickly. "Will you give it to him and wish him Godspeed? We had not time to say goodbye."

She knew that sounded too plaintive and was ashamed of her own need, but the stable boy's face softened. "I will." He received the hairpin from her as graciously as a courtier, bowing his head. "He will be safe, my lady. He is a great warrior."

This was so close to what she had said to comfort the maid that Alyson smiled. She thanked the lad and watched him weave back into the press of men and horses, then sagged, the smile dropping from her lips. She knew Guillelm was a fighter, of course she knew, but war was war. A stray arrow, a sword thrust and her dragon's fire and dazzle might be extinguished. And he was so bright, so obvious a target . . .

She could not bear to be parted from him in this way. Whatever the danger, however foolish or selfish her action, she had to go with him. Why not? Other women went in war trains—camp followers and the wives of soldiers. She was a healer; she could be useful. There was her sister, too, and the other nuns, women who might appreciate her care, if she could saddle her horse and ride out unnoticed in this battle horde.

Alyson was lucky—her mount was stabled at the very end of the block, with a stall full of straw and feed between her and the other horses. Keeping to the shadows, she reached Jezebel without raising any alarm and was slipping a bridle over the mare's narrow head when she heard Guillelm's bloodcurdling war cry. Even as she froze, chilled by the almost demonic shout, her husband rode past the stable, raising his sword arm and yelling, "Ride to St. Foy's! Ride!"

"We ride!" the answer rumbled from two score and more throats, and they were off, thundering out of Hardspen at full gallop.

Alyson had no time to saddle her horse. She cast herself onto the mare's back and pounded out of the stable yard, her borrowed cloak and hood pulled low over her head to hide her face and hair. Glad there was no moon to light her clothes or show off her shape, she urged Jezebel on and joined the cloaked and hooded squires at the rear of the column.

Guillelm spurred Caliph to greater speed, leaning forward in the saddle to give the massive warhorse his head. Aware of the dark ground rushing under his heels, he was merciless in his riding, never slowing down, careless of obstacles. Reckless as he was, the stallion drove through shadows on the track, leaping over fallen branches and churning up a miasma of dust. A fox darted across the road, the white tip of its tail a banner amongst the dark green and black of the wayside hazel and hawthorn, but Guillelm was not to be diverted. "Forward!" he yelled, running Caliph straight at a sapling growing in the middle of the road. He felt its leaves slap against his foot and heard the wheeze of horses and men, falling behind, but he did not draw rein.

Women were in danger. *Nuns* were under attack by a creature he had spared. He knew from the sweating, exhausted messenger who had ridden out from the village close to St. Foy's that the men there had sworn to defend the convent if need arose, but what could an aging, ill-armed militia do against mercenaries? If any died, man, boy or woman, Guillelm knew he would be to blame. Whatever excuses a confessor might make for him, he had allowed the Fleming to leave Hardspen with his men and weapons. He had made a serious misjudgment in trusting the word of Étienne the so-called Bold: The man had broken his knightly promise. If Étienne had ever joined the forces of King Stephen or the empress, the venture clearly had not worked and so he was back in the area he had terrorized so readily before, looking for easy plunder. And if one had the stomach for it, a convent was the easiest target of all.

Alyson's sister was at St. Foy's.

Cursing, Guillelm rode harder still.

Numb with grief and the pounding ride, Alyson saw the flames and heard the sickening roar of burning timbers through the trees, before the column reached the convent. Breasting the rise in the rutted road, she groaned and almost lost her reins, instinct alone saving her from being pitched headlong from Jezebel's back. Around her she heard shouting from the squires, saw their pallid, sweating faces.

Below, stretched before them in the downland valley, was a scene from hell. The church of St. Foy's was wholly ablaze, spiraling plumes of fire and smoke spilling from the roof of the nave and leaping out of its shattered windows. There were prone bodies, suspiciously still, lying like broken toys in the garden where only a few weeks earlier she and her sister had walked in peace. Of the mercenaries there seemed no sign, except for one stray riderless horse, careering round and round in the road outside.

"Have any survived?" hissed a squire and Alyson, not trusting her voice, pointed back to the church, where a few limping figures seemed to be trying to beat out the flames at the base of the building, without success. The convent wall had a massive breach in its eastern side and as Alyson watched, willing herself to nudge her horse to a final effort but unable to force her frozen limbs to move, she saw the roof of the nuns' dormitory cave in with a splintering crash.

"Tilda!" she shrieked. Flinging herself off the shuddering, rolling-eyed Jezebel, she ran down the hill, not caring if the Fleming's men were there or not.

Suddenly ahead of her she saw Guillelm appear in the gap

in the convent wall, carrying a trembling figure in his arms and leading a dazed old man by the shoulder.

Even as she rejoiced that he was safe, that the mercenaries truly had fled from her lord's strength and righteous anger, she realized her mistake. Catching a flurry of movement in the corner of her eye, she turned about, swerving just in time to avoid the rushing mount of one of the squires who passed so close to her that she felt her cheek grazed by the lad's stirrup. But it was not his headlong dash she had sensed, or even heard above the general din of the fire, shouting and galloping horses. Instinct guided her to look farther back, up the hill toward the trees crowning the top of the ridge, and yes! There it was: a figure, stepping out of the woodland. As he emerged from the shadows of the trees, he was skylined a moment, his wiry, mail-clad shape clear against the summer stars. It was too dark to see the knightly device on his armor or cloak, but he was no ally—his war helm was closed and he carried a sword in one hand and a crossbow in the other.

Alyson began to run again, to Guillelm, aware she had only seconds, instants, before the enemy raised his helm and wound up his deadly crossbow.

He would shoot at Guillelm—

"Down! Get down! Get away!" Yelling warnings, she ran straight at Guillelm, her one thought to save him, her only wild plan that if she could not make him hear her warnings, she might spoil the aim of the enemy archer.

Ignoring the growing pain of her heat-seared lungs and her fading, tiring limbs, she screamed again, "Get down!" and now Guillelm heard and saw her, shock and horror warring in his face, his mouth forming the question, "How?"

"Down!" Alyson cried, but she was too late. She felt a punch slam into her shoulder, spinning her round so that she fell backward, the breath knocked out of her. She tried to move, to reach

Guillelm, shield him, but as she raised her head a jolt of agony drove through her body and she blacked out.

Guillelm reacted without conscious thought. He lowered the shocked, sobbing prioress gently onto the ground and seized the quivering arrow shaft buried so sickeningly in Alyson's shoulder, determined to draw it out before she came round from her faint.

Even as he worked, images flashed constantly before his eyes. Alyson running toward him, arms outstretched, making herself a target. Over and over, he saw the bolt thud into her slender body, saw her feet actually leave the ground as she was flung around by the force of the impact. She had been shot in the back and he had done nothing to save her; worse, he had not even known she had joined the war band. He had been so keen to lay sword against sword with Étienne the Bold, who, cur that he was, had turned tail the instant he saw him, riding through the smoke and soot of the burning convent.

"Ah!" Although he tried to be steady and careful and the crossbow bolt came out cleanly, the sharp, decisive tug hurt her—Alyson came out of her swoon with a shriek of agony.

"Sssh, sweetheart, it is done." Guillelm wanted to cradle her but dared not; he could not bear to hurt her again. Kneeling by her, he packed his cloak around her body, terrified at how cold she was. Her shoulder was bleeding freely and that must be good, for the ill humors would be washed out.

What if the crossbow bolt was poisoned?

What if she died?

"Live, Alyson," he whispered, too afraid to be angry at her. He should have known she would attempt something like this; she was never one to sit still when those she loved were under threat. Where was that sister of hers? The Flemings had herded the nuns into the courtyard while they torched the buildings. None had been harmed, so where was she?

Blinking away tears, he raised his head and met the pasty faces of the squires. The lads had dismounted and gathered round, forming a shield with their horses. *Too late,* Guillelm thought bleakly.

"My lord, we did not know . . ."

"Truly we never suspected . . ."

"She moved so swiftly, ran right amongst the horses . . ."

"We could not stop her!"

Their excuses died away and they hung their heads.

"What can we do?" asked one.

Guillelm raked them with furious eyes. His knights were still searching for survivors in the wrecked convent—friends or foe—but these useless, lumpen youths should be good for something.

"Get me that archer," he spat.

"I will do so, my lord." Fulk stepped into the circle, glanced at Alyson's still body and then turned, shouting for his horse.

"Sir—"

At first Guillelm thought it one of the squires, or the half-blind old militiaman he had led to safety from the burning church.

"Do not scold them, sir. I rode in disguise." The small, breathy voice was Alyson's. She was looking at him, her eyes dark with pain and fear.

"Peace!" Guillelm took her icy hand in his, trying to will his own heat into her. "We shall have you home safe, soon enough."

"I am sorry to be so much trouble." Alyson tried to raise herself on her elbow, gasped and fell back.

"Alyson!" For a dreadful moment, he thought she had died, but then saw the quick rise of her chest and realized she had passed out again. He should lift her from this burnt, wrecked ground as soon as possible, but what way would be best? In his arms, on horseback? On a litter?

"Give me your cloaks!" he snapped at the hapless squires. "Cover her with them. You! Bring me the infirmarer! You! Make a fire here! You! Find Sir Thomas." He almost said Sir Fulk, his natural second-in-command, but Fulk was off on another necessary task and one he longed to accomplish himself, though revenge on the archer would not save Alyson.

Live, please live, he thought. It was a prayer and wish in one.

"Where is that infirmarer?" he bellowed, above the steady weeping of the prioress. He was growing incensed with the lack of speed of everyone about him and exasperated with the cowering, wailing nuns who had trailed after him like ducklings following their mother as he carried the helpless, vacant-eyed head of their order away from her devastated convent. If Alyson's sister was in that drab company, why had she not come forward to be with her? Was she so withdrawn from the world that even the sight of her own flesh, broken and bleeding on the ground, stirred no passionate care? "Is there no one?"

"I am here, Guido." Calm as a rock in a sea of troubles, Sir Tom leaned down from his horse. "What say I find something to use as a stretcher?"

"Do it," Guillelm answered curtly, "and tell your men to search the infirmary for potions and such." A late thought struck him, but he could not feel ashamed at it, not with Alyson injured beside him. "See if any of our own men are hurt, and tend them."

"They will not be hurt. Men never are." A small, slim nun emerged from the smoke, her arms full of books and manuscripts.

"I am Sister Ursula, who was once Matilda of Olverton Minor," she said, calm as glass. "I have been in our scriptorium, where our true treasures are stored. The mercenaries did not recognize them as such." Slow, careful, she laid the books on the ground and only then looked at Alyson.

"Your infirmarer?" Guillelm asked, as Sister Ursula's lips moved in prayer. His hands itched to shake her out of her complacency; was this woman human? "Your sister is still bleeding."

"The infirmarer is dead." Sister Ursula opened her eyes, fixing Guillelm with a stare of utter dislike, mingled with distaste. "Our sister in Christ passed away eight days ago."

"Mother of God, have you no one who can help my wife?"

"Do not blaspheme against the name of our blessed Lady of Heaven."

Sister Ursula stared at a kneeling squire striking sparks off his knife to light a small, swiftly gathered bundle of kindling until the youth shuffled out of her path. She knelt beside Alyson, facing Guillelm across her sister's body. "I will pray."

"Please—" Guillelm felt to be out of his depth dealing with this smooth, polished creature. He felt to be drowning in her piety. If it had been a man he would have appealed to honor or come to blows. How did women deal with each other? He thought of his sister, Juliana, but their relationship had been oddly formal, she being so much the elder and out of reach of sibling contests.

Rivalry. The answer came to him as he recalled the scrapes and scraps that he had seen and sometimes intervened in between brothers. It was a risk to employ it against women, but what other tactic could he use? Luck and recklessness were all he had left.

"If she could speak, Alyson could tell us how to treat her," he remarked, adopting Sister Ursula's calm tones while around him his squires and gathering knights held their breaths against the approaching storm. *Gently—he had to do this right.* "She is an excellent healer."

Sister Ursula said nothing.

"She told me you had no diligence in such matters," Guillelm went on, lying shamelessly and, worse, feeling no guilt as he did so. "That you love books more than people."

"She is wrong," said Sister Ursula.

"You put your skill above hers, then? I have seen no other to match her, even in Outremer."

With a small shake of her head, remarkably like Alyson's, Sister Ursula unclasped her palms.

"I thought her judgment a little harsh, but I see that she was right. She said you lacked the healing touch."

"What nonsense." Sister Ursula rose to her feet. "Build up that fire," she commanded. "I must have more light."

Chapter 16

Alyson remembered little of the return journey to Hardspen. Drifting in and out of a fevered consciousness, she was aware in snatches. Guillelm's anxious face, leaning over her. The constant, throbbing pain in her shoulder. The hard, uncomfortable litter, made of lashed-together branches, that felt like a bed of bones. She tried several times to tell Guillelm that, on their slow ride home, but could only manage "Bones."

He misheard and gave her a drink, something cooling. It tasted strange, as if it was a potion but with parts missing. She could not say what it lacked.

Tilda was in her dreams, sometimes lying beside her, sometimes wiping her face and hands. Her sister never smiled and did not speak to her.

There was weeping, too, a boy or woman crying. It tore at Alyson because she could not help.

Sleep was easier and in sleep she felt nothing. She treasured sleep.

Guillelm offered the prioress his horse, Caliph, and safe haven within Hardspen: a living space and refuge while messages were sent out to other convents within the order, pleading for places for herself and her homeless, beleaguered flock. Sobbing, all the nuns gathered round him to thank him, which embarrassed him greatly. On the journey, the prioress continued to weep while her shivering, sooty-faced charges plodded along the track with their pitifully few belongings, retrieved from the ruins and bundled into rough homespun blankets. As they traveled, the nuns settled into a dull, stunned quiescence, almost as disconcerting as the prioress's endless grief.

"They are women," Fulk remarked dismissively. He walked with Guillelm, the crossbow he had taken from the mercenary who had shot Alyson slung over his back. He told Guillelm that he had ridden down the archer and another straggler from the mercenaries. "They died screaming," he said with relish.

Guillelm clapped him on the shoulder but could find no words of thanks. Alyson was not screaming, but she might die. Her sister had washed out her wound with one potion and packed it with fresh cloths, ripped from Alyson's own gown, remarking casually that Alyson might be given another potion to drink "whenever her pain is too great." Otherwise, she had offered no comfort or hope. Seemingly indifferent to Alyson's suffering, she positioned herself at one side of the litter and occasionally wiped beads of sweat from her sister's forehead. She appeared more concerned with the well-being of the convent's books and manuscripts, keeping them close beside her on the litter, sometimes dusting them off, running her fingers down the spine of the largest Bible as a devoted wife might trace her fingers down her husband's back—as Alyson had with him and might never do again.

Alyson had sneaked out with the squires. Alyson had saved his life, shielded him with her own fragile, slender body. Her courage appalled him. He was ashamed of his own rude health and yes—yes, he was angry at her. To put herself in danger for a sister who did not care—it was love but it was also pride and folly. To do what she had done for him—did she not think? Had she forgotten her reason? He wore armor! The crossbolt doubtless would have pierced it, but he was the leader; it was for him to undergo such trials, not her. Did she think him feeble? Or did she not care that his own men might think him weak or easily duped?

But she was so white, lying amidst the tatters of her torn gown. As part of the madness of this entire night he missed her silk veil and found himself wondering what she had done with it. Was it pinned under that shabby, cow-brown hood?

"Hurry," he muttered, aching to take her in his arms and race back to the castle. Biting down on the order to march, he told himself that they had to be slow, or her wound would bleed more. The nuns would not be able to keep pace, either, apart from Sister Ursula, who glided along beside Alyson's litter in the middle of the column, easy as a shadow.

Finally the tall walls and keep of Hardspen crawled over the horizon and Fulk shook his arm. "Leave everything to me, my lord," he said in a low undertone. "I will send out riders to the castle, ensure all is made ready for our return, and for the comfort and housing of our unexpected guests."

Grateful for his support, Guillelm nodded. "As you ever did in Outremer, Fulk."

His seneschal gave a small bow. "I am glad you remember."

Sister Ursula tried to keep him out of the main bedchamber while Alyson was being tended afresh, but Guillelm insisted on staying. "She is my wife."

"And it is a pity that you did not take better care of her," Sister Ursula replied. "But then I have heard that you were ever reckless, Guillelm de La Rochelle."

The stinging rebuke made him boil with rage. Conscious

of Gytha's sympathetic look, the cowering embarrassment of the other maids, he moved again toward Alyson.

A black-robed arm stopped him. "I will tend her." Sister Ursula turned back to the parchment-pale, still figure. Alyson looked scarcely more than a sleeping child, her huddled shape lost in the great bed.

"Please, let me help. Let me do something."

The nun ignored Guillelm's plea. Briskly, she stripped Alyson of her cloak, veil, gown and undershift, asking at the same time for this and that salve to be put within her reach—salves taken, with an irony that did not escape Guillelm, from Alyson's own potion store.

"Gytha, help me turn her," Sister Ursula ordered. "Osmoda, bring a candle closer. I need to be able to check that there is no iron left in the wound."

With Guillelm left standing, feeling anxious, frustrated and useless, by the foot of the bed, Alyson was rolled onto her stomach. Even in her drugged slumber she moaned, wincing.

Sister Ursula washed the wound in Alyson's left shoulder and sniffed it. "Deep, but wholesome," she announced. "Whoever removed the arrow did so cleanly enough." She glanced at the row of bottles and basins by her feet. "We should pray first, before I use any of these potions or salves. It is God who heals, not us."

"Wait," said Guillelm, as Sister Ursula piously pulled the rugs away to kneel on the bare flags. "What are those other marks on her body?"

The nun ignored him, stepping back from the bed. "I have changed my mind," she said. "Any of my prayers would be better offered up in the chapel, in the company of my order."

Before Guillelm could even think of stopping her, Sister Ursula slipped through the door and was gone.

Guillelm crouched in her place. The gouge in Alyson's back, slicing diagonally across the top of her shoulder blade and piercing through to just beneath her collarbone, was bad enough, although Guillelm had seen similar injuries inflicted on soldiers in Outremer and the men had always survived. She was less cold to touch now, and the bleeding had stopped: the dressings that her sister had earlier packed so tightly against the torn muscle, sinews and chipped bone had staunched the flow. He tried to think of the remedies the Arab doctors had used but could not remember any. The shock of seeing Alyson hurt had turned him simple, it seemed.

And there were those other marks . . .

Guillelm gripped the edge of the bed, disbelief and anger exploding in his mind. "She has been beaten, many times," he said. He was struggling to keep still—his body and spirit were screaming for revenge. He raked a hand across his chest, unaware that he was drawing blood.

"Who did this?" he demanded, his free hand hovering a palm-span above the line of one long, ragged scar, tracing its painful track from the small of her back to the middle of her thigh. "Was it her father?"

Osmoda whimpered and tottered for the door, intent on escape, but Gytha said and did nothing.

"Answer me!" Guillelm punched the bed head, hearing its timbers crack and splinter. Transfixed on the threshold, Osmoda flinched, her scrawny face showing pure terror, but the old nurse, although her complexion changed from apple red to chalk white, looked at him with eyes full of understanding.

"She would not let me see her naked," she said. "I suspected but did not know for certain until recently."

Osmoda moaned and fled, the wide sleeves of her gown slapping against the stones of the corridor as she hurried away.

"How recently? And who?" Such was the force of Guillelm's building rage that he no longer could contain it. He shook with it and the great bed also shuddered. "Mother of

God, I have never willingly hurt a woman and I have no wish
to start now, but if you do not tell me—"

Gytha plucked one of the salves off the floor and started to
draw a sheet over her young mistress. When Guillelm reached
across the edge of the bed and seized her wrist, she raised her
eyes to him again.

"It was her father," Guillelm stated. "Sir Henry was ever
strict."

"Sir Henry was not an easy man, but he loved his daughters.
He would not raise a hand to either." Gytha's eyes were warm
with a certain sympathy that sent a stake of pure ice through
Guillelm's vitals. He shied from the idea, his eyes unwillingly
drawn to Alyson's old hurts. There were long, thin lines running
vertically and horizontally across her back, buttocks and legs.

"Birch rods," Gytha said softly, "sometimes a belt. It was
not her father."

"It was mine." Guillelm sat down hard on the stone flags
and hid his face in his hands. The knowledge shamed and un-
manned him. "Why?" he said. Alyson had been his father's
guest at Hardspen, had been set to be his betrothed and yet
Lord Robert had done this. "How could he?" he whispered.

Now Gytha did cover Alyson with the sheet and began to
smear a lavender-scented salve around the area of the wound,
although careful not to touch the wound itself. She worked
with a deftness that surprised Guillelm, although in these past
few moments he had thought himself beyond shock. "Why?"
he asked again.

"Your father drank and was fond of it, particularly malmsey
wine." Gytha passed the pot of salve to Guillelm and indicated
a small raw place on Alyson's forehead. When he gently worked
some of the salve across the graze, the nurse resumed her story.

"He could not always hold his drink. He became . . . tetchy,
quick to take offense. The pages and maids kept out of his
way at such times, or Alyson would send them away, out of

range of his fists. He would pull her hair. Once I saw him slap her. He demanded her obedience, said he would not commit to their betrothal until she was bent to his will."

Moving with great care, Guillelm handed the salve back to the nurse. "I had wondered why my father and Alyson had not been formally betrothed, especially when Alyson and her people moved to the castle."

"Your father did that. He liked to keep her in doubt."

His father had always done that filthy trick, Guillelm remembered.

"He may have been a lord, but he had no honor." Gytha cleared her throat. "I am sorry to say this, my lord—"

"No, 'tis best I know." So much now made sense: Alyson's reluctance to speak of his father, her sudden, inexplicable looks of fear. "She must truly hate me and mine," he said bleakly.

"Never, my lord!" Gytha shook her head so strongly that she loosened one of the pins from her head rail and it flew from her head, bouncing on the flags. "She would hear no ill word about you from anyone. There was one evening, soon after her own father had died." Gytha pursued her lips and was silent.

"Tell me." He dreaded to hear more but could not leave it so. "Please."

Gytha sighed and settled on the edge of the bed, absently rubbing her knees over and over.

"Lord Robert had been drinking hard that night. He called you a lost son, said you were worthless, reckless, useless. My lady Alyson flared up at once. She leapt from her seat on the dais and told him to his face that you were three times the worth of any man.

"Lord Robert stalked from the hall at that. A few moments later, a squire came to my young mistress, told her she should join your father in his great chamber."

"His bedroom? But they were not plighted."

"Indeed they were not! But what could my lady do? She was in his house. Her father was dead. She had no protectors.

"I followed her that night."

"That night? There had been other occasions?"

"When Lord Robert summoned my lady to his chamber? Yes. Too many times for my peace of mind, I can say! When I asked Alyson about them, she said Lord Robert scolded her. About her gowns, for one matter, and her learning for another. He thought her altogether too showy. He took her book from her and burned her dresses, all but the plainest.

"But I was speaking of that particular night," Gytha went on, while Guillelm listened to Alyson's light, fast breathing and the unearthly sound of the nuns in the chapel, singing, and wished his father into the darkest, deepest, hottest pit in hell. "That night, I followed her."

"So you said."

"Be not so sour, my lord, for it is good I did. You were a thousand leagues off in Outremer and my bird had no one else to look out for her. None but her own wits, and sometimes these failed when her temper overcame her. Mind, I think your father provoked her, too, so he had an excuse to punish."

"And he did so here." Guillelm looked about the main bedchamber, trying to conceive of the shadows and horrors the room forever would hold for Alyson and feeling a tremendous shame and despair. "A pity he did not die of a surfeit in the great hall, first."

"It would have saved my lady much hurt."

About to say more, Gytha paused as Alyson turned on the bed, her legs thrashing briefly beneath the linen sheet. She quietened and Gytha said quickly, "I am glad you removed Lord Robert's treasure chest from this room. He bent her over it, you see, while he chastised her."

Guillelm tried to swallow and found he could not. Tomorrow

he would be burning that chest, he vowed, but tonight he had to know all, every grotesque detail. "You are sure of this?"

Gytha nodded. "I saw with my own eyes! The door was ajar. He was very drunk, you see. He was using his belt, laying on harshly. I stopped him that night by screaming outside the chamber that I had seen an intruder in the castle, close to Alyson's room." The nurse gave a grim smile. "He came out quickly enough from his chamber then, you may be sure! He was ever jealous of my lady, convinced all men were spying on her."

This was too close to what Guillelm himself felt at times and he hung his head, overwhelmed afresh with shame. "He did this because of me? Because she had spoken up for me?"

"For other reasons, too, my lord. You must not reproach yourself."

How can I not? Guillelm thought, wondering how his father had faced his own confessor, how he had lived with what he had done.

"Why did she say nothing to me? I would have understood."

"Can you imagine my lady wanting to spoil your good memories of Lord Robert by confessing any of this to you?"

"I have no good memories to spoil." Guillelm sighed. "Tell me this once and be done."

Gytha rubbed her knees more and said in a hushed quick way, "I do not know the whole tale. I only learned what I did that night because I saw Alyson before she had time to collect herself." The nurse glanced at her former charge, a slow blush stealing into her plump cheeks. "I fear I took advantage of her moment of weakness that night and persuaded her to talk by claiming that if she told me a little of what had passed between her and Lord Robert I could advise her on how best to please him and avoid such—"

"Please him!" Enraged afresh at his father, Guillelm could say no more.

"I am not proud of what I did." Gytha sighed. "But, then,

I truly feared for her." Her lip curled. "I would not treat a dog as he had dealt with her that night! When I brought her out of the chamber, she could scarcely walk, she was shaking so much. And this was not the first time, no! The first I knew of it, but Lord Robert had whipped her before. For smiling too broadly at Sericus, a lame old man whom she has known since she was a child! She asked me, then, as we limped slowly back to her room, if she had done wrong. Lord Robert made her doubt herself."

Gytha talked more, a sordid, pitiful story that revealed Lord Robert as a bitter misogynist, intent on breaking Alyson in every way he could. His father had wanted her powerless and a victim and so had kept her in doubt of her own place at Hardspen—delaying their formal betrothal, denying her the clothes fit for her station, forbidding her to visit or see her friends, giving her no keys to the store chests. She had sat with him on the dais in the great hall but had not been allowed to speak, even if a villager from Olverton came and asked for audience with Lord Robert.

"All this within the month she stayed with him," Guillelm muttered, grinding his fists into his eyes, trying to rid himself of the unwelcome pictures that were now branded into his brain. He had known his father was a narrow, vengeful man but even so—

"Mother of God!" he burst out.

Gytha nodded. "He was eaten alive by jealousy, possessed by envy. Every day was worse than the one before. He would smile and say honeyed words to her, let her think he was content, that he approved of her and then he would change: draw back, become cold, not speak, summon her to his chamber.

"I know this is a terrible thing to say, but the summer sickness was a blessing. With so many falling ill, Lord Robert had to allow her to practice her healing arts and allow her more freedom. When he was taken sick"—Gytha touched Alyson's still hand, clasping the pale cool fingers in her own chapped palm—"I cannot pretend I was not glad."

"I want to kill him," Guillelm said. "Grind and break his bones—"

"Would you become another Lord Robert?" Gytha snorted. "He is already dead and buried, as well you know! Can you think of nothing better than that?"

Astonished at her forthrightness, Guillelm fell silent.

"Yes," he said, after a long, tense moment. "Yes, I can, and I will."

"Good!" Gytha rose off the bed. "And I will fetch Sister Ursula to tend my lady now. She has prayed enough for one night."

Chapter 17

Alyson leaned back against the pillows and looked at the parchment in her lap. Guillelm had found it for her from somewhere, and ink. He said she could use it to write down her potions, or the tithes that Olverton owed the church, or poetry or stories she remembered—anything she wanted.

"The Arab doctors believe that when a woman is sick or injured, she must have everything she desires," he had told her. "You are to indulge your every whim."

Carefully, using her left arm, Alyson reached for her cup of mint tisane, conscious of the stretch of the healing sinews in her shoulder. It was ten days since she had been brought back to Hardspen and every day saw her stronger, more interested in her surroundings.

She could not become any more interested in Guillelm than she already was, but she was becoming anxious of how she might appear to him, with her bandaged shoulder and unwashed hair. It was a small reassurance to her that he seemed equally anxious to please her; whether because of the Arab doctors or for his own reasons Alyson did not know, but she reveled in his attention.

Five days ago, he had carried her outside their chamber to

a made-up bed on the highest point of the keep, well out of range of archers, he said. There between the battlements, on the very roof of the castle, he had made what he called a paradise: a private, hidden garden.

Paradise it was, Alyson thought, sipping her tisane and watching the swifts tumbling in the cloudless blue skies. The canopy set above her soft mattress creaked softly in the breeze. She had cool drinks waiting for her on a low table beside her couch, and pieces of fresh white bread and honey to eat. There were seven low wooden tubs set out over the roof filled with earth and turf and flowers—roses, lavender, marigolds, hyssop, speedwells and buttercups.

"I carried the tubs up here, and the earth," Guillelm said, grinning at her exclamation of delight. "The nuns planted the flowers; I was merely their water-bearer."

He did not mention her sister and Alyson did not ask. She felt too weary to delve more deeply into where Ursula might be. Not with her, certainly. She had not seen her sister since the night she had been injured, and even now she was not sure if Ursula's presence had been a dream or not.

But she was very glad of this high, private garden. The sight and scents of the flowers eased her. She watched a bumblebee, dusted with pollen, flying among the lavender, and a white butterfly basking on top of the battlement walls and felt truly safe, as she had as a child. She was happy to stay out here from sunrise to sunset.

She dozed, stirred, ate some bread and honey and took up her quill. Gytha, sitting on a stool close to the canopy, put down her spindle and spread a rough cloth over Alyson so she would not spill ink on herself or the linen sheet.

Smiling her thanks, Alyson began to write. Though she had not asked Guillelm for the parchment, she was pleased he had found it for her and flattered that he had remembered her love of reading and writing. She had written two letters every day for the past five days: one for Guillelm, and one for herself.

She always began with her letter to Guillelm, before her shoulder ached too much. Aware that his skill in reading was not as great as hers, she wrote in a large, even hand. It was more of a simple "good-day" to him, a scrap of contact between them.

> My dear lord,
> I trust that your time with the armorers is well spent this morning. I await your company this afternoon.
>   With faithful obedience, Alyson

Then, because Guillelm always asked if she was sufficiently warm or cool, or if she was thirsty or hungry or bored, she added,

> I am very comfortable, counting the bees on the marigolds, drinking a mint tisane that is cooler and greener than the grass on the downs. I have no pain.

Except the small hurt of missing him, to which she would not admit.

She tore off the strip of written parchment, tied it with one of her ribbons and held it out to Gytha.

Her nurse rose off her stool, "I will find a page to take it to him," she said and wandered off to do just that.

Alone on the roof, Alyson listened to the nuns singing in the chapel below and after a while picked up her quill again. She hummed as she wrote, happy at the task. It was a sweet, secret pleasure to confess her thoughts.

> To myself, Alyson of Olverton and Hardspen,
> Today by the grace of God I am stronger. My shoulder gives me less pain, although it itches greatly. I would

scratch myself like an old boar against a young oak tree! I dare not tell Guillelm of this, though every day when he comes he asks how I am faring.

I wonder if I may see Tilda? It is strange to think of her as Sister Ursula. Sometimes I wonder if I recognize her high, shrill voice issuing from the chapel, where the nuns seem to spend most of their time and sing the holy offices. I wish she would visit me. Perhaps I should ask Guillelm if I might go down to the chapel and see her instead.

I wonder when Guillelm will come? I pray it be soon! This paradise he has made me is so lovely. He says that in the gardens of Outremer there is running water, and many small fountains. That the air is full of spices and the very trees have fragrant leaves. Two days ago, he carried a great cauldron up to this garden and filled it with water and sprays of lime, so that I might have my own scented shade. I laughed when he used a ladle to water the tubs of lavender and marigolds, and he flicked water at me. Yesterday he brought the merlin up to this place and flew her from the battlements. He tells me that Sericus has taken over her daily care and that he seems to have an aptitude for the art of the falconer. I spoke to Sericus again about the wolf that is terrorizing the country and he told me that there have been no more sightings. Perhaps it has died, or perhaps the villagers and cottars have been able to scare it off. I am glad of this, for the threat of the wolf has been preying on my mind.

My lord sleeps in the great hall with his men. Every day, it is a grief to me. I would ask that we both sleep here, in our private Eden, with the stars as our roof, but I lack courage, or perhaps it is strength. Often I am so tired by sunset that I do not even know that Guillelm has carried me down to the great bedchamber until I find myself waking indoors the following morning.

But enough of sadness. It is the duty of a wife to accept the wishes and actions of her husband. In many ways, my lord dragon is attentive and winning. He courts me in many ways. I know that I repeat myself, that writing this again is perhaps a waste of precious parchment, but the memories are also precious to me.

I wonder what he might bring to me today? On the first day he carried me to this paradise, he bathed my hands and face with rosewater. He said the ladies of Outremer used rosewater to add bloom to their complexions. I wanted to ask him then about Heloise but was too cowardly. He said I smelt sweeter than the rosewater, and he kissed me. I teased him by asking if I should wash him first before I kissed him and he lightly tugged my hair, then drew back as if I was as lethal as wolfsbane. I thought I had lost him again to his strange dread of women, that he would leave me stranded on the roof of Hardspen for the rest of the day. But he did not! My lord did not. Instead, he showed me a wonder of Arabic learning, an astrolabe. Stargazers use them to track the motions of the heavens. He also showed me new ways of counting, far easier than tallies. He learned the numbers from an Arabic farrier in Nazareth, a man called Unur. The Arabs count in batches of ten and have a wonderful empty number, called zero. It is a perfect round circle. I drew one with my quill on Guillelm's palm, and he drew one on mine. I did not wash my hand for the rest of that day.

Alyson stopped writing and rubbed her aching shoulder, then her wrist. After a drink of her tisane she resumed her letter.

My lord has played me songs from France and the Holy Land, on a small harp that looked like a child's toy in his huge hands. He plays well and sings clearly, though he says his voice is too deep to be truly excellent.

My lord has promised to teach me some dances from Outremer, when I am allowed to rise from my sickbed.

Yesterday we played chess. He told me that he and Unur of Nazareth often played chess together. The piece we call a queen, Unur called a vizier. I won our game and Guillelm has asked me for a rematch.

Once, when my stomach rumbled with hunger and he heard, Guillelm laughed and sent down to the kitchen for meat. He cooked a dish himself, on a brazier of coals. Pieces of lamb threaded onto a thin stick, flavored with mint and onions. He said such cooked meat could be bought from street cooks in any large town in the Holy Land. It was delicious.

I think Guillelm is planning something, though he will not answer my questions when I ask after the heralds and messengers that I see pounding out on horseback from Hardspen throughout the day. I would ask Sir Tom, but he only wants to play chess with me. As for Fulk—

Alyson brushed the end of her quill thoughtfully against her forehead. By one single, violent act, Fulk had regained Guillelm's approval and he now strolled about Hardspen with the mercenary's crossbow as if it were a personal badge of honor. He was careful to visit her every day, always at the beginning of Guillelm's own time with her and always asking after her injury. He brought her a gift: a flute she had not quite enough breath to play.

Fulk had also found her herbal, which Lord Robert had taken from her.

"Mother of God, I have been scouring the store rooms for days for this!" Guillelm said, highly gratified and taking the leather-bound volume from Fulk with a grin of pure delight. "Where was it?"

"In a grain bin in the stables, my lord," Fulk answered quietly, bowing to Alyson as a faithful retainer to his lady. "I am glad to be of service."

That had been two days ago and since then, the leather-bound book lay untouched on the low table. To Guillelm, Fulk was a changed man, his gift and attentions to Alyson proof of that change. "He is capable of great loyalty, once he chooses to give it," he said, adding quickly, "If he is involved in some malice or deceit, I shall discover it. Fulk was ever a poor liar."

Alyson sensed that Guillelm was not as confident as he wanted to appear over his seneschal, but mindful of his and Fulk's long years together in Outremer, she did not voice her suspicions. True, Fulk had found the herbal, but how long ago? The pages did not carry the scents of the stable. She considered it much more likely that Fulk had discovered her book somewhere within the castle and had hidden it within his own personal things, waiting for the perfect opportunity to produce it, the very moment when Guillelm would be most likely to be pleased.

Perhaps I am too wary of Fulk. He is in my lord's favor—not as high as Fulk himself might wish, but Guillelm is no longer sharp with him. Fulk makes himself busy with whatever plan Guillelm is hatching and is amiable with me. I only wish that it was not Fulk who had found my book. I wish his sly, creeping fingers had never touched it. I wish Guillelm had not told him about my lost book.

No, I am being unfair, Alyson thought, and deliberately scored through the last sentence. Above the scratch of the quill, she heard voices. Swiftly, hoping the ink would not smudge, she rolled up the parchment and placed it under her pillow, preparing to greet her maids.

Gytha and Osmoda helped her out of bed and down the stairs to the bathhouse. "Your lord wanted to bathe you himself," Gytha was saying, "but I told him no."

"Gytha, you had no right."

Her nurse clicked her tongue. "You would have him see you with a pus-filled shoulder?"

"It is not pus-filled!" Alyson panted. She was rapidly growing weary with even this brief outing and her legs trembled and ached. Supporting her under her right elbow, Gytha shook her head.

"Believe me, my lady, a little mystery is just what you need," she said. "Think of the ladies of Outremer, with their veiled faces. Think of the womenfolk of the infidel, hidden behind the latticed shutters of their harems, courted by pining musicians and poets who fall in love with their very shadows." Gytha had also listened to Guillelm's tales.

Alyson was too breathless to answer.

Later, in the bath, she asked, "Has my lord seen me?"

Osmoda, more simple than Gytha, said, "What do you mean?" but Gytha understood. "He has seen and he knows all, my lady," she answered firmly. "I told him."

"Gytha!"

"It needed to be said," her nurse responded, folding her arms across her broad bosom and tapping her foot. "He saw the marks! Would you have Guillelm think it was *your* father who had treated you so?"

Alyson cowered in the tub. "Does he think me ugly?" she whispered, dreading the answer.

"No," said Osmoda, too quickly.

"We should wash your hair. There is still blood on it," said Gytha.

"Gytha?"

Her nurse lifted a kitchen ladle and gestured for Alyson to bow her head. Alyson sighed as the warm water streamed over her hair and bounced on her shoulder. The water made the wound itch less and for that she was glad, but not for Gytha's stubborn silence. "Gytha, please."

"I swore to my lord that I would not tell you, but if you knew what he was doing for you, you would put such foolish ideas out of your mind." Gytha poured another ladleful of water over Alyson's back. "Wait and see, my lady," she said, relenting a little. "Have faith."

Chapter 18

Word had gone out: Lord Guillelm de La Rochelle was host-ing jousts at Hardspen. The peddlers arrived before the knights—such travelers always seemed to catch the news first—and when they had pitched their tents and stalls within the bailey and laid out their wares, Guillelm sought out Alyson on her roof garden.

He found her clipping the lavender and frowned. She clicked her fingers at him. "I am strong enough to do this, my lord. You need not scowl."

Guillelm snorted and threaded his thumbs through his belt, wanting to kiss her and more. She was not quite her nimble self and her face still had a pale, gaunt cast, but she was healing.

He took the pouch from his belt and swung it before her puz-zled eyes. "You need to keep your strength so that you can carry this," he said, dropping the pouch into her free hand.

"This is heavy, dragon."

"As is any bag of gold. Are you going to put that knife down and come with me?"

Her eyes sparkled. "To where? Why do I need a bag of gold?"

He grinned. "To visit the traders." Guillelm rippled his fin-gers at her. "Shall we go shopping, sweetheart?"

She smiled, tilting her head to one side in that endearing way that always made his stomach flutter and his heart race. "Will one bag of gold be sufficient?" she teased.

"It had better be, wench."

Walking steadily so as not to overtire her, Guillelm wandered about the bailey with Alyson. The traders had indeed come, and more of them than he had hoped: lithe, brightly clad folk with marvelous goods and news. Barter for local wool, leather and beer for flint, cooking pots and salt was in full swing. Children darted amongst the crowds of cottars and villagers, hawking beads and linen ribbons.

Arm in arm, like any other young couple, Guillelm and Alyson strolled about. Clutching the bag of gold made her fingers ache after a while and so Guillelm took it back, joking that now he had the purse strings again. Alyson meanwhile took a lively interest in everything, pausing to admire the goods spread over the grass. She stood for a time watching the sun on new cups and basins—so long that Guillelm was taken from her side by some matter of land rights.

Alyson walked on, shaking her head at a woman who offered her armloads of furs. She passed Sericus, head down in the thick of haggling for pepper, then quickened her step, drawn by a mass of people round one trader.

Even at the rear of the crowd she could see over most heads if she stood on tiptoe. The trader, recognizing the small, dark beauty as the lady of the castle, pointed with a slim hand. "Lady, if you will, I shall show you gems worthy of your breeding. For you, there is nothing more fitting than garnets." He spread a necklace like a magic mist over his fingers and showed a brooch in the palm of his hand.

Alyson moved in slowly through the crowd. Though she had longed to find a bookstall—where perhaps she would discover a manuscript that would please her sister—Guillelm would have this brooch; the dark fire of the gemstones matched his eyes.

The necklace of red stones was given to her to touch, the trader holding a pair of looped earrings beside her hair. Too late, as he placed the jewelry on her open palm, Alyson jerked back her hand. The garnets dropped on the ground between them.

"Forgive me, I cannot take them," she said, dry mouthed. She was too ashamed to admit that although she was lady of Hardspen, she had no means to reward the trader.

Alyson swung round and moved back into the crowd, almost trampling Edwin the shepherd in her haste. She begged his pardon and would have gone, but the man called her back.

"I owe you for helping me," he said, dark eyes sharp, and with no further words to her, Edwin began bargaining. He got both brooch and necklace for a lamb, shrugging off Alyson's thanks. "Give them to the lady," he told the trader and turned his back on the affair.

Warily, the trader dropped the pieces into her hands. The crowd applauded, and Alyson felt a change amongst those watching. She looked up into Guillelm's face and smiled, and he held out his hand to her.

"I have something to show you that will match those jewels," he said. "In that large tent close to where the juggler is performing." His eyes crinkled in private amusement. "Come."

The striped tent was owned by a clothier and his wife and, clearly against Alyson's arrival, they had set out several gowns on their long polished trestle table for her to consider.

"Take any or all," Guillelm instructed in a low voice. "Do not worry about payment."

Alyson ran a finger over the fur collar of a winter gown. "These are my size," she murmured, and looked closely at her husband, paring his fingernails with a knife. "I have missed my perse-colored gown these past few days," she remarked.

He shrugged. "After your . . . skirmish with the archer, that dress was nothing but rags. I took it away."

"To give to these good people as a template?" Alyson asked softly. She tugged on Guillelm's sleeve, made him duck his head as she hissed into his ear, "Have you had these poor folk laboring with their needles all night?"

"Hardly!" Guillelm answered at once. "They have been here two days and, if you must know, I gave them your gown when they arrived." He bent his lips to her ear. "If the clothier's wife looks a trifle red about the eyes, it may be because last night she and her man were drinking in the great hall till the early hours. You heard nothing of that feast because you were already snoring when I carried you to our chamber."

"You cannot silence me by embarrassment, my lord."

"No, but I can make you blush," said Guillelm, releasing her with a gentle tweak of her sleeve. "What do you think of the scarlet dress? Or that one in white and gold? Or the green and yellow?"

Alyson had never bought clothes before—nor did she now, she thought wryly, for Guillelm insisted on paying for a whole trunkload of gowns, undershifts, veils, ribbons and cloaks. When she laughingly protested at the cost, Guillelm countered, "How can you grant me favors at the forthcoming jousts and wrestling matches, if you have no fresh combs? How can you meet your friend Petronilla, or Lady Edith, if you have no new gowns? How is your shoulder?" he added slyly.

She burst out laughing. "You ask me how I am, after such bounty? A joust here? Dragon, you give me so much." In truth, the idea of a joust alarmed her, though she knew it to be a true manly sport, but to know that Guillelm had taken the trouble to find her oldest friends, to invite them here to Hardspen, when Lord Robert had driven Edith's messengers away—

Suddenly she was weeping into her hands, overwhelmed. "Forgive me," she managed to whisper from her closing throat and then she was conscious of being bundled, gently but firmly, out of the tent. Although the day was warm, Guillelm swept his cloak around both of them, shielding her from curious faces.

"Now what is it, sweet?" he asked, scooping a tendril of hair away from her eyes.

"Nothing! But to see my friends again, after so many seasons . . . and a joust here . . . Men die in such things." Alyson gulped, aware she was making little sense. She wanted to beg him to take care but was afraid he might be offended, think her interfering. She took another deep breath and tried again. "My shoulder is healing well, thank you, my lord."

"So, we are full of the Eastern courtesies I told you of, are we? I think I prefer a more English informality." Guillelm wrapped the ends of his cloak more tightly about her narrow shoulders, pulling her closer. "Like this."

"People will see!" Alyson exclaimed, at once scandalized and delighted.

"Indeed," Guillelm said gruffly, ashamed as he misinterpreted her moment of freezing delight as fear. Their meeting, which had begun so excellently, seemed to be going from bad to worse. "Please forgive my action. It was foolish."

Although he was a head taller than her and broader, Alyson felt herself relax. Lord Robert would never have admitted anything he did or said was foolish. She touched his arm, brushing a rose petal, fallen from their roof garden, off his shoulder. Against the backdrop of the keep, his starkly handsome face and bright hair lent him an unworldly air, like a fallen angel.

"There is nothing to forgive," she said softly.

He bowed his head toward her and they stood together in quiet, Alyson aware of his light, slow breathing, Guillelm lost in the moment entirely. Out of the shadows, from an unseen booth, drifted the mellow, haunting sound of a rebec: someone playing a lament. People strolling about the bailey paused to listen, their figures as insubstantial to Alyson's dazzled senses as the smoke from a distant fire.

"Are you real?" Guillelm murmured. "Is this a dream?" The sound of the rebec wound about them as he lifted her hand and kissed her palm, her fingertips. He ran his thumb lightly down her arm. "You are so pretty."

"No—"

"Yes, you are." He drew her back into his arms. Alyson leaned against his shoulder. When she threaded her arm around him, he sighed.

"Do you know the tune being played?" he asked. "It sounds very old, very beautiful."

"Sorry, no."

"Do not be, sweet. There is no need to know." He rocked her lightly, in time to the slow rise and fall of the music. "Only remember."

His eyes held hers. "Alyson?"

She smiled, knowing why he had stopped, why he was so suddenly tense. It really was her move. "All is well," she said, and she took his face gently between her hands and kissed him on his mouth.

Guillelm spent the rest of the day in a happy fog, though he could have strangled the page who had interrupted his deepening embrace with Alyson to say that the first of the knights had arrived. It was no one he knew, a younger son of one of the local landowners, keen to better his fortune through keeping the horse and weapons of those knights he vanquished. There would be many younger sons arriving, Guillelm thought, and knights weary of fighting for King Stephen or the empress and looking for easier spoils. He had warned his men to look out for any troublemakers—he wanted no battles to erupt at Hardspen between the factions of Stephen or Maud.

Soon after he had greeted the gangly, young knight who had ridden in on an old chestnut horse, a wagon of women-folk arrived, escorted by stripling archers and a dozen sturdy, experienced retainers. Alyson, who had stood patiently beside him while the acne-scarred knight had nervously recited the names of his kindred and promised his obedience to the lord and lady of Hardspen, gasped and drew back.

"Petronilla," she moaned, as if in despair, rather than glad-ness. "How very elegant she is!"

Guillelm saw a pale, moon-faced woman with sparse blonde hair leaning from the front of the wagon, waving. To him, her white features and dress were as insipid as milk, but Alyson was flicking hopelessly at her own gown as if it was spattered with dust.

"I have no time to change," she was saying.

Guillelm turned his laughter into a cough and shook his head. "I will bring your Petronilla and her ladies to your par-adise—after you have changed."

Alyson laced herself swiftly into her new scarlet gown—she knew red was Guillelm's favorite color—and ran up the long spirals to the roof garden. She had scarcely recovered her breath when Guillelm appeared, escorting Petronilla.

"My dear creature, how brown you are!" Petronilla ex-claimed the instant Guillelm disappeared downstairs. "You are almost as dark-skinned as your lord, who is as tanned as one of my father's peasants."

Two light kisses landed somewhere in midair close to Alyson's ears as Petronilla swept about the garden, leaving a trail of snapped-off flower heads where the long sleeves of her gown had caught against the sides of the tubs and a sweet, rather sickly scent of violets. Gaping at her friend, whom she had not seen for two years, Alyson realized she had forgotten how talkative Petronilla was.

"Not that Lord Guillelm is anything like a peasant," Petronilla went on, dropping her pet squirrel onto Alyson's couch and frowning at the simple wooden cups that had been left on the low table. "I suppose that his blond looks are quite handsome, if you like the brooding sort. It is a shame he is so big. No large man is ever graceful and his bones will pain him and grow crooked before he is much older."

"Not if I can help it, Pet," Alyson answered mildly.

"Do not call me that name! So childish." Petronilla stepped back from the battlements with a shudder. "I told my women to be careful with that, and now it is quite spoilt," she remarked coolly, referring to some calamity Alyson had not seen. "Edith would say he is almost a fashionable knight, your Guillelm: his color is right but not his size—much too lumbering! Edith sends her apologies, by the by. She cannot come because of a stomach chill."

"I am sorry for that," Alyson replied, her mood sinking further. She had forgotten how Edith's easygoing charm had smoothed relations between them all. Without Edith she was finding Petronilla a trial. "How are you, Petronilla?"

"I have a mark on my hand that I hope you will take a look at."

"Of course."

"And the skin around my elbows looks dry."

"I have a salve that may help you there. Shall we go down to my potions room?"

Petronilla beamed. "You can meet my maids, too, and see my wagon. Father had it made for me specially, with extra cushions; you know how easily I bruise! More than Edith, although she is a redhead. No dashing bachelor will look at her

now she is three-and-twenty; she will have to settle for a
widower, or a man like your Guillelm."

"Then Edith will consider herself fortunate," Alyson
replied, considering this brittle-tongued, wispy woman and
recalling the chattering, golden child she had been, beloved
and protected by everyone. Petronilla had always been so glad
to try her salves, too.

That interest between them at least remained, Alyson
thought, leading the way as Petronilla seized the leather lead
of her squirrel and dragged the squirming creature off the
bed. "How are your parents?" Alyson asked above the squirrel's squeals of fear and indignation.

"Father is looking for a good marriage for me. He has been
approached by several knights, but none have really caught
my eye and he knows that. Mother says that with my beauty
and wealth I can take my time. We heard about the attack on
St. Foy's, by the by. Someone told me that your sister is staying here. Are you not afraid that your bear of a husband will
alarm her? She was always mistrustful of men."

"My sister is a deeply religious person. She spends her day
in the chapel, in prayer and contemplation," Alyson answered
doggedly, depressed that Petronilla had learned about Sister
Ursula so quickly. "The nuns are devastated about the loss
of their home. Guillelm tells me that the prioress is shocked
beyond measure that their convent should have been attacked.
She and the nuns rarely venture from the chapel."

"Even so, Matilda is your sister—"

"With her sisters in Christ in such a wretched state, Tilda
cannot leave them." Alyson took a deep breath. "Forgive me,
Petronilla, my sister is of course Sister Ursula now. She has a
different name and a different life."

Alyson felt Petronilla's hand drop onto her injured shoulder
and bit her lip hard to stop herself from crying out. She turned
on the narrow staircase, trying not to flinch or show her distaste

as she stared straight into the young woman's delicate face and
hard, narrow eyes, glinting with curiosity.

"Do you not miss her?"

Alyson nodded, hoping that would be enough. She heard
Petronilla take in another breath and braced herself for more
painful questions.

"I see you have not grown as much as a finger-width, by
the by," Petronilla exulted, touching the crown of her head
as if in comparison, her fingers idly checking that her jeweled
fillet was perfectly arranged on her yellow curls. "You are
quite as small as a cottar's child."

"I know I do not match the fashionable forms of beauty,
any more than does my lord," Alyson replied, in what she
prayed was a good-humored way. She turned and resumed her
downward climb, quickening her pace so that she and Petronilla soon would be joining others.

"Perhaps you could cover your hair," Petronilla trilled happily, tripping on the steps behind Alyson, her breath hot on
Alyson's aching shoulder. "And never wear a drop-waisted
gown or belt; that would draw attention to your short legs.
Hush!" This said to the squirrel, scrabbling on the leash by
her feet.

"What do you call the creature?" Alyson asked.

"Mother said it had a name; she gave it to me as a contrast
to my coloring. Perhaps you should have a pet."

"I do not know if my lord would allow that," Alyson replied
in mock-seriousness, breathing a sigh of relief as she stepped
out of the keep and Petronilla was surrounded by her ladies-
in-waiting.

Alyson found supper in the great hall that evening a trial,
after a long afternoon spent with Petronilla and her maids
happily burrowing through her stores of potions and salves,

trying at will what they fancied. It was the first time she had dined in public since her injury and she had hoped to be seated by Guillelm, but he, Fulk and Sir Tom were absent, still at the tourney ground seeing to last-minute preparations for the jousting that would begin on the morrow.

Sitting in Guillelm's place, Alyson knew she should be the gracious hostess. There were a score or more of young knights and their squires, all strangers to Hardspen, who had arrived throughout the day, lured by the promises of winning renown and rich prizes. Seated among Guillelm's veterans, the new men nervously picked at their trenchers or were drinking deeply, with a grinning bravado.

Aware of Petronilla on her left, scarcely touching her meat, Alyson was increasingly mortified as the meal progressed. Hardspen had no resident minstrels, for Lord Robert had disliked music and neither she nor Guillelm had yet had the time to appoint any players. They were "entertained" by several traveling musicians who had arrived for the jousts and who, despite Alyson's and Sericus's best efforts, frequently beat their drums or blew their whistles in opposition to each other.

"At least there are no jugglers," Petronilla remarked when Alyson felt compelled to apologize.

"We could hold a court of love," Alyson suggested, blushing deeply as she spoke. "My lord told me that in southern France and also in Outremer, the ladies of the courts there encourage the young knights to speak of ideal love, to make music and compose poetry in honor of their chosen beloved."

"What else did he say?" Petronilla asked, sitting up and becoming more animated than she had been for the past hour.

"I forget," Alyson answered. She would not admit to Petronilla that only yesterday evening, dozing in the great bedchamber after her bath, Guillelm had sent her a single white rose by way of a smirking Gytha and the carefully written note: *To my bright-eyed wife, whom I miss and who misses nothing.*

"What do you think?" Alyson went on, rousing herself from her pleasant reverie. "If I instruct the servants to move back the trestles, arrange the benches around the fire space, I think your maids would be interested," Alyson added, seeing one of Petronilla's ladies-in-waiting valiantly trying to stifle a yawn.

"I am sure they would be." Petronilla drummed her fingers sharply on the high table. "Yet I think we both know that only one woman here is the ideal of beauty."

"Yes, I am beginning to understand that," said Alyson, wishing Guillelm was with her to catch eyes with, share the moment.

Or would he? As the long night continued, Alyson heard a dozen or more chants—she could not, even at her most charitable, call them songs—to high, cruel beauties, with golden locks, green eyes, skin as white as ivory, bodies as tall and shapely as that of the Roman goddess Venus, all dressed in silver and white with bracelets and fillets of gold. Petronilla, in a pale primrose-colored gown and white veil, took the young knights' fumbled "prayers" to their ideal lady as no more than her due, turning her own gold bracelets on her wrists. Her maids, trim and pretty in gowns of light green, whispered behind their hands to each other and pointed at one slim young warrior or another. Feeling both ignored and conspicuous with her blood-red gown and black river of hair, Alyson sat small on Guillelm's great chair, only waiting for the "love court" to be done as she watched the smiling Petronilla and wondered afresh about the courted, desired and unattainable Heloise.

Chapter 19

The next time Alyson saw Guillelm was the following morning at the first joust. Sir Tom came to escort her to the tilting ground and was remarkably closemouthed about what was planned.

"You will see soon enough, Alyson," he said, tapping the side of his mangled nose. "Guido says he wants it to be a surprise—a pleasant surprise."

"Men trying to batter each other to the ground?"

Sir Tom gave an amused cough. "Aye, well, Guido did say your views on tournaments were unusual. I suppose with your being a healer . . ." He smiled at her and offered her his arm. "I think this first event is more of a pageant, a kind of acted story, as is seen with the mystery plays." Through the mesh of facial scars his eyes were wary yet bright. "It is your lord's own idea. Some of the ladies may be taking part, to bestow favors and prizes."

Petronilla would enjoy that attention, Alyson thought. She turned back, looking the way she and Sir Tom had come. They were walking steadily to an area on the downs enclosed by a long series of ropes draped at regular intervals with Guillelm's own standard and circled by onlookers and hawkers.

On the most sheltered side of the down, out of the gusting breeze, a stand had been erected, with benches and chairs. Beneath the bright awning and canopy, she spotted Petronilla and her ladies, seated with goblets of mead, beckoning first to one hovering page and then another.

"The distribution of favors seems to be in full swing," Alyson remarked. "Have they been here long?"

"No, but my lord wished you to appear last; he wants to bring you to the high seat himself, as a mark of honor." Sir Tom scratched at the long scar zigzagging through his black beard. "I suppose you have a favor for him?"

"I have." A certain wistfulness to his question made Alyson add, "One for you, too, Sir Tom, if you will wear it."

She expected thanks, or shy pleasure, or even polite acceptance. Instead, her strapping escort said quietly, "No thank you, my lady," without quite looking at her.

"As you wish." Hurt by his refusal, Alyson glanced about rapidly for something to remark upon, to heal this sudden rift between them. "There are no horses."

"No, my lord instructed that the knights should fight on foot. He wants no mounted battles ranging from village to village. He says the country is wrecked enough already, from the king's and empress's skirmishes. Here he is," Sir Tom added, in obvious relief.

Alyson's spirits leapt at the sight of the tall, sinewy figure striding away from the shadow of the stand toward her. Dressed in plain battle armor, carrying his helmet in one fist and with the fingers of his other hand drumming against his sword belt, Guillelm was grimly solemn.

His mouth in that line is like his father's, Alyson thought. Despite her bold intentions, she quailed a little as she stepped ahead of Sir Tom.

"How now, my lord?" She sucked in her stomach and flicked her hands along the waist and flanks of her gown, making the skirt billow in a shimmering red tide. Heartened by Guillelm's dark eyes ranging over her, she was poised to offer him her own, deliberately original favor—very different from the scraps of cloth, trinkets or gloves usually given, hers was a letter on parchment, steeped in lavender, wishing him good fortune in the jousts.

Then she saw them. A finger ring on a cord, tied onto the shoulder of his mail. A ribbon, threaded round his belt. Another ribbon, pinned to his cloak.

Alyson closed her fingers round the parchment till it crackled. She wanted to rip these other favors off him, demand he wore none but hers. *Do not say anything,* she thought, but she snapped her fingers and heard her treacherous tongue saying, "That ring will surely cut your face, dangling on that cord."

Guillelm turned his arm this way and that. "It may." He answered as if indifferent to her concern, and he did not say who had given him the ring.

"Why accept it, then?" Alyson persisted, aware of Sir Tom frowning, knowing she was probably making too much of the matter.

"A knight is very discourteous if he does not take what is offered to him, especially if it is from a lady," Guillelm answered, still reasonable.

But this issue of accepting favors is more than being polite—what of my feelings? Alyson tried to think of a prayer to stop her temper. But she could do better than blind anger. Focusing her hurt, she unclipped a key from her belt.

"Here is my favor, sir, the key to the great bedchamber."

Guillelm's eyes narrowed. "I need no key—but I will take it, and that other offering in your hand."

"It is mine to give, or not."

Guillelm hooked his thumbs into his sword belt. "Before God, you are still a thoroughly provoking wench. Why can you not hand it across? You know you wanted to only a moment ago."

Was this in jest or earnest? Reminding herself he was not Lord Robert, Alyson wet her lips with her tongue and plunged on. "I, too, know how to tilt and joust, my lord."

"Indeed you do." Ignoring Sir Tom's muffled exclamation, Guillelm dropped to his knees before her and removed a long, slim knife from his belt.

"This blade I took from Hasim of the black rock fortress. I would that you receive it into your care, my lady, as my favor to you."

His face was open, young-looking, his dark eyes without guile. He meant it as an honor, Alyson realized, as a sign that she was his equal. Hoping her eyes would not blur with foolish tears, she clasped the smooth handle of the knife.

Guillelm lifted his hand again, palm upward. "I have a splinter—"

Alyson touched the dark needle of wood embedded in the broad base of his thumb. "So I must be like Saint Jerome with the lion and remove this man-made thorn from your paw, yes, dragon?" As she spoke, Alyson noted the bruising round the base of his thumb and the reddening of the skin close to the splinter. It would hurt, but she knew to say nothing as she began to cut out the wood, her fingers deft but slow, to reach all of it.

"Sir Tom, will you find me a cup of wine?" she asked.

"Mother of God, I need no numbing draught," Guillelm protested, holding his hand steady as a rock as she pricked and eased the gleaming tip of the Arab blade under the core of the splinter.

"It is to cleanse the wound," Alyson replied, flicking the shard of wood off the knife. "There! I have it out. Thank you, Sir Tom." She poured the cup of wine over the gash, which though shallow scarcely bled. "'Tis done."

Aware of Guillelm's closeness, his living warmth and scent, the strange intimacy that drawing out a mere splinter had evoked between them, she kissed his hand and raised her eyes to his. "I would suck the wound if I suspected poison. Should I do so?"

"A tempting offer." Still kneeling, he leaned forward and kissed her healing shoulder. "I fear I must decline, bright-eyes. I would not have you endanger yourself any more, especially for the sake of a splinter off the chapel door."

He was smiling, but mention of the chapel reminded Alyson of the nuns. Priests she knew disapproved of the violence of tournaments and jousts; she could well imagine her sister's icy comments on what was happening at Hardspen.

Guillelm's words confirmed her fears. "I tried to speak with your sister but she would have none of me. The prioress did not even allow me to cross the threshold of my own chapel."

"If that door had been a man's throat, it would have been crushed," said Sir Tom under his breath, and Guillelm agreed. "I admit my temper was not of the best, especially since your sister—"

He broke off, but Alyson finished the rest in her mind. Her sister had not asked after her, had shown no interest. Suppressing a sigh, she asked, "Are my sister and her companions well?"

"They sing heartily enough," answered Guillelm sourly, "so I think it is safe to assume that they are in excellent health." He gave a low whistle. "Truly, the scarlet suits you, Alyson. You are as perky as a bird."

Perky, Guillelm thought, groaning inwardly in despair the instant the words escaped from between his teeth. *Can I do no better than that?*

Perky. She had never been called that before. Alyson smiled and removed the crumpled parchment favor from her pocket. "For you, my lord."

"Will you tie it on for me?" Guillelm tapped the middle of his chest. "Here?"

Silently, Alyson untied one of her blue hair ribbons and knotted it about the parchment. As she fastened the whole to

Guillelm's mail she felt his breath on her forehead and sensed the rigidity of his hands, stock-still against his sides.

"What is that scent?" he asked. "Lavender?"

"It is." Alyson patted the parchment and raised her head, almost starting when she realized how close Guillelm's lips were to hers. "Is there anything else, my lord?"

Guillelm patted the parchment in turn, giving a grunt she hoped was one of approval. "In Outremer, as you know, the rose is for healing and for love," he murmured. "What of lavender, here? I think it may be the same." His voice grew softer still. "I hope it is."

Sir Tom cleared his throat. "Guido, the joust. Everyone awaits your presence."

"They will wait a little longer." Guillelm traced a finger lightly across Alyson's bottom lip, the small caress deepening the gleam in his eyes. "Why no red ribbon for me, sweet?"

"Blue is the color of the blessed Virgin Mary, the color of protection," Alyson said quickly, her mouth aching and tingling from Guillelm's touch. She did not want to admit her wary superstition of red and blood, did not want to confess her feeling of ill luck about his wearing her favor almost as a target right above his heart. "Should we not make haste?"

"For certain we must." Absently straightening a crease on his parchment favor, Guillelm climbed to his feet and offered Alyson his hand.

With Sir Tom limping a step or so behind, they made their way to the jousting ground, Guillelm lifting the rope enclosing the area so that Alyson need not duck. From the stand she caught the glitter of gold as Petronilla turned her head, switching her attention from the milling squires to the lord and lady of Hardspen. Today, Petronilla and her ladies were clothed in white and gold, their long veils edged with golden thread.

Alyson sensed Petronilla's probing eyes assessing her red gown and quickly suppressed an impulse to brandish her new dagger; Petronilla would consider such a token unfeminine. Besides, Guillelm was now addressing the spectators in the stand, the traders, servants and villagers sitting three to four lines deep around the roped-off ground, and the knights clustered within it, checking their weapons.

"Fellow knights, ladies, gentlemen and women of the road, villagers and woodmen of the downs, I, Guillelm de La Rochelle bid you welcome to these jousts on behalf of myself and my lady Alyson. I hope you enjoy this day. May God and all his saints keep you and your champions safe. May they capture many prizes, with courage and skill."

There was a brief patter of applause, swiftly dying away as Guillelm stalked across the flat open ground toward the middle of the jousting area. Feeling his hand gripping as tightly as a snare about hers, rushing and almost missing her footing to keep pace, Alyson found herself too breathless to protest at his speed and too preoccupied with avoiding the cattle and sheep dung and the various stacks of weapons gathered at several points throughout this roped-off space to ask why a tent had been erected in its center.

The tent was circular, with a roof of blue and red stripes. Its cloth walls were tied back to its framework and its awnings were raised to show off a gorgeous interior: lamps and couches of gold, chests with their lids thrown open to display the plate and coins within, a table covered with swords and daggers, another table stacked with papers.

Astonished that such treasures should be displayed inside a jousting ground, Alyson realized that Guillelm had been less reckless than first appeared. The tent was set upon a raised platform of earth, as tall as herself, and surrounded by a wall of armed men, standing shoulder to shoulder with interlocking shields.

Guillelm marched to a seven-man gap in the shield wall, where a series of roughly cut earth steps led up into the heart of the mound. His standard was draped across the bottom of the steps and another flag fluttered on a pole at the top of the earth staircase.

Guillelm stood with his back to the steps and raised his free hand for silence. "Today there is much bounty to be won," he went on. "Prizes of combat, the arms and horse of the vanquished—that goes to general custom. Also there are other prizes." He pointed to the striped tent on the man-made defensive rampart. "Do you see the pavilion above me? It is the tent of Hasim of Outremer, won by me as a spoil of war. Within it are chests of treasure, grants of land, weapons from the finest smiths in the East. These are the prizes to be bestowed upon those she favors by my wife, the lady Alyson. It is she whom you knights must impress with your daring and more especially your honor: the manner of your victory and your mercy to those whom you vanquish."

As more applause and a hum of excited talk broke out from the spectators, Alyson stared at her husband. The gifts he had spoken of were generous, largesse on the scale of a king. "These are truly mine to give?" she asked softly, her voice cutting through the excited yelling and stamping of feet. She heard her name being bellowed around the jousting ground like a lucky charm and gave one of her hair plaits a nervous tug.

"Grants of land?" she queried. Land was more valuable than gold. Land provided the means of growing food, of shelter, of life, and Guillelm was awarding lands in her name. The man whom she chose would swear fealty to her.

"None of the fields or woods are from your Olverton estate, my sweet," Guillelm replied quickly. "I would not give to others by taking from you."

"No, no, dragon, you misunderstand. What I meant—" Alyson tried to explain but her sense of gratitude and sheer surprise made her tongue and wits sluggish. "You are most generous," she began, stopping altogether when Guillelm grinned and suddenly hoisted her into his arms.

"Look well on your excellent lady, knights!" he shouted. "Today she is your queen!"

Alyson's protest was lost in the roar of approval from the crowd. Torn between indignation at being displayed like a banner and a curiously satisfactory kind of vanity—people were staring at her, not Petronilla—she again attempted to thank Guillelm, but he now added the final, unbelievable instruction.

"Knights! To obtain the favor of my lady then you must fight me, here on this ground, by this stair. Any who succeed in passing me and climbing up to the pavilion shall be said to have won. Do not dare to touch her, not even so much as a fingertip, but come at me however you wish! One at a time, in pairs or in a score of flashing shields, swords and maces! I will take you on in whatever numbers you like! I too fight for the lady Alyson and for her I will struggle against all the world!"

Alyson gasped as she was lifted higher.

"I am the dragon and she is my prize!"

"No!" cried Alyson, appalled at these new revelations. "It cannot be! I am a healer, I will never consent to such folly—"

She spoke to the air. Guillelm had already set her down and stepped back, taking guard against the steps. She whirled after him. "My lord, this is madness."

Guillelm smiled. "Peace, Alyson. Our swords have not been sharpened and I will check my blows."

"Even with blunted weapons it is dangerous. Please, my lord, stop this now!"

About to add, *For my sake,* Alyson saw the bright, possessive pride in Guillelm's dark eyes and wished she was with her sister in the chapel of Hardspen, anywhere but at this jousting ground.

"Do you know what Hasim used this pavilion for in his fortress in Outremer?" Guillelm asked, as if she had not spoken.

Discouraged, Alyson shook her head. How could she make Guillelm understand? *I am not a toy,* she thought, but he was too full of his own answers to heed her.

"The tent was set up in his pleasure gardens, within the harem." Guillelm paused, a fleeting expression of wonder and sadness playing across his stark features. "I remember there were bowls of flashing mercury within the tent, and couches garlanded with the flowers of the orient, and carpets. Such carpets, Alyson! Thick, lush coverings of blue and red and gold, spread upon the ground itself.

"Perhaps we can use the tent in a similar way here, after the jousts," he went on. "Make it our own secret place."

The idea was appealing, Alyson conceded, but then doubt took over. Had Heloise possessed such a pavilion? Had she entertained Guillelm on a couch strewn with roses and mint?

Fighting that image, Alyson found herself remarking tartly, "And what of the women, my lord? The women of the harem who used this tent?"

Guillelm sighed. "Yes, you are right to remind me. Hasim's women screamed when they saw me but truly they need not have feared. Neither I nor my men touched them. Their families ransomed them and saw them safe."

Hasim's women. And she was Guillelm's woman—as he himself had said it, his prize. The thought thrilled and depressed her afresh.

Seeking a diversion, Alyson realized with some relief that Fulk and Sir Tom were tramping across the jousting ground to join them.

"I believe Fulk would speak with you, my lord," she began, but it was Sir Tom who called out, "Good speech, Guido! Now allow me to escort your lady to the stand—though I see few takers for your challenge."

It was true, Alyson realized. The young knights clustered about the jousting ground seemed in no hurry to arm themselves. In twos and threes, ignoring the increasing boos and jeers of the crowd, they whispered together like gossiping tailors, apparently reluctant to move.

"Perhaps the knights are not inspired to take up arms for such a cause," Fulk put in, with a quelling glance at Alyson, adding now that he was level with her, "None wear the Hardspen favor."

Fulk had his back to Guillelm, who did not hear his seneschal's latest sly dig, but Sir Tom blinked and roughly caught the man's arm, dragging him to one side while he hissed something urgently into the leaner man's ear. Whatever passed between them Alyson did not catch but she was glad—Fulk's glower when he returned to her side was a joy to behold.

"How now, sir?" she asked sweetly, wishing for an instant that she was a man, to fight Fulk openly. Or to fight Guillelm. That battle would be short, she thought, gauging the length and strength of his bronzed shoulders and arms. She shivered, whether with fear or desire she could not say.

Marking her trembling, Sir Tom coughed. "I will fight, Guido."

"No!" Alyson stepped between the two men. "No, this has gone far enough."

"It has not even begun yet, woman," grunted Guillelm, staring down at her with that infuriatingly superior "leave this to us men" look. "Though for the sake of your tender nerves, Tom and I will be as mild as fresh milk to one another." He glanced over her head. "Still, it must begin soon, before the crowd begin to throw benches onto the ground, instead of stones."

It was true, Alyson realized. Spectators were tossing pebbles at the squires and a few were already sizing up the lingering knights. "Why can we not have a play here, like the mystery pageants?" she burst out. "Everyone who wished then could take part."

"Not just the knights, you mean?" Fulk was on to her meaning at once but he gave it a darker twist. "Would you perhaps prefer, madam, that Lord Guillelm is the prize-giver here and you the fighter, with that new shiny dagger?"

"And my lord tied to a post or chained to a rock, like Andromeda in the legend, and me the dragon, fighting off those who come to claim him?" Alyson demanded, nettled by Fulk's wheedling. "I think not!"

"You know, there is some virtue in that idea," Guillelm remarked, drumming his fingers thoughtfully on his belt. In a single swift action, fluid as the merlin when she stooped, he thrust his broadsword into the parched earth at his feet, burying more than a third of its blade, and came at her again.

"Do not!" Alyson warned, clicking her fingers angrily at him, but before she could swerve or try to thrust him aside—which she knew, maddeningly, was frankly impossible for her—she was aloft, and heading for the pavilion. She pounded her fist against his shoulder, forgetting for an instant he wore mail and yelping as her hand scraped on the small metal rings. "Guillelm, put me down!"

"In good time."

She was pressed so tightly in his embrace that she felt his slow heartbeat, the thick band of muscle beneath his ribs. Sucking in air to protest anew, she sneezed as strands of his thick blond hair blew across her eyes and nose as he lowered his head.

"Does your shoulder pain you?" he asked gently, serious after his earlier teasing. "Do you truly wish to withdraw, my Andromeda? I swear I will not chain you anywhere, but to defend you against all." He lowered her onto the second step.

"I would tie her, or she will be intervening in every single fight," Fulk remarked, adding quickly, "I jest, of course." He turned away, stepping back to yell insults at the lagging knights.

Guillelm watched him leave through narrowed eyes.

"Damn the man," he muttered. "He had sense and grace enough in Outremer. Has English ale addled his wits?"

"Forget Fulk," Sir Tom said quickly. "But if Alyson is staying here, bring her a chair!"

So Alyson found herself a part of the joust, sitting on a high-backed seat at the top of the earth steps, within the shade of the red and blue–striped pavilion. Hailed publicly—by Guillelm himself—as the Andromeda of Hardspen, with Guillelm the lethal dragon of the story, prepared to fight any who tried to reach her, she watched with mounting alarm as four knights, armed with swords and clubs, finally made an attack.

Am I wrong to loathe this? Alyson thought unhappily, gripping the arms of her chair so tightly that her fingers and shoulders ached. She feared for Guillelm and even more for the young knights, two of whom had patches of stubble on their youthful faces instead of full beards and the other pair so weedy they looked like birch saplings in armor. Beside them Guillelm was as big as a troll, with a troll scowl on his face. She could see his expression only in profile, but what she did see sank her spirits further.

To turn away would be an insult to the courage of these warriors; she had to keep a steady countenance and watch. Though she was not in chains like Andromeda, that was her ordeal. *But unlike Andromeda I want the dragon to win . . .*

She prayed to Christ and to the saints, determined not to flinch as the four young men lunged at her husband, their blades grinding against his broadsword. Across from Alyson's lonely vantage point, Petronilla and her ladies chattered and pointed and giggled in the stand, a tumbler practiced back-somersaults at the side of the stand and the other spectators roared on their favorites and yelled for more ale. She saw Guillelm parry one blade after another, his sword arm almost too fast for her to follow, saw him buffet one warrior and knock him flat; drop his weapon, grab two more and hurl them away, dizzy as whipping tops; take up his sword again and slash it across the helm of the remaining challenger, straight at the youth's staring eyes.

The crowd were on their feet, laughing as the four tottered from the field, jeering at their stricken expressions, cheering as another clutch of boy-soldiers sprinted for her place. Charging from the base of the earth steps, Guillelm smashed through the shield of the lead knight as if it were no stronger than the shell of an egg, seized his opponent's mace and tore it from him, using the mace to club the knight's thrashing legs. Alyson heard the crack as mace met bone and she dry heaved. She kept still as the knight fell, clutching his knee.

Amazingly, as if he sensed her concern, Guillelm turned to her. "I checked the blow," he said. "Aside from bruises tomorrow, the lad will be whole."

Before she could answer he swung the mace again, catching another assailant in the stomach. The man doubled over, gasping, and his squire darted onto the field to drag him out of harm's way. Another unarmed squire lunged at Guillelm, hands clawing for one of the favors pinned to his strapping body. Guillelm cursed and swatted the boy away.

And then Alyson saw the new threat emerge from the shadows of the stand, using the futile attacks of the younger knights as cover. No youth this, but a veteran, with strong boots, dull but well-maintained chain mail and his shield arm more muscled than his sword arm. He moved as deftly as a prowling spider and covered the ground between the stand and the earth steps in a series of well-judged sprints, winding in his track so as to keep out of Guillelm's immediate sight.

He is going to reach the stairs, Alyson thought, as Guillelm fought five more knights at once, using the flat of his sword. Inexplicably she felt a chill. The veteran knight was a stranger to her but behind his visor his eyes were hard.

He is coming after me! Alyson remained frozen in her seat, her limbs locked in horror as the older man clubbed down a yawning man-at-arms close to the stairs with the hilt of his sword and leaped through the gap before any of the other soldiers could react. His act was against the rules of the joust, but this quick-moving, agile warrior had forgotten or ignored the idea that the joust was a contest, not war. He was snarling as he slammed his blade home into its sheath, climbing the bank on hands and knees and still invisible to Guillelm, who was boxing the ears of a young knight who had tried to bite him.

"Do that again, lad, and you will have no teeth!" he bellowed, missing Alyson's shout of "Behind you!" altogether. Two knights leaped upon his back and started to throttle him with their maces.

"Stop!" Now Alyson found she could move, but her way to Guillelm was blocked by the older knight, who rose up beside her chair.

"You will cut yourself with that, pretty," he said, and ignoring Guillelm's specific command that no man touch her he ripped her new dagger from her belt.

"No!" She flew out of the seat after it, grappling with the laughing warrior.

"Alyson!" The yell ripped from Guillelm's lungs, echoing round the ground as he shook off the two and launched himself at the stairs. There was a rush of light, cool and shade, and a jolting crash. His shoulder barged into the stranger knight's, snapping the man's shield arm and knocking him down.

He swung his sword and the veteran's sword shattered, fragments of metal hurtling over the ground. Alyson heard the man shriek as Guillelm hauled him away from her, tossing him down the man-made hill.

* * *

Guillelm sank to his knees beside Alyson. Battle-hot and burning, he took her in his arms. "Are you hurt?"

"No." Alyson swallowed, and her pale, narrow head, translucent in the sunlight, found Guillelm's battle-battered features. He flinched against a look of judgment and yet there was none, only a clear, tear-bright gaze. "He was so determined to win."

Bile rose in Guillelm's throat. He swallowed the bitter mouthful, conscious of a throbbing in his arm, of the twittering of the crowd, of the bruised knights groaning. One of his men—Fulk or Sir Tom, probably—had ensured the older knight had been removed from the ground.

"You will not hurt him more?" Alyson shuddered and clung closer. "Please promise me you will not."

"Why? Why should he matter to you?"

"He does not." Alyson smiled bleakly. "But you do." She touched the ragged parchment favor over his heart. "I would not that you have his . . . injury on your conscience."

It would not be on my mind at all, Guillelm thought, too wise to admit that. "Very well," he said. "For you." He would tell Tom to get the fellow out of Hardspen, without horse, without armor, without sword. "I am sorry, sweetheart."

She smiled again, a more genuine smile this time. "For being so reckless in your fighting that you make my heart race fit to burst for worry of you?"

"No, for being too careless of your safety. That was reckless, and wrong."

He ignored the rules, not you, Alyson thought. She reached up and planted a gentle kiss on his cheek.

"I forgive you," she said.

Chapter 20

The joust at Hardspen had lasted three more days. Long days to Alyson, who, since her near-disastrous encounter with the older knight had sat more conventionally with the other ladies in the stand, where Petronilla had regaled her with gossip. How she had ever been this woman's friend was a mystery, but not so much of a mystery as where Guillelm spent his nights. He had told her the merlin was sick and fretted if left alone.

What about me? Alyson had thought, too humiliated to ask her question aloud. Besides, without even being asked, Guillelm had given an answer: "Whenever we come to sunset and the end of the day, you are more than half-asleep. So far I have carried you to our chamber every night and you have snored on my shoulder."

"Why must you sit with the merlin?" she had asked once.

"She feels at ease with me," Guillelm had said, and Alyson had forced herself to be satisfied with that.

Now, sitting with her in their high rooftop garden, Guillelm looked up from whittling a small wooden flute with his knife—he was in the habit of fashioning such toys whenever he had a quiet moment; he said he did not like to be idle. So far, she had a whistle, as did most of the pages in the castle. It was, in Petronilla's words, a new fashion.

Petronilla had left that morning, her wagon creaking under the weight of her luggage. The men entering the jousts were already gone and Sir Tom was talking about leaving, although now he was in the mews, fussing over the merlin. Alyson had considered asking Sir Tom if Guillelm really was in the mews all night but had decided she did not want to know.

"How is your shoulder?" Guillelm blew some sawdust away from the half-finished pipe and threw it down in his lap. "Would you like more salve on it?"

Alyson squirmed slightly in her chair. Her shoulder was itching less than it had done but any contact between Guillelm and herself was to be savored. Or was that desire only on her part? Had he asked simply from courtesy? Sometimes she was certain he loved her and wanted nothing more than to be with her, to touch and kiss and more. Was she right?

As she said nothing, made no move, Guillelm cleared his throat and tapped the key on his belt. "I still have your favors from the joust. Perhaps we should use this one and retire downstairs." He smiled. "We would be more private there, and more comfortable."

"If it please you." *Fool!* Alyson castigated herself. *Smile at him, let him know you welcome this chance to be alone. At least nod your agreement.*

But already she was too late. Sericus and Fulk invaded the roof-garden at a furious pace, Fulk first.

"Lord! You must come! Messengers from King Stephen and the empress are at this moment within your great hall, both demanding urgent speech with you, and their pages are fistfighting on the floor!"

"Mother of God, man!" Guillelm jumped to his feet. "Two boys scrapping and you do not stop it—no one has sense to part them? What is everyone doing in the great hall, lounging about with their thumbs in their mouths?"

"Placing bets and egging each boy on, no doubt," Alyson remarked, also climbing to her feet. "Throw a pail of water on the pair and tell them it is with my compliments; the envoys will accept that a lady is mistress in her own house and take no slight from it. I will tell them the same and say the brawling disturbs the nuns who are staying with us, if need be."

"A double warning, then," Guillelm grunted, irritation giving way to amusement as he stood at the stop of the staircase and bawled down an order involving water, buckets and a good aim, but Fulk was not finished.

"The king's messenger was a knight at this joust only yesterday. He still wears the favor of the lady Petronilla."

A sly jibe from Fulk that no knights except Guillelm had worn hers, Alyson recognized, but she answered calmly, "Then that knight will know that a lady's wishes are always to be followed. Should you not go with your lord?" she added, as Guillelm disappeared down the spiral steps after a single lingering look at her that spoke eloquently of his frustration. She, too, was disappointed and she especially had no wish to go down to meet the envoys and their disheveled pages on the arm of her least favorite seneschal.

Without a farewell, Fulk turned and stalked downstairs, leaving Alyson and the wheezing Sericus. "Take my arm, Sericus, if you will," she said, intending to support him as discreetly as possible down the long treads of stairs. "What is it?" she asked, as the old man made no move except to rub his rheumy eyes and then his lame leg. "Sericus?"

He looked at her then. "The wolf has returned."

Alyson felt as if all the breath had been punched from her lungs, but there was worse.

"A cottar's child is missing, a little girl. Stop, my lady!" Sericus put an arm out to prevent her hurrying after Guillelm.

"I told Fulk and he said both wolf and child must wait until after the lord of Hardspen has seen the messengers of the king and the empress. To do otherwise would be an insult which neither Stephen nor Maud would forgive or forget."

"But a child is gone, Sericus!"

"I know."

"For how long?"

"Two days."

"Two days!"

"The cottar did not dare to interrupt the joust."

Alyson wanted to put her head in her hands and weep, but that would help no one. "Can you gather a hunting party?" she asked. "Beaters for the woods, men or boys who can shoot a bow? The family of the cottar—can they bring any weapons? I will ensure that if they are due to do any work on my lord's fields or in my lord's holdings, then they will not suffer for missing today and joining us."

Sericus mouthed "Us?" in sheer horrified astonishment, but before he could protest, Alyson passed by him.

"I remember well being a little girl. I know I can guess better than any man where a girl-child might run and hide. I know the woods well here," she went on, taking the steps two at a time. "I know the land hereabouts as well as any man. If the cottar can show us where the child went missing we can start from there. Come!"

Guillelm watched the envoys of the king and the empress leave and smiled. There had been some tricky negotiations over the past hour but he had managed to promise nothing too great to either side. He stretched in his chair, cracking his shoulders, and wondered where Alyson had got to. Perhaps she was with the sisters of St. Foy's in the chapel, talking to her own blood-sister.

"I hope so," he said aloud, thinking he must tell her how the bucket of water had worked at once and the whole incident had ended in laughter, even for the hotheaded pages. Stretching again, he realized he was hungry. Was it too soon to nag the cooks?

A shadow moved at the back of the hall, solidifying into a familiar figure. "Thomas!" Guillelm bawled out in sheer good humor. "How is the merlin?" In truth, he hoped the bird was now eating well and regrowing some of its shed feathers; he wanted to spend his nights with Alyson. *If they were at least in the same chamber, that would be a start—*

One clear look at his companion's face had Guillelm out of his chair and striding from the dais. "Thomas? What news?"

Let this not touch upon Alyson, he prayed, but surely that was impossible. His wife was safe and healing, snug on her roof-garden at the very top of the keep. How then could Sir Tom's grim face be connected with her? "Speak!" he commanded, a coil of dread winding tight about his guts.

"The lady Alyson has gone hunting a wolf that made off with a child," Sir Tom said bluntly. "Fulk has just learned that she and a ragtag party of old men and boys have been gone this past hour."

Rushing off to save another without thought for her own recent injury—that was Alyson all over. Guillelm longed to box her ears but even more find her, hold her tight, make her safe.

"Saddle my horse," he said through bloodless lips.

"Already done. Fulk has gathered our best trackers."

Guillelm nodded. "Then we ride," he said.

The child of the cottar had done what Alyson would have done at the same age if chased by a wolf. She had scrambled into the tallest tree she could find and, when Alyson and her party of archers and villagers spotted her, close to the track she had used to gather firewood, she waved and shouted to them gleefully, her tears of fright forgotten.

Soon the wiry eight-year-old was tight in her mother's arms, gabbling tales of her adventure as her mother rocked her on her lap, the pair of them sitting on a fallen tree trunk while the archers prowled through the undergrowth, seeking tracks. The wolf had been scared off by their approach, but the child said it had emerged from the middle of the woodland, where she herself had been forbidden to venture. "I keep to the track at the edge of the wood, as I am told," the child piped, receiving a kiss from her mother as the woman tried to untangle burrs and leaves from her daughter's grubby yellow-brown hair.

The thanks of the cottar to Alyson were heartfelt. "You have given us back our lives, my lady, with this our youngest, our only daughter," he said. "If there is anything we may do for you, please call upon us."

"Any help we can give, it is yours," the wife of the cottar agreed, glancing at Alyson's slim shape.

Guessing what help she meant, Alyson asked, "How many children have you?"

"Five, your lady, and all living, thanks be to God," said the cottar, squeezing his wife's shoulder. Standing beside her, one could see the love between them, warm as the summer's day.

"I will remember your kind offer, Harland, Elfgiva." With a nod to both, Alyson spurred Jezebel forward before these two handsome, sinewy, rose-complexioned and above all loving parents noticed the tears in her eyes. To Harland and Elfgiva, a daughter was not a disappointment, but a treasure.

"My lady!" One of the squires clutched at her saddle. "What must I eat for a headache?"

"Drink less beer!" called back another squire, to general laughter.

Alyson chuckled too and was about to lean down and suggest another "cure" when the squire released her saddle and straightened, like a man on sentry duty. She heard it as well, the galloping of many heavy horses.

"Sericus! Gather everyone about in a circle, archers to the front!" she ordered, shielding the cottar's family with Jezebel's broad flanks. Who was this, breaking through the stands of elders and hazel at so furious a rate? Please, God, not Étienne the Fleming, returning again to wreak more havoc.

She saw Guillelm's fluttering standard and breathed out in relief. A shout of joy broke from her lips as Caliph burst into view through the trees and Guillelm hurtled toward her, ahead of all his men. He was bareheaded and she could see his face.

He was not smiling.

They returned to Hardspen in silence, where Guillelm issued swift orders that the wolf be hunted down by what he called a "proper" party of men and dogs. Lunch was yesterday's bread and soft new cheese: a snack since the cook had not known at what hour any of them would be dining.

"My lady will be spending the afternoon in the solar, at her needlework," Guillelm announced to the astonished company in the great hall—none more surprised than Alyson herself.

Leaving her bread, she leaned across her seat to murmur, "You know there is no solar here at Hardspen."

Guillelm shook his head. "I had your previous bedchamber cleared out while we were eating, and tables and chairs taken in. That will be your solar. It is large enough for you and your maids."

"But I thought—" Alyson stopped, disappointed that she and Guillelm would not be spending time together on the roof-garden. "I have stills and potions to work on," she remarked, shocked when Guillelm took her hand in his and said softly but firmly, "No."

"What are you saying?" Alyson felt a chill of alarm. Farther along the table, Fulk was openly grinning.

"I have decided, wife, that in future you shall be best employed inside this castle. Hardspen is a bare place—" Ignoring the sword and shield of his famous ancestor on one wall, Guillelm swept an arm up to the high rafters as if to illustrate his point. "Other ladies do embroidery and tapestry to add warmth and color to the rooms of their menfolk. I have decided that it will be more fitting if you follow their example."

Do not argue with him before Fulk and his men, Alyson scolded herself. "As you wish, my lord," she agreed, while her stomach coiled itself into knots of rage. "For this afternoon."

"All afternoons."

How had he arrived at this folly? Of course she knew—she could hear Fulk's insinuations in Guillelm's every boorish idea. Alyson put a hand to her mouth, as if stifling a yawn. "I had no notion you were so ordinary in your expectations, my lord."

Next moment, Alyson felt a heavy hand upon her back. She moaned, the pain of her injured shoulder jolting through her nerves, and would have tumbled from her seat, had Guillelm not been there, tugging her none too gently off her own chair onto his lap.

Ever the jester, Thierry called out some ribald comment in French but Alyson had ears only for Guillelm's searing whisper.

"I barely touched you then, Alyson, and see how you flinched! Your shoulder is not even half-healed and yet you shame me by cavorting around the countryside on a wolf chase! When I found you this morning, were you about to dig a wolf pit yourself, too?"

"That is not fair!" Alyson hissed back, stung by the truth of his words and even more by the hurt shining in his eyes. She wanted to give an account of herself, not to win but to give him a reason for her actions so he would understand she'd had no choice. "I never meant to shame you—"

She stopped, overcome for an instant by a burning sensation in her throat, the prelude to tears. Digging her fingernails tightly into her palm she regained some composure and continued. "I knew you could not set out yourself because of the envoys and yet with a child missing there was no time to be lost."

"You did not think to send me a message? I would have sent Fulk and a troop of men out immediately."

And would Fulk have acted promptly, for the child of a peasant? I think not. Alyson stared at her hands. "I did not think I should disturb you," she said, as much as she dared admit. "I realize I acted impulsively." She forced herself to raise her head and look him in the face. "I am sorry. Truly, I thought you would be pleased."

She hoped to see forgiveness in her husband's compelling eyes, a gentling of his lips. To her inward dread, his harsh features remained locked in a frown. "Pleased that my injured wife is putting herself in peril? There cannot be any more of this, Alyson, even if a child is in mortal danger." Guillelm's right hand tightened about her narrow waist. "Promise me there will be no more, or I shall have no peace."

"My lord!" Fulk had no qualms in interrupting their conversation. He clearly felt himself in the ascendant; now he pushed himself away from the table and the dais and walked toward Alyson and Guillelm, glowering at a hunting dog that had crept into the hall until it slunk off to the lower tables. "My lord, be not harsh to your lady. She is young and unschooled in the ways of a large household."

He smiled at Alyson—that is, he showed his teeth—and added, "Will you see Sericus now, my lord?"

Now you have said enough words to act as fat on the fire of Guillelm's anger, Alyson thought, but said quickly, "I would send Sericus on an errand."

"You have done enough," Guillelm said. "Now I will have my say."

Alyson met his steely glance, inwardly sending a prayer to Christ that she had not made matters worse. "What business have you with my seneschal?" she asked, fearing the answer.

"Bring him inside," Guillelm said to Fulk. He tipped Alyson off his knee. "Call her women."

"Talk to me," Alyson said, hating the pleading note in her voice. "Guillelm, you cannot fault the loyalty of Sericus—"

"Not to you, perhaps, but where was his sense?" Guillelm's large hand captured both of hers and he dragged her close again. "If I choose to punish that old man for his folly, then I shall, and that will also be your chastisement. Get to your solar, madam, or I will have your women carry you there."

Hot speech flooded Alyson's mind but she was mute, shocked. She had not seen Guillelm this coldly stubborn before. Seated beside him, Sir Tom was shaking his head. On the tables below the dais, men were suddenly busy with their drinks or dice. *I have no allies here,* she thought. *They all think I was wrong.* "Dragon, please—"

"No more." Guillelm released her and Alyson forced herself to walk away from him, her footsteps crackling on the freshly strewn rushes and meadowsweet.

"Excellent, Guido," remarked Tom, clapping a flea on the back of his neck. "I have seen you deal with lepers with more care."

"It is not Alyson whom I blame." Guillelm could not drag his eyes from the straight-backed, retreating figure. He longed to rush after her and somehow make everything right between them. He wished she would look back, just a glance over her shoulder. Then he would not have to live with the dread that she was as angry with him as he had been with her—an anger on his part that he suspected was unwarranted, in spite of Fulk's snide comments.

But if she had been injured on the wolf hunt, or worse—his mind shied from the final thought, his thoughts leaping back as if from the jaws of the wolf itself. He could not stand to think of Alyson hurt. She had been hurt so often at Hardspen. What kind of man—of husband—was he that he could not protect her from her own fierce charity? He should have remembered about the wolf himself, sent out hunters days ago, before the joust, and not trusted to that old fool Sericus, who had told him the beast had vanished.

Alyson had also vanished. He watched the shadowy entrance for several more moments, hoping against hope that she would return. Even to have her quarrel with him would be a relief because it would be contact. She was gone now and he felt bereft: stupid, arrogant, unreasonable and, more than anything, alone.

"Where is Sericus?" he demanded. He and Fulk had not yet entered the great hall. What was keeping them?

"That old man did the best he could." Tom again, an unwelcome conscience. "You should not vent your spleen on him. It is unfair, as your lady says and—"

"When I need your advice, Thomas, I shall ask for it." Guillelm glowered at the entrance but still the two seneschals did not appear. Instead a page scampered over the rushes, missing his footing once on a discarded meat bone. Before sprawling full-length amongst the milling dogs, he righted himself in time and gabbled his message.

"Lord! The holy Sister Ursula is outside the hall this very moment, with Sir Fulk and Master Sericus. She begs leave to speak with you."

As Guillelm cursed under his breath and rose, braced for another chilly encounter with Alyson's sister, Tom put down his cup.

"Will you tell her anything?" he goaded, in a low, carrying voice. "I for one wish that you would share with Alyson's sister the real reason why Alyson was asked for no favors at the joust. Did you not notice how that blond piece Petronilla preened over the many trinkets she gave out? Women care about such matters. If you told Sister Ursula the truth, she would tell Alyson."

"I think that unlikely; they are not close. Besides, the joust is over." A fiery jealousy was burning in the pit of Guillelm's belly. He wanted to slam Tom's head into the trestle for even raising the subject. "I admit I was wrong, Tom—I did so at the time and I do so again."

"Yet you say nothing to Alyson herself. Do you wish her to feel entirely friendless, wondering why no knight approached her?"

Feelings, thoughts, guesses—Guillelm felt to be in a trap of his own devising, and the knowledge that he had created this current bad blood between Alyson and himself made another burden. "She has me. She needs no other defender."

"And do you think Alyson remains convinced she has you now, this moment? Guido! How can you be so thickheaded?"

Very easily, Guillelm admitted bleakly. He knew he was being stubborn. He knew he should have spoken to Alyson earlier about her favors and the joust; he knew—

"Enough!" Guillelm slammed back his chair, saying to the page, "Lead on, boy." The sooner he could be finished with the nun and seek out his wife to forge some kind of peace with her, the better.

Sister Ursula was waiting on the stairwell where, if Guillelm had known it, Alyson had waited a few months earlier, on the night he had returned to Hardspen. Standing beside her, Fulk wore the bright look of a fellow conspirator.

"Where is Sericus?" Guillelm asked him.

"I suggested that my sister's seneschal leave, to give us

some privacy," Sister Ursula answered and, before Guillelm could protest, "Sericus was ever . . . partial to my sister, and this gentle knight tells me that you and Alyson are estranged."

Guillelm stared at Fulk with raised brows. "You have been busy."

"I speak only the truth, my lord."

"Leave us." Guillelm spoke as curtly as he had done to the page.

"You doubt his loyalty," Sister Ursula remarked when she and Guillelm were alone.

If I do, it is no concern of yours, Guillelm thought, though he said nothing. Again, he was ashamed of Fulk, and of his own misjudgment. He had been almost willfully blind, reluctant to admit to the man's glaring faults because of his excellent fighting skills. Habit and old companionship could not easily be set aside, but Fulk had made no effort to outgrow his prejudices. Guillelm's own small hope that his seneschal would mellow in time toward Alyson was revealed as futile.

Putting that thorny matter aside for the moment, Guillelm studied the svelte, black-robed figure before him. He chose to be blunt.

"You are pleased to think that Alyson and I have fallen out."

Sister Ursula clasped her bony hands together, as if in prayer.

"Why?" Guillelm persisted.

The nun shook her head. "I am here, as a mark of penance, to speak for my order," she said through pursed lips.

Guillelm put his right hand behind his back and made a fist of it. He could sense Sister Ursula's distaste of him, revealed in her rigid stance and in the way she would not look at him directly. Yet she had been speaking to Fulk and the pair had looked easy together.

Heloise too had laughed and joked with Fulk in Outremer . . . Swiftly, before the old bitterness overwhelmed him, Guillelm tried again. "First answer me this. Do you not wish Alyson to be happy?"

"I wish her to be alive." Now Sister Ursula raised her face to his, her narrow features schooled into a mask of loathing. "You men! All you think of is war and killing! The prioress wants me to beg you that you allow us to stay on at Hardspen for a little longer, when I—"

"Gladly," Guillelm intervened, but Sister Ursula would not be denied.

"In a castle full of the same brutes who would have cut us down in our convent without a qualm!" she retorted. "It is madness! Evil." She raised a quivering hand toward Guillelm, her index finger thrust out like a dagger. "You are evil, my lord de La Rochelle, for you have murdered others and will do so again—including my sister!"

"Stop!" Guillelm sprinted ahead of the nun as she turned to go back to the chapel, using his own body to block the stairs. "Do you think that habit gives you the right to say anything you please? What do you mean? I would never, never harm Alyson!"

"You want a son, do you not? An heir? Men always do!"

She has gone mad, Guillelm thought, as Sister Ursula leaned closer, her eyes wild as she prodded his chest with her finger. A cascade of words broke from her mouth, and from sheer shock he sat down on the stone steps, listening in appalled fascination to her rave.

"You took Alyson when you must have known that the womenfolk in our family are fated to die in childbirth, so do not speak of never harming to me! You knew she wanted to be a nun! You might say you know differently, but Alyson would say the moon was made of gold because of you! I think she is either bewitched or terrified. She does not know her own mind."

"And you do."

"No! But Christ knows! God knows!" Sister Ursula straightened, tucking the simple wooden crucifix that hung around her neck out of sight as she smoothed down her habit. The action seemed to calm her; when she spoke, her words were more measured.

"Every woman in our family, without exception, has died in childbirth. My mother, her mother, the sisters of my mother, my great-grandmother. If you care for Alyson as you claim, then you will allow my sister to depart with my order when the time comes, to spend a period of contemplation and prayer with us. Allow her that space and peace so she may come to know what God desires for her."

Sister Ursula withdrew by another way, leaving Guillelm sitting on the stairs, staring at the soot-encrusted walls and seeing nothing.

He was still there when a boy came later, to light the torches.

Chapter 21

Perhaps their marriage should be annulled. Alyson would then be safe. Alyson would be able to pursue her true vocation. She loved learning.

The nuns of St. Foy's had thought they were safe, until the Fleming had attacked. There was no safety in this world. Perhaps Alyson would not be like the women in her family. Perhaps she would have an easy pregnancy and birth.

If they ever joined in love . . .

Brooding, horrified by what Sister Ursula had told him, Guillelm went about Hardspen that night without any sense of hope or joy. Fearing his own temper, he avoided Sericus and never sent for the man. After supper, he hunkered down in a stairwell and watched Alyson leave the solar for the garderobe, dreading that a page or maid might spot him, or a knight find him, or worse, Alyson herself see him and ask what he was doing.

What am I doing? Guillelm thought. He was a coward not to approach Alyson, unkind in leaving her to wonder how matters stood between them. He had ordered her to the solar; now he should seek her out. What could he say? "I will release you from our vows"? Was that what she wanted?

"I do not believe it is," he said aloud, "but perhaps I am mistaken."

For now he waited, his body stiffening in its cramped, huddled stance, his ears straining for the sound of his wife's returning steps.

Why? Alyson thought as she sped, head down, away from the garderobe, half-fearful, half-longing that she would encounter Guillelm. Why had he been so loving, so attentive through her fever and injury, and why now was he changed? Anger she could understand—he had been in a righteous temper over her wolf hunt, but as the day had dragged on and he had not come once to the solar, she began to fear that he had really abandoned her.

Please let him be furious with me but not cooling, not indifferent, she prayed. *Please let him come, if only to say goodnight.*

I am wishing so hard to see Guillelm that I am imagining him in the strangest places: as a shadow in the corner of the stairwell, below that unlit torch.

She stopped and listened intently, hearing no sound but distant clattering from the kitchen and great hall, a page playing on his new whistle somewhere within the keep, plus her own increasing heartbeat. She had to take a breath and then she sensed it: a difference in the space and air between herself and the stone walls and steps. Alyson squinted; there was something on the stairs, a darker block, solid and unyielding.

"My lord?" She scarcely dared hope. "Guillelm?"

The shadow moved, growing larger and blacker for an instant before Guillelm threw back the hood of his dark cloak.

As if drawn on invisible strings, he stepped toward her.

"I am sorry," he said. "You are wholly excellent and good, but I cannot live with anyone. How we are"—he spread the fingers of both hands, lifting them to her—"is wrong. I was wrong to think I could live with anyone, even you."

Something broke within Alyson but she dared not sag. Pierced beyond tears, she thought only of Guillelm, how hard this must be for him. "Dragon, is this what you truly desire?"

He lurched closer, eyes blazing, then whirled aside, striking the wall with his fist. Alyson cried out as she heard his hand slam into the stones but Guillelm never made a sound. He put both hands behind his back.

"It must be," he said. "You must be safe." A spasm crossed his haggard face. "It is the will of God." He lowered his head.

"Do you believe that?"

Guillelm stared at her, unblinking, as if he would fix her forever within the orbit of his eyes. He said nothing.

Alyson walked softly along the corridor to join him in the shadows, dreading that every step she took might see him break from her and stride away, leaving without a backward glance. Hope and fear warred in her but she had to know, she had to risk the question that was pounding in her head.

"Why do you believe it?"

He shook his head. "You should leave. This place is full of chills and darkness. Bad air."

"I will leave after you."

Neither of them moved.

After a moment, Alyson shivered, and Guillelm swept off his cloak and handed it across. "Please, take it. You are cold."

"Thank you." Dare she suggest they share it? "I will sit. My feet are cold."

"Here." Guillelm knelt and rapidly unlaced his boots. "Slip these on, over your own shoes and stockings."

He did not want to leave! As he sat beside her in the corner, with his shoulder against one wall and his back to the other, Alyson almost broke down in sheer relief. As it was, she could not manage to place his boots over her feet; her fingers were trembling so much they would not work.

"Let me help." Deftly, Guillelm eased the boots onto her feet and tucked the ends of his cloak about her shoulders. Crouched close, she noticed that one of the heels of his own leggings was threadbare.

"I should darn your hose," she remarked, "that is, if you will allow it."

To her horror, the thought of not darning Guillelm's clothes herself, of the dread possibility of never darning his hose, spilled tears from her eyes.

"Hush, sweetheart. Please do not cry." Kneeling, he rocked her in his arms. "Hush." He kissed her forehead and the top of her head. "Mother of God, I never meant to cause you such grief, Alyson. I want you to be happy. Happy and safe, like your sister."

"Tilda?" Alyson called her elder sibling by her old, secular name but in a flash she understood. "She has spoken to you!"

"Hush." Guillelm squeezed her waist and drew back. "All that matters is that you are safe." From his lips it sounded like an urgent prayer. He reached toward her to brush a wisp of a curl away from her ear, then froze. "I am sorry," he said. "Perhaps, in the circumstances . . ." He coiled his fingers into a loose fist and lowered his arm, moving as slowly as a starving man. "I am sorry to have disturbed your peace."

"Peace is not what I want," Alyson whispered, mopping the last tears from her face. She felt like a tightrope walker at a fair, buoyed by hope, edging her way to the truth but with danger on every side. "Safety—if it is the barren safety of a nunnery—is not what I want."

Amazement broke through the rigid mask of Guillelm's features and his eyes became alive again. "But your sister and your father—both of them at different times told me that learning was your dearest desire!" He clasped her hands, raised them to his lips. "When we did so badly together, when you froze, each time I came near, I thought they were right. That I was being selfish, keeping you here."

Alyson said nothing but her expression must have told him what she felt because he gathered her close again, with a befuddled look of wonder playing across his strong face that almost made her laugh.

"Truly, you are happy with me?" he asked.

Alyson cupped his chin in her hand, her whole body thrilling at the contact. "If I freeze, dragon, it is with rapture," she murmured, blushing to be admitting this but determined to free her husband once and for all from his demons of self-doubt. *And from Heloise . . .*

"What a fool I have been." Guillelm kissed the tip of her nose and, when she smiled, brought his mouth down on hers in the kind of embrace that Alyson had been longing for and dreaming of for weeks.

"We should move from here," she remarked, alerted to the world again by the spitting of a torch that was almost burnt out.

Guillelm smiled and wound his arms more tightly around her middle. "Move all you wish," he said. "You can squirm as much as you please from me. You are as light as a crane fly, even with my boots."

"A daddy longlegs?" Alyson queried, giving the common name. "If you think that, I can do this with impunity."

She tickled him under the arms until he grunted with laughter, seizing her wrists and bringing her eager hands onto his chest.

"You know well how to divert me, dragon," she said, her fingers combing through the springy golden fuzz as she traced the outline of his collarbones.

"You also," Guillelm answered, closing his eyes a moment and groaning something softly in Arabic.

Spread-eagled on top of him, their bodies separated by no more than a few threads of cloth, she could feel the heat and muscular power of him. More intimate things, too.

"Someone may find us at any moment," she said.

"So roll off me," Guillelm suggested, lowering his arms and closing his eyes again. "Or shall we sleep here? Give Fulk something new to grumble about."

Alyson smiled.

They did not, of course, bed down on the stairs, but neither did they retire to the main bedchamber. No sooner had they slowly disentangled themselves and dusted off their clothes than Fulk found them.

"My lord! I did not think to find you here." He gave Alyson a brief nod, both greeting and dismissal, and returned his attention to Guillelm, now pulling on his boots. "My lord, a troop of men have been sighted on the downs, riding to Hardspen. They bear the standard of the Knights Templar!"

"An excellent company," Guillelm remarked, cool where Fulk was visibly excited. "I shall ride out to meet them. Have my horse made ready."

"Already done, lord," said Fulk, smirking at Alyson. "This way—" He stepped before her, preventing any words of parting she and Guillelm might have shared.

Alyson returned to the solar. It was perhaps a discourtesy, not going back to the great hall to wait for and to greet these knights, but, from what she knew of them, her company would scarcely be welcome. The Templars were warrior-monks who eschewed women. What had brought a company of their order to Hardspen? She suspected Fulk had sent one of the knights a message. Fulk would be delighted; to him, she and Guillelm were already estranged and now, with the appearance of men who were pledged to fight in Outremer, what better way to remind his lord of their former time together in the Holy Land? These strangers would drink with Guillelm and his men, and reminisce on the old battles fought and won, and all the while Fulk would be watching, hoping to draw Guillelm back into that world.

Knowing this, it was hard for Alyson to remain with her maids, trying to work on a piece of embroidery by a dim, flickering candle while shouts of carousing drifted through the keep. It was a great risk, she knew, but tonight would be a test: Would Guillelm miss her?

He did send word, requesting her presence in the great hall, an invitation Alyson politely declined. For the next hour she sat half in dread, half in hope, listening for Guillelm's rapid step outside her chamber and imagining his face as he burst into the cramped solar to fetch her himself, but no man came near.

The maids around her worked quietly at spinning or their own embroidery, their heads bowed. The silence became unnerving and Alyson asked for a song.

Sitting on a stool with her back against the wall warmed most directly by the room's small brazier, Gytha looked up from rubbing at a comb with a piece of rag. "I have done better than that, my lady," she said, rubbing at her knees instead. "The local wisewoman is here. Eva is taking a bite to eat in the kitchen and will be with us directly."

Glad of any change, the maids broke into a muted chatter, but Alyson was more suspicious. "Eva is a recluse, living in the woods, and she just happened to walk into Hardspen this evening?"

"That is so," answered Gytha firmly, her ready blush betraying more.

"After you sent for her?"

"Perhaps," Gytha admitted, adding in a softer voice, for

Lindsay Townsend

Alyson's ears alone, "After seeing you and your lord together on the stairs, before moonrise, I should think you will be glad of her skills. She has philters and spells to guarantee a male child."

"You spied on me, Gytha?"

"Only for a moment, my bird," replied her old nurse imperturbably. "And I kept these others away. To be sure, you do not spend your private times with your husband in ways or in places that most wives would call productive, but it was a start."

"Gytha! No more." Alyson's face was burning as the door to the solar opened and Eva the wisewoman was admitted, shedding her bulging pack before the tumbling flames of the brazier and the keen faces of the maids.

Chapter 22

Eva was a tall, sinewy woman of two and thirty, veiled and gowned as modestly as a nun. With quick, brown eyes, a ready smile and red, work-roughened hands, she looked like a laundress or a kitchen maid. There was nothing unusual in her appearance except for a faint red birthmark under her right ear, shaped almost like a pair of lips.

Alyson tried not to stare at this mark as Eva explained the various uses of her potions and sweet-smelling unguents. Too distracted by what Guillelm was or was not doing to concentrate on the wisewoman's smooth, soothing patter, she agreed with all of Gytha's suggestions as to what she should buy. When wine appeared in her hand, she drank it to the dregs, although she knew by her first smell and sip that her drink had been laced with a sleeping draught. Anything, including an evening of oblivion, was better than wondering if Guillelm would leave his fellow campaigners and join her.

In the morning, learning that Guillelm had come to the solar but had been turned away by the other woman, who told him roundly that their lady was soundly sleeping, Alyson felt a little easier. He had intended to spend the night, not with the Templars, but with her.

"He wanted to carry you back to the main bedchamber," Gytha went on, pausing as she teased out a knot in Alyson's hair with her comb, "but I told him you had given strict instructions not to be disturbed by anyone."

Alyson sat up straighter on her couch, her head suddenly, appallingly clear. "You had no right. He will think—"

She broke off, aware of the maids listening and of Eva, deftly lifting her pack onto her shoulders, giving her a cool, careful look.

"Thank you, my lady, for allowing me to stay the night," the wisewoman said as the silence stretched on. "It is good for me to come away from my man and the little ones. He appreciates me more on my return."

She bid the other women farewell, leaving the door to the solar open to admit the fresh morning air. Crossing the threshold, she turned back. "There is a festival in the village of Setton Minor this day. I know this because my man comes from there and he has prevailed upon me to join him in their merrymaking." She smiled, softening the plain contours of her face, then continued, "The people there have heard of your rescue of the cottar's child. You and your lord would be welcomed and greatly honored. Will you come?"

Alyson's first instinct was to say yes, but would Guillelm agree? As she hesitated, Eva added gently, "I hope you will, my lady. It is a time when all may forget their cares and the busiest of men and women may remember each other."

And their vows, Alyson thought, and she smiled. "We will come," she said.

Perhaps I have done a very foolish thing, but I cannot help it, Alyson told herself. Part of her wanted to dance and clap her hands, seize the first clean gown she could find and rush to Guillelm. It was a wonderful chance for them to be alone together for an entire day. No Hardspen. No Templars. No Fulk. She and Guillelm could be like any other young couple at a festival. The freedom of that idea made her giddy.

The clever, careful potion-maker in her urged caution. Patience and persuasion were the keys. If Guillelm thought that he was being ordered to attend this event, he could easily refuse.

Leaving Gytha and the other maids to air and tidy the solar, Alyson slipped into the empty main bedchamber, where she dressed with particular care. A pale blue gown, to complement her eyes and coloring. Her hair bound tidily but not too severely into a single plait, and her head covered by the beautiful silk veil her husband had given her. The whistle he had made for her hung from her belt. A gold necklace and a silver coronet. Her most comfortable shoes, because she intended that she and Guillelm would walk to Setton Minor. If they rode, Caliph and Jezebel could prove too alluring to thieves, and Guillelm might be tempted to bring the merlin on a saddle perch. She was determined that all of his attention would be on her.

Guillelm woke, clearheaded, in the great hall. It was still very early. No others were stirring, not even the servants or the nuns in the chapel. When would that little community be moving on? he wondered. He knew the prioress was awaiting word from her own superiors, but he was surprised at the tardiness of her order. As Sister Ursula had pointed out, the nuns were in a castle full of fighting men.

It was a mistake to think of Alyson's sister, and what else she had said. All thoughts inevitably led to Alyson. He had missed her so much last night. Every moment, as he sat amongst his own men and the Templars, speaking of Outremer and the endless bloodshed spilt in the name of God, had driven home how alien that world had become to him. He no longer lusted for glory, or fellowship in arms. He was sickened and, yes, bored by the talk of killing. He longed for Alyson's quirky, mettlesome conversation. Her missed her laughter, her smile, the way her eyes darkened to a more brilliant blue when she was interested in something. He missed the smell of her hair, the touch of her hand on his, the feel of her flawless skin. He missed everything about her. He was mad to be separated from her.

Leaving the soldiers and squires rolled into their cloaks, the Knights Templar snoring to a man, Guillelm rose and strode from the hall.

He wanted to return to the solar at once and carry Alyson off with him, but he forced himself to wash first and comb his hair. Returning to the main bedchamber for a fresh undershirt, he met Alyson coming the other way.

The sight of her robbed him of words. Without any conscious choice, he opened his arms and she ran into them. They clung to each other.

"I never want to be in a nunnery," Alyson was saying, and Guillelm answered, "I know. I understand that now. I do."

She drew back a little to look at him. "Truly, dragon?"

"Truly, my most excellent girl."

He kissed her: lips, eyes, nose, throat, ears. The taste of her was sweeter and more heady to him than mead and she kept pressing her lithe form tight against his, whispering his name over and over.

A crowing cock somewhere in the bailey alerted Guillelm to the passage of time. "We cannot keep meeting in the castle corridors," he murmured, nibbling her ear.

"I know a place."

"Only say, sweet, and we shall go to it."

She stood on tiptoe and whispered a name into his ear, and so it was agreed between them.

On the way to Setton Minor they talked. Alyson began it, saying again that she had no wish to enter a nunnery, that it had been a childhood desire, long outgrown. For his part, Guillelm apologized for threatening Sericus.

"I was wrong to speak of punishing the old man. I spoke out of anger and concern."

"Concern?" Alyson was onto the word in an instant.

Guillelm scowled. Reminding himself yet again that the small, dark woman strolling hand-in-hand with him across the downs was not in any way like Heloise, it still took a leap of faith to admit this next. "I was desperate with worry for you. I wanted to blame someone."

"But Sericus takes my orders, not the other way round."

"I know. I am not proud of how I behaved. Nothing will happen to him, I promise."

"Thank you."

"No! You should not thank me. I was wrong, altogether wrong." Guillelm felt a drop of water on his face and for an appalled moment thought his shame was breaking through into tears, but a glimpse of the darkening sky in the northeast warned of an approaching storm.

Alyson tugged at his hand. "We can seek shelter ahead, if we hurry." She pointed to a small wayside barn, its thatched roof a bright yellow against the flower-studded green of the downland. It was the only cover for more than a bowshot's length in any direction.

Another splash hit his face and Alyson pulled at him again. "Run!"

They skidded along the gently undulating track, each stumbling in their haste. Passing a spring welling forth from an outcrop of flint and chalk and a shrine with two ancient wooden crosses, each garlanded with flowers, they reached the barn just as the rain began in earnest. Another few steps and Guillelm shouldered open the barn door, to be met by a mound of new hay, a scattered collection of rakes and, straight in the doorway, a wooden plough riddled with woodworm.

Alyson sneezed at the dust and Guillelm quickly pulled off his cloak, draping it over the plough. They sat down on the threshold, leaning against the plough, facing the rain.

"This may last a long time," Alyson remarked, glancing at the sullen gray clouds.

Guillelm, yearning to embrace the subtle lines of her profile, the sweet contours of her shape, could only answer, "It may."

"Will you host another joust at Hardspen?"

The question was his chance and he grabbed it. "Alyson, at the joust, the favor I gave you—did it please you?"

"Very much." Alyson lifted her hands off her lap to show the dagger tucked into her belt. "Did my tokens please you, dragon?"

Guillelm nodded, now hearing Tom's warning being bellowed in his mind. He had to say this. "You would have been asked for more favors and not only from me, except—"

He broke off as she turned her head to look at him. Her eyes widened slightly, then narrowed. "Sir Tom would not take a favor from me," she remarked. "Was his refusal anything to do with you?"

Conscious of a building sneeze and a general tightening in his chest, Guillelm nodded. "I was jealous." Wretched, aware of how pathetic his actions had been, he rubbed fiercely at his itching nose. "I told every man who entered the lists that if they received so much as a smile from you, they would have to fight me."

"What?"

"I warned every knight that if they wore your favor I would

challenge them—ow!" He flinched as Alyson jabbed her foot against his leg.

"You deserve no less," she said, her words as rapid as the bouncing rain. "I sat for hours with no champion, while that simpering Petronilla loaded rings and ribbons on dozens! It was the same at our Court of Love! Her looks were praised to the heavens! And now you tell me it was because all these men were cowards and dared pay no suit to me because of you?"

Abruptly, she started to laugh, snapping her fingers at him. "Your face, Guillelm! If I but had a mirror here . . . So you were a very jealous guardian of my honor, were you? I vow, it is a better explanation for me than that my looks were somehow amiss, not fashionable, but had you so little trust of me?"

Her moods were like quicksilver, but he saw the real danger of her last reproof. "Never! I have always trusted you, sweet. You—but not myself."

"Ah. The dragon temper." Alyson glanced at him sidelong, her face disconcertingly unreadable. "I suppose if you could not rein it in, you were wise to warn the others, but next time"—she tapped his knee with her knuckles—"you shall bear my granting favors, and with a good grace. I am no ninny, to toy with a man's affections, neither yours nor another's. All I give tokens to shall be as brothers, and they will know it."

"Yes, wife," Guillelm answered, tightening the hand she could not see into a fist as he imagined the clamor round Alyson. The very idea gnawed him like a canker. "You are very just."

Above them thunder rolled and Alyson laughed afresh, her eyes as brilliant as the flash of lightning forking over the downs. "We do not have to hold these tourneys so very often." She took his hand in hers and kissed the long scar close to his thumb. "Be at peace. I am."

She snuggled against him, as sinuous and unconsciously appealing as a kitten. Aware of a different heat pounding through his veins, Guillelm waited. He sensed she had more to say.

"I love watching the rain." Alyson held a hand out into the downpour.

"You always did."

They were still and quiet, Guillelm content to inhale the smell of her hair and feel her, warm and soft against him. For how long they were like this, in half-dream, half-dozing state, he had no idea.

When he stirred again to full wakefulness, Guillelm realized that the rain was still falling. It was almost dark outside, a late afternoon turned into an early twilight by the weather.

"We have lost more than half a day," he said wonderingly.

"I know. You were sleeping so well, I did not like to disturb you."

"Really?" Astonished that he had slept at all, Guillelm thought he would say nothing more of consequence but suddenly found new, dangerous words dropping from his mouth like broken teeth.

"I know how my father treated you."

Beside him, he felt Alyson stiffen.

"I am sorry," he said. "I will never forgive him."

"To forgive is a hard thing," Alyson agreed. "But you must not blame yourself."

"We were never close but, even so, I feel responsible for his misdeeds. Afraid, too. I am his blood. Perhaps as I age, I will grow more like him."

"Never fear that!" Alyson shook her head. "You are nothing like Lord Robert. Not in any way."

"But sometimes you seem to freeze when I approach. I feared then that you were thinking of him, comparing us, reminding yourself that I was his son—"

"Never! As I told you, dragon, if I go still, it is with rapture, not fear." She would not hurt him by confessing to the odd memory-flash of Lord Robert's cruelty when they themselves were close. Such unwanted remembrances had nothing to do with Guillelm and herself, and she was determined they would throw no more shadows.

"Pray God you are right." Guillelm gently touched her head. "How could he strike you? Beat you? He could not have loved you—no man who loves a woman would ever seek to hurt her."

"There are other ways of hurt." Alyson knelt up so that their eyes were level. "I can bear it no longer," she said simply. "I have to know. Who is Heloise? What did she do to you?"

Guillelm sighed. "Before I tell you of Heloise, I must explain about my older sister."

He took her hand in his, comforted and reassured when she gave his fingers a gentle squeeze. Heartened by the gesture and by her steady blue eyes, he took a deep breath.

"Juliana is trapped in a loveless marriage. I did not recognize it as such, when I served her and my brother-in-law briefly as squire, but even at twelve I thought Juliana cold to her husband, unnecessarily reserved. Once I found her crying in her solar. She told me then that all men are brutes—those were her exact words: 'Knights or peasants, men are brutes, slaves to their base passions. Soon enough, you will grow up and be like all the rest: the charming, fresh-faced younger brother who runs to bring me my book or cushion will be as sullen and determined of his rights as Oliver.' Oliver is her husband, a dour, laconic fellow who never praises when he can carp. I did not understand then what Juliana meant about rights, but I learned. I learned especially in Outremer, where some poor women have to sell themselves to put bread in their children's bellies. They know too much about the rights of men!

"Soon, I was more than ready to believe my sister's dismal prediction regarding men. I had seen it too often, played out in alleys when besieging forces broke through. I witnessed how soldiers hurled themselves upon unwilling girls and women. I tried to stop it, but other commanders told me it was the sport of war, that it was the nature of the beast. I remembered what Juliana had told me, and agreed.

"Of course, Heloise was nothing like a common camp follower or courtesan, forced by circumstances to give her unwilling body to greedy, careless troops. When I met her, I began to entertain the hope that my sister could be mistaken and that not *all* men were brutes."

Thunder cracked again, farther away this time. There was more lightning, but Alyson paid it no attention. "I know that she is blond," she remarked, as if that was of great significance. She flicked at her own plait, a nervous, defensive gesture. "Fulk said she is very beautiful."

"Fulk is an idiot." With his thumb, Guillelm traced the line of Alyson's veil, marveling at the feel of silk against silk. To him, her flowing black tresses were richer than any gold, but how could he persuade her of that?

"Heloise bleaches her hair," he lied. "There is very little of nature in her. She uses many arts to enhance her looks."

"She is charming?" Alyson prompted, a question Guillelm wished she had not asked. "Enough," she added quickly, sitting back on her heels. "If it pains you to speak of it, then let it go. It was many years ago, in another country."

"No, sweet, you deserve the truth."

Guillelm stretched out his arm and drew her close, heartened when she did not stiffen. Burning inwardly at the memory of the entire episode with Heloise, he began to speak.

"As I say, when I encountered Heloise, I was already convinced that women despised men, especially men like me: the big, clumsy kind."

"You are not clumsy, dragon! Not a bit."

Guillelm kissed her in thanks, then kissed her again for pleasure.

"If you keep interrupting, I shall never be done," he warned.

"Why should I not interrupt, when I am kissed for my trouble?" Alyson responded pertly, which made him want to embrace her afresh.

Fighting down his desire, Guillelm resumed his account.

"I met Heloise at a joust in Outremer. She sent me a favor to wear. I was amazed. Ladies of my uncle's court in Poitiers had rarely granted me favors and I had grown accustomed to the same and worse treatment in the East.

"After the joust—in which I won Caliph—Heloise sought me out. I remember she was dressed all in white. She was radiant on that hot, dusty afternoon. She brought me a covered silver chalice of wine. She called me 'my terrible beauty.' I was flattered."

Guillelm sighed, looking down at the top of Alyson's lowered head, wishing he could see into her mind. She was so still, so quiet, he hardly knew how she was receiving this sorry story.

"She had a rich town house in Jerusalem. From its roof you could see over the grain market to Tancred's Tower. I fell into the habit of calling there, whenever I could. She always received me. I took her gifts: game, flowers, a poem I had written in mangled Arabic. She smiled at my spelling mistakes."

Alyson inhaled a slow, deep breath but said nothing.

"She would have no other rivals to my affection. Somehow, she heard that I had a liking for small, dark women and she scolded me for days, threatening to deny me her company. At the time I thanked God that she had never learned anything particular of you, Alyson. You were still my ideal, but your father had made it very clear to me that he would never consent to a match between us. I was trying to make some kind of life for myself. All other black-haired, zesty, vivid beauties were too strong a reminder of you, whom I had already lost.

Heloise was tall, voluptuous, pale as a winter new moon. I told myself I was smitten with her.

"She encouraged me. She allowed me to kiss her hands. She teased me into washing and kissing her feet. She spoke of the lands I should be granted in the East. She admired my battle prowess. When she at last admitted me into her inner chamber, with no chaperone present save a Greek maid who knew no French, I took it as a sign and spoke my suit, offering Heloise my hand in marriage.

"She refused me." Guillelm felt his mouth twist downward. "How she refused me! She told me I was altogether too big and brutal, that I would burn any woman to ashes in a wedding bed. I remember her laughter as I stumbled from her house. I remember the Greek maid, laughing and pointing, and Heloise, cool and poised, lounging on cushions, picking the petals of the roses I had brought her and tossing them on the floor."

Guillelm fell silent. Around them, he heard the drizzle of the departing rain, the faint alarm call of a blackbird. He waited and felt his companion shudder, but there was no sound from her.

"After that, I knew it was no use," he said. "I knew what I was to women. Juliana had warned me, and Heloise confirmed it. I was a brute male, a warrior, nothing more.

"Then I returned to England, to Hardspen. And I found you again, sweet, brave Alyson, who has never feared me. I thought, I hoped—I prayed things would be different between us. I hoped my love for you would make the difference. I am sorry it has not."

"But it has," Alyson said.

Chapter 23

She touched his arm, relieved when he did not flinch.

"You are no brute," she said softly. "You never were."

"Truly?" He looked at her, the ashlike, dull dread in his eyes terrible to see.

"Yes." She took him by the shoulders. "You are too big to shake, or I would do so. Do you think I care what an Eastern harridan says about you?"

"Truly?"

Alyson nodded and, utterly exasperated, snapped her fingers. "Of course, you great fool! Do you think—?"

Her tongue was stilled from the rest of its complaint as Guillelm wrapped his arms about her, his whole being transformed into a fiery glitter and brightness. His eyes gleaming, his stern face glowing, he pressed her close to his heart. The heat of his strong body made her gasp.

"Do you love me, sweetheart?" he murmured. "Can you love me, just a little?"

"Yes!" Alyson whispered. "Yes!"

She gasped a second time as his lips embraced the curve of her breast. She was intoxicated, but not by wine. By Guillelm. Increasingly daring, she parted the neck drawstrings of his shirt and burrowed her hand inside, reveling in the feel of his solid body. His chest was crisscrossed with curling golden hairs and, on his left side, by a ridge of scar tissue running down the length of two ribs. She drew back the shirt further and kissed the taut, tanned flesh, close to the scar and then on the scar. His ribs moved under her lips as he inhaled sharply, not releasing the breath until she teased her fingers over the powerful band of muscle across his stomach.

"Mother of God!" she heard him hiss, his big hands circling her breasts in gentle, almost lazy sweeps that made her entire body quiver with need. In that mysterious, secret place between her legs, Alyson felt to be melting into sweetness— she was lost in his touch and in touching him. She loved his long flanks and his back, so broad that when she wrapped her arms about his shoulders, her hands could scarcely meet. She loved his shaggy golden eyebrows and his long-fingered hands with their pads of callus on the palms and the fingertips that could probe and stroke. She loved his full, sensual mouth and did not care that his heavy runner's thigh imprisoned both her legs. In the faint yellow glare of the storm, he was like a statue of a pagan god come to life.

"So beautiful," she murmured. He was so wonderfully hot, his athletic, robust body both smooth and at the same time rough-skinned. Touching him, Alyson thought of Caliph, recognizing in Guillelm the same compelling vigor.

She ran her thumb along the length of his nose, giggling as he caught her thumb between his lips and sucked it. His eyes flashed as he watched her, ravishing her with a glance, and his mouth was bent into an indulgent smile.

She did not want this moment to end, but outside the barn there came a pounding of feet. As she and Guillelm broke apart, a gap-toothed boy almost impaled himself on the plough inside the door.

"My lord! My lady! I have a message for you!" he yelled, shaking his dripping head and spraying them with water drops.

Guillelm glanced at Alyson, who was standing poised on the balls of her feet, her hands bunched into fists. "What are you doing?" he snorted.

"I could say the same of you," Alyson retorted. In leaping to his feet, Guillelm had swept her behind him, and not all that gently. Each had attempted to shield the other from a possible attacker.

He smiled, a little grimly, she thought, but his answer was amused. "Peace, wife. I *am* a soldier. Now let us hear what this fireball has to say. Your message, young man?" he demanded.

Alyson quickly turned her back to reorder her gown with hands that were far from steady, but the boy was far too excited at the prospect of dealing with a real crusader to pay attention to her, a mere woman.

"Mistress Eva charges me to tell you that she and the villagers of Setton Minor will await your coming another day, for today is now too wet for the festival. She bid me give you this."

He handed over a bundle and then was off again, sprinting across the downs with wild abandon, as agile as a pine marten.

"How did Eva know where we were?" Guillelm asked.

"She is a wisewoman, doubtless with her methods of divining," Alyson answered, kneeling back amidst the hay. She was so deliciously distracted by Guillelm's declarations and embrace that she could scarcely concentrate; it took her three attempts to untie the bundle.

Inside was a precious scrap of parchment, on which Eva had scratched the following.

> *My lady, consider the barn your castle for today and tonight. Use anything within it as you please. Burn the plough, but not, I pray you, the rakes. If you stay you will have good fortune. The pie is venison.*

"She has sent us some goodly provisions, this Eva," Guillelm exclaimed, as Alyson spread the bounty before them.

"Mmm," Alyson agreed. There was indeed a venison pie, dark maslin bread, dried apples, nuts and soft cheese. In addition to the food, there were two woolen sheets, big enough for two to lie between. Alyson lifted one, brushing its rough warmth against her cheek.

Eva must have talked to her nurse, she thought, for the last thing she drew from the bundle was a salve. The wisewoman had tied a strip of parchment round the earthenware, round-bellied jar, with the instruction, *For my lady's shoulder. A salve of garlic.*

Alyson blushed. The healer in her knew that garlic was a good antiseptic, but she also knew that the bulb was said to be an aphrodisiac.

She glanced at Guillelm, hoping her desire for him did not show in her face. "If we are to reheat this pie we shall need a fire."

Guillelm reached across her to the woodworm-ridden plough. "Then I shall break this up for you." He walked out again into a darkening landscape of rainbows and puddles, whistling as he went.

Later, after she had cleared away the rakes into a corner and swept an area clear of hay and chaff, Alyson laid the plough-turned-into-firewood on the "hearthstone" of a low-level boulder. "This will smoke, I fear," she said.

"I do not care," Guillelm replied.

In case she sounded too brazen, Alyson stopped herself in time from saying that she did not care at all, either, but that was still true; she was too happy.

It was a strange intimacy, working companionably and almost silently with the man she loved to prepare a meal and a bed for the night, on the downs where only sheep lingered. While Guillelm went off to refill their water flasks at the spring, she said a prayer to the Virgin, and to Jesus, then busied herself making the fire.

She had a good blaze going when Guillelm returned. As she saw him crossing the downs, threading surefootedly amongst the grass and heather, Alyson was transfixed by love and then laughter.

"What have you been doing?" she burst out, unable to contain her giggles. He seemed to have gained an instant gourmet's stomach; his linen shirt bulged above his belt and pouched in ungainly folds round his normally sleek middle.

"Kindling for tonight," he said, patting his heather "stomach." Nodding approval at her fire, he stalked into the empty space of their barn. "If you want to spread Eva's bedding in our sleeping place"—his face broke into a wolfish grin—"you may do it in any way you please, wife."

Wife. She was truly his wife. Hugging that marvelous knowledge to herself as Guillelm piled the kindling by their firestone, Alyson made two rough "mattresses" of hay, covering the smaller with her own cloak and Guillelm's and the second with Eva's blankets. Presuming nothing—although part of her was scandalously tempted to drag their bedding into one glorious heap—Alyson was already half-regretting her action when a deliberate snapping of twigs made her look up straight into her husband's face.

His expression was impossible to interpret but as he fed the fire with more wood, his words were clear enough. "We will freeze that way. We need to bundle together tonight."

"But it is summer," Alyson answered, mentally scolding the rational part of her head for mentioning that fact. What did it matter? Bundling, as Guillelm put it, was what she wanted. Finally, they would be in bed together.

"It is warm now," Guillelm replied, moving away from the

fire to draw the two rough mattresses together. His amused voice came out of the semidarkness as he respread the sheets and cloaks, making a single bed. "It is clear you have never had to take a watch through from dusk to dawn, my girl."

"Why would I? I am a healer." She was laughing, making a joke, but Alyson grimaced as she said it. A shadow seemed to pass over her and she trembled. Was this how the rest of the evening and the night would be—this muddle of longing and regret because she was not sure who would make the next move between them? *I have vowed to seduce him,* she thought, defiantly raising her chin.

"And I am not your girl anymore," she went on, unsure if she was being pert or merely petulant.

Amazingly, Guillelm seemed to understand her tumbled feelings, her lack of sureness of how she should act now. His smile filtered to her through the smoke. "No, by God! You are my woman now."

He moved back to the open door, pointing to the darkening vault of heaven. "Venus is rising. Can you see her?"

"I think so." Alyson padded toward the fire and Guillelm. As she drew near, he caught her gently round the waist and lifted her closer.

"It is clearing. The skies will be full of stars tonight," he said, turning away to give her time to regain her breath and smooth her gown. "Look—there is Andromeda, without her dragon."

He pointed as Alyson stood beside him, close enough to smell the fresh water on his skin. He had washed himself at the spring. Trying to distract herself from his disturbing presence, she followed his pointing arm as he named several stars.

"I know few stories or legends for these summer stars," she said softly, ashamed of her admission. Her parents had never been able to share any tales with her, and when she had once asked Gytha, her nurse had claimed she had forgotten. "They are very beautiful," she added.

Through the arching roof lintel and above the hissing fire, far above the tops of the tallest tree or hill, the stars slowly filled the sky, brighter than pearls. Some seemed almost blue-white in their brilliance.

"I have always loved the night sky," Guillelm said. "The scents of an eastern garden at night, the call of owls. When I was in Outremer I would lie awake listening to the little owls hooting at each other."

He and Alyson listened as two barn owls called again and again, the sounds drifting slowly away on the still air.

"I used to listen for bats," Alyson said, smiling at the memory.

They remained silent together a moment longer, each aware of the other.

Dropping another twig onto the fire, Guillelm's hand found both of hers and raised them gently. He cleared his throat, as if about to admit a shameful thing. "As you know, I like to cook, when I can. Shall I treat your shoulder with that salve and then heat up our supper?"

Gratitude flowered again in Alyson. "Yes, please," she answered, still partly astonished that she was alone with him and that she moved him—as clearly she did.

Kneeling beside her on their springy, seductive, sweet-smelling bed of hay, Guillelm hoped that she did not realize what effect she was having on him. Although it was a rainy midsummer, he was still very hot, and not from his earlier brisk walk to the spring. He was pleased that his clothes hid the most obvious signs of his arousal. Smoothing a salve made from crushed garlic onto the very top of her shoulder— working with her gown merely unlaced and not even peeled away from her back—should not have been in any way erotic, if only because of the salve's pungent smell, but touching Alyson made his senses explode.

"We can eat soon," he said. Food was not what he wanted but Alyson might be hungry. The edges of her healing wound were as pink as a peony. Delicately, so as not to hurt her, he trailed his thumb down the delicate line of her spine. Sensing her shiver, he steeled himself to his task again.

"We can use the bread Eva gave us for trenchers," he remarked, as the savory smells of the pottage and pie filtered through the barn. He had already burned his fingers on the earthenware crocks when he placed them in the ashes of the fire, but he was not about to admit that to his nervous little healer-wife.

"There are the dried apples, too," Alyson said in her low, warm voice. "We can roast them."

"I can roast them. You need to pamper that shoulder."

Conscious of his own rigid discomfort, Guillelm sat back on his heels. He wondered when he would be able to walk to the fire without hobbling in an undignified crouch. "It is good English food, but scarcely the exotic dishes I hoped to serve you," he growled.

Alyson smiled and shook her head. "To me, it is a feast."

Under the bright stars, with the air about them perfumed with hay and woodsmoke and the savor of venison and roasting apples, they shared their simple meal. To Alyson, water had never tasted sweeter. To Guillelm, day-old maslin bread had never been so delicious. The crab apples burst in their mouths like a draught of hot spiced wine.

Relaxed and replete, they ate the soft cheese and then the hazelnuts, rolling the shells between each other, making a game of it.

"There are the owls again," Alyson said, tilting her head to listen.

Guillelm watched the firelight play over the fragile bones of her face. He wanted her. He had wanted her for a long time.

"Dragon?"

Something of his tension must have shown in his face. He attempted a hasty smile that felt more like another of what Tom called his "gravestone grins."

"Guillelm, what is it?" Alyson reached toward him.

"No," he warned darkly. "Not unless you take it further. Much further."

She could do this, Alyson marveled. Moving from their hearthspace, she glided lower on their rough bed. She placed a hand on his foot, her palm covering the ankle bone, and looked up at the man she loved.

Guillelm's dark eyes bored into hers. "I have always wanted you," he said.

She had not touched him with such leisure and intimacy since their bath together. Alyson took off his shoes and ran her hand along the length of his lower leg; one hand and then the other, learning him over again. He quivered under her hands, the sinews and muscles tensing, feeling harder than bone but warmer. Through his thin leggings, the hairs on his legs were surprisingly soft, his flesh solid and at the same time yielding, both rough and polished. His eyes never left hers.

"I know I have sometimes been curt with you." His speech came in stops and spurts as she curved the fingers of her hand across his knee. "People are always around. It has driven me mad. Not being able to touch you when I want to, to hold you—"

His large hands bunched into fists by his side, then unclenched. He was sitting on their mattress with his back against the greater mound of hay, his legs thrust straight out in front of him. He was breathing slowly, deliberately, and a strong, dark tide of color had risen in his tanned, handsome face. The firelight threw the intent brightness of his gaze into stark relief.

"Alyson," he said urgently, using her name almost as a plea.

He was waiting for a word from her, she realized, holding himself until then under an iron restraint.

"I am sorry," she whispered. "I do not mean to tease you."

Now that she finally had Guillelm where she had dreamed of having him for so long—alone, finding her desirable—she was suddenly besieged by a thousand doubts of inexperience. What if he expected a miraculous seduction? "I do not want to do anything wrong."

She was blushing, no doubt scarlet in the face, but she knew she must not look away from him. She wanted no shadows, no Lord Robert or Heloise between them. *Surely I can do this,* she thought. *I love him.*

Alyson withdrew her hands and knelt up on the prickly mattress, undoing her belt and then the plait of her hair with cold, fumbling fingers. It was harder for her to hold his eyes than it had been for her to keep her ground against the knight at the joust who had tried to attack her.

"I want you to hold me," she heard herself say. "Please, Guillelm. Hold me. Love me."

He was already moving. In the space of a breath, Guillelm enveloped her in a rib-crushing embrace, his face flooded with energy. "Mother of God, I was afraid you would never ask! Alyson, my wife, my sweet little healer."

He kissed her lips, forehead, nose and throat, saying again, "I was afraid I had lost you, that you perhaps had changed in your feelings toward me."

"I changed to you?" Alyson wondered. "I thought the same. The very same."

Each began to laugh in sheer relief, laughing afresh when

a fox yapped from somewhere on the downs outside, as if in protest at their levity.

"Come here." Guillelm swung her up into his arms, rolling off the bed and carrying her closer to the fire. "Let me look at you."

For Alyson, the gentle collision of his chest and flanks against her body robbed her of words and even thought. She could only feel, skin against skin. Her arm, pressing against Guillelm's belly.

He kissed her throat, sending a lazy wave of pleasure sweeping through Alyson's body that made her toes curl.

"I love you," she said, the words easy to say because they were true.

Brighter than the tumbling flames, his eyes and face glowed with feeling. "You are so lovely. Let me see you—all of you."

He began to tease her blue gown off her legs and higher, gently trailing the soft linen past her thighs, her hips, her slender waist.

"Put me down, please," Alyson begged, longing to be free of the clinging cloth.

He did so instantly, his face showing an uncertain shyness that she was almost ashamed of evoking. "It is all right," she said.

Swiftly, before she lost courage, Alyson unfastened the lacing of her gown and stepped out of the loosened garment and her white undershift, hanging both over a nearby standing rake. The silver coronet followed, and the rest of her jewels dropped into a small, glittering heap onto the dirt floor of the barn. Standing stiffly, naked and never so glad of her unbound flowing hair, she spoke with her head down, staring at Guillelm's well-shaped feet.

"Dragon, I am—"

She was not certain what she would have said next, only that she was here, but Guillelm said gently, "Sssh." Stepping across the dry earth, he embraced her again, enfolding her in his arms with such a look of wonder and desire that she blushed and closed her eyes.

"You are beautiful," she heard him say. "Beautiful and honorable and appealing. A man would have to be dead not to be bewitched by you."

He lifted and carried her back to their bedspace, laying her down on her cloak. Stripping off so swiftly that he was almost a blur of movement, he came beside her and drew her closer still, so that she was lying full length on top of him.

"A little less hard for you, I think, than the ground, even with our bedding." He blew softly on her eyelids. "Are you ever going to open your eyes?"

Stubbornness urged Alyson to respond to such a direct, amused challenge, but she was distracted by strange, new sensations. With her breasts pressed against Guillelm's chest and her nipples brushing against his chest hairs, her breath seemed to have dissolved into her throat. Her slender legs, long for her height, rested on his, her toes pressed against his calves. He shifted under her, moving slowly so she could accustom herself to the touch of a man in this way, his thighs supporting her easily, their muscled potency as hard and flawless as new iron. His entire body seemed as enveloping and comforting as a hot bath. But it was not a passive reassurance. She could feel his obvious arousal. His entire skin seemed to crackle with energy. The firm embrace and gentle clashes of their bodies made her mouth dry and Alyson shyly conscious again of that place between her legs.

"Alyson?"

He moved again as she ducked her head and burrowed her face against his shoulder, wishing she was more strutting, more like the deadly Heloise. She found everything about him intriguing yet familiar; this embrace was new to her and yet it felt right.

"This is not something you learn from potions or books," she admitted, kissing an old scar close to the beguiling crease of his right elbow.

"No, little healer. I know it is entirely fresh to you."

The solemn tenderness of his voice made her feel welcome in his arms and more confident, so that when his hands began to caress her, she allowed her fingers to wander, too.

"God!" His breath came in rapid gasps as Alyson's hand flowed down his right flank and across his lower back, exploring that powerfully seductive hollow close to the base of his spine. "Your hands. Your fingers!"

"My shoulder is healing and my fingers are fine," Alyson said, a little smugly, part of her reveling in his clear response, the way his legs jerked and his hips rose from the mattress, inviting her to go further, touch more. Then she too was lost in sensation as Guillelm turned them both slightly so that she was still supported in his arms but more side-on, and the fingers of his left hand were cupping her breast and the fingers of his right hand stroking her back, lower, then lower.

"So lovely," he said. He kissed her, his mouth and tongue flicking and teasing against hers, his thumb softly circling her perked nipples.

Murmuring reassurance as his stretching hand glided over her jutting hip bone, he touched as if she were as delicate as rare glass. "Look at me, sweet."

How do I open my eyes? Alyson wondered, her body sunk in an intoxicating wonder. Then she gasped, her eyes flying open as Guillelm fondled her bare bottom. He smiled at her, a certain tension in his eyes.

"There is more," he said, rolling her closer to him, kissing her again, stroking her naked form from the top of her spine down to her calves.

"Your skin is finer than silk," he muttered, trailing little kisses down her breastbone and across each breast. His hand never left her bottom, his palm rubbing over the soft mounds, his fingers circling each cheek until she felt dizzy with a building excitement that seemed to begin in her loins and extend in a whirling, stomach-buzzing sweep to her breasts and throat and lips.

"Guillelm!" Her legs stiffened and her bottom raised in response as he touched her in a way no other man had ever done. Almost stunned with these new feelings, she reached out for him, her groping fingers freezing in a moment of delicious shock as she encountered his hard maleness.

"Do not touch me now," he groaned as if in pain, moving back from her slightly, out of her reach but still within his. "You are entirely too sweet and this is a journey that's better if we go together."

His other hand relinquished her breast and dipped lower, fingers stealing softly between her legs to the tight black curls where Alyson had never before been caressed.

"Please—" she gasped. His big hands, one covering and smoothing over her bottom, the other spiraling still more deeply into her most intimate place, were dissolving all sense of place or time or even shame. She clung to him, lifting her mouth to be kissed.

"I do not think I can bear this," she whimpered, surfacing after a long, passionate embrace. She felt herself hovering on the edge of something explosive and at the same time sweet—as if she might die but be glad of the dying.

"Trust me, Alyson," Guillelm whispered. "Please trust me."

His voice and his kiss calmed her, though the sweet tension remained and grew tauter. He was above her now, smoothing back her raveled hair, kissing her breasts, always touching her as he moved his body over hers, never crushing her with his weight but giving her time to familiarize herself to this change.

"I do trust you," she said, her answer ending in a strangled intake of breath as his fingers pleasured her again.

He moved closer, encouraging her now to wrap her arms around his middle, breathing teasingly into her ear as their thighs collided. Alyson felt as if she was in a golden haze, with the firelight and Guillelm's tantalizing kisses and his hard, blazingly warm body covering hers. Her sense of expectancy increased as she felt him lower himself into her, her body pliant and trusting, her eyes open, gazing into his.

He growled something in Arabic she did not properly hear and then began to move within her, kissing her deeply.

Alyson felt a sharp, brief pain and then only a luscious, melting joy, wave after building wave. Sensual and overwhelming, it caught her up, sending her on a dizzy, speeding journey of devastating bliss. She heard Guillelm shout her name and saw his face tense and then flame into an exultant, almost savage release.

Clasped in each other's arms, they tumbled together over the brink of delight into ecstasy.

Snug in Guillelm's embrace, Alyson stirred early the next day. In the pinky-gray predawn light and the dull orange glow of the sunken fire, she watched him sleeping, wondering at everything that had happened.

Their union of last night—had it finally laid Guillelm's demons to rest? Were they now truly husband and wife? The holy church stressed that the sin of lust should be fought. So had they come together in love or lust?

Surely we came together in love, she thought. She had told Guillelm she loved him. He had spoken of his love for her and although he had not said the words, "I love you," his every action showed it.

Then why does he not tell you? A new voice started up in her head, sounding like the sneering whine of Petronilla. Dismissing the voice, Alyson concentrated on Guillelm.

In this predawn light he looked younger, almost a youth, although there was a strong shadow of golden stubble along his jaw. His lashes curled against his tanned, lean cheeks like wisps of the finest silk. His bright hair was longer than when she had first met him, spiking in little tufts over his ears and beyond where he wore the collar of his mantle . . . when he was wearing it. At the moment he was wonderfully naked, bundled together with her under his cloak, which certainly did not cover much of him, sprawled out as he was in sleep. She nuzzled his bare shoulder, wondering what it would be like to kiss his slumbering mouth.

Almost as if he had sensed her thought, Guillelm tightened his grip around her middle, then relaxed with a sigh of wake-fulness and opened his eyes.

"Good morning." Rolling her on top of him again, he kissed her forehead, then her mouth, re-covering her carefully with his cloak. "You slept well, I trust?"

"Extremely, thank you," Alyson stammered, conscious again of her own nudity and blushing under her husband's in-tense, knowing stare. Lying on top of him, she could hardly fail to notice his rapidly increasing arousal, nor her own re-sponse to his long, sinewy body. But it wasn't even morning!

"We should go," she began, willing herself to move but failing miserably when Guillelm smiled at her.

"Everyone at Hardspen, if they have any sense, will still be in bed. As we are, I believe." He raised an eyebrow. "Rather an eccentric couch, I know, but comfortable, I trust?

"Alyson?" Guillelm touched her cheek with his fingers. "Have I shocked you with this? Do you truly wish to rise? Be-cause if you do, then we will."

He would do this for her. He would forgo his own need. He trusted her choice. Was that not caring? And love?

Then why does he not say the words, "I love you"?

Chapter 24

Alyson and Guillelm returned to Hardspen in the midafter-noon, wandering back to the castle by way of a high, winding droving road that avoided the flooded river plain and water meadows. They did not hurry and Alyson was glad that Guillelm seemed in no more haste than she was to go back to their every-day lives.

As they approached the main gate, it opened and a lone rider with two other horses on long leading reins cantered out to meet them. Alyson felt a prickle of cold temper, mingled with unease, run down her back as she recognized the riderless horse as Caliph, and the glossy black mare as her own Jezebel.

Fulk jumped down from his irritable bay stallion and began talking at once, his nasal voice raised to a half-shout, as if he intended that others should hear him, as well as Guillelm.

"My lord Guillelm, you are needed. I know that you left word where you were yesterday, you and your lady, but my messen-ger did not find you at Setton Minor and you have been sorely missed. Thomas of Beresford left for his manor this morning. The nuns of St. Foy's have also left. Their sister house at Warren Applewick, some three and thirty miles from here, have offered them a permanent sanctuary at their convent. Some of the knights of the Temple are their escorts on the journey."

"That is noble and kind," Alyson put in, determined not to be ignored. Fulk wore no helm today, or armor; he had mud-spattered leggings and a badly dyed scarlet mantle. His gray hair was greasy and uncombed and he had not shaved, but he looked altogether too pleased with himself. The red pimples across his nose and cheeks seemed bigger and more noticeable than ever and his thin lips seemed locked into a steadfast half-smile.

Holding Caliph's reins out to Guillelm, Fulk deigned to glance at her but addressed Guillelm.

"The leader of the Templars staying with us, Sir Michael of Normandy, wishes to have urgent speech with you, my lord. It concerns the safety of your very soul."

"What?" Guillelm was already laughing.

"What?" Alyson's prickle of tension flared into alarm. She wanted to ask *What have you done?* but knew she would have no true answer from Fulk. Conscious that with Sir Tom leaving Hardspen she was without a doughty ally, she now asked, "Where is Sericus?"

"Abed, lady. I heard a rumor yesterday that he had taken a chill."

"Steady, Alyson." Guillelm squeezed her shoulder, misunderstanding the depth of her concern. "If Sericus is out of sorts he will doubtless enjoy your fussing, but we shall see him hale and thriving again, hopping about the castle." He turned to Fulk, his look less kindly. "Never mind this nonsense of souls. Hand my lady her horse and help her to mount. Do you expect her to walk into Hardspen while we ride?"

"Nay, Guillelm," said Alyson quickly, distressed at the thought of Fulk touching her. "Sir Fulk was merely being a little tawdry through prudence, as at the joust."

"Before God, you are right," Guillelm muttered, recognizing her point immediately, along with the reminder of his own jealous antics. "Fulk, I beg your indulgence."

"There is entirely no need," Fulk said, very affable, bowing and handing Alyson the reins to her horse. "If you will permit me?"

He did not say "my lady," Alyson realized—a tiny thing, but one that deepened her growing sense that something was very wrong. If Fulk was up to no good again, then he had chosen his time well, with Sericus ill, Sir Tom gone and the nuns of St. Foy's going. Pretending not to notice Fulk's outstretched hand, she pulled herself deftly onto Jezebel's back and took a moment to arrange her skirts.

Fulk, however, was not interested in what she was doing; he had planted himself even closer to Guillelm and was even now repeating his warning. She caught the words, "soul," "your well-being," "Sir Michael" and "no time to be lost."

"Peace, man, we are coming," Guillelm interrupted, winking at her.

It was the last time she saw him truly smile for the rest of that day.

Entering the great hall, Alyson felt an outsider. The sense struck her instantly, even more forcefully than when she had been at Hardspen as a "guest" of Lord Robert. There were no other women in the echoing, high-ceilinged room and the men sitting at the trestles, talking quietly, paring their fingernails, scratching for fleas, roughing with the dogs, were strangers. No Sericus, nor any of the other old-timers who knew her. No single man of Guillelm's command except Fulk.

"Our men are at the practice ground," Fulk explained, catching Guillelm's questioning glance.

"All our men?" Guillelm seemed as suspicious as she was, Alyson thought, unless that was wishful thinking on her part.

Staring at the knights ranged about the hall, she found herself missing even a rough flirt like Thierry. None of these Templars smiled at her.

They were drinking and eating nothing, she noticed. Instead, as she and Guillelm walked into the hall they stopped chatting and straightened on their benches, solemn as the keenest of novice students at a cathedral school, and all facing the dais.

From the rim of her vision she saw Guillelm touch the place on his belt where his dagger was, as he jerked his head up to scan the walls.

"Where is the sword and shield of my ancestor, Thorkill of Orkney?" he demanded, pointing to a patch of stones beneath a window slit. There a faint outlining of fire-soot showed where these arms had recently been displayed. "Why have they been taken down?"

"They are here, my lord de La Rochelle," the leader of the Templars answered, pointing to a space behind his high-backed chair on the dais. "I ordered it done. These are pagan weapons. We are warriors of Christ."

Sir Michael of Normandy, his face hidden—deliberately?—by the hood of his cloak, shot back his plain cuffs and gripped the arms of his chair. Almost as if he were lord here, Alyson thought, sickened by a dread that would not abate. She was horribly conscious that the nuns who could claim equal spiritual worth with these fighting monks had already set out for their new home, escorted ironically by a Templar escort, but there were still too many Templars left at Hardspen. She counted a score in the great hall and still had not finished as Guillelm spoke in answer to Sir Michael.

"I am lord. Those weapons should not have been removed." Releasing her hand from his, Guillelm glared at Fulk. "What is going on?" he demanded softly. Fulk did not answer.

As three men stood by the door into the great hall, barring the way, Alyson scanned the room, seeking another escape.

Unless they could fly, there was none. She tugged urgently on Guillelm's cloak, whispering as he lowered his head to her, "Can you throw my veil and this necklace through one of the window slits? Would that alert your men?"

"It is already in hand," he whispered back. "No harm shall come to you, I promise."

"Please, my lord. All will become clear." Sir Michael nodded his hooded head and several knights rose from their places. They placed two chairs in the middle of the hall and then withdrew.

"Please, sit," Sir Michael suggested.

Guillelm handed Alyson into a chair but remained standing. "If I do not receive an explanation, Sir Michael, you will regret it."

"You mean, I will not live to regret it." Sir Michael answered, his smile visible even with the cloak hood and shadows shielding most of his face. "I have heard from your comrade of your prowess with all weapons, including knives. But think! If you hurl your dagger and kill me, my men will cut you and your lady down."

His features etched into deep lines of harsh disgust, Guillelm turned to Fulk. "Will you escort your lady outside?"

Alyson drew in breath to protest, but Fulk stared at the floor rushes and did not stir.

"What price, Judas?" Guillelm demanded, as his seneschal remained silent.

"Lord Guillelm," Sir Michael interjected, "you must not think too badly of Sir Fulk. He serves a higher master than you, as do we all." He touched the red cross conspicuously embroidered on his mantle. "And in his concern for you, he turned to me for help. You are not yourself, Guillelm de La Rochelle."

"Say plainly what you mean, man," snarled Guillelm.

Sir Michael finally drew back the hood of his cloak,

revealing a long, faintly equine-looking face and an utterly hairless head. Alyson noted the marks of shaving on his narrow skull and the marks of fasting in his pale, gaunt cheeks, bloodless mouth and dull, unblinking drab brown eyes. A pitiless ascetic, she guessed and, from the wary, cold glance he gave her, a man who disliked women as greatly as Fulk did.

This dislike was confirmed by what he said.

"This morning my men arrested a local female, a so-called wisewoman, Eva."

"You had no right," Guillelm ground out, his tanned face flooding with rapid color. "The Templars may be a powerful order, but even their writ does not run in the borders of another lord's lands. Justice is for the ruler of England, and for me, who holds these lands in the name of the sovereign."

"Which ruler, though?" Sir Michael asked mildly. "King Stephen or the empress?"

"You still had no right," Guillelm persisted.

"In matters concerning religion and the church I have more rights than you," Sir Michael replied. "The pope will uphold my claim of jurisdiction."

A spasm of scorn crossed Guillelm's face. "You would send petitions to Rome because of one local woman? What did she do, forget to bow as you passed?"

"She is a witch, my lord. There is the very sign of evil upon her flesh: two red marks close to her ear, the place where Satan kissed her. She has been arrested and shown the necessary instruments of inquiry—"

By which he meant instruments of torture, thought Alyson, with a shudder.

"She has confessed to her witchcraft and has named two more of her coven. Freewoman Gytha, a former nurse, and—"

"Folly!" Guillelm bawled. "The women are no more witches than I am!"

Sir Michael shook his shaven head, steepling his fingers together on the smooth wood of the dais table. He was sitting at the high table, almost in Guillelm's place, and he spoke with unconscious arrogance.

"In your present condition, my lord, I find your assertion unconvincing. You clearly have been bewitched and by none other than that woman who sits beside you, staring at me as brazenly as any man."

Sir Michael lifted something from his lap and placed it on the table with an audible snap. "This potion was procured by your wife from the witch Eva to use against you. It was found amongst the possessions of the nurse Gytha, who is the confidante and gossip of your wife. Gytha confessed freely that the potion is witchcraft."

Alyson freed her dry tongue and forced herself to speak. "A love potion, no more." She knew Gytha. Her poor old nurse would not have been able to resist the idea of a charm to help Alyson and Guillelm in bed. "Such things are harmless."

"Witchcraft," Sir Michael repeated with relish. "And evidence to be used at your trial."

"Think, Guillelm!" Fulk broke in. "If she is found guilty of witchcraft, your own reputation will suffer unless you put her aside and annul this marriage. You may lose Hardspen!"

Alyson trembled at the threat, but not because of Fulk. Now surely was the moment where Guillelm would declare his love, where he would openly pledge himself to her. She looked up at her husband—after last night, her true husband—and willed him to answer.

"I do nothing on your say-so, Fulk," Guillelm responded, without even glancing at her. "Alyson and I were wed in church. She is mine, my wife."

Alyson gasped as, still glaring at Fulk and Sir Michael, he reached down and spread his hand across her stomach.

"She is carrying my heir."

That was it. No words of love. No public declaration of his feelings. Hard, practical reasons; she was his, and his broodmare.

A tear rolled down her cheek and before she could prevent it or hide her distress from the corpse-pale, grinning head of the Templars, there came a thunder of knocking on the door and Thierry shouting, "Guillelm!"

"Here and whole!" Guillelm yelled, straightening to confront Sir Michael. "I am not so old nor so young as to fall into any trap," he said. "I saw dust by the jousting ground and sent a message."

"How?" Fulk asked, flinching as he realized how far he had revealed his part in the Templar's conspiracy.

Now Guillelm smiled, although to Alyson it seemed his face was no more than a mask. She sensed the dragon anger boiling beneath his grim exterior and, despite her own bitter disappointment and her renewed revulsion for Fulk, she trembled for the man. His punishment would be far worse than riding in full armor for a day.

But Guillelm was answering Fulk. Alyson scrambled to attend.

"The lad who delivered me a message yesterday was shadowing us today. I spotted him almost at once, but for the sake of my lady's gentle heart I let him be. When I saw the rising dust on the practice ground and realized just how many men would have to be there to make it, I disliked it. So I nodded to the boy, jerked my head. He is a quick study; he was off for the jousting ground in a moment. I cannot guess what he told my men, what plea he made on my behalf, but it was enough. They are here."

"We have reached a stalemate, Lord Guillelm," Sir Michael remarked, grasping the new situation at once. "What do you suggest? An ordeal? Champion against champion?"

No! She would defend her own honor, Alyson thought. She pushed herself off the chair. "I will prove my innocence and sanctity," she declared, her voice ringing clear to the rafters.

"I and my nurse Gytha and the woman Eva will go live with the nuns of the former convent of St. Foy's. We shall join them at the convent of Warren Applewick. We shall pray with them, and God and the Holy Virgin will protect us. We are no wrongdoers."

"Well said, my lady," came a new voice, as Sericus, with Thierry covering his scrawny body with a shield and men loyal to Guillelm streaming past them, now tottered into the great hall.

Guillelm said nothing.

Chapter 25

"You have been wise." Sister Ursula paused in brushing her sister's hair, an intimacy Alyson had been glad of, until she realized that her sibling was taking their moment alone together as another chance to drive home her argument.

"As you say," Alyson demurred. Having walked all day, leaving Gytha and the wisewoman Eva to ride on Jezebel, she had reached the new convent of the former sisters of St. Foy's with her legs aching and her whole body weary. That had partly been her intention, to tire herself so she would sleep quickly and not lie awake fretting, but she was too exhausted to dispute with her sister. "Is my lord well?" she asked.

"He is dining with the abbess and the prioress in the guest house," replied Sister Ursula stiffly. "Why were you walking with him today, Alyson? You should have treated your journey here as a pilgrimage and eschewed his company."

"Peace!" said Alyson, using Guillelm's own oath. She had walked with Guillelm in the company of his men because not to do so would have caused her almost unendurable pain. As it was, to be separated from him at all and especially in these circumstances, with the threat of witchcraft hanging over her, was vile. She found that the space beneath her breastbone actually ached, that there seemed an absence in the very center of her.

She glanced about the bare whitewashed cell that would be her sleeping place for this and for how many other lonely nights, seeing the tiny posy of flowers in the wall nook by her thin, narrow bed without any real pleasure. She could not even take the trouble to discover what the flowers were.

Am I going to be like this forever? she thought, panicking at the idea. Everything seemed dulled, purposeless. She told herself it was shock, horror at Fulk's treachery and the Templar leader's malice, but she knew it was more simple and terrible.

Walking with Guillelm, she had hoped he might say the words she ached to hear from him. But though in parting by the convent gate he had clasped her so tightly to him she could hear his racing heart, though he had whispered, "Sweetheart, take care. This will not be for long—I swear I will challenge the pope if I need to so that you are safely restored to me!" he had not said, "I love you."

"When he leaves tomorrow, I will not see him for many days," she said, finding it some relief to speak of him, however obliquely. "Do they serve roasted fruit at the abbess's table here? Guillelm enjoys those. And mulled wine." She had been planning many variations with spices and the rare sugar to try on him, especially as the winter months drew on. "I trust they do not oversalt the fish. I know he dislikes that."

"I neither know nor care," was her sister's bald response, accompanied by a fierce pull of her brush that tugged at the roots of Alyson's hair. "Such worldly concerns are not for me, and they should not be any part of your life."

Sister Ursula banged the brush down on the edge of the bed. "Yes, you flinch now!" she spat, her green-gray eyes flashing dislike, her thin face one long grimace of reproach. "Why did you not flinch away from him? You know the fate of the women in our family! I have heard him, braying his manhood in the very church of this holy place, asking the abbess to pray for his unborn son!"

Not for me. Alyson was glad to be sitting on the edge of the bed. As her left foot went into an agonized cramp she almost cried aloud, although not with her body's pain. *I have not been rejected. Guillelm respects my decision and sees the logic of it. It is the safest way for Gytha and Eva. Being here saves them from the questions of Sir Michael and possibly even torture. Guillelm's mother died in childbirth and he knows too well the history of the women in my family. Perhaps he is right to ask for prayers. What else can he do? It is women who bear children. I am not being abandoned.* Trying to be resolute, she limped to the door of her cell and opened it.

"Thank you." She could scarcely look at her much-loved sister, buried in her black piety, her thin fingers stroking the cross at her neck as if to wipe away the contagion of any human contact. "I wish you good night."

"Pray God protects you from the consequences of your own sin and desire," Sister Ursula retorted, determined as she had been in childhood to have the final word. She glided past Alyson, leaving without once looking back.

Life in the convent settled for Alyson into a bland, color-less existence. Gytha and Eva were put to work in the gardens but Alyson was told that digging was not seemly for one of her status. "It could also injure your child," the abbess con-tinued, smiling at her charge and glancing at the fine silver altar crucifix that Guillelm had left as a gift.

"Then allow me to work in the infirmary," Alyson pleaded, but again she was denied.

"No. For you, I think that your innocence is best proved here, in our church." The abbess brushed some stray pollen from a vase of drooping lilies off the altar cloth, looking round the

convent church in the same satisfied, managing way that a
house-proud wife might check over her stores. "Remain in
church from your time of waking to your time of retiring and
pray. God and the world will then see your purity."

"May I have a little parchment, so I may write to my lord?"
Alyson asked.

The abbess, still brushing pollen, shook her head. She was a
small yet angular woman, seemingly fashioned of straight lines,
so that in her plain gown she seemed like a black cube. Her wide
face, with its heavy jaw and narrow brown eyes, radiated nothing but honest good nature. "You have no need to write, my
child," she replied. "He knows where you are. You are safe here
and at peace. You must direct your thoughts to God."

Alyson prayed in the convent church. She joined the nuns
in all their services. She swept and cleaned the church, taking
care not to disturb the nuns who entered for their own quiet
contemplation, or those who changed the flowers. She asked
for nothing for herself and learned not to approach her own
sister, who resented being singled out, or to ask for news of
Guillelm. Kind but implacable in her own sanctity, the abbess
believed that talk of husbands in a nunnery was inappropriate. She never answered Alyson's questions.

The days drew on. Speech was not encouraged in the convent and Alyson saw Gytha or the wisewoman Eva only with
the width of the church nave between them. At night she
prayed on her knees in her cell, longing to speak to Guillelm,
to share with him the snippets of news she gleaned from the
nuns about the civil strife between King Stephen and the Empress Maud, and to hear about him in return. Was he safe?
What had happened to Fulk and the Templars? More selfishly
perhaps, did he miss her as greatly as she missed him?

When she first began to feel sick, Alyson thought it was

because she was pining. In the refectory at meals she avoided the game and poultry dishes that the convent were allowed to serve in addition to fish and vegetables, telling herself she did not fancy the rich roast duck. Even a liking for hot blackberry tisane was nothing new. It was only when her breasts began to feel tender and her monthly course did not come that she began to wonder.

Was Guillelm right? Was she with child?

That night she dreamed of Guillelm. She dreamed they were together again in the barn, only this time the night was fine and dry, spring rather than high summer.

"I ache here." In her dream, Alyson placed a hand on her breasts. She was so tender there that she could no longer sleep upon her front, and the fabric of her tunic felt tight and harsh.

It was a warm, breezy night and they had lit no fire. Guillelm lifted the wooden whistle from Alyson's lap and laid it aside. "Untie your tunic, sweetheart. Let me see."

He crouched so that the moon could shine upon her breast and laid hands on her, his firm touch surprisingly comforting. "Look up." He stared at the prominent veins below Alyson's collarbone. A smothered laugh escaped him. "We should be in the lambing field ourselves."

Guillelm touched her throat on the big life-vein. "You know what it is, Alyson. Part of you knows. The part that has caused your mind to give me these words within your dream."

Alyson looked down at herself. She put a hand on her taut stomach and sucked it in. So tiny, it could not be felt as yet. She felt old, mortal, her own childhood gone forever. She thought of the women in her family, fated to die in childbirth. She lifted her head. "What should I feel?"

"Nothing yet, the baby is too young to be moving within you," answered Guillelm, deliberately misunderstanding her. He caught Alyson against him, both of them kneeling, and rocked her.

"Peace, peace," he whispered, as she remained stiff. "There will be time enough. Our child will spend three seasons within you—you will love each other by then."

With Guillelm's dream-acknowledgment of the child as his, some of the fear and numbness ran out of Alyson. "Are you glad?"

Guillelm nodded, laying his bright head against her shoulder. For a time all was quiet, their dream-world still, then Alyson felt him start against her. "Listen, the first lamb born!"

Alyson heard the fragile, bleating cry for herself and something woke within her—soon that would be her child, Guillelm's child. She sprang to her feet. "Who shall we tell?" she cried. "Who first?"

She woke on her own question, already knowing the answer.

Chapter 26

She felt guilty, stealing away from the convent during the silent predawn hours, before the first service. Without parchment, she had no means of writing a note to the abbess to explain or apologize for her absence and she dare not wake her sibling; she was certain Sister Ursula would raise an alarm to prevent her going.

Walking barefoot from her cell Alyson had several nerve-jangling moments. The tiny creak of her door as she eased it open seemed as loud as a horn blast. The broken snore of a sleeper in one of the other cells convinced her that she was discovered, until the steady, heavy drone began afresh. Another few steps and she froze, spotting a moving shadow, which turned out to be nothing more than the abbess's pet tabby cat, Nero, stalking the corridor. The painted eyes of a statue of the Madonna reproached her as she passed the statue's narrow window niche but now no others saw her.

So far, the abbess's instruction that she, Gytha and Eva be housed not in the more lavish comfort of the guest house but with the novices and nuns in the general dormitory had worked to her advantage—no one expected her to take flight from here, in the midst of so many other sleepers. Alyson grimaced afresh at the thought but kept on. Unbarring the final door and closing it slowly and softly behind her, she stepped outside into the pinky-gray morning.

In the clammy, dew-laden air she took several steadying breaths and laced on her shoes. Careful to walk all the way around the courtyard, keeping close to the walls in case any should spot her crossing the cobbles that she herself had swept only the evening before, she made for the small stable block.

In the straw-scented barn she knew she would not find Jezebel—Guillelm had taken the mare back with him when he left—but she hoped to find some mount she could use. There her luck failed. Aside from the abbess's gray palfrey—which Alyson dare not borrow—there was only a drab mule, which she sensed would bray loudly if approached. Smiling grimly at the recollection of her sister's accusation of Guillelm "braying," she retreated rapidly, hurrying from the convent on foot by way of a small eastern gate. Blinking into the yellow glimmer of the rising sun, she turned southwest, toward the distant church tower of Saint Michael. After Saint Michael's would come Saint Jude's and after that she would truly be on the road to Hardspen, on the road home.

She walked until she was certain she would be out of earshot of the convent and then ran, anxious to put as much distance as she could between herself and the nuns.

Fixing her eyes on the tower of Saint Michael, she began by cutting across country, blundering once through a patch of thistles that tore at her gown. Behind her, faintly, there were voices shouting and fading; her departure from the convent may have been discovered. Ignoring that, Alyson ran on—she was running more slowly now, making for the track she knew was at the other side of the upcoming wooded valley, pacing herself so that she could breathe but not think. The early sun flashed in her eyes, its heat already as humid as a summer afternoon. There was a rumble in her ears like thunder, but it was her own pounding heartbeat, urging her to greater speed.

Alyson sprinted off the balls of her feet. Her hair broke free of its plait. She flew down the dry stream bed of a water course, her toes scarcely rocking the round yellow pebbles, and her feet bit into mud as she entered the green twilight of the wooded valley. There her speed was checked by the thick undergrowth of hazel and her own weariness.

She slowed to a walk. The bed of the stream grew sloppier, soothing her burning feet. Deeper in the wood she heard the trickling sound of water; a spring welled out from a bank and ran over the grass to the stream bed. Alyson cupped her fingers and drank.

Suddenly she was weeping into her wet hands. What was she doing? Sneaking away from her hosts, deceiving nuns, rushing off with no coherent idea other than to see Guillelm again. Would he be pleased to see her? *Please let him be pleased,* she thought, while a darker voice in her head added, *If I am with child, please let us both survive.*

She stretched her hand across her stomach. *Be safe,* she pleaded to the tiny, fragile life within, another soul, the fruit of her and Guillelm's love.

Did he love her?

"Enough!" Alyson said aloud, mopping the last of her tears away from her cheeks with her fingers. Even where she did not keep to the winding road, as now, she would have a long, exhausting trek today. "Save your energies for the journey. Do not talk. Do not think. Walk."

Alyson walked on through the woods. She was glad to be taking a shortcut through here—had she kept to the turf-and-stone track that snaked up and down beside this wood, she would have added another mile or so onto her trip—but this was

no carefully maintained royal forest. In this wood, there were no
ditches to keep deer in or out, or woodmen coppicing oaks and
limes; it was in truth a long, narrow strip of straggly trees, some
old and rotting, others hung about with lichen. It smelt of musty
rooms and the only birdsong she heard was the frequent, scolding alarm call of the blackbird.

She moved quickly, wary of disturbing animals—either the
two-or four-footed kind. No boar grazed here, Alyson noted
with relief, seeing no characteristic score marks on the tree
trunks, but she noticed badger hair on a stump and fox tracks
near to a small muddy pool in the middle of the wood. From
there she could also clearly see the farther edge of the wood and
now she quickened her steps, keen to be out in the fresher air
again and back on the road.

Then she heard it. A whistle that was not a birdcall, answered by another. Ducking under the low branches of a
chestnut, Alyson pelted for deeper cover, a stand of hollies
where she could hide until the men had gone. Had they seen
her? Worse, were they tracking her? Whoever they were,
Guillelm was not part of their number; he would have
shouted, made himself known. Had they seen her?

Risking a look back, Alyson recognized an emerging shadow
and instantly flattened herself onto the damp earth, praying the
man had not spotted her. He was still on horseback, jabbing and
slashing at the undergrowth with his sword, a boyish, childish
gesture except that his face was taut and red with anger.

It was Fulk.

Where was she? Fulk had watched her leave the convent and
from the instant his men had brought word of her movements
he had followed her sneaking progress. No doubt she was heading for Hardspen, but to him it no longer mattered. She was
outside the convent, having deliberately left sanctuary. She had

put herself outside the protection of the holy place. She was his now.

Fulk tightened his grip on the reins, angry that the search was taking so long. Everything had been clear until she entered the wood. He should never have hung back, but then, he had expected her to keep to the road, where a single lone female could be easily ridden down. He had planned to seize her a mile away from the convent, out of sight of anyone, but by fleeing into the trees the cunning witch had escaped. Not for long, though. Once captured, she would be blindfolded, taken to a more private spot and then—

He closed his eyes, sending a prayer of thanks to God. Sir Michael, that great Templar knight, had been right. His advice had been timely.

"If you wish to recover your lord's good graces, then I would suggest you strike camp close to the convent, and wait," Sir Michael had told him as they had shaken hands in parting. "Those women will betray themselves: One or all of them will flee sanctuary and when they do, you will know who is guilty. It is a proof your lord will not be able to ignore. A witch cannot bear to stay by a holy place."

Fulk opened his eyes, catching a flash of blue-purple off to his left, shimmering against the browns and greens of the trees and earth like the brilliant plumage of a kingfisher. As two of his men hauled her out of a mess of holly branches and dry leaves, Fulk permitted himself a grin—Alyson had been found by her own female vanity, by a scrap of veil, fluttering in the breeze.

Chapter 27

Blindfolded and gagged, her hands tied by a thin cord that cut so badly into her wrists that she could feel a trickle of blood on the sleeves of her gown, Alyson was flung facedown across the back of a horse. A nightmare ride followed, where every step of the horse's hooves jolted up through her body like the punch of a hammer. She could do nothing to protect herself from the searing pain in her breasts and stomach, and each time she shifted slightly on the plunging horse, trying to ease the agony of her ride, a heavy mailed hand slammed into her back or brutally thrust her head down again. She rode with her face thrust against the flanks and neck of her mount, waves of sickness rising in her gorge, her teeth aching as she bit desperately into a filthy rag Fulk had forced into her mouth. Her only relief now was pride, that she would not scream. Dizzy with the relentless, thunderous motion, clammy with dread that she would fall or be pitched forward into the rushing void, she vowed to herself that when they stopped, wherever they stopped, she would fight. Whatever happened, Fulk would not make her scream. He would not make her beg.

Some long time later, when her muscles felt flayed and her arms gone numb in their sockets, a gobbet of dirt struck her in the face as whoever was riding the horse above her reined in with savage force. She was hauled off the sweating charger with as little ceremony or concern as if she was a bale of cloth and dropped onto the ground.

Despite Alyson's best efforts, her legs were shaking so badly that they buckled and she sprawled forward. While she was prone, a man grabbed her arm and she curled inward, instinctively shielding her belly from kicks or blows, but instead her bounds were efficiently cut, her blindfold tugged off and her gag removed.

"Thank you," she tried to say, but the soldier, who was a stranger to her, shrugged and put a finger to his lips and stepped back. He had a young-old face, lined by exposure to strong sun and a bush of russet hair, that curled in a way Petronilla would have envied.

"Eustace does not understand you. He speaks only French." Fulk stood before her, hands on hips. He wore gloves of mail and she wondered if she had been put across his horse, an almost unendurable thought.

"Where are we?" she asked quickly, if only to spare herself his gloating smile.

"These men with me are all loyal to me," Fulk continued, as if she had not spoken. He watched her struggling to sit up amidst the dry grass and ferns with the same cool patience a spider uses to watch a fly. There was no pity or care in his look.

"May I have some water?" Alyson asked. She loathed the thought of having to deal with Fulk, but deal she must. She forced herself not to touch her stomach; there was no way she could check on the babe within, if there was a babe. Would a child survive such a ride? What if she should miscarry? What if the child was harmed in some way, deformed? Her mind flashed to a terrifying image of Guillelm, his face warped in disgust, repudiating both her and her baby.

"Water," she croaked, close to tears, repeating her request in

Latin as she tried to remember the same word in French. "Please?"

Fulk merely stared at her. The strange soldier, Eustace, who had cut her bonds, touched his hand to his own water flask and then turned his back.

Alyson almost howled with despair. She glanced past Fulk and her possible ally, who was now striding away, shouting something in French over his shoulder about making water, and she looked to the rest. She knew there were others; at least three men had wrestled with her when they had caught her.

Five men circled her, tall and implacable as standing stones, in gray armor and plain brown mantles. None wore any insignia, she noticed, no device to show which lord they served. Three wore helms and she could not see their faces. The other two were unknown to her. She might have seen them at Hardspen, but she could not swear to it.

The red-haired stranger knight, the only one who had shown her any gentleness, had vanished into a stand of trees.

"Where are we?" she repeated.

This time Fulk deigned to answer. "Somewhere you should recognize."

It was a place she did not know. A roughly circular clearing in a stretch of forest. About them were massive beeches and oaks, and beyond the clearing the understory enclosed them like living curtains, the hazel and elderberry bushes heavy with growing nuts and berries that shone in the sunlight. Within the clearing itself there were orchids flowering amidst old tree roots and stumps, their bright glossy petals flickering like dragon tongues amidst the sandy, grassy base of the woods.

"Did my lord Guillelm bring me here?" she asked, speaking his name like a charm.

If she hoped for some sign of shame or disquiet amongst the half-dozen warriors loyal to Fulk, she was to be disappointed. They regarded her gravely, unsmiling, one thoughtfully scratching at his beard, another addressing a remark to his closest companion that she did not understand.

Fulk thoughtfully translated. "Piers is from Brittany. He says that now he can see you properly, he can understand how you bewitched our lord."

Piers added more, which made Fulk twitch like a horse stung by a fly. Scowling, he made a cutting motion with his hand and Piers fell silent.

"Do not try to dissemble to me, Alyson of Olverton." White spittle gathered at the corners of Fulk's mouth as he raised his voice. "You are sitting in a circle you yourself have made, a witches' circle. You came here many times this summer, with the woman Eva and the woman Gytha, to make your foul magic."

Affirmative grunts of agreement issued from the other men as Fulk named her supposed coven, although Alyson could not be sure how much of her speech with Fulk was understood by them. It made her task of argument that much harder, but she had to attempt it. If she could only delay whatever Fulk had planned for her until she could make an escape—

"Really?" She tried to sound as bored as possible, while she scanned the horizon. Where was the red-haired knight? Had he perhaps had a change of heart and gone for help? Even as she dared to consider that, her hopes were dashed. She heard him beating back through the forest and a moment later he too was in the clearing, taking his place in that ominous circle of men.

She used Guillelm's name a second time, praying that she might inspire a fear of retribution in these men, if not fealty. "If you are sure of this, Fulk, then why do you not bring your charge before our lord Guillelm?"

"And have you maze him again out of his wits? I think not."

"Does my lord dragon seem dull-witted to you, Fulk?"

Fulk's face darkened. "Where you are concerned, he has

shown neither wisdom nor seemliness. If you had not interfered, my lord would have returned to the Holy Land to fulfill his true destiny, fighting the infidel. He should be there now, defending Outremer."

Fulk took a step closer to her, his hands raised before him, making a protective cross.

"I have a cross, too." Alyson lifted the small silver crucifix that the abbess had given her from her neck, dangling it aloft on its chain so that the men could see it. She kissed the cross and wound the chain about her fingers. Still unsure if she rose that she would be able to keep her feet, she knelt instead and began to recite the Creed.

"Stop!" Fulk bawled. "You shall not profane such holy words with your incantations! You are a witch! You have already done enough!"

"What have I done, Fulk?" Alyson goaded, aware, as Fulk seemed not to be, of his men watching him, their faces carefully blank.

"You!" In four strides, the Frenchman reached her and yanked her upright by her hair, laughing as she screamed in pain and insult. "Treacherous, foul, evil! Witch!"

His hands were in her hair, dragging and tearing, and still the accusations poured from Fulk, each one blistering in its rage and hurt.

"It is thanks to you I have lost my place! It is thanks to you Guillelm told me to quit his service! It is thanks to you I have no lord! You have done this to me!"

"No!" Alyson cried, grabbing Fulk's wrists to stop him. "You have achieved this yourself, by your own spite! Do you not understand? We could have been friends, but you always saw me as a rival."

"Witch!" Fulk thrust her away and kicked out at her. His men murmured, anxiously shifting from one foot to the other, but none of them intervened, not even as she tottered.

Afraid to turn her back on Fulk, Alyson scissored two fal-
tering strides and then regained her balance. Straightening,
she faced him. Between the time she had last encountered
Fulk and now, the man had lost weight. Already rangy, he was
now gaunt. His gray hair was lank, his hooded eyes bright
only when he berated her.

Despite what she had endured from him, Alyson felt a
shred of pity.

"Fulk, why did you not leave with Sir Michael?" she asked
softly. "I am certain he would have welcomed you into his
service."

For an instant, Fulk seemed to recognize her sympathy, but
older, fiercer resentments and jealousies took hold. "You dare
to offer comfort, witch," he snarled, "when it is you who have
sought to destroy me?" He pointed to the encircling men.
"Were it not for these stalwart warriors for Christ, who have
chosen to follow me into exile, I would be alone."

"I am sorry," Alyson said. Part of her ached to take Fulk
in her arms, to give him the kiss of peace. The man was in
such pain.

"Sorry? You shall be sorry! You shall be tried—and found
wanting!"

The veins in his throat and neck bulging, Fulk yelled a
series of orders in French and Alyson was seized again.

Her "trial" was brutally short, and painful. Slung between
a birch sapling and an elder bush, suspended between the two
trees by ropes attached to her wrists, Alyson was forced to
stand, half-hanging from her arms. Her toes scarcely brushed
the soil and within moments of being left in that degrading,
captive position, she began to shake. Tremors as fierce as a
fever ripped through her body. She was terrified for herself
and even more for her child but dare not confess her preg-

nancy to Fulk. In his maddened state who knew what further atrocity he might conceive against a possible spawn of a devil? He had already convinced himself that she was utterly evil.

His voice ran on, relentless and hard as an avalanche of stones as he called on his loyal men to witness her depravity. Breathless from being almost crucified between the two trees, Alyson could hardly answer his hounding questions, much less interrupt his tirade.

He spoke in a mixture of languages, English and French, until she was completely bewildered. Light-headed through lack of water or food, her throat bone-dry, her chest aching, her arms and legs burning with pins and needles, Alyson struggled to retain consciousness and make some reply. She knew she had to fight—even though Fulk had said these men were loyal to him, they must not be entirely sure, or he would not be having this mockery of a trial. If she could only make them see their commander was mad . . .

Please, a keening voice in her head pleaded. *Please, God, let Guillelm find me.* But her thoughts were dark. He had not said "I love you." If he found her now and heard Fulk's accusations, whom would he believe? *Please believe me. Please believe in me.*

"She is evil," Fulk ranted, striding about the clearing, eloquent with malice. "She uses potions to bend men's wills to her own. Lord Robert died in her care. Who is to say he was not poisoned by her? I have a witness who swears that she killed him by such foul means."

"Where is this witness?" Alyson wheezed. "Produce him."

"So that you may bewitch him, too? I think not."

"What does he look like?" Alyson took in the deepest breath she could manage. "What is his name?"

Fulk hesitated. "Edwin, no Edmund. What does a name matter? He saw you give Lord Robert poison! You admit your maid bought a love potion and what is that, if not another kind of poison? The worst kind, for it manipulates the very hearts of men. And there is more . . ."

Alyson lost the rest of what Fulk was saying. When she came round again, Fulk was still accusing her.

". . . As with the father, so with the son. My lord Guillelm has already lost his place in Outremer, thanks to her. How long will that female let him live?"

"The abbess allowed me to stay in her convent—"

"You lied to her! You fed her a potion and tricked her!"

"Which, Fulk?" Alyson gasped. "A lie or a potion?"

"So you admit it? You are condemned by your own admission!"

"Not so!" Alyson cried, as Fulk said more in French, words she did not understand but which had the men with him nodding and frowning. Where was the red-haired knight Eustace, who had cut her bonds? Alyson attempted to find him, to catch his eye, but she could not see him. Her sight was beginning to darken again.

She savagely bit her lower lip, straining to keep awake, and almost screamed in horror. She had blacked out, and in that brief time Fulk or his men or both had built a pyre about her. Her feet rested on logs and twigs, branches and dry grasses were stacked against her legs, rising up to her waist. Thrashing in her bounds, writhing and desperately kicking the branches away, she cried out in Latin, "Before God and all the saints I swear that I am innocent!"

"No, you are guilty!" Fulk yelled, piling kindling back around her. "You shall burn!"

"Mother of God, help me," Alyson prayed, her whisper cracking as the dreadful nightmare of her plight overwhelmed her. Surely not even Fulk would do this? Surely his men would stop him?

Guillelm! Where are you?

"Send a thunderstorm, send rain." Her mouth was trembling so much she could hardly form the words.

Dragon! Save me!

"If you do this, you will forever lose Guillelm's favor!" Alyson panted, determined not to flinch as Fulk tried to set a spark to the kindling. "You are not being true to your own nature—you are a defender!"

Fulk, crouching amongst the kindling, raised his head. "You are making the fire die!"

"God is with me," said Alyson. She tried to say more but could not; a chill of terror spiked through her head and heart and vitals, freezing her. *What have I ever done to you?* she wanted to say to Fulk, but she did not even know if he would hear her.

"Fulk, you must let me go." Desperate, she lied, "Fulk, you must let me go, for I have more to confess!"

That cut through to the core of his obsession. In an instant he was climbing over the rough fagots toward her, his lean, gaunt face ablaze with a lust of curiosity. "What more? What?"

"Untie me!" In a fading effort, Alyson shook her arms, lashed to the elder and birch trees that arched above her head. "If you would have me speak"—she paused to suck in another awkward breath—"you must let me breathe."

Dislike and greed warred in Fulk's face. Greed won. A knife flashed like two lightning bolts, and Alyson's bonds were severed. She would have sprawled on the mess of kindling and branches piled about her legs had Fulk not dragged her free.

"Tell me. Give me your confession, witch!"

He was sweating as much as she was; a rank foulness filled her lungs and made her dry-heave.

"Need drink," she whispered. "I thirst."

A battered leather flask was held her lips and she drank, the sweet, good water clearing her head. As her blurring double vision cleared, she realized that another of Fulk's men, not the red-haired knight, had given her his water. She nodded her thanks and through his visor, a pair of bright, embarrassed eyes blinked and would not meet her gaze. The knight shifted slightly and she felt herself leaning against a braced leg and flank. Without his support she would have fallen; as it was she could just keep her feet.

Fulk knocked the flask from her shaking hands. "Speak! I have waited long enough."

The man supporting Alyson suddenly shouted, lowering her hastily to the ground. Still yelling at Fulk, he stepped over her, drew his sword and pointed. "The dragon!" he screamed. *"Nous sommes tous morts!"*

Trapped behind the man's legs, Alyson looked where he was pointing and understood. Sinking back on the earth, she closed her eyes, letting her weariness take her where it would.

It was Guillelm. He had come for her. She would be safe now. It was over.

Chapter 28

Guillelm saw her fall and vented a bellow of rage. There were five scampering stick figures between him and Alyson and he wanted there to be more; more to mow down and destroy.

If they had hurt her, if they had harmed her in any way, they would know such agony before he had finished with them!

Slash them, cut them, kill them, trample them, they shall not escape, they will burn in hell and still know my anger.

The stick figures, tiny, pale, moving as jerkily as puppets, are huddled together. I can ride them down, gore them into the dirt. But Alyson would not want that. She is a healer.

Guillelm leaped from his horse and drew his sword. Behind him, now a long way off, he heard the red-haired follower of Fulk call out, as the man had done earlier, when he had been combing these woods. Tom would deal with that; Guillelm had to reach his wife.

He advanced, brushing aside the other men's feeble challenges like chaff. They struck at him and once he felt a sharp tear in his arm, a gash that stung and filled his head full of angry bees.

"Alyson!" Using her name as a paean, he rushed forward again, his pace quickening as he saw Fulk draw his own blade.

* * *

Beside her, Fulk spun round and tried to run into the forest. He had not gone above five paces when there came a new bellow and Sir Tom was there on horseback, barring the way, a sword in his left hand. Sir Tom advanced and Fulk retreated, making a dash for another part of the woodland.

As he passed her, Alyson caught his sword arm and clung on, praying her strength into her hands.

With a squeal of rage, Fulk tossed her off and lunged with the sword. The blade sang past Alyson's head and struck one of the logs intended to be used for her burning. Sir Tom was yelling but Guillelm, coming at a sprint, shouted, "Mine!" and, seeing Fulk's movement to stab with the sword again, threw back his arm.

There was a flash of light and Fulk tumbled away, a knife glancing off his shoulder. In shadow, Guillelm knelt by Alyson, unfastening his cloak. She spoke to him. "You came for me."

"Little idiot. Of course I came for you." Guillelm shook his head. As he leaned across and his hands wrapped her gently in warmth, Alyson felt the touch of water on her face. It surprised her, his weeping.

"How? Why?" she began, but when she moved her arm—which was only just beginning to return to life as the blood pulsed painfully back into her wrists and fingers—and tried to touch Guillelm's hair, he drew back.

"Are you hurt?" he asked. He was running a hand over her head, neck, throat, arms, flanks—all over her, as if to check she was whole. Even as she was, stunned with everything that had happened, Alyson felt a spiraling tingle of desire.

"No, no," she answered hastily, catching his fingers in hers before she forgot herself completely and launched into his arms. Then she saw the red staining through his sleeve. "You are bleeding!"

"'Tis nothing, a scratch." Guillelm turned quickly, to hide

the injury from her. "But what are these marks, upon your wrists?" Abruptly, he scanned the bundles of wood and kindling, the broken branches in the elder and birch trees. His face darkened. "That evil, treacherous bastard—

"Fulk!" he roared, still crouching over her. "I challenge you! Fight me, damn you!"

She could feel the heat of his rage and yet he clasped her gently, rocking her to and fro as if she were a babe in arms.

She had yet to tell him about their child, if a child it was. "Guillelm—"

"No, sweet, explanations as to why you are out of the convent must keep." He glanced at Sir Tom, who had dismounted and approached. "Tom."

"I know, Guido. I will take care of her for you." With a tiny grunt of discomfort, Tom sat on the ground beside Guillelm and cradled Alyson off Guillelm's knees onto his own. When Alyson started to protest that she needed no one to "take care of her," Tom tightened his arms about her and brought his mouth to her ear.

"This is the only time, wench, that I will ever have you anywhere near my lap without your ever-anxious husband gutting me. Now be still and let me savor the moment." He was smiling as he said it, though his eyes were strained. He gave her more water to drink, muttering "Steady," as she tried to take a huge gulp of water to soothe her parched throat.

Tom tried to block her view of the clearing with his own large head, but Alyson tugged at his cloak.

"Must see," she choked, for she knew Guillelm had risen and left her side.

"For sure you must," Tom sighed and he positioned her so she was sitting half on the ground with her back resting against his broad chest.

"He is hurt!" Alyson murmured, seeing a trickle of blood falling from Guillelm's arm onto the grass and ferns. "I must go tend him."

Tom wound one of his legs across hers, pinning her. "Let him be. I have seen him fight with worse."

Fight? Alyson tried to warn Guillelm: that he should not do this; that he had already attacked and driven off most of Fulk's straggling group of soldiers; that Fulk no longer mattered; that it was over. She could not find the breath to shout, and as she struggled, Guillelm spoke.

"Wherever you are, Fulk, whatever tree you are hiding behind, come out! Fight me, one against one. Whatever happens, your men may go free. Face me! Fight me!"

He began to chant something in a strange mixture of French and Arabic.

"What is he saying?" Alyson asked Tom. Tom shook his head. Exasperated, she snapped her fingers. "How did you find me? Tell me that, at least."

Sir Tom cleared his throat, his tone amused. "Guido said you did that trick with your fingers. I did not quite believe him. You are a fiery creature, mistress Alyson."

"How?" Alyson repeated, her eyes fixed on Guillelm as he stalked across the clearing, the evening sun throwing his tall shadow still farther. "Oh, God, he will be killed. His arm is bright with blood!"

"Someone may be killed, certainly," Sir Tom grunted. "No, you stay still. You cannot help him now. Listen! Listen, Alyson, show that good sense that Guido praises you for so much. We found you because your man wanted to see you, because he rode over to the convent in desperate hope of seeing you."

"Truly?" Alyson hugged that knowledge to herself. "Really and truly?"

"Truly, Alyson, and if you keep interrupting me I shall never be done. So we rode to the convent, and what we found was a full hue and cry over your going missing, but Guido guessed you had taken the road back to Hardspen. 'Whatever we do, whatever we plan, we are one,' he told the abbess. 'I know what she will be doing. She must have cut across country, and that is how we have missed each other.' He was right, too—we had not ridden a half-mile away from the convent when his trackers spotted Eustace of Normandy in the woods off the road. He was not easy to miss, since he was sprinting toward the road, waving his arms."

"Is Eustace a tall, weather-beaten man with red curling hair?"

"How did you know that? No matter, you are right. It was Eustace, who had gone off with Fulk when Guido told Fulk to leave his service." Sir Tom's battle-scarred face colored with embarrassment. "The fellow must have had a change of heart."

"Fulk would say I had bewitched him."

"If any are bewitched, it is Fulk himself. The man was always wild with ambition, but now he has become obsessed."

At the edge of Alyson's vision, she saw Sir Tom make the sign to ward off the evil eye. "What he did here, what he was about to do, was madness," he said.

"Fulk was convinced he was right."

"In that he has not changed," Sir Tom replied. "He was ever one to judge harshly and narrowly. Once in Outremer—"

Alyson waved her hand to silence him. "What is Guillelm doing?" she asked.

Throughout her hasty, whispered conversation, her eyes had not left her husband. Guillelm had been walking up and down the clearing, nodding to his own men who had ridden out of the woods. Those loyal to Fulk had already fled— Alyson could hear them dimly, pounding along the road—or were sitting or lying at the edge of the clearing. Some were clearly wounded, others looked as dazed as she was. She noticed them because Guillelm had noticed them and had called to his own troops to tend them. Of Fulk there was no sign.

Now Guillelm had completed four full circuits of the clearing, scanning this way and that, into the trees and undergrowth and beyond, when he picked a pebble from the earth. Still in midstride, he hurled it at an elder bush. In a snapping of twigs the bush seemed to explode; the dark purple juice and pulp of the elderberries splashed against the nearby trees like blood. As Alyson shivered, Guillelm feinted a throw at a low canopy of scrubby brambles, then jerked round and tossed another stone into a squat, dense holly tree.

"He is trying to shock Fulk into breaking cover," Alyson said.

"Yes," Sir Tom agreed. "But he will not do it. Fulk's an old hand at this."

Guillelm stopped, scooped up a handful of dried grass and struck the edge of his sword with something Alyson could not see. Sparks flew and the grass caught fire, smoke and bright orange flames rolling from Guillelm's outstretched hand into the sky.

"Meet my challenge or burn!" he roared. "Mother of God, I will burn all these woods from here to Hardspen, but you shall not escape me!"

"He would, too," said Sir Tom, half-admiring, half-remonstrating. "That is my wild, mad dragon."

"Mine, too," said Alyson, coughing as the smoke coiled into her lungs. "I can sit and watch no more."

In a spurt of her old familiar speed, she evaded Sir Tom and, before he could prevent it, pushed herself to her feet.

"Fulk, fight me!" she cried. "If I am a witch, as you say, you need have no qualms in warring with a woman. I challenge you!"

"No!" Guillelm shouted, skidding round to her, flinging his flaming torch aside. "Never!"

As one of his men scrambled out of the woods to stamp out the torch, Guillelm was running to her. At the sight of his stark, set face, Sir Tom backed away, but Alyson held her ground. She was almost too weary to move. Summoning the last of her fading energy, she called out, "Are you a coward, Fulk? Or afraid that you are wrong?"

Fulk stepped out from the cover of two rowans, growing so close to each other their branches interweaved. He walked around a patch of dog's mercury and nettles, his sword and helm blackened with smeared mud, a long dark cloak wrapped around his armor and trailing over the grass. His face was, if possible, even more gaunt.

"I am not wrong," he said.

At the sound of his voice the muted speech of Guillelm's men as they scoured the woods was cut off sharply, like a musician placing his hand upon the harp strings to kill the sound. Faces appeared at the edges of the clearing as the men came to listen.

This was the moment, Alyson knew. She touched the cross the abbess had given her. "I swear that I am innocent. I did not flee the convent. I chose to leave it."

"Why?" Fulk demanded.

Alyson knew she should not hesitate, but she hated the idea of telling her very personal news to everyone in this clearing. "That is between my husband and myself."

Fulk could not contain his dislike. "We all heard the vow your husband took at Hardspen, madam, on your wedding night. Shall I remind you of it? 'We may share the same bed, but we shall never lie together in love.'"

"Stop—" Tears pooled into Alyson's eyes as she remembered. "Why say such things now?"

"Because he knows he is a dead man," muttered Sir Tom somewhere behind her.

"He would make himself a dead man," said Guillelm, coming beside Alyson and putting himself between her and Fulk. "But I am not sure that he is worthy of being killed."

Fulk backed up several paces, his face panic-stricken as Guillelm cast his sword onto the ground and opened his arms. "See me, Fulk. I am wounded and unarmed. We would be a match. Come at me, not my wife. For Alyson is my true wife, to have and to hold until the end of my life, and I put my faith in her."

Alyson gasped at his use of the words of the marriage ceremony, at the reminder of the sacred promises they had made to each other. She understood them as never before, and in speaking them, Guillelm was showing her that he felt the same.

"For Alyson I would face any ordeal," he said, "any trial. I know she is innocent, although in truth I would defend her even if she were guilty, she is so excellent to me. I love her. Do you hear, Fulk? I love her!"

Fulk gave a low cry and moved away, but no one was watching him. All eyes were on Guillelm as he turned, emotion brimming in his face, his forehead, cheeks and chin red with feeling, sweat darkening the blond hair plastered to his temples. He was as weary as she was, Alyson realized, as worn down with worry. Almost of its own will, her hand rose and she touched his ear where a branch had scraped across it, drawing a speckle of blood. She wiped the blood away.

"Your arm," she whispered. It was still bleeding, though less than before.

"It is of no matter," he said softly. "Nothing matters but that we understand each other."

He took her hand and kissed her fingers one by one. "I love you," he said. "Can you not see this? I have always loved you."

For the second time he opened his arms and Alyson fell into them.

Sometime after, when Guillelm left her a moment to fetch his horse, Alyson remembered the others, and Fulk.

"Gone," Sir Tom said bluntly, when she asked. "Ran off the instant Guido said he loved you. The fellow can run back to Outremer for all I care. We are well rid of him."

"Yes," said Alyson, though she was thinking of Guillelm again and those marvelous words, "I have always loved you."

It was her deepest wish come true.

Chapter 29

They returned to the convent. This time, Alyson slept in the guest house, with Guillelm beside her. There were things to discuss: the return of Eva to her woodland cottage, and Gytha to Hardspen, but first Alyson told him her own news.

Sitting side by side on their bed, he heard her out gravely, in silence. "You are sure of this?" he said at last.

Alyson sensed him watching her as she fed their small brazier fire with twigs. "As sure as I can be," she answered. Was he pleased? she wondered, a little of her earlier jubilation and confidence draining away. "You did say that you would not annul our marriage because I could be with child," she went on, her voice becoming higher and faster. "You were right, Guillelm."

"Mother of God, girl, I said that to Fulk! I spoke the only language he would understand, but if you think I meant it, you have less wit than our merlin." He wrapped his arms about her, tossed the rest of her twigs onto the fire and kissed her deeply. "I would never give you up. Unless you wished it, and even then—" He kissed her again. "No, I do not think I could do it. You will have to put up with me forever, sweetheart."

"And you me!" Alyson said quickly, kicking teasingly

against him to feel his hard, masculine strength. To her surprise he released her at once, his face contrite.

"I have hurt you?" he asked. "The baby?"

"We are fine." Alyson took his large hand and placed it on her stomach. "We shall be well. All will be well, Guillelm. I know it."

"You do?" His features buckled in relief. "Oh, that is excellent!"

He swept her against himself, kissing her over and over, telling her how much he loved her. Suddenly, he stopped again. "You are sure?"

Alyson nodded. She was sure. Her sister's dark predictions and her own tragic family history had no more power over her. She did not know why or how, but she knew she would be safe.

Now, taking this knowledge as a gift, she sought to reassure Guillelm further. "The abbess says I will have a safe pregnancy. So does Eva the wisewoman."

He believed her, although the abbess and Eva had said no such thing. But then, Alyson thought, snuggling down in the wide bed with its wolfskin furs and soft pillows, a wife did not have to tell her husband the truth all the time.

Epilogue

It was spring, season of new lambs, as it had been in her dream. Guillelm was with her, as in the dream, much to Gytha's red-cheeked chagrin.

"It is wrong, my lady! A man at a birthing! It is not seemly!"

"Peace," Alyson gasped, clutching her husband's hand more tightly as another pain crested within her. He knelt by her bed, mopping her hair, giving her weak ale whenever she thirsted and above all, holding her hand. He had come to the main bedchamber the moments her pains had begun, sensing what was happening even before the wisewoman Eva had been summoned.

Eva now packed more rushes under Alyson's hips, remarking, "In the village, the menfolk often stay. Someone must tend the other children and the fire and keep the animals away. The other wives help when they can, but that is not always possible. I think it a good thing the husband sees how brave his woman is, bringing his children into the world."

"So does this husband," growled Guillelm, saying to Alyson. "You are doing well, sweetheart. I am so proud of you."

"Push, Alyson," Eva broke in. "Push hard."

Sweat stood on Alyson's forehead as she obeyed. For an instant she felt to be splitting in half and then, dimly, she heard a cry and Eva's glad shout, "An heir for Hardspen! My lord, here is your son!"

"Let me—" Alyson craned forward to see, her arms outstretched, just as another fierce pain flattened her back onto the bed.

"Alyson!" Guillelm hugged her, hiding his face. "Breathe, little one. Excellent! Keep on."

He spoke calmly but she felt the strong tremor through his body as he watched her struggle. She was glad he was there but sorry, too; grateful for his support but sorry he should be cast in so helpless a position. He was the one who usually did the fighting!

She tried to smile, to reassure him, but then sneezed instead, a sudden spasm that sent a whiplash of swift, slithering pain through her body.

"My lady, there is another child!" Eva exclaimed, and within an instant a second high, wailing cry filled the chamber.

"Alyson, we have a daughter," Guillelm said, kissing her cheek. "Twins! Boy and girl and both healthy! See them, they are beautiful . . ."

Through blurring vision, Alyson saw Guillelm, his bronzed, scarred hands cradling two tiny bundles.

"An easy birth, especially for twins," Eva was saying. "The lady has been blessed."

"Such, tiny, perfect fingernails," Guillelm marveled and Alyson smiled, sinking into a delicious, pain-free slumber.

As sleep took her, she heard Guillelm say softly, "I love you, Alyson."

I love you, my lord dragon, she thought in return, resting safe and secure in his arms, with their babies, their children, between them.